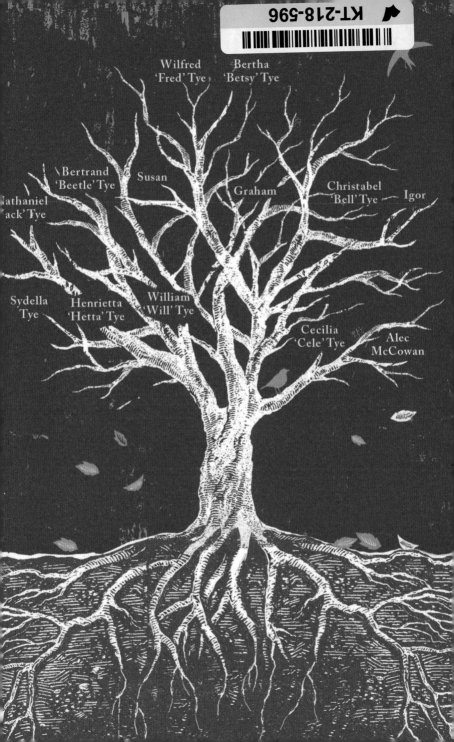

Cousins

Cousins

SALLEY VICKERS

VIKING
an imprint of
PENGUIN BOOKS

VIKING

UK | USA | Canada | Ireland | Australia
India | New Zealand | South Africa

Viking is part of the Penguin Random House group of companies
whose addresses can be found at global.penguinrandomhouse.com.

First published 2016
002

Copyright © Salley Vickers, 2016

The moral right of the author has been asserted

Typeset by Palimpsest Book Production Limited, Falkirk, Stirlingshire
Printed in Great Britain by Clays Ltd, St Ives plc

A CIP catalogue record for this book is available from the British Library

ISBN: 978–0–241–18771–5

www.greenpenguin.co.uk

Penguin Random House is committed to a
sustainable future for our business, our readers
and our planet. This book is made from Forest
Stewardship Council® certified paper.

*In memory of my parents and their friends Ram Nahum,
my godfather Arnold Kettle and his wife Margot
(from whom I learned to 'yield on unessentials').*

*And for my Party siblings, Heather and Andrew Gollan and
Martin and Nick Kettle, whose lifelong friendship has been
among the best of legacies, with my love.*

Heart of the heartless world,
Dear heart, the thought of you
Is the pain at my side,
The shadow that chills my view.

The wind rises in the evening,
Reminds that autumn is near.
I am afraid to lose you,
I am afraid of my fear.

***

And if bad luck should lay my strength
Into the shallow grave,
Remember all the good you can;
Don't forget my love.

John Cornford

PART ONE

Hetta

❧

I

When a persistent ringing startled me from a sleep of unusual contentment I swear I knew it was Will. My grandmother claims that the women in our family are blessed with second sight. Certainly my intuition has always been sharp. But maybe it was simply that Will was the person in our family most likely to be the source of a late-night phone call.

The phone had stopped ringing and had started again by the time my father got to it. I could hear him in the hall below sounding apprehensive and annoyed. And then I heard his voice change and become urgent.

He was calling my mother, who joined him in the hall, and hearing the note in their combined tone I got up and went halfway downstairs and sat on the landing, which is where I used to sit when eavesdropping.

Through the banisters I could partly see my parents in their pyjamas. My father was holding my mother, who was crying. She rarely cried so I knew this was serious.

I waited a little on the landing but the worry of not knowing what had happened was too great so I ran down the remaining stairs.

'Hetta!'

'Dad, what is it?'

I was right, it was Will. At first I thought he must be dead but it turned out to be worse than that.

At the time I was immersed in the Brontës and saw myself as Emily, wild and poetical and in love with her brother. So it's hard to say how far I felt the gravity of what had happened as a real event, rather than a drama in my Brontë persona. All I understood then was that Will was in hospital and that both my parents were to go at once and that I was to drive with them to Cambridge.

We left Dowlands, our house in Northumberland, there and then and I have always believed that we were still all in our pyjamas but reviewing everything now I can see that was unlikely. Maybe only I was. I certainly slept in the back of the car because I awoke to hear my parents talking in the voices people use when they don't want to be overheard.

My father was saying, 'It's Nat all over again'.

I know I heard this and that it isn't the construction of hindsight because my Uncle Nathaniel was hardly ever mentioned and his name had a special allure for me. He was my father's elder brother and was killed in a climbing accident, the kind of event which my tragic imagination relished.

I had written some poems in my Emily Brontë mode for my dead uncle, one of which began:

> *Oh you who are lost to us, still you are with us,*
> *Lost in the flesh but here in the heart,*
> *Still we shall mourn for you, though we are silent,*
> *Dumb though we be we are never apart.*

As far as I remember it went on in a similar vein and I doubt it improved.

I don't recall my mother's reply but maybe for the first time I had some sense of what the death of my uncle might have meant to his family and it was fear that made me exclaim, 'Will's not dead, is he?'

My mother was more level-headed than my father and would certainly have tried to soothe my fears. But anxiety had been awoken, a real and not a dramatic anxiety, and I was no longer consumptive Emily Brontë with a poetical tempest raging in my breast but robustly hale, sixteen-year-old Henrietta Tye, whose brother Will, it seemed, had suffered some appalling injury.

My father said now, 'How long for Christ's fucking sake before we get there?'

I know I am remembering that accurately as he never said 'fuck'.

My mother was driving. Like Granny, she was a better driver than her husband, just as she was more competent at all forms of handiwork. She taught me, as, more successfully, she had taught my elder sister Syd, to use a drill and to plumb; while at the time I found this freakish, subsequently I've been grateful to her since it has saved me hundreds of pounds in plumbing bills.

I should explain that my sister's real name is Sydella but inevitably she has always been referred to as Syd. And because I felt that this had shaped my sister's rather hearty personality I insisted on 'Hetta' early in my life to avoid any possibility of 'Henry'.

Syd by this time was married and living in Jordan and Will had essentially been away since he left for university. So I was the only child still at home, which was sometimes a bonus but sometimes horribly lonely.

It felt lonely now with no one beside me to share this catastrophe.

'Is Cele coming?' I asked.

'I'm sure she'll have been called,' my mother said.

Cele was our cousin Cecilia, the only child of our father's sister Bell, and when she was younger she stayed with us almost every holiday. She and Will were always very close. They were only five months apart in age so it seemed quite natural that they should do things together.

I could tell our mother didn't quite approve of Aunt Bell. I wouldn't go so far as to say that she *dis*approved but taking Cele in as often as she did was probably her way of indicating that Bell wasn't much of a mother. But maybe there was another reason why Cele was so readily made part of our family.

Will was originally one of twins but his sister died soon after they were born. I took, as we all do, the world I grew up in for granted. But looking back on events now I seem to see that for as long as I can remember there was a kind of blur, a tinge of melancholy at the outlines of Will's personality.

Of course none of this occurred to my sixteen-year-old self that night when we drove to Cambridge. We arrived just before five in the morning and as we drove into the hospital car park I heard the ducks laugh. It is still very dreadful to me to hear that sound, that harsh sardonic noise which seems to say 'You think you know everything, you human fools, but you know fuck-all'.

The laughter of the ducks met us as the sky was turning from green to a cruel orange. There was some heat between my parents over parking at the hospital. My father wanted to leave the car just anywhere and when my mother said, 'We don't need the car being towed away on top of everything else,' he snapped, 'For Christ's sake, Susan, he might be dying and you're worrying about parking restrictions'.

His words and the tone he used – my parents rarely rowed – frightened me to the tips of my fingers. From where I supposed my heart to be all down my arm like an electric shock ran the terrifying thought: Will is going to die.

2

Will didn't die. When I eventually saw him, which was not till the following morning, he was unrecognizable. He lay unconscious, his face puffed and hideously discoloured, with a huge white collar supporting his neck and a kind of helmet over his head, like a boxer or a biker. A tube had been slotted into his throat and a terrifying mechanism was helping him to breathe. The sheet and hospital blanket were draped over a frame, forming a sinister-looking tent over the bed, his shoulders were bare and a liquid was being dripped into his left arm. He looked neither as if he were asleep nor as I imagined a dead person might look but like a non-person, belonging to no-man's-land.

There had been a move by my parents to prevent my witnessing all this but Granny said with unusual firmness, 'Of course Hetta must see her brother'. She must have feared that I might never see him again.

Holding her hand tight, I went in to see Will.

Cele was sitting by the bed. She barely looked round as we entered. Her hand on Will's reminded me of the Rodin hands she had taken me to see when I stayed with her in Paris. Except that Will's hand was covered with sterile dressings.

There were only two chairs in the room so I stood awkwardly by Granny, not knowing how to react.

'Can he hear us?' Granny asked.

Cele shrugged; her eyes, which she always dismissed as 'gooseberry-coloured', were glassy with tears she was trying not to shed.

'Let's suppose he can,' Granny said. 'Will, darling. It's Granny here. Granny and Hetta. We're all here with you, beside Cele.'

'He knows I'm here,' Cele said, with what I sensed was irritation.

'Of course he does,' Granny said. 'I was just placing us for Will.' She sat down, deliberately calm although I knew how she was feeling.

Standing in the narrow room, with Will all white on the stark metal hospital bed and Cele and Granny so obviously holding back tears, I began to weep. I was always a crybaby; as the youngest, I was the conduit through which the collective family tears were let. I stood there, weeping them out and trembling.

Granny and I left Mum and Dad and Cele at the hospital and Granny took me back to their house in Ely. She drove very steadily until quite suddenly she pulled off the road with, 'Sorry, pet. I need to stop for a moment'.

We had pulled up by a field of cows and she opened the window on the passenger side, my side, and said, 'How now, brown cow'.

It was a brilliantly sunny day and we sat there in Granny's little white Fiat by the ruminating cows and the ditches full of cow parsley and hovering flies. I remember that for the first time I wondered why cow parsley was called cow parsley and what, if anything, it had to do with cows. It was the kind of question that in other circumstances I might have addressed to Granny.

When we set off again she drove in silence and when we got to their house, near the cathedral, Grandpa was in the living room waiting for us. His arthritis made him slow and he was struggling out of his chair as we came in, his face crumpled with concern, but before he could frame a question Granny said, 'Will's still unconscious but he's alive.' Then she said, 'Fred, darling,' and took his face in her two hands and, very tenderly, kissed his forehead. I'll always remember her doing that.

Despite the sun, I was shivering and she said, in the brisk voice she employed when attempting to keep our spirits up, 'Fred, I need tea and Hetta probably needs a bath. Is the immersion on?' They never did put in central heating.

She ran me a bath, dissolved an aspirin in water and poured me a glass of milk to wash it down. I drank it in the bath. My brief sleep in the car, on the journey down to Cambridge, seemed weeks away now but when she tucked me into bed I felt I was never likely to sleep again.

'What will happen to him?' I asked.

'I don't know, lamb,' Granny said, 'but he's alive and these days they can work miracles.'

She sat by me till I fell asleep, as she always did when we were small.

The next few days are a blur. My recollection is that Cele found a room in the hospital and Mum and Dad stayed in a hotel. Syd, who flew over from Jordan, must have stayed there too. Mum would have wanted her nearby. I stayed on in Ely with Granny and Grandpa, which I was glad of.

I was no use to anyone. Nor did they want us at the hospital where Will's condition was 'critical'. I think now we must have been allowed to see him that first morning because they were afraid he might not survive.

During those anxiety-ridden days Granny liked to take herself off to the cathedral. 'You don't need to be of a religious disposition to enjoy the quiet of a great cathedral,' she said to me once. She could be defensive over anything like that in front of Grandpa.

I would have gone to sit in the cathedral too but I stayed with Grandpa, because I knew Granny would like me to, and let him read to me from the translation of the *Aeneid* he'd been occupied with since he retired.

The school I attended was the local comprehensive, the kind that didn't teach Latin, and while I knew of this project of Grandpa's I'd never had anything to do with it. But Will had been involved in the Virgil undertaking since he was very young and perhaps I obscurely felt that this was a way of being in touch with him. Of us all, he most shared Grandpa's enthusiasms and, although Grandpa would have fiercely denied it, Will was his favourite. I knew that this accident would hit Grandpa especially hard. It was from the roof of King's Chapel that Will had fallen and it was because of Grandpa that Will had gone to King's.

There was some bother about Will's college rooms, which meant that at some point I went with Granny to help to clear them.

The only time I'd visited Will at King's his rooms had been a mess – littered with socks and underpants and old newspapers, with unwashed plates, congealed brown sauce on them, lying about and dead matches and cigarette ends all over the floor. At home, Will's room had always been an inviting jumble of books, collections of flints and stones, shells, feathers, animal skulls, birds' nests, a glass tank where he had once kept newts, a cage which had been home to Hermione the hamster, motorbike parts and ancient implements, rescued from neighbouring farms, hanging from the rafters. Now, by comparison, these college rooms looked very stark; the books were stacked in neat piles on the clean floor, there was a single armchair and no pictures or anarchist posters on the walls. The bedroom gave an impression of a monk's cell: very few clothes in the chest of drawers and nothing in the wardrobe but a leather jacket which looked brand-new and which I'd never seen Will wear.

I requisitioned some boxes from the porters for the books while Granny went to move her car. But as I was carrying the second box, which I'd over-filled, a book toppled out and a passing student picked it up off the cobbles.

'Are you Will Tye's sister?'

Reluctantly I admitted I was. I didn't want to have to talk about Will.

'I remember you visiting him once. Is he OK? Only we heard . . .'

'I don't know,' I said. 'He's still in hospital.'

'Oh God, how awful. Can you . . .'

'I'm sorry, parking wardens,' I said, hurrying away to avoid hearing whatever it was he wanted me to do.

I had the book I'd dropped still in my grasp. *The Night Climbers of Cambridge*. It was not the first time I'd heard of these madcap climbers and when I'd loaded the box on to the back seat of Granny's car I took another look at the cover. A black-and-white photo of a young man climbing a building.

Covertly I opened the book and recognized, from another picture, the spires of King's Chapel which stood so majestically before me.

'Is that all, darling?' Granny asked. She looked dreadful. Instinctively I tucked the book down the side of the box so that the title was not on view and got in beside her.

That was May 1994, when everything changed for my family.

3

It has been suggested that I set down what I recorded in my diary and what I can remember and what I have subsequently been told of all that led up to this event which affected all our lives. And while nowadays I have some slight reputation as a writer, I cannot say if I shall ever make our story known to a wider public, or to anyone beyond those who played a part in it. Maybe not even to them, at least for a while. Enough harm has been done, God knows. But for myself it will be a comfort to try to lay out my complicated thoughts about what happened in our family, to unpick some threads where they have become tangled in my mind and follow others to see if they form some pattern.

And if at times I have had to imagine what occurred to those who have chosen not to tell their own stories or are not here to tell them, I hope I may be forgiven. I have tried not to take liberties and only to fill out as best I can, from what I know of them and from what has been vouchsafed to me, what their thoughts and reactions and responses might have been.

Though Will was always 'Will' to us, his given name was Wilfred. He was named after Grandpa, who, coming from an ancient Northumbrian family, had been saddled with a very grand set of names: Wilfred Acton Lancelot. But in fact, as long as I knew him, Grandpa was only ever known as Fred. He was a committed socialist and Granny used to joke that he called himself Fred after Engels. Anyway, Fred suited him.

Granny was a Tye too. She and Grandpa were first cousins and Granny had a line she liked to spin which was that she only married Grandpa so she could keep her own surname. She was christened Bertha, which she hated, but was always known as Betsy, except to Grandpa, who occasionally referred to her as 'Guns', after the Big Bertha gun. To understand this you'd need to know that as well as being an ardent socialist Grandpa was a pacifist and had been a conscientious objector in the war.

Our father was named after Bertrand Russell, who was Grandpa's favourite philosopher because he was against religion and for pacifism. His sister, my Aunt Bell, was Christabel, after Mrs Pankhurst's daughter, 'which', I once heard my mother say acidly, 'tells you all you need to know about the Tyes'.

If Dad couldn't have been less philosophically minded, Aunt Bell could hardly have been more unlike the famous suffragette. She took not a scritch of notice of human rights, only of her own rights, which she interpreted liberally. Bell showed early promise with the violin and a great career was predicted for her when she won a scholarship to the Royal College of Music, where Cele's father was a tutor. He taught Bell harmony, engendered Cele and then disappeared from their lives.

After Cele was born my aunt gave up the violin, which was a pity but they needed money and fiddlers are poor earners. She took a job as housemother at a boys' prep school in Durham, which took overseas pupils as boarders. She got the job because when she was only fifteen the headmaster had fallen, with adolescent passion, in love with her and had nursed a soft spot for her ever since. That was the kind of thing that happened with Bell.

House-mothering was not the most suitable employment for her. She had had Cele too young to be readily maternal and, as Mum liked to say, Bell didn't see the point of boys until they grew into long trousers. Her job also caused a minor friction with Grandpa, who disapproved of private education in spite of – or because of – having himself gone to a famous public school. But as he had given away all the family funds with which he might have helped out there was nothing he could do about his daughter's means of earning, and money was badly needed since Cele's father provided nothing.

I suspect that the headmaster would have bent the rules and allowed Cele to be educated free alongside the boys, but Bell sent her to the local primary. It was a grim one but it was Bell's gesture towards Grandpa, who was much more shocked by her association with a private school than by her having an illegitimate child.

Our grandfather, as I explained, was ideological, unlike Granny, who mistrusted 'principles'. But she was mostly tolerant of Grandpa's quirks, though she was not afraid to laugh at him about them. At some point she inherited from her godmother Staresnest, a remote cottage on Exmoor. Granny was truly bothered that Bell had had to abandon her musical career and she minded that because of Grandpa's socialist principles they were in no position to help financially. So, following her philosophy of damage limitation, she gave Bell the cottage.

Aunt Bell's hospitality in the cottage depended on her relationship with her current lovers, who it amused my father to refer to as 'the applicants'. For some reason there were no lovers there the Whitsun when our mother was laid low with a slipped disc. Cele must have pleaded for Will to stay at the cottage and I expect Aunt Bell was happy enough to agree because Will absorbed Cele's attention so completely that this relieved Bell of any responsibility for her daughter's entertainment. At the last minute, I suppose because of our mother's back, I was packed off to go to stay with them too.

It was a long train ride from Northumberland and Will ignored me for most of the way. I finished reading my comics and then amused myself staring out of the window and making up stories about Moonblossom, the fairy with silver skin and silver hair I had invented as my companion and who at that time went everywhere with me. I expect Will was reading Sherlock Holmes. He was always one for crazes and he had a big Conan Doyle phase around that time. I was not quite seven and used to being ignored by him. I never minded much because Will was also protective of me and would have fought anyone who tried to harm me. It's hard to convey quite how special he was but as a small child I would have done anything for him. He was someone who always minded things tremendously. I've never met anyone who cared quite as passionately as Will did about the things he cared for. Except Grandpa maybe.

Besides being fearless – or so it seemed to me – Will had an explorer's initiative. We had been at Bell's for less than a day when Will found a place to swim near Cow Castle, the Iron Age fort that stood about five miles down the river that flowed past Staresnest. While the river was good enough near the cottage for fishing for minnows, it was too shallow for swimming. But down-river, by the ancient mound, the water ran deeper.

We were country children and had grown up with the countryside our domain. And while Cele officially lived with her mother in the cramped school flat in Durham, she spent so much time with us at Dowlands that she counted as country-bred. For all her delicate looks she was physically strong. She had to be to keep up with Will.

She carried me piggyback part of the way to the Iron Age hill fort where, on an oxbow bend of the river, under Will's direction, we built a dam constructed of rocks and flotsam and some useful rubbish from the abandoned gypsy encampment on the opposite bank. The summer before a man had been spotted there cooking what rumour claimed was a squirrel over a fire. The gypsies had gone, leaving several car tyres, a clapped-out pushchair and some broken sheets of asbestos, and Will and Cele pirated these to fortify our dam.

The others had swum and I had paddled in the shallows, and we were on the bank, letting our bodies dry in the unusual warmth of the late-May sun, when we heard a horrible row downstream. Will jumped up, pointing at the small round head of a creature swimming for its life.

It was the first time I'd seen an otter, though I recognized what it was. We watched as, confused by the baying of hounds and no doubt crazed by the sense of peril, the otter began scrabbling desperately over our dam, its paws slipping on the corrugations of the asbestos. Will grabbed my towel and waded downstream. I saw him wrap the towel round his hands, making a kind of sling, and lean down and lift something out of the water. He hurried back cradling a towelled bundle in his arms.

The otter must have been exhausted as it lay quite docile, shuddering from time to time and rolling back its lips to expose freckled pink gums. A rank smell of fear was exuding from its damp pelt.

'Here,' Will said, 'you stay and see those bastards off.' He walked to the gate that opened on to the water meadow, nursing the otter in my towel.

Following orders, we stood on the bank, and when the pack of hounds and hunters came by we waved and squealed and generally acted like the kind of girls Will had ensured neither of us wanted to be, and told them their quarry had gone 'that way', pointing upstream.

'Little beast,' said a massively built man with a florid face, stopping to wipe his forehead with a handkerchief. He looked like a caricature from the old bound copies of *Punch* someone had long ago left in the cottage. 'We nearly had the little devil but he slipped away from us.'

We waited till the hunt had rounded the bend in the river and then flew over to Will, who was kneeling under a tree nursing the otter. When he saw us he said, 'His paw looks as if it's gone. Bloody, *bloody* bastards'.

I began to cry because one of the otter's back legs was horribly mangled where the dogs must have got him and the paw looked as if it was barely attached. 'Shut up, Hetta, we don't need crybabies,' Will said. I expect I did shut up because he had a temper and I was scared of rousing it.

Cele said, 'What should we do?'

'Take him back with us, of course. We can't leave him here. Those bastards'll get him and if they don't a fox will.'

The otter seemed as willing to be resigned to Will's command as we were. Swaddled in the towel, the poor creature made faint mews and occasionally a high chit-tering sound, and the damp little body made frantic twitches and jerks. But the chase and the pain must have depleted its instinct to escape and Will had that touch with animals so that they seemed to know they were in safe hands.

'We'll have to find a vet,' he said.

We carried the otter back, or Will did, to the cottage

and applied pink Germolene to the wound and offered him mashed sardines from a tin, which he spurned. It was a dog otter.

One of Bell's lovers must have appeared around this time, because I remember some man drove Will and Cele with the otter to a vet they tracked down in Mine-head. I know I stayed behind and Aunt Bell played Snap with me, which was kind of her as games bored her. In fact the game bored me too – all I wanted was to know what had happened at the vet's – but our mother had raised us with a strict regard to manners and I knew to pretend I was enjoying it.

After a bit Bell put down her cards and said, 'God, Hetta, isn't life just utterly bloody sometimes, don't you find?' I've always remembered this because I was grateful to her for talking to me that way. She never made any concessions for children being children.

When the others came back their report was gloomy. The vet had said he would do his best, he felt the paw might have to be amputated, but he'd give it a go at healing first. Will had held the poor fazed creature in the towel while the vet injected him with an antibiotic and cleaned the wound and placed a splint and bound bandages round the hind paw.

The next morning I was permitted to go with them to see how the otter was doing. His eyes were open but glazed and when the vet opened the cage he made no effort to escape.

'He's not going to recover. He's better dead than

lame,' Will said. Because I still believed that emotion had the power to alter circumstance, I protested; but the vet agreed with Will's verdict.

He must have trusted Will, the vet, as he allowed him to hold the otter while he administered the fatal injection. The slight little body went limp at once and we took him back with us and buried him at the bottom of the garden, with a gravestone made from a slab of rock with 'RIP Otter' scratched on it with the point of a diamond brooch that Will had instructed Cele to 'liberate' from Bell's jewellery case. Only diamonds, he explained, were sufficiently sharp to cut stone. Afterwards he was unusually angry, even for him, and swore at Aunt Bell when, quite mildly, she objected.

4

Among Bell's 'applicants' were three principals, who came and went according to a system that was mysterious to us and, now that I think about it, was probably no system at all. More like pot luck, I imagine.

There was Kenny, an eye surgeon, tall with a head of fading yellow hair and matching teeth. I disliked him because he made a fetish of not washing his hands. 'I'm a surgeon,' he used to proclaim, 'there's no point in washing. It does nothing to the significantly dangerous germs.' Then there was Alastair, a Scottish civil engineer, a thin, reticent man with a prominent Adam's apple and going prematurely bald. We liked him better than Kenny, who didn't like children at all. But Alastair was awkward and his conversations with anyone under the age of twenty were for the most part strained.

Our favourite by far of Aunt Bell's admirers was Robert, whose occupation I never knew until lately. Robert was slightly overweight and wheezed asthmatically when he walked and he wore what we called 'fancy' socks, though now I see they were highly fashionable and certainly expensive. Among the applicants, Aunt Bell liked Robert the most too. I could tell this because, while she never made any open effort with her appearance, she always looked her best when Robert was around.

Robert liked books and the theatre but above all he liked music. Part of his appeal for Aunt Bell must have been that he took her to the concerts and operas where orchestras were playing with which she must once have aspired to perform. To her credit, she never gave any sign of resenting this; but that she regretted the loss of that potential life you could see in her enthusiasm for her outings with Robert.

It might have been Robert who drove Will to the vet's that Whitsun when we found the otter. I can't be sure. I do know that the summer of that same year, a time when Robert regularly took his wife on an opera tour, Aunt Bell was off somewhere in Europe with Kenny and was to follow this, presumably in one of her efforts at even-handedness, with a trip to the West Highlands with Alastair. Will and Cele were to spend part of the summer with our grandparents in Cornwall.

It wasn't until Grandpa's heart began to fail that my grandparents moved to the house in Ely. When they first retired, they went to live in a place called St Levan in Cornwall. Quite recently, Granny told me that she'd felt it was best that they not live too near Dowlands and I suppose Cornwall was about as far removed from Northumberland as you could get. But the reason she always gave when we were children was that she hankered after a milder sea to bathe in.

Both Granny and Grandpa loved sea swimming but

the seas of the North-East are perishing and only children and the foolhardy submit their flesh to that icy water. In Cornwall there were no strictures about catching cold. We were issued with bald towels, which rather than absorbing the damp simply ensured that the salt abraded our skin, and if we were caught shivering we were told to run up and down the beach to get warm.

It wasn't hard to see where this spartan attitude came from. Grandpa had a theory he would never explain (probably because, as Bell said, it was inexplicable) that burning coal was unfair to miners. When he was a conscientious objector he'd become friendly with other COs who had been drafted down the Durham mines – in the days when there were still working mines – and this had led to a stubborn refusal on Grandpa's part to allow fires except in the most exceptional circumstances. Although coal fires had long been left behind, this attitude had become a habit so that our grandparents' house was needlessly cold. Only Bell, with her beautiful woman's knack of getting her own way, could really shift Grandpa from this position and get him to put on the heating. Bell had made an early decision to rebel against any form of asceticism.

But although our grandparents' houses were cold their home was always warm because the welcome was warm, and we children were always happy there. Grandpa wasn't bothered about the kinds of rules and regulations that plague children, and was generally occupied with his books in an absent-minded, easygoing kind of way, and

Granny enjoyed indulging us, so there was a comfortable tranquillity in the atmosphere which Dowlands lacked. For one thing, we were allowed more autonomy than we were at home. Granny used to send us off on explorations, providing us with maps and compasses and local bus timetables, and packets of sandwiches in greaseproof paper, Marmite or peanut butter, and usually either a wormy apple from their garden or a blackening banana – for some reason all their bananas were speckled and over-ripe. We were sent off out with no safeguards beyond Grandpa's maxim of 'Use your common sense'. Will and Cele's favourite activity was to swim when they could at Port Chapel with Cele's namesakes the seals.

When she was small Cele couldn't quite manage 'Cecilia', and pronounced her name 'Seal', so seals came to have a special significance for her. And for years, among the family, this was how her name was spelled. A relative of Granny's had had a sealskin jacket, from the days when killing animals for their pelts was acceptable, and from this had been made an amazingly lifelike toy by a woman who worked at Dowlands when Granny's grandparents lived there and who, according to Granny, was really the person who had brought her and Grandpa up. When Cele was around four or five she discovered this toy seal, which became her special companion. Given that Bell was not exactly affectionate, I imagine Seal was a comforter and Cele was inseparable from him and slept with him until she was quite old. It was only when she had to leave home for school, and had also to leave her namesake behind, that to avoid schoolgirl sniggers from her peers she hit on the spelling of her name which has stuck.

There was a feature of the visits to our grandparents which had a lasting significance for Will and Cele.

I've explained about Grandpa translating the *Aeneid*. I think it was really to ensure he had something to get his teeth into when he gave up his job in adult education that Granny suggested this exercise. He'd worked all his life with ideas, and with nothing to feed his intellectual appetite he would have been at a loss and probably driven Granny to distraction. But, much as she loved literature, the *Aeneid* wasn't to Granny's taste and Grandpa wanted company to discuss his translation with. He always needed an audience. So at some point, I can't say exactly when, in order that they could be involved he began to teach Will and Cele Latin. And there was this too: for all Grandpa's radical views, he was still basically in favour of an old-fashioned education.

Apart from Greek and Latin, Grandpa was fluent in French, German and Russian, which he learnt during the war at the height of his obsession with the USSR – and Will inherited Grandpa's gift for languages. It sounds eccentric, and I suppose it was, but my grandparents were eccentric and my impression is that Will, at least, enjoyed these sessions. He probably liked the idea of being eccentric too. And maybe that is why neither of the cousins for years ever mentioned to the rest of us

what it was that they did with Grandpa when down at St
Levan.

It isn't only matters like sexual abuse that children
keep to themselves. Children need secrets. For years I
kept perfectly harmless possessions that no one could
have minded my having – a Dinky car with only three
wheels that I found on the beach, the exquisite bleached
skull of a tiny bird and a glittery ring I'd blown my holiday money on – under a floorboard I'd prised up with
the Swiss Army penknife that Grandpa had given me,
and for which he'd got into trouble with Mum. (The
knife was a secret too. She confiscated it, but having ferreted out her hiding place I discovered and retrieved it.)
Bell wouldn't have been interested in Cele's accomplishments anyway and our mother might not have quite
liked Grandpa teaching Will – she was odd about
Granny and Grandpa, though she was always careful to
speak well of them in front of us. But you couldn't help
picking up a reserve.

The result was that no one who had a part in Will and
Cele's formal education had any notion of their prowess
in Latin. At some point, Grandpa must have decided to
teach Will Greek too. Or perhaps Will asked to learn; he
might have done, because even at primary school he was
always more taken by any subject that was not on the
curriculum – I remember that at one stage he had an
ambition to go to sea and taught himself the Morse
code. In any case, he kept it from our parents. I don't
think it ever occurred to Grandpa to mention it to

anyone. And Granny – well, Granny never disclosed anything that she felt wasn't hers to give away.

So it happened that most mornings at St Levan, after breakfast and before they were let loose on the world, Will and Cele sat in the cold kitchen at the red Formica table taking it in turns to read aloud from the *Aeneid* and then translate. Thanks to Will's native ability and Cele's desire to please, they were by this time accomplished enough to have become Grandpa's sounding boards.

The summer after we found the otter Cele turned thirteen. Her birthday was 2 August, an inconvenient date for Bell, who, released from the duties of house-mothering, was desperate to be off on one of her jaunts with whichever of the applicants was available. So if Cele was not with us at Dowlands during the summer holidays, she and Will would often be down at St Levan with Granny and Grandpa.

I know from Cele's diary that she spent her birthday of '84 there because she describes choosing her birthday supper – fish and chips, followed by summer pudding – and her presents: a watch from Granny, and from Grandpa *The Ragged Trousered Philanthropists*. She doesn't say what Will gave her. Maybe nothing. He wasn't one for presents. It goes without saying that neither card nor gift arrived for her from Bell. There's a pathetic postcard from Ravenna stuck in the diary, post-marked late in August, with 'Darling, have the happiest birthday ever. Present when I get home' written in Bell's extrovert hand.

The day after the birthday it was business as usual and Cele and Will sat down with Grandpa to the *Aeneid*. By this time, Grandpa had reached Book Seven and Cele had the lines *saevit amor ferri et scelerata insania belli,/ira super* to read aloud.

'This happens to be a rather important moment,' Grandpa apparently said, his voice, I can imagine, a little over-emphatic.

Cele said she didn't understand it. She hadn't the same natural aptitude as Will and went along with this exercise, as with so many things, to fit in.

'Virgil is giving his opinion on war,' Grandpa explained. One of the reasons he was so keen on the *Aeneid* is that he considered it a great anti-war poem.

Will suggested, 'War is insane?'

It strikes me now that, without really understanding what he was doing, Grandpa was unconsciously recruiting Will, not so much to a cause as to be of his mind, one of his inner party. Cele records Grandpa saying with unusual fervour, 'Virgil is describing how easily the desire for destruction is kindled – the "accursed madness of war" he calls it.'

Later when they had set off down the coast path to swim, the cousins discussed this moment. It was Cele who uncharacteristically wondered, 'Do you think Grandpa really regrets what he did in the war?' As a rule, she took any such observations from Will. Or maybe she was different when it was just the two of them.

'You mean what he didn't do in the war?' Will asked.

He was at the age, they both were, when, if you are going to be political at all, you begin to become politically aware. Although Grandpa's pacifism was a well-established fact, it was one of the several no-go areas with our parents and I doubt that Cele and Will had talked much before about the First World War and Grandpa's father dying and how it might have affected him. But now they did, all the way to the beach. Apparently Will said, 'You can see what all that has done to Dad.' Cele's diary doesn't enlarge on what he meant by this and I wish I could have been there to ask him. Cele knew all too well what it was like to grow up without a father but she makes no mention of this either.

5

The long train rides from St Levan often resulted in Will arriving back at Dowlands with some new scheme. Travelling back from Granny and Grandpa's that summer, he decided it was time he and Cele executed a long-conceived plan to build a tree house. Although Dowlands itself was not large, it had once commanded considerable acres but by the time my parents came to live there the land had shrunk to a grassy area surrounded by a ha-ha, now more a ditch full of nettles and thistles, which encircled a run-down walled garden. Long ago this garden had been laid out, not by Capability Brown but by a lesser-known contemporary, but its elegance had been lost through years of inattention, though our occasional odd-job man, Steve, did his best to keep the beds in some sort of order.

Our mother's family had farmed sheep for generations and Mum had rented back one of Dowlands' lost fields where she grazed her Swaledales. It was in this field, in one of the tall sycamores, that Will had planned the tree house. Granny, who's a gardener, detests sycamores because of the way their seedlings spring up uninvited, but they make excellent trees for climbing.

Naturally, it was Will who masterminded the construction: the selection of discarded planks, lifted from the outhouse, or tranches of rotten fencing. Tools were filched from the cellar, from whose steps our father would occasionally shout, 'What fiend in human form has pinched my hammer?'

One of the reasons I was so attached to Cele was because she was kind to me. Syd had been kind enough but in a managing sort of way, and Will, who could be incredibly kind, could also be quite cruel. But Cele, perhaps because she understood the misery of feeling excluded, was always sensitive to my – or any – distress.

There was a period, a short period mercifully, when I suffered from nightmares, probably due to a sadistic teacher at my school. I remember once I was in the grip of a nightmare – some current *Doctor Who* monster was pursuing me – when I was woken to Cele's voice saying, 'It's OK, Hetta, it's only a dream.' It was at her insistence that I was permitted to observe the construction of the tree house. But I was under strict orders from Will not to be a pest.

A plank they were hauling up swivelled round on its axis and crashed down again. I was standing below and the plank just missed my head and I must have screeched.

Cele shouted up, 'Will, be careful, that nearly brained her!'

'Hetta, what did I tell you? Get out of the way. Where's the saw?'

Cele had been charged, as less likely to be intercepted and questioned, with the task of lifting the saw from our father's toolbox. She passed it up to Will.

'Shall I come up?'

'Hand me up the plank again first.'

She heaved it up and Will swung it over and began to saw, while I did as ordered and cleared off to collect honeysuckle. There isn't a scent in the world to match that of damp honeysuckle. I heard a yelp and a thud but I thought it was just Will chucking the ends of the planks down.

But when I looked it wasn't a plank; it was Will himself. He was lying on the ground and it was apparent from the blood spurting from his arm that the saw had severed something vital.

Cele had ripped off her T-shirt and was wrapping it round his arm. To my horror it hardly staunched the blood. In the blink of an eye the faded cotton was becoming a threatening scarlet. She started to pull at the belt of her jeans, which stuck fast in the loops, so she kicked off her shoes, dragged down the jeans to yank out the belt and bound it round the improvised bandage. Then in nothing but her knickers she tore through the nettles and thistles in the ha-ha.

Steve was weeding the bed by the house as she charged through the front door. To this day, she told me, the sweet scent of phlox makes her feel slightly sick. The next part I can't really remember. There were raised voices and people making frantic telephone calls and I seem to see, though this may be one of those later reconstructions, a dead pale, somehow shockingly shrunken Will being carried off on a stretcher. I don't know if Cele went with him in the ambulance to the hospital. I know she'd have begged to go.

The Blue Room, where Cele slept with Will when she visited, was at the top of the house under the roof, which was a constant source of stress to Dad as it was always needing repairs. At night you could hear skittering sounds behind the chimney wall. I was scared of rats and thought Cele might be too, sleeping alone, and I stole up after lights out and got into bed with her. She was curled up with her seal, holding Will's pyjamas to her face and crying.

Aunt Bell was out of reach and out of contact but Cele would have stayed on at Dowlands anyway. I doubt they could've got her to go. Each day she disappeared and I would wonder where she had gone. But I know now that she had climbed to Saint Cuthbert's chapel.

Granny found this ruined chapel when she lived at Dowlands during the war. And when, for a term, I had a crush on a teacher who ran the local archaeological society, which led to my joining it, I was able to tell Granny that there was evidence of some sort of structure there as far back as the eighth century, when all those old Celtic saints were supposedly roaming abroad. She was thrilled. Granny knew a lot about the Celtic saints and she was particularly fond of Cuthbert.

I can see why, as even by saintly standards Cuthbert sounds special. There are many stories about him. 'Apocryphal they may be,' Granny used to say, 'but even apocryphal stories can have truth in them. The deepest truths, sometimes.'

We children were all animal lovers and we liked it that Cuthbert was too. There was one story we liked in particular. Cuthbert's monastery was on Holy Island, which on a clear day you can almost see from the beach near Dowlands. The saint, it seems, had a strong feeling for the sea and made a practice of wading into the water at night to pray. Two of the nosier monks followed him, no doubt hoping to find their bishop up to no good. They must have had a long cold night of it as Cuthbert only waded back to shore as dawn was breaking. But while their hope of a juicy scandal may have been disappointed, what these spies did witness were two sea otters which had followed Cuthbert out of the water and were apparently trying to dry his feet by rubbing them with their pelts. It was this that led Cele to Cuthbert's chapel when Will was injured. A saint so honoured by otters might, she hoped, be called on to help a boy who had tried to save an otter.

The chapel stood by one of Northumberland's many holy springs where miracles of healing were supposedly performed and Cele used to go secretly to collect water to take to Will in hospital. And while the damage was severe – Will had severed an artery and damaged a vertebra in his neck and had to wear a collar for months – he did recover, so maybe the saint did help. Will's arm thereafter bore the track of a long scar, which brought on a wave of guilt in Cele whenever she saw it.

Evidently she had taken the wrong saw from Dad's tool-box, the big jag-toothed one which was unwieldy. It had caught in the plank of wet wood and stuck and it was in yanking it out that Will had plunged the ragged blade into his arm.

6

During the nights that followed this accident, Cele began to try to calm her fears by counting. Our mother had taught us the old shepherds' way of reckoning – 'yan, tan, tethera' – and while the rest of us dismissed this as one of Mum's sheep-farming idiosyncrasies, which we tended to mock, it seems that poor Cele found it soothing. The sheep helped for a while but then, finding their effectiveness lessening, her nightly accounting turned to the hootings of the tawny owls which lodged near our house, or the sharp cries of gulls, in from the sea to escape coming storms.

I knew nothing of this until a few months ago. I had come ostensibly to visit Mum and Dad but I was anxious to speak to Cele and I arranged to meet her on Holy Island, where she works now, guessing that she would talk more easily there than at Dowlands.

We met at the Castle Hotel by the ruins of the medieval priory that stand over Cuthbert's monastery and after I had bought us both a drink we sat on a bench outside. You get a good view there of the same sea into which thirteen centuries ago Cuthbert waded in order to pray.

My cousin told me then how the urge to count had imperceptibly passed into the daylight hours: the number of strides up the hill to the chapel, and then, as part of her psychic bargain with the taciturn saint, the number she could reach while holding her breath. 'If I can count to one hundred, two hundred, three hundred and hold my breath, will you save Will?' Once she fainted by the stream and when she came to heard her own voice saying in her head, 'If I lie here while I count ten thousand, will you save him?'

Like water first trickling then, gathering in weight and momentum, finally bursting some barrier whose flimsiness becomes apparent only with its destruction, the need to quantify experience flooded her daily life. From the moment when light seeped through her closed lids, and even beforehand at the hinterland edges of sleep, she had to count: forwards, backwards, in all kinds of permutations, engaged in absurd subtractions – start from a hundred and go backwards subtracting by the two times table, no, start from ten thousand and go backwards in multiples of three. Start from . . . Start from . . . Start from . . . It never stopped.

The result was that long after Will was out of hospital and mended Cele became less and less able to communicate properly in everyday life. Her ability to form friendships was trammelled by the remorseless inner idol that demanded an absolute subjection. If you can hold your breath till you count to three hundred the ceiling will not fall in; if you can do the nine times table up to twenty-four that aeroplane will not drop out of the sky; if you, if you, if you . . . Her formerly wide-ranging attention was cruelly enslaved to perpetual calculations.

As the obsessions mushroomed – count to exactly sixty before the clock ticks on; hold your breath till you get this exact, do it again, do it again; stand on one leg until the next plane passes over, then hop to the next corner till the next; do it in all four corners, now backwards – her anxiety mounted. Worn ragged by the strain, she grew more and more reserved.

By this time she was at the local comprehensive, one of those massive concrete constructions, the pride of seventies architects and endorsed by educational reformers, where it was easy for a shy, recessive girl to disappear. It was an irony, but not an atypical one in Cele's life, that she lived close by in a precious little prep school where her mother supposedly acted as 'mother' to pampered rich kids. Homework, with which she struggled alone because it never crossed Bell's mind to help or to enquire how her own daughter was managing, became an enduring battle since every task required in preparation some enervating mental sum. Her capacity to discuss, to form sentences, never mind to imagine, dwindled; her mathematical ability was confined to mental arithmetic (where constant practice made her shine); the one subject, Latin, where thanks to our grandfather she might have excelled, had no place in the school's curriculum.

Once when Kenny had come to stay and Cele apparently treated him to monosyllabic answers to his uninterested questions, she heard him suggest to Aunt

Bell that 'the poor little monkey' be sent away to school.
She had by this time perfected the habit of listening
behind doors and Aunt Bell's voice was distinct. The
suggestion from Kenny terrified her, but to her surprised relief Bell pronounced a seemingly categorical
'Out of the question.'

She said she couldn't imagine why her mother would
voluntarily keep her at home and for a few days she
basked in the comfort of being wanted, until something
happened which made her realize that the grounds of
her mother's protest were other than maternal.

She was listening outside Aunt Bell's bedroom again,
this time to a conversation her mother was having on
the phone. Bell was talking to Granny and Cele heard
her mother say, 'She irritates me,' and then lower her
voice so poor Cele was left straining her ears and wondering what was to follow from that cruel dismissal.

Hearing all this for the first time that day by the ruins
of the twelfth-century priory, I reflected how I'd always
smugly considered myself rather superior in my
sensibilities.

'Cele, I had no idea,' I said. I felt deeply ashamed at
how insulated from her suffering I had been.

I've said she was always kind. 'How could you have,
Hetta? You were what? Seven then? No one knew. I
didn't really know what was going on myself.'

We sat there in the weak February sun as she described
what followed from Bell's casually hurtful words.

It seems that Granny was dispatched to inspect St

Neot's and the following term, without much discussion or any explanation, Cele was packed off to board there.

St Neot's was closed down long ago. I doubt it would fulfil any modern educational criteria, state or private, but back in the eighties things were generally laxer. From what I can work out, it was really a school where reasonably well-heeled parents could dump girls they were tired of or could think of nothing else to do with. Not delinquents, not crazy girls, just girls who for whatever reason didn't fit in.

Poor Cele was terribly unhappy there. Bell was supremely unmaternal but to be sent away felt like a final abandonment. Even Granny and Grandpa in St Levan were miles away and the much vaster distance from Dowlands, which had basically been her home, was an anguish for her. Especially the distance from Will. It was very wrong of them to allow this. I know Granny felt she should have made more protest.

Miss Finch, the Head of St Neot's, was an oddity. My guess is that there had been some past scandal which had led to her departure from more conventional educational establishments. Certainly she had a lover, which added to her glamorous reputation among her pupils as it seems she took no trouble to conceal him. The lover, Colin Chance, was supposedly a social anthropologist and taught the girls what passed for science, though this seems mainly to have involved self-regarding anecdotes about his fieldwork in Africa. An old alcoholic called Mr Mackenzie, probably unable to find employment elsewhere, taught maths. Of all the St Neot's staff Cele liked Mr Mackenzie best because he was also in charge of cricket, at which Miss Finch, ahead of her time, believed passionately girls could excel, and lacrosse, which she maintained developed firm breasts. Mr Mackenzie, lacking breasts, knew little about either sport, which suited Cele perfectly as although she had a good eye and was a swift runner she had been encouraged by Will to despise any form of organized games. Mr Mackenzie perhaps shared this prejudice as he made no fuss about her always choosing a position at cricket in deep field to which she customarily took a book.

The one place where Cele said she felt a little at home at St Neot's was the garden. This garden reminded her of Dowlands, and Mum's Swaledales, as it sloped down to a ha-ha below which lay a field let out to a local farmer. When Cele felt homesick for Dowlands, she got into the habit of slipping down to the cover of a boulder just above the ha-ha, where she would read in the company of the mildly grazing sheep.

One afternoon, she looked up from her book to the enquiring face of Miss Finch, who politely asked if she was interrupting.

Cele could only deny this. She said that her headmistress stood there, saying no more, with Cele hoping like mad that she'd go away and leave her in peace. As always, in this as in almost every situation, she began to count.

And then Miss Finch came out with an unnerving observation, 'Counting the sheep, Cecilia?'

The question made Cele blush. She never did work out how her headmistress had seen within her so accurately. But in the light of what Cele went on to tell me I have wondered since if Miss Finch maybe shared with her pupil this or some similar disability: events revealed that they may well have had some undisclosed feature in common.

Miss Finch asked Cele whether she 'might like to go and talk to someone clever at helping people with hitches'.

Years of living with Bell had made Cele money-conscious and all she could think of in answer to this terrifying invitation was 'Wouldn't it be very expensive?'

Her headmistress apparently brushed this objection aside. It wasn't for years that Cele learned who it was who had funded her.

A week or so later, Miss Finch informed my cousin that Mr Chance was to drive her to Truro the following morning where she would be seeing a Dr Keynes.

Colin drove her in his Morgan. To be squashed in a sports car so physically close to the man reputed to be her headmistress's lover left Cele paralysed with embarrassment. Happily for her, Colin drove in silence, which he broke only when they reached Dr Keynes's office. She had the impression that he was angry at having been saddled with this task and when she got out of the car he sped off again almost before the car door was shut, yelling, 'I'll pick you up in an hour. If I'm not here, wait.'

Dr Keynes turned out to be a short man with a

clipped beard, which gave an impression, Cele said, of a well-disposed Mephistopheles. He tried to put her at ease by saying, 'This is probably a frightening experience for you, Cecilia. New experiences are, especially if to do with doctors. But I am not a medical doctor.'

The unmedical doctor opened a door into a room with many paintings on the walls and two chairs. Outside, through the window, she could see a garden.

He indicated she should sit. 'That chair's yours. Nicer for you to have the view of the garden. Do you like gardens?'

'I thought it was a trick question,' she told me, as we sat drinking beer that February day. 'But he was just breaking the ice.'

'Then,' she said, 'there was an awful silence while I tried to think of what to say and at last, out of sheer embarrassment, I asked, "What kind of doctor are you?"'

'I'm a psychologist,' Dr Keynes explained.

Cele was none the wiser. There wasn't much psychology in her background. Nor in mine, come to that.

'I'm called an educational psychologist,' he told her, 'but I don't have much to do with education. It merely means I see schoolchildren.'

There didn't seem to be much to say to this either. After a further silence Dr Keynes apparently relented and asked, 'I wonder why you suppose you're here, Cecilia.'

Cele told him she didn't know.

'Obviously,' she told me, 'I did know. But also I didn't. He asked me if I'd like to guess why I was there and I was too frightened to say "No, I wouldn't" so we sat in more silence for so long I thought he'd gone to sleep. I was in agonies about what to do but in the end he took pity on me and asked, "Might you like to guess why?"

'I would have liked to say "No" to that too but I was far too shy. So we sat in more silence until he took pity again and asked, "What do you enjoy doing, Cecilia?"

'I didn't know what he wanted me to say so I said something like, "Oh messing about, I suppose."

'Anyway, then he grilled me. No, "grilled" isn't fair. He was cleverer than that. I liked him actually. I sometimes think I might have died if it hadn't been for Dr Keynes.'

'And messing about means . . . ?' Dr Keynes asked my cousin, all those years ago.

'Doing things with my cousin Will.'

'You see a lot of Will?'

'Mostly in the holidays.' All holidays it had been till then.

'And Will is where?'

'Northumberland. He lives there.'

'And your own family? You see them?'

The truth was that Aunt Bell, having dumped Cele at the school, had contented herself with writing a few postcards during the first term, after which she rarely communicated. Years of practice meant that Cele hardly missed her mother. But children are ashamed of their parents' defects.

'My mother. I don't really have a father. My grandparents live in Cornwall. Granny comes to see me here sometimes.'

'And your grandfather?'

'He doesn't drive and he doesn't like cars. I see him in the holidays.' And then, because it was something to say and the pressure to say something felt unendurable, and maybe too from a desire not to show off exactly but to show she was not, as Grandpa would say, a duffer, she said, 'We read the *Aeneid* with him.'

'Do you indeed,' Dr Keynes said. '*Lacrimae rerum.*'

7

The next time Colin took Cele for her appointment with Dr Keynes he was late seeing her. He apologized for this as he showed her to the chair overlooking the garden.

'Sorry for the wait. Am I in your bad books?'

No one had ever asked her such a question. But he had mentioned books. 'I brought this.' She held out the red-jacketed Loeb edition of the *Aeneid* that Grandpa had sent on one of Granny's visits.

('Really I only took it to have something to say,' she told me that day on Holy Island.)

Dr Keynes took it and it opened at the page where a line was marked by a faint pencil star, inscribed, I suppose, by Grandpa: *sunt lacrimae rerum et mentem mortalia tangent.*

Dr Keynes read it aloud. '"There are tears for things and mortal matters touch the mind." A line that fame hasn't tarnished.'

'It's our grandparents' code. LR.'

'I see.'

'It's not code really.'

'Shorthand?'

'It's a sort of a joke between them. They joke a lot.'

This was true. 'LR' was the kind of thing they would

say if, for example, Grandpa broke a plate. He was always breaking things.

'"Tears for things" is rather a sad comment, isn't it?' said Dr Keynes. 'Aeneas lamenting his lost comrades who died in the war.'

As Cele said, we never really thought about its significance.

'Granny and Grandpa don't say it sadly,' she said.

'And how about you, Cecilia? Do you feel sad?'

There was another of those pauses during which she was aware that she was supposed to come out with something significant and was rescued by the sight of a large tortoiseshell cat balancing on the fence. 'Is that your cat?'

'That's Hector. Do you like cats?'

We liked all animals. 'Yes.'

'And do you have a cat?'

'They do at Dowlands.'

I should explain here about Mrs Mahoane.

Mrs Mahoane – Old Moanie, as we called her – who had some forgotten connection with Mum's family in Wooler, was what was once called a PG, or paying guest. I don't imagine PGs exist nowadays. She occupied two rooms, including a sitting room where she 'took her meals' on a trolley. She honestly spoke like that. We used to imitate her saying she had 'a partiality' for beetroot and because she was greedy and a messy eater the embroidered tray cloths on her trolley, which were a counterpart to her language, were always stained slightly pink. Her bedroom was originally a small room off her so-called sitting room. But at some point she must have given our parents money because after Syd left home her bedroom became Old Moanie's and Old Moanie's former bedroom was converted into her private bathroom.

A dark shadow of insecurity about money hovered over my family. The house 'ate money', we were told, and it was tacitly understood that the roof or the blocked guttering or the rotting windows justified the presence of Mrs Mahoane. Whatever the reason, we children were solid in agreeing that she was a nasty old woman, one we resented being told to feel sorry for.

Among our many reasons for disliking Old Moanie was her antipathy to animals. She claimed to 'suffer' from an allergy, which meant that our cat Ribby and her several kittens were constantly having to be removed from her room. Ribby, like many cats, had an instinctive grasp of where she was least wanted.

Will in particular hated Mrs Mahoane because he once saw her throw Moppet, one of Ribby's kittens, out of the window. Will yelled at her that she was a 'vicious old cow' and was ordered by Dad to apologize when she furiously complained. When Will refused he was forbidden TV until Dad either caved in or forgot about it.

When Cele told Dr Keynes about Ribby's kitten he said, 'Ah yes. Ribby from *Samuel Whiskers*. That was nasty of her,' in a tone of such sympathy that she told him how we used to say that Samuel Whiskers and Anna Maria lived behind the skirting boards in the Blue Room at Dowlands.

'Dowlands is where Will lives?' Dr Keynes asked, and she explained how it had once belonged to Granny and Grandpa's family but that Granny had given it to Dad. It was only when Cele was recalling this that I wondered how that gift had come about. It's interesting what you take for granted as a child.

When we had finished our beers that February day, we left the hotel, Cele and I, and walked down to the seashore, where little buff-coloured birds were running to and fro along the wave line, probing the damp shingle with their beaks for prey.

'Dunlin?' I asked.

Cele nodded. She knew far more than me about the local birds.

'I think it was his knowing about Samuel Whiskers that made me tell him about the tree house,' she said. 'Do you remember, you came to see me in the Blue Room when Will was in hospital because you thought I might be scared of rats on my own. I was so grateful.'

'You blamed yourself?' Dr Keynes suggested. 'For Will's accident?'

'I took the wrong saw.'

'But it wasn't you who cut Will's arm.'

'I don't think he blamed me.'

'But you blamed yourself.'

'I was stupid.'

'Cecilia, is there a voice in your head telling you that you are stupid?'

That frightened her. 'No.' She didn't want him to think she was mad.

'You made a mistake,' Dr Keynes said, 'and the trick of life is to make the mistakes as fast as possible, not try to avoid making them.'

'But he might have died.'

'He might. But he didn't. And it strikes me that Will also made a mistake. You can't nab all the mistakes for yourself, Cecilia.'

Holy Island is a misnomer. It is only an island twice a day when the tide comes in, flooding the causeway that connects the quasi-island to the mainland. Cele had to get back to work and I had to get back across the causeway before the tide turned. We walked up to the ruined priory and I kissed her goodbye and made as if to go. But she stopped me, her hand on my shoulder.

'Do you remember the otter at Staresnest?'

I hadn't in fact completely remembered. I had forgotten, until she reminded me, about Bell's diamond brooch.

'I told Dr Keynes about it. I told him how Will had held the otter when he had to have an injection.'

'I wasn't there for that,' I said. I realized that this still rankled.

'Weren't you? I didn't remember. But you were with us when he had to be put to sleep?'

I nodded.

'What I remembered thinking at the time was that I would never have had the nerve to do that, to hold a creature while it was being put to death, and when I said this to Dr Keynes he said – he was looking out of the window at the time which he did when he had something to say that he didn't want to sound too heavy – "Maybe if it had been down to you alone you would have found the nerve." And then he said, "I do wish Hector would refrain from shitting on my young delphiniums." And I said something like "I don't think I cared about the otter the way Will did."'

A cloud of redwings and starlings was passing over high above in the slate-grey sky and Cele shaded her eyes to watch them.

'I'll never forget what he said to me after that,' my cousin said, still watching the birds. 'He said, "Yes, you need either to care very much or not at all to kill a fellow living creature."'

8

That summer, it seems Cele told Will about Dr Keynes. She was worried about doing so because she guessed he would disapprove but she was unused to keeping anything back from him.

Will was more than usually scornful. 'Freud is complete bullshit. You know that, don't you? He'll expect you to fall in love with him.'

I wouldn't have seen this then, any more than Cele would have done, but Will would have resented any threat to his position in Cele's affections.

'I won't.'

'He'll expect it so I expect you will. Unless you have already?' He looked at her with his unblinking stare.

'I haven't in the least,' she protested. 'Anyway, he's not a shrink.'

'What is he then? Do they think you're barmy?'

Even without the excitement of his driving her way in excess of the speed limit to her weekly appointment with Dr Keynes perhaps she would have fallen in love with Colin anyway – though when I say 'in love' I mean 'in fatuation' – because if anyone was, Colin was fatuous. But not to a lonely girl who had never had much attention paid her nor ever had a very high opinion of herself.

One day that autumn term, after Colin had collected Cele from her appointment, the Morgan began to shudder and they finally came to a halt. Colin got out, inspected the tyres and opened the car's bonnet, from which issued scalding steam.

'Shit. I'll have to ring the AA.'

This was before mobile phones were common. A roadside pub was visible a hundred or so yards up the road.

'Fucking bloody nuisance,' Colin kept saying. Teachers were not supposed to say 'fuck' in front of pupils. I expect that had an allure for Cele. It would have done for me.

It had begun to rain and she was wearing only a cardigan over her school dress. Before they reached the pub Colin took off his waxed jacket. 'Here, don't get wet.'

'But what about . . .'

'Don't fuss. I can't stand fussers.'

Colin used the phone at the pub to ring the AA and the school to tell them what had happened. He came to find her in the pub lounge where he had parked her. 'They'll be here within two hours – sweet Jesus. So, Cecilia, here we are. How old are you?'

'Fifteen.' Her birthday had been that summer.

'Right. Then we can risk a drink without me being sent down for corrupting a minor.'

'I've often been in pubs,' she said, blushing.

This was true. Something I've not explained is that Will had begun to frequent pubs. And when Cele was with him of course she went too. Although he was small and slight, he somehow gave an impression of being older than his age. And although Cele was both taller and older than him he made her sit outside. Lemonade shandy had been Will's choice of drink for her.

Colin bought her a shandy and himself a beer.

'Entertain me, Cecilia. Tell me about yourself.'

'There isn't much to tell.'

'There must be. What d'you talk about to old What's-up? Dr K?'

'Nothing much.'

Colin laughed. 'You mean I drive you there all that way week after week for you to sit in total bloody silence?'

Stung, she said, 'We talk about Virgil sometimes.'

'Virgil? Not your usual schoolgirl reading.'

Anxious now not to be dismissed as a show-off, she told him about Grandpa and learning Latin with Will, which made her blush still more. To her horror, Colin placed his hand under her chin and turned her face towards him, forcing it upwards so she was looking into his eyes.

'So you're in love with your cousin Will.' He laughed again, and while I wasn't present myself I hear it as a mean laugh. 'No harm in that. It's legal between cousins. Another shandy? Though why in God's name you like that undrinkable stuff . . .'

She accepted another drink, though the shame of having chosen something he so clearly despised fuelled her hot skin with more fire. Poor Cele. It's truly terrible to have all your emotions displayed so readily for all to see. When Colin came back with two refilled glasses he said – I know this is right because she said she could never forget it – 'Have you fucked your cousin yet? Here's your kiddies' pop.'

The idea of doing anything so gross with Will felt sacrilegious. He laughed again. 'Have you fucked anyone, Cecilia?'

'No,' she said, hating him.

'That's a pity,' Colin said. 'You're a pretty girl. Very pretty, in fact.'

Looks were never thought important in our family. But Cele was Bell's child, and in her mother's eyes she was counted as plain.

9

Will was unlucky in being a December child. Mum and Dad used to combine his birthday and Christmas, which meant he received more extravagant presents than might otherwise have been given but I suspect left him feeling short-changed. As a rule, Cele spent his birthday with us, staying on after Christmas while Bell swanned off to enjoy herself elsewhere, and there was a tradition that we all went to the Harbour Café at Seahouses for scampi and chips to celebrate. But that year for some reason, possibly one of Bell's infrequent outbursts of conscience, Cele spent the whole of the holiday abroad with her mother and maybe this was why Will's fifteenth birthday fell rather flat.

GCSEs were due to come in the following year, but because he was so bright Will had been moved up a year at school and he sat what must have been the last set of O levels. I remember him in those days revising hard. He spent a lot of time in his room, playing his flute late at night, or jazz on the music centre Mum and Dad gave him that year.

During those same Christmas holidays Will took me to a jazz gig up at Berwick. It was the first time I heard live jazz and I was beside myself with excitement and deeply flattered at being asked. I wonder now why he wanted me there and how he persuaded Mum and Dad to allow me to go. Maybe I was some sort of substitute for Cele. Maybe it was the fact that he knew our parents would not be in favour of my going and he needed to assert himself and just wore Mum and Dad down. Will could always do that when he set his heart on anything.

Stu, the older brother of Will's friend Jesse, drove us to Berwick in his van and on the way back, after the gig, Will recounted the massacre of the Highlanders at Culloden by the Duke of Cumberland's men, which he must have been studying for his history O level. He told it so vividly that I have never forgotten that story. You could tell that Jesse and Stu were captivated too.

Will sat nine O levels that June and it wasn't till the summer holidays at St Levan that the cousins met again.

Granny and Cele drove to meet Will at Truro and it was then that she became conscious of how much he had grown. There had been scarcely an inch between the cousins. Now she was a good two inches taller. Will hugged them both, and holding him she smelled the familiar smell of his skin. But she also smelled something less wholesome.

That evening, after dinner, which would have been shepherd's pie, Granny's customary welcome dish whenever any of us visited, Will suggested a walk. It was a chilly evening and the weather had turned to drizzle.

Cele made some expression of reluctance, because she would rather have stayed in and talked, but Will said, 'Oh come on, don't be pathetic. A walk will do you good.'

He was parodying Mum, whose solution for all ills – 'a breath of fresh air' – we children mimicked. But Cele says she felt something beyond his usual teasing in his tone. And she half guessed where they were heading. Not to the Hind and Hounds, which lay close to our grandparents' house, but to the Green Man on the outskirts of the village.

Will strode in with the confidence he always displayed at any potential challenge and ordered a Jack Daniels. Cele, whose taste for shandy had been squashed by Colin, asked for a tomato juice. When Will came over with the drinks, she suggested that he ought to be careful because of Granny and Grandpa and he rounded on her.

'Jesus, Cele, don't you give me a hard time, I'm up to here with that.'

The way he downed his drink bothered her. He got himself a second Jack Daniels and she ordered a packet of crisps and they sat in silence, which was quite unlike them, until she asked, 'Who's been giving you a hard time?'

'Oh, Mum and Dad. Me and Jesse got a bit pissed at the Anchor and the publican shopped us. To hear my doting parents carry on you'd think I'm an incipient alcoholic.'

Cele was fond of Jesse but he could be wild. 'I hope you're not.'

'For fuck's sake, Cele. I expected you at least to be on my side.' The injustice of this made her eyes well and Will said, I expect nastily, 'You know I can't stand girls who cry.'

'It's just . . . I was looking forward to seeing you.'

'Well I'm here, aren't I, so let's have fun. God knows I could do with some fun.'

But they didn't have much fun. Not even on her birthday. He bought her some rubbishy scented bath stuff from the village shop – she told me she would rather have had nothing than that – and was rude about her reading Terry Pratchett. Most nights he went off to the pub, sometimes with Cele on the pretext of an evening walk, more often alone, because even for Will she couldn't summon up the face to deceive our grandparents. He took to letting himself out of the house when Granny and Grandpa had gone to bed. They retired early so it wasn't difficult. And he would ask Cele to wait up to let him in.

He was never obviously drunk, she said. But he was moody and his face had a look she'd not seen before.

Cele had promised to ring Colin at some point in the holidays and, while Will's presence had inhibited her, the trips to the pub left her feeling deserted. One day, when Granny had asked her to post a letter, she nipped into the village phone box and rang Colin's number.

He was offhand when they spoke but suggested a meeting in Penzance. She said it was easy to fob off

Granny with a story of meeting a friend from school but
Will asked questions.

'What friend?'

'Oh, just a girl at St Neot's.'

'What's her name?'

'Florence,' said Cele, ad-libbing the name of someone
she would never bother to go out of her way to see.

'You've never mentioned her.'

'I've not seen you for ages. She's new.'

'New friend or new at the school?'

'Both. Look, it's just for the afternoon. We're going
shopping. You hate shopping.'

'I'll come anyway,' Will said.

He did, following her from the bus to a shop where
the mythical meeting with Florence was supposed to
take place and where luckily he left her. 'I'll be at the
pub. Come and find me when you're done with your
friend.'

There was something aggressive in the way he said
'your friend'. There was no way he could have known
about Colin rationally but I don't believe that it is only
the females in our family who have second sight.

Although we talked about it that day on Holy Island,
there have been very few occasions when Cele has spoken about her affair with Colin, and always briefly. I have
never wanted to question her further, so I don't know
when precisely she and Colin became lovers. I do know,
because this she did confide, that undressing her in the

flat in which he lived in a run-down house owned by the school – but clearly not too close by for his movements to come under scrutiny – he announced with monumental crassness that he'd been waiting for her to 'come of age'. So it must have been some time after her sixteenth birthday, that summer of '87. What she did tell me is that from this time on she began to skip her appointments with Dr Keynes. It was because of this that she and Colin were found out.

The cancellations appeared in the monthly invoices which were sent to Robert, to whom Bell had appealed for funding Cele's so-called education. Robert, noting the missed sessions, felt duty-bound to alert the school. Thank God for Robert, though it's also the case that without his deep pockets Cele would never have been sent away. Anyhow, she came back from an afternoon with Colin to a request that she report to the Head's room.

Miss Finch didn't actually accuse Cele of anything but she had clearly worked it out. She was, Cele said, fair, even with the pretty sure knowledge that Cele had been carrying on with her own lover. But it was plainly unacceptable for a pupil to be conducting any kind of sexual liaison.

At sixteen, the school-leaving age, she was able to leave St Neot's without giving rise to any more comment than that it was unusual for a girl to be taken away midterm. It was presumably considered best that Cele come to us at Dowlands. Our grandparents would have been too close to Colin and Dowlands was always basically home for Cele.

Colin apparently told Miss Finch that Cele had a crush on him and that he had been in a quandary over how to handle it. She herself had admitted to nothing more than that she had skipped some appointments with Dr Keynes and had been 'driven about' in Colin's car. Nonetheless she arrived at our home under a vague cloud. There must have been some anxiety about what had actually been going on but any discussions were kept firmly from me. My parents were not prudish exactly but they were not too comfortable about sex. What stays in my mind is that Will must have guessed about Colin since he behaved as if he was absolutely livid with Cele.

If Will couldn't attract someone's full attention he could generally summon discord. He had always been prone to lash out, but in the past his tricky moods had swiftly evaporated and he was just as often sunny. He had no obvious reason for ill humour. He had done spectacularly in his O levels and talked excitedly about his liberation from the 'dreary' comprehensive, where I was soon bound. But, icily and pointedly, he ignored Cele.

I could tell she was miserable. She was probably missing Colin too, though she told me that the person she missed most was Dr Keynes. He wrote to her once and she showed me the card on which he had written in neat black italic script *Remember to make the mistakes as fast as possible.*

It was during this period of exile from Will's attention that I really got to know my cousin. And I was grateful for someone to make my tea when, exhausted in that wrung-out way that besets you on the edge of adolescence, I arrived home after a mile and a half's trudge from St Aidan's, the local primary school. Mum had returned to supply nursing and for a period Cele became my surrogate mother. She baked scones, made bread, she even made my bed for me and tidied my room, which was a godsend as the state of my room was a regular bone of contention.

Cele was naturally tidy but a further expression of her obsessive compulsive disorder was that she had become a demon cleaner. I find it astonishing that no one, not even Granny, commented on this or ever thought to ask why. Cele asked me once, during this period, if the various pencil scribblings on my bedroom walls were precious, and after I had dismissed them as childish nonsense I arrived back from school one afternoon to find that my walls had been washed clean. Even the skirting boards were pristine. For this short while, our house was treated to the cleaning regime of a Swiss clinic while Cele worked out her misery in an extensive programme of housework. Only the Blue Room, where once she had slept with Will, was exempt because it was pointedly denied her.

She and I spent a good deal of time during those few weeks tramping the long beaches while Teasel and Trug, our terriers, ran for sticks which we hurled obligingly into the foaming waves. I went with her once to the chapel. She never made any mention of the saint but I've learned since that he was in her mind.

10

Cele's stay with us at Dowlands ended abruptly when out of the blue it was decided by Bell that she should be sent abroad. This was, as Dad put it, a 'very Bellish' solution, though it was in fact Granny who came up with the suggestion of where Cele might stay. Marie Bazinet was the daughter of Marion, an old university friend of Granny's, and Marie was looking for an au pair with whom her children could read and discuss English literature. Cele, having spent so much time at Granny and Grandpa's, was always a reader, though to be fair to Bell she was a reader too and that was the one aspect of Cele's education you could say her mother had taken a modicum of trouble over. So Cele was packed off to Paris as a kind of literary ambassador, where I imagine she was considered to be out of Colin's reach.

I didn't visit her in Paris then, though I did later, but when she returned that summer she had acquired a new sheen. She arrived bearing gifts – a Babar clock for me, picked up in a Paris flea market, a leather-bound notebook for Will, a silk scarf for Mum – and wearing a blue workman's jacket over a very short lace skirt. Mum looked askance at the skirt and Will initially sustained his cool manner to her but he allowed her to accompany him on evenings when he was out with his Seahouses gang. I suspect he was showing her off – though I doubt that Cele would have recognized this.

Among the things that had changed with regard to Will and Cele were their sleeping arrangements.

One consequence of Mrs Mahoane's presence was that for years we had no spare bedroom. Dowlands was one of the smallish country houses built in the eighteenth century in these parts; apart from Mrs Mahoane's occupancy, two of the back rooms were so damp they were only used for storage. Perhaps it was this, or perhaps it was merely the effect of the status quo, but Will and Cele had continued to share the Blue Room longer than might otherwise have been thought suitable, one of those behaviours that with hindsight appear strange but are taken for granted at the time. Cele was so much our sister that I doubt if any of us considered there might be any other kind of relationship between the cousins. Certainly it had never crossed my mind. But with Cele's expulsion from St Neot's the matter of where the cousins slept must have been discussed because thereafter Cele was assigned the room off the kitchen, known as the ironing room. The decks were cleared of the bundles of crumpled clothes that generally were deposited there and this change marked in my mind other changes between my brother and my cousin.

One was Cele's new command of French. She didn't – her character hadn't altered so much – make anything of this, which would have provoked the kind of put-downs at which our family excelled. But her reading gave it away.

We were in our kitchen and Cele was sitting in her time-honoured place on the floor with her back to the Rayburn. She always felt the cold. The thermometer had dived that summer and we were experiencing one of Northumberland's cold snaps. I was at the table trying to draw Ribby in her basket – I was going through a phase when I had decided to become a children's writer and illustrator like Beatrix Potter – when Will came in with muddy boots and issued a rather imperious demand to put on the kettle for tea.

Cele was reading *Le Grand Meaulnes* and whether because she was reading French or for some other reason this must have touched a nerve in Will and sparked what to my knowledge was their first outright row.

Cele ignored him and carried on reading. I think she was genuinely absorbed and may not even have heard Will, but that in itself would be enough to make him cross.

'Away with the fairies?' This was an expression which we all loathed since it was used by Miss Hunt, the sadistic teacher at the primary school we'd attended, the one who had given me nightmares.

Cele stopped reading and stared up at Will.

Will could outstare any of us. 'Aren't you going to say something?'

'I don't have anything special to say,' Cele said and put the book back up as if she intended to go on reading.

Will leapt across the kitchen and grabbed it from her. Had Cele grabbed it back I suspect that the clash would have resolved in laughter. Instead she simply got up and walked out of the room.

Will stood there holding the book and probably feeling stupid. He glanced at the page and then slammed the book face down on the table – we'd been brought up by Granny to be fussy about books and he would never normally have done that – and marched out after her.

He didn't come in for supper that evening. It was a rather dismal meal and Cele excused herself, saying she was tired, and went off to her bedroom. I guessed she was wishing herself back in Paris with the sympathetic-sounding Bazinets.

I don't know what made me wake in the night but I saw from the Babar clock that it was 2 a.m. It was the summer before I moved to my secondary school and maybe that prospect pulled me out of sleep. I was very concerned about the uniform.

Our mother was of the view that we not only could but should 'make do' and I was to be kitted out in the various hand-me-down skirts that had belonged to Syd. Syd and I were quite different shapes and I was not convinced that the skirt, which my mother had claimed she had altered, would be either short enough or the waistband tight enough to fit my waist. The skirt was in the room where Cele now slept, waiting for the end of the holidays to be ironed ready for school. My plan was to smuggle the skirt out of the house and throw it away and then act innocent over its disappearance. I was by now practised at this and felt only slightly ashamed that my mother never worked out what had happened to the various unwanted hand-ons I discreetly disposed of.

The moment I opened the door I knew there was no one there. You can always tell a sleeping body, however quiet. I was so sure that I switched on the light. The bed was as neatly made as it had surely been left that morning.

Curiosity, a childish voyeurism, who knows what mixture of emotions known and unknown, or more likely half known, led me stealthily up the creaky stairs to the landing at the top of the house by the Blue Room. Privacy never having been an issue, no one had ever thought to block the gaps between the ill-fitting door and its frame. Through these cracks I could see a faint light and hear sounds. Will and Cele's voices. At first I supposed they were arguing. But listening more closely alone on that dark stairwell I began to blush.

There was a moth which had flown in at the window and was now unable to navigate its way out. As the voices rose to an odd pitch, the moth began to flap at the cracks in the door frame, drawn, in that inexplicably suicidal way moths have, towards the light. Something about this frantic futile fluttering scared me; it seemed to echo the strange fluttering of my heart and I turned and hurried back down the stairs as quietly as I could.

My brother and my cousin were not arguing. They were making love. I knew it as surely as I had ever known anything and the knowledge brought with it feelings I could neither recognize nor accommodate.

Cele was like a sister to me and equally, I had supposed, a sister to my brother. Overhearing the passionate consummation of two people I was so close to was a profound shock, one that registered in my physical being so violently that I can feel the trace of it still today. I was eleven so of course I knew about sex. Or rather I knew the details. But sex is not about detail. The 'facts of life' are myth and fantasy, poetry, stories half grasped, the unanswerable questions of fear and desire – most powerfully fear of desire.

What I blunderingly overheard that night brought with it intimations of realms of experience that I had only dimly sensed. It was to become a moment which haunted me, haunts me still. I came to feel like a traitor within the gates of a paradise that was never mine to enter and at the same time, though this I only felt much later, a witness who could vouch for the truth of that paradise.

But the chief feeling I had at the time, as I crept back to my bed, was shame and embarrassment – an embarrassment which transferred itself to the school skirt, which I had failed to be rid of and which I rejected with unusual scorn when I was asked to try it on for size.

11

The autumn when I started at the local comprehensive was the start of Will's second year at the sixth-form college in Berwick. I think I have said that there was no Latin taught at our comprehensive, and since no one knew of the lessons with Grandpa it hadn't been among Will's O levels. But at the Berwick college Latin A level was one of the options.

Will, who had excelled at every subject, was taking, as boys who showed any talent for the subjects did, maths and science for his A levels and it was characteristic of him to antagonize his teachers by skipping his regular classes and making friends with the teacher of a subject for which he was not down to sit. The Latin teacher was young and approachable, it was his first teaching appointment and one day Will met him at the pub where the teacher confided that the college had decreed that they would drop Latin the following year if there continued to be insufficient demand.

Thanks to Grandpa, Will was very familiar with the set text, Book II of the *Aeneid*. He wouldn't have divulged this to boast – more, I imagine, to be matey. The teacher was concerned for his job and Will was naturally sympathetic to anyone in trouble with the establishment. So the upshot was that, without anyone at home knowing, and really only to help someone he had taken to, Will signed up to sit Latin A level.

I don't know how much Will and Cele communicated at that time. I scanned the post with a curiosity which added to the guilt I felt at being privy to their secret. Will was less available to me than ever. When he wasn't in Berwick he was perpetually going off to see Jesse Arnedale, who I guessed was his alibi for the pub. By now I believe he had begun to drink seriously.

If you ask me why, I would have to admit that I cannot say for sure. Partly boredom: the Northumberland countryside, idyllic for us as children, offered little for us to do as we grew older. Partly, I suspect, a kind of swagger. Partly, I am sure, because he was missing the old intimacy with Cele. But maybe too it had something to do with his being so spectacularly bright. It's easy to underestimate the pressure this brings. I have always been grateful that any talent I have been granted has taken time to show.

In our family's case, the pressure to succeed came from Mum. Mum's family were tenant farmers and had had little formal education. Her parents, our other grandparents, were not unintelligent – but they were, I suppose, what not Granny herself but her and Grandpa's sort would call 'uncultivated'. I can see now that, while she would have attacked anyone who suggested this, Mum was in fact secretly ashamed of her own parents' lack of sophistication. Considering how close they lived to us we saw very little of them, though Mum always put this down to the pressures of their hard-working farm life, for which the rest of us, including Dad, were made to feel guilty. What is certainly the case is that Mum had a need for us all to excel which had something to do with a competitiveness with Granny and Grandpa and their background. Mum had a way of saying 'intellectual' which was a form of condemnation and yet, perversely, Will especially was her bid for intellectual confirmation. But Will never wanted to stand out, or not in that way. Jesse and the gang down at Seahouses had barely more than four GCSEs apiece.

Whatever the reasons, Will's drinking meant that relations with our father were becoming more strained. The drinking itself was rarely tackled but the unpredictable moods it brought out in Will clouded the atmosphere. Dad, who generally ducked confrontation, was at a loss to know how to deal with a son whose energy and blitheness had developed into a surly belligerence.

I was having a bad time too. I'd fallen victim at my new school to a bully, a pale-eyed, flaxen-haired girl called Pauline Crowsdale. Years later, I spotted Pauline Crowsdale at Newcastle station. I didn't introduce myself. The slight fair girl had become a bulky beat-up woman, depressed-looking and too aged for her years. But in those feral childhood days her word at that school acted as law.

I don't know why she took against me. Maybe it was no more than that she had found a weapon she could use and that alone made me the object of her spite. By one of those strokes of bad luck that can dent a childhood, she discovered that my sister was known as Syd. Taking her cue from this, my tormenter decided to call me Henry and declared that I was really a boy and had a penis tucked away in my underwear. The only sure disproof of this, she declared, would be for me to reveal my unadorned vagina, something I was naturally desperately keen to avoid. My unwillingness to expose myself was, according to Pauline, a sure sign of the accuracy of her diagnosis. And of course I never told my family about this humiliation.

So I, who had always been the cheerful easy child, moped about the house that Christmas. Will was hardly around and my parents, noticing I was less than happy, though they wouldn't have fathomed the reasons, decided that a change would do me good. That half-term, with the help of Granny's friend, I was dispatched to Paris. Cele could be relied on to take care of me and the visit, it was suggested, would help improve my French.

The Bazinets were bilingual so I don't know that it helped my French but it helped me in crucial other ways. In fact it was a life-saver. Paris was heaven for a pubescent girl: fabulous fashion, strange foods and scents, paintings, architecture – the sight of the proportions of a French window still takes me back to being not quite twelve – and above all the hospitable Bazinets.

The first impression I received of the Bazinets was

that their apartment near Saint-Sulpice was alive with music. Both Marie and her husband Philippe, as well as their children, played. Marie was a piano teacher, and also played the harpsichord which contributed to the graciousness of their big light sitting room. It was a lovely room, overlooking the church.

Marie, the daughter of Granny's old friend, must have learned from Granny something of my cousin's history. I see now that Granny, distressed over what had happened to Cele at St Neot's and maybe too distressed at her mother's neglect, had thought of Marie as a safe haven for Cele. Her role as literary resource for Marie's children was probably cooked up with Granny's connivance.

Marie was a naturally solicitous woman anyway. I could see why under her care Cele had begun to thrive and the Bazinet children, Cele's supposed charges, were unlike any children I'd encountered. At home, we were always being reminded of our manners but in practice this amounted to being no more than not openly rude. It was the young Bazinets who first acquainted me with the subtle value of charm. Sabine and Théodore were polite but not too polite, pleasantly but not officiously sociable and, compared to me, shamingly well-versed in art. They were already accomplished musicians, without any of the showing off or fear of seeming to show off that I was familiar with in England. Rather than scorning my philistinism, they seemed to take pleasure in transforming me into a fit companion for their world.

Secure in this enchantment, I fell head over heels in love with Théodore.

There's a song Granny sometimes plays on her old vinyl: *There's a last love/And a first love/A best love/And a worst love.* I suppose we all imagine that our first love will be our last but as it happened Théodore really was – and is. Of course by that age I had had crushes: Peter Tyke at my primary school and Jeff Denny, the garage hand from the car repairers Dad used, who faintly resembled Trent Reznor of Nine Inch Nails. But Theo was different because he also fell in love with me.

It was Theo who introduced me to football and football became one of my ways of escaping my family. No one in my family cared about sport. Syd, who was physically heavy, made a virtue of disliking exercise and Will was too rebellious to believe in teams. I was thrown when Theo asked what football team I supported and it was simply local geography that made me say 'Newcastle'.

'The Magpies they are called?' he suggested.

I grasped gratefully at this prompt and from that day became a devoted Newcastle supporter.

Years later, when I confessed my ignorance, Theo said, 'I knew you knew nothing really, but I was sorry for you coming from this cold-sounding family.' I was defensive at the time only because he was right: compared to the Bazinets my family was cold.

I came home restored by Theo's affections and bolstered by my new-found enthusiasm. Quite quickly my football expertise, and maybe the boosting effect of

Theo's affections, gave me a position in my class. A gang of influential boys became my allies and with their backing Pauline Crowsdale's taunts faded fast.

But matters were not going so well with Will. He was spending more and more time in Seahouses, from where he would ride back dangerously drunk on the motorbike that he and Jesse had put together from what looked like scrap. There were many late evenings when I helped him in through my bedroom window, from the outhouse which abutted the house and was child's play to climb. More than once he passed out on my bed, leading me to spend nights on the floor, sick with worry that I would not be in time to wake him early enough for him to make his way undetected up to the Blue Room.

It was one such exploit that led to the row over Mrs Mahoane. Mrs Mahoane had continued to be a thorn in our sides. Although she insisted that, being a light sleeper, she was 'obliged to wear earplugs' – revolting little waxy balls which she left by her bedside – she was always complaining about noise at night, from which we deduced that she left off the earplugs in order to catch us out. After one evening when Will had come home drunk and had thrown gravel up at my window, she claimed to have opened her own window 'to see what all the noise was' and to have been hit by a stone.

There was certainly a mark on her neck but nothing that a handful of gravel could have caused, even supposing, as the aggrieved Will put it, 'I was such a bad shot that I'd got her fat face by mistake'.

Dad had his suppressed-anger look. 'If you'd been drinking, your aim might well have been boss-eyed.'

Will suffered from the drunk's certainty that alcohol only improved his faculties. 'Fucking liar. I never threw anything at the fat cow but I will if she doesn't watch out.'

A couple of nights later, Old Moanie advised Dad that Will had woken her again. In fact he had not been out, as I could testify, but he was punished anyway. It wasn't the punishment he minded as much as having Old Moanie's word taken over his. Will was rarely untruthful, and he rarely bothered to deceive, which was part of his problem with Mum and Dad. If I had less of a rocky ride it was partly because I was a much smoother liar.

Two nights after this, a small rock crashed through Old Moanie's window, spraying glass fragments everywhere. She came knocking on our parents' bedroom door in her big floral nightgown and Will was immediately summoned and asked to account for himself. He had had just enough time to climb into his pyjamas and to hiss at me that I was to please keep my mouth shut. I would have done anyway. Dad grilled me the following day but I am glad to report that I gave away nothing, and his confidence in my veracity remained unquestioned.

Mrs Mahoane left, after issuing a bill for the repair of her mother's bureau, allegedly damaged by the rock.

'Good fucking riddance, mad old cow,' was Will's verdict.

'The "mad old cow" helped us keep up the house. I shall have to ask you to help me in future with any repairs because, thanks to you, we are now going to be considerably short of funds,' was Dad's aggrieved rejoinder.

But although Will would have been happy to help Dad he was never asked.

These were some of the most discordant times I remember in my family. We had had rows, like any family, but the whole drift of the family ethos was to steer clear of dramas. The atmosphere now became tense. My solace was the letters I received from Theo. I have them still in a lilac box faintly scented with mignonette, which he gave me before our first parting.

Cele also wrote – to us all collectively but more often privately to Will. I steamed one of these letters open but I was overcome by such dismaying guilt that I barely took in the content and I cannot now say if I read what I believe I read, which was Cele making a solemn promise never to see Colin again.

12

I was waiting in the kitchen, hoping for a letter from Theo when the post came and I immediately registered the significance of the manila envelope addressed to Will with the London postmark. I left it on the table but had gone out long before he came down for breakfast so I wasn't around when he read the news.

He wasn't around either when I came back for lunch but the envelope was open. His results were unheard of levels of failure – Ds in Pure Maths and Physics and a fail in Applied Maths. When he did come in, clearly the worse for his visit to Seahouses, he referred to this with an appearance of unconcern. 'Dunno that I want to go to university anyway. Academic life is pretty shit.'

Dad's response to this was typical. 'In that case, old son, you'd better look for a job because I'm not going to support you.'

It was fair enough for Dad to feel that he could not support us indefinitely but there was no question that he had some problem about money. He was a consultant at the hospital and by this time Mum was working almost full-time, so they can't have been that short. The generous explanation is that this was a reaction to an unnecessarily straitened childhood, but you could also say that Dad was simply rather mean. And I felt too that Mum's comment to Will – 'You've only yourself to blame' – was another form of meanness. As Bell said to me once, 'When it comes down to it, Hetta, there *is* only oneself or someone else to blame.'

Some days later, with Will about to embark on what Dad dismissed as 'another hare-brained scheme' – which was no more than a plan to go off on his motorbike around the world (an outcome that might have spared everyone a truly impossible grief) – a second manila envelope arrived. For the Latin A level, Will had sat a different board. Our parents had been kept in the dark over the fact that he'd been entered for this exam but I don't think it was to slight them that on reading the result Will immediately rang Grandpa.

I was eavesdropping, as usual.

'Hi Grandpa, how are you? And Granny?'

Grandpa by this time was already growing slightly deaf and with the converse logic of the deaf he tended to shout into the phone so I could hear not his words but his unmistakably emphatic voice.

I noted a certain pride in Will's response. 'Pretty good, yes, thanks. Yeah, yeah, I know that wasn't so clever. But listen. I just got the Latin result. I got an A.'

Even I, from my hiding place, could hear the enthusiasm resounding from the other end of the line.

The Latin result took the wind out of our parents' sails and for all their reservations about Grandpa they didn't hide the fact that they were relieved. Anything, I suppose, to quash the proposed motorbike adventure. And for the first and only time in all the years I knew him, Grandpa initiated something that wasn't political or to do with his own work. He asked Will down to St Levan, because, he said, he'd 'come up with a plan'.

Grandpa, quite out of character, had got hold of the A level syllabuses for Greek and Ancient History and he was offering to coach Will in these subjects with a view to his sitting the exams that summer. And, painful as it is to say this, I imagine that our parents were only too glad to have their obstreperous son out of the house and off their hands. In the event, it turned out that he had read most of the Greek texts already and, as Grandpa put it, 'the Ancient History is only a matter of general knowledge' (which tells you a lot about Grandpa, who never grasped that his standards were maybe unusual). Will entered himself for two more A levels and at Grandpa's suggestion applied to read Classics at King's.

I don't think, I really don't, that Grandpa pulled any strings. That would have been too great an offence against his principles. What he did do was take up this matter of Will's future as a project and poured his energy into it for reasons that I only later understood. Reasons of . . . well, I suppose it was his attempt to put something right. Something 'right' for himself, that is.

I dare say the name Tye rang bells. The Director of Studies in Classics had apparently been taught by a contemporary of Grandpa's. Whatever the reasons – Will's intellectual ability was unquestionable and he had that string of outstanding O levels – he was offered a place at King's on condition he got As in his exams. And when that was exactly what he did the family breathed a sigh of relief, assuming that the recent turbulence had all been merely a troubled adolescent spell which was now safely over.

I am hazy about how Will spent his time before going up to Cambridge. He stayed away from Dowlands and then, of course, I missed him. I had resented him. But he was always exciting. He had a way of setting the air alight and it was strangely uncomfortable suddenly becoming an only child. Most of the time he spent down in Cornwall with Granny and Grandpa, where he got involved with a music festival.

Syd never got past Grade Two piano. I banged my way through various piano exams and somewhere around Grade Five my lack of talent was acknowledged and I was allowed to give the piano up. Will, however, could play any keyboard like a demon. He had taught himself the flute and while he was at the sixth-form college he had started to play the sax.

Granny says, 'Never say "if only",' generally following this remark with 'If only I never said it myself'. But if only Will had stayed in Cornwall and gone on playing the sax, if only he had gone roaring round the world with Jesse, who was at heart a decent boy, if only, *if only* people would just let other people be . . .

13

The first time I travelled any distance alone by train I was thirteen. Will had sent me a postcard (a vintage black-and-white photo of Lenin) inviting me to visit him in Cambridge over the school half-term and I was so thrilled that I begged and begged to be allowed to go. I find this quite touching now. Aunt Bell had mentioned that she was going to London and after a lot of parental discussion it was agreed that I would travel down with her on the train from Durham and, provided she put me on the train at King's Cross and Will met me in Cambridge, I could go.

I was in awe of my aunt but the journey to London was entertaining as she kept me amused with various stories about Dad when he and she were little, stories which, on reflection, tended rather to glorify her at Dad's expense. She also lent me her *Vogue* and *Harper's Bazaar*, which I devoured hungrily. She was wearing a fitted suit made of a soft lavender tweed. I had tended to consider tweed suits the province of sensible middle-aged women till I encountered Bell in that one. I suppose she was travelling to a tryst with one of the applicants.

I was alarmed, though not very surprised, when at King's Cross my aunt abandoned me with a cheery,

'You'll be OK now, dear. They'll flag up the platform number on that board there.' In fact I felt quite proud of myself for negotiating the crowded station and making my way to the correct platform.

It was even less of a surprise when there was no Will to meet me at Cambridge. I asked at the station about buses and caught one that dropped me by the market. The clocks had not yet gone back, the evening was still light and I found my way unaided to King's.

I remember how impressed I was with Will's rooms – 'rooms': not a single room but a bedroom and a study with an imperious stone fireplace, before which I saw one of Granny's home-made rag rugs, on which a plate I recognized from Mum's wedding dinner service, piled with cigarette butts and beer-bottle caps, reposed.

I dutifully visited the Fitzwilliam, because my parents would expect a report, and Will took me punting because I begged him to. It was autumn, not the punting season, and this was his first experience of what is quite an art but he manoeuvred the boat skilfully before carting me off to the Granta where we sat outside and he bought me a cider. That seemed very glamorous too. And at the Granta he introduced me to a friend of his, Harvey.

Harvey was chattily affable in a way that I instinctively mistrusted. He questioned me with a seeming interest which I recognized as fake. But that was all I saw of Harvey on that visit.

I heard more of him when just before Christmas Cele reappeared.

She had finished at the Bazinets. Theo, who to my untutored ear already played the cello like a professional, had been sent away by a regretful Marie to a school which specialized in music. Sabine was by now apparently eagerly reading all the English classics. So, with sadness on both sides, Cele's official role with the Bazinets had come to an end.

My school term hadn't finished so when supper was over I went to my room to do my homework and it was not till near bedtime that Cele tapped at my door. She was the only one who did this – the rest of the family simply barged in.

I asked about the Bazinets. It was too important to me for me to be able to disguise my concern.

'We'll stay in touch,' she assured me. 'You'll see Theo again, I'm sure.' Of course she had divined the state of my affections.

She enquired after Pauline Crowsdale, who by now had dwindled to a minor irritant, and I asked, 'How's Will?'

I knew that Cele had visited Will before she came up to Dowlands and I had imagined it as a lovers' reunion. But in fact, she told me then, they had had a heated argument.

It was one of the rare occasions when she spoke to me about Colin, which shows how agitated she must have been. Evidently, while she was still in Paris Colin had turned up out of the blue at the Bazinets' apartment. He had winkled her address out of a girl at St Neot's with whom Cele had vaguely corresponded.

Probably the poor girl was the latest target for his ego. Really only to avoid a scene, Cele had gone out to dinner with him. I don't know what went on between them and I don't know how Will discovered this. He may have simply guessed, because he knew Cele so well and she was never able to conceal any guilty feelings.

He needn't have worried because Cele hadn't at all wanted to see Colin. 'He showed off his French in front of the Bazinets,' she told me. 'It was mortifying. I couldn't wait for him to leave.'

I think myself Colin was fundamentally a woman-hater. Philanderers mostly are. But Colin for Cele was only ever some kind of fill-in. For Will. Or maybe for her father. Or maybe it was her way of unconsciously getting a bit of her own back on her mother, beating her at her own game. I don't know. What I do know is that he wasn't really important. He came to seem important, which somehow counts.

Anyway, after this row with Will, Cele had determined to put the whole Colin episode behind her and had rung Colin to ask him to return various letters she had sent him. I can see why she might have been worried about these. Colin was vicious and he wasn't above blackmail. He replied, suggesting a meeting. She was so anxious to draw a line under that relationship that she went all the way to Truro to meet him and she said that her heart started to thud so violently on her way to this assignation that she wondered whether she was about to have a heart attack. But apparently Colin never showed up.

She had come up to us at Dowlands after this, praying that Colin was out of her life and that would now be that.

The Cambridge term, which is absurdly short, had already ended but she reported that Will had said to say that he was 'busy with various activities'. I suppose he was still very angry with her. She was vague with my parents about what these activities were and they didn't press her. There was always an unspoken hovering sense that with Will they were keen not to rock any boat.

The other thing that had bothered Cele was Harvey. 'He sort of hung about,' she said. 'It was difficult getting Will to myself.'

'I didn't like him. He's creepy,' I offered.

She had a way of frowning when she was troubled. 'He lives out but I got the impression he's used to sleeping in Will's rooms in college. I mean I was staying there.'

'Yuck!' I was flattered to be granted this hint of her relationship with Will. 'D'you think Harvey's gay?'

'Maybe.'

'But Will isn't, is he?' I was being sly because I was pretty sure from what I'd overheard that he wasn't.

She looked quite cross at this and said, 'No, but so what if he was.'

I apologized and she said, more gently, 'It's more that I don't think Harvey's a good friend . . .'

And there we left it, as far as I remember, at least for the time being.

When Will arrived, late on Christmas Eve, he was

outwardly in sparkling form: amusing, expansive, flamboyant. With hindsight too flamboyant. His mood, as Granny said, could always reach to heaven and back down to hell in an hour. Our family celebration was always on Christmas Eve because on Christmas Day itself, by long tradition, Dad did duty at his hospital. For years Dad acted as a hospital Father Christmas, which I'm sorry to say I found embarrassing, and on alternate years we visited either a children's or an old people's home. It was good of my parents, and characteristic of them, but I can't say I enjoyed it.

That was a Christmas that especially sticks in my memory as Syd joined us. She was so much my senior that I saw little of her as a child, and seeing her then it was more as if a young aunt had come to visit. She was larger than ever – 'bonny', as Bell spitefully put it – but she looked happy.

What I noticed was that Mum's mood lightened immediately on Syd's arrival. Poor Mum. Will was constitutionally so unlike her and I'm afraid I wasn't too congenial either. Syd was the child most akin to Mum and it must have been hard to have her favourite living so far away, especially in such an alien place as Jordan. She had gone there originally to work for a schoolfriend's father's firm, but she must have had her own reasons for straying so far from home.

I felt quite jealous too, not because of Mum's obvious preference for Syd but because Will seemed suddenly so pally with her. They laughed riotously together and recounted episodes from their childhood in which I'd had no part. They'd had some competitive game which he resurrected, to do with throwing stones across the ha-ha, which Syd took to with great gusto and loud belly laughs. But I see now that this was partly Will getting his own back on Cele.

I don't know if it was because Syd was to be there but Will had brought us all presents, which was itself a novelty. A basket, I think, for Mum, a bottle of Armagnac for Dad, there was a CD – or was it a video? – of Spike Milligan for Syd and I was given a dear little carved squirrel he'd found at a stall in the market. To Cele he gave a cardboard box beautifully wrapped in green tissue paper. She opened it after the rest of us had opened ours and I was the only one placed to observe her face. Her expression matched the contents of the box which, I could see, was quite empty.

There was a gift tag attached to the tissue paper with something written on it. I slyly watched Cele read it but nothing showed in her face to enlighten me.

On Christmas Day loyalty sent me out with our mother on what Will referred to as her 'calves-foot-jelly rounds'. Syd came too, for which I was grateful as for the last few years Will would have none of these missions and Cele, the most merciful of us, whose sense of loyalty meant that she had formerly always accompanied us, stayed at home that year. I imagine she was hoping to explain matters to Will.

The fire, which was always lit in the sitting room on Christmas Eve and maintained throughout the Christmas period, was out when Mum and I got back from the grisly old people's home. Dad was still at the hospital playing Father Christmas in his silly beard and there was no sign of either Will or Cele.

I was disappointed because I was looking forward to the game of charades that we traditionally played on Christmas Day and which acted as an antidote to the good works. Mum was preparing the lunch of cold turkey and salad and after I had helped to lay the table I slipped into Cele's room. Mrs Mahoane's room had become mine and Cele was now in my old room, where some of my outgrown toys were stowed.

At thirteen I no longer played with toys, but for all Mum's promptings I was still too attached to them to hand them on and I'd decided that, if discovered, my story was that I was in search of my old blue monkey, who had been my first Christmas gift and whom I often brought out at Christmas. I knew he was stashed in the storage box on top of the wardrobe and I climbed on a chair to fetch him down to act as my alibi while I investigated Cele's things.

She had not unpacked her suitcase and I riffled through some lace underwear and found a pack of contraceptive pills and Mitsouko by Guerlain in her sponge bag. There was a book on the bedside table – *Le Rouge et le Noir* – and marking the page was the gift tag with Will's handwriting on it.

> *Yet each man kills the thing he loves*
> *by each let this be heard,*
> *some do it with a bitter look,*

some with a flattering word,
the coward does it with a kiss . . .

Hearing the back door open, I quickly replaced the tag, grabbed Monkey and fled. But it was only Dad coming in. The four of us ate lunch with Dad and Syd gamely making poor jokes and Mum unable to suppress her annoyance at Will and Cele's absence.

After lunch I went to my room to read. I was reading my way through *The Once and Future King* which Grandpa had given me because it was written by his old schoolmaster. I'd just reached the story of Lancelot and Guinevere's adulterous affair and I was feeling sorry for Arthur. It's hard not to when you've followed him from his childhood as the lowly Wart. I read on, losing myself in the story, until I heard the back door again.

It was twilight. A crowd of rooks were wheeling past, their ragged wings etched clear against a petrol sky. Looking down I saw that Dad had gone outside and was watching the birds too. He liked birds. It was one of the few ways in which he resembled Granny. As he stood, another figure, wearing a woolly hat that snuffed out the upper part of the face, came towards him down our drive.

I thought from the shape that it was Cele but the voice filtering up to me as I opened the window was not hers. Running downstairs I suddenly knew who it was.

Harvey was standing by the fire warming his bottom and our father, at the sideboard, was pouring a drink. Harvey looked at me as I came into the room with that unappealing affable smile as if we were old friends.

'Hetty! Oh, ta,' to my father who was handing him a glass.

'Hetta,' I corrected him, hoping I sounded cold.

'Well,' Harvey said, 'down the hatch then. Cheers!'

I don't believe he was public-school. But he put on this obnoxious public-school manner, which was supposed to be amusing.

I stood there feeling unamused and he must have picked this up as he smiled in that slimy way he had and said, 'You all right, Het-Het-Hetta? How's school?'

Over a second drink, into which I observed Dad pouring a rather less generous measure of vodka, Harvey explained that Will had invited him to stay, that he had hitched his way from Cambridge, expecting to have to stay a night en route but had struck lucky with a lift from a couple on their way to visit a relative in Berwick.

'An old dodderer and his beady wife. My bet is the only reason she was keen to see his aunt over Christmas was to make sure she dropped her doubloons their way when she dropped off her perch,' was how he described his benefactors. These people had been generous enough to go out of their way to leave him at the bottom of our drive.

It was plain when Cele and Will came home that Harvey's presence was going to be contentious. Cele's face, coloured by the cold wind and looking quite lovely, instantly shadowed at the sight of the interloper standing before the fire. I can see him, legs straddled in that awful cocksure position that certain men adopt. My mood plummeted at the thought of him staying. Our parents were inclined to be over-hospitable. Whatever they thought of Will's guest, politeness would ensure his staying as long as he chose.

But he didn't choose to stay long. After a few days, with Cele looking glum and Will becoming increasingly loud-mouthed and objectionable, he and Harvey took off, ostensibly to walk Hadrian's Wall. The bottle of port, Dad's annual reward for playing Santa at the hospital, was found to be missing from his car. And while Dad believed he had left it at the hospital, I was sure that Harvey was the culprit. Though Will might help himself liberally from the already opened bottles or decanters, it would be out of character for him to steal. As I think I've said, he was rather innocently honest.

I don't remember what Cele did when they left. Mum and Syd had got into a huddle and Cele, who for so long had been a surrogate daughter for Mum, might reasonably have felt left out. My recollection is that she hung around for a few days and then went off to London where Bell had commandeered a flat from someone she had met on a cruise. I remember the news of this cruise causing comment. Cruises weren't at all Bell's sort of thing.

I spent the rest of the holiday finishing *The Once and Future King*. I can't stand the Disney kind of Arthurian romance but I still enjoy that version.

14

For the rest of Will's first year at university we hardly saw him. He came home for a few days at the start of the Easter vacation having grown a beard and wearing a terrible green woolly hat which, I suppose to annoy Mum and Dad, he declined to take off at mealtimes. He sank fairly quickly into a vague boredom and then gave some excuse to go off to be with Harvey.

Cele came to us for the Easter weekend. There had been some talk of her training as a French-language secretary (I think that's what they were called). I don't know what that might have involved but it had come to nothing. Maybe after her time in Paris she wanted financial independence. Anyway, she had found a job as a receptionist in a GP's surgery, a position which came through a contact of Kenny's.

Alastair had apparently resigned from the list of Bell's applicants but Kenny lingered on. And there was Robert. But Robert had a wife. And soon after this we learned that a new applicant had arrived in Bell's life.

I know now that it was because of Robert's wife that Bell went on the cruise in the first place and that she went with the intention of finding a replacement for Robert. A mistake. Robert was a match for her and if ever there was a woman who needed a match it was Bell. Graham, the fellow passenger whom she met in the Straits of Gibraltar at a vodka-and-caviar evening, had important pluses in his favour: he was divorced and he was a successful businessman. But he was very slow on the uptake and spoke in clichés. Bell should have had an inkling at least, when to everyone's astonishment she announced her engagement to Graham, that a character so alien to her own would come to be irksome. But she had that trait that I've observed in attractive women: a belief that they can shape their own happiness in the way they can shape men's fascination.

Graham's pre-eminent advantage was that he had what Granny called 'means'. These included the vast flat in South Kensington where Cele stayed that Easter. Bell may have felt it was worth trading variety for steadiness and luxury but I'd like to think she also felt some compunction over her daughter.

One of the consequences of Bell's proposed marriage was that she decided this was the moment for Cele to meet her father. We were all very curious to hear about him. He turned out to be an elderly Russian, much older than Bell in years and appearance, with a straggly Rasputinish beard (quite unlike Will's bushy one). Cele found her lost father living in a flat, jam-packed with furniture and hung with icons, in a red-brick mansion block off the Marylebone Road. She said that the carpets were filthy, covered with a patina of animal fur, and the scent of incense failed to disguise a pervading smell of cat pee.

The only feature of Cele's missing parent that Bell had revealed was that he came from a noble Russian family. If this was really the case, then from Cele's account he had travelled some distance from his roots. Apparently he sat by a coal-effect electric fire with one bar burning, a long-haired Persian cat on his lap, chain-smoking and rocking all the time on a chair piled with cushions, which made her wonder if he had a bad back.

He offered her some old biscuits which he must have been hoarding for years, the kind that were once called squashed flies, on a dirty plate with a faint gold emblem that might have been a relic of the noble past. Cele was too shy to refuse the biscuits so she ate two, to pretend she really liked them, while he asked very formally after her mother whom he referred to as Christabel. He enquired too about Cele's music and when she disclosed that she neither played an instrument nor sang he lost any appearance of interest in her and began to stare at the clock on his table, which she was amused to observe was an hour slow. This was May and the clocks had gone forward two months earlier.

Bell, who was avidly awaiting Cele's report, was annoyed at her description and became vocal about her former lover's looks. 'Igor was exquisitely beautiful when I knew him.' She was clearly offended at the idea that she'd had an affair with someone as unattractive as Cele made him sound.

Bell's wedding was very luxurious – in Granny's words, 'vulgar' – though I must say I enjoyed it. The ceremony took place in the town hall but the reception was at a hotel, marmoreal in decor, with deep carpets, decorated with pink orchids and overlooking the park. Bell wore a cream Dior suit in which she looked stunning. To be fair, although she enjoyed looking good, I don't believe she cared particularly about clothes; or jewels either, though her engagement ring was a massive diamond. Graham wanted to show her off. I suppose to him she was a prize.

Syd flew from Jordan to be at the wedding and arrived with a man in tow, who caused general surprise by being extremely good-looking. He was also quite a few years younger than her, despite having already fathered a family. I liked Omar. I sat beside him at the wedding breakfast, at which he ate very little and chain-smoked throughout; afterwards, when there was dancing to a live band, he flung me about in a kind of exuberant polka. I decided that it was shrewd of Syd to settle in Jordan where large women are considered sexy and handsome young men are attracted to the maternal.

The job that a rather moth-eaten Kenny, who also appeared at the wedding and was introduced to Graham as an 'old friend', had put in Cele's way was with a GP practice in the Finchley Road. Bell's new circumstances were proving useful: they provided Cele with accommodation, which in London, even in the nineties, was not cheap. And in turn Cele began to provide Bell with a bulwark against a rashly acquired husband. Although Cele had grown up with her mother's casual indifference, she must have longed for a closeness that had been at best fleeting. And now, thanks to Graham, she and her mother became, for a spell, almost companions.

They went together to concerts and, on Graham's Coutts account, to the stalls at the Royal Opera House. They also made trips to Staresnest, where it was said that Graham never wished to go and where occasionally Kenny joined them. Bell no longer wanted Kenny to herself but he'd clung on like an old burr. As Kenny had grown shabbier Cele had grown fonder of him. She said once that she had wondered if her mother wished she had married Kenny rather than Graham. But as Will said, Bell had not married Kenny for so long that she couldn't alter the habit.

Not long after she returned to Jordan, Syd caused a family upset by writing to announce her own plans to marry. She'd come back that Christmas especially to tell our parents, but faced with Mum's vocal rejoicing at the return of her eldest child, Syd had flunked the revelation that her stay abroad was to be permanent. She wrote, not too tactfully, to say that it was Bell's wedding that had given her 'the courage to break the news' of her own imminent wedding. Omar, she explained, although married already, could under Jordanian law take another wife. But in practice, Syd assured us, he was planning to live only with her.

Our parents took this hard, Mum especially. Syd, as I've said, was the child closest to her in character and inclination but also, although like most parents she cherished the notion that she was liberal-minded, the prospect of a polygamous Muslim marriage horrified her. There was a terrific argument over the phone which ended with Syd declaring that if they were going to take that line she wasn't inviting them to the wedding, which led to further dramas. I had contracted glandular fever and had been off school pretty much since the wedding, and was in that restless, bored state that attends convalescence. So when Granny invited me down to stay at St Levan I was glad to accept to be away from all the family fuss. It was on that stay that Granny and I had a conversation about love.

I was recounting how badly my parents were taking the news of Syd's proposed marriage and relishing my disloyalty.

'Well, you know, Hetta, there's no knowing where love will take us,' Granny said when I mentioned the polygamous marriage. 'Love is stronger than morality, thank heavens.'

We were in their garden, folding sheets from the washing line. It was really rather an ugly garden, a dog-leg shape, marked out with a rickety fence, but Granny had made it beautiful with the kind of flowers you see in the illustrations of old-fashioned children's books: nasturtiums, marigolds, zinnias and heliotrope, which she called Cherry Pie.

I can see her so clearly that day – with the spires of hollyhocks behind her, Ribena-coloured and that papery sherbet yellow. She grew them from seed in shallow wooden trays in her shed.

"'The heart has its reasons of which reason knows nothing,'" she said, flapping the sheet down against her flat-as-a-board stomach and piling it into the basket, which had done past service for many cars, trains and piratical ships.

I guessed she was talking about herself and Grandpa, though at that time I knew very little about their history. I knew very little about Pascal either but I liked those words.

15

I stayed at St Levan long enough to recover. Grandpa and I watched football on their black-and-white TV set – they were the only people I knew who still only had black-and-white TV – and I watched the racing with Granny. Her mother was Irish and grew up with racing stock and she and Granny used to bet on the horses. Granny could still enjoy what she called 'an occasional flutter'. And I lounged about in their garden, eating unripe apples from their tree and chocolate fingers and reading *Sense and Sensibility*. I decided that even if I was supposed to prefer Elinor, I much preferred Marianne. And to break the journey home I stopped off at Bell's flat in South Kensington.

Cele had suggested that I go to meet her after work so I went by tube to Swiss Cottage and walked down the Finchley Road.

When I finally found the practice, Cele was busy with an anxious-seeming old man who was fretting about his wife's prescription. I was impressed at how she dealt with him. The old man's flies were half undone and a bit of his shirt was poking through the zip. His raincoat was stained and the collar askew and covered in dandruff. But Cele had her hand on his arm and was speaking to him in what we as children used to call a 'proper voice', that is, not one adopted for children or idiots.

I sat down in the waiting room and read a feature on acne in an out-of-date magazine, which advised me to be sure to keep my face and hands clean and not to eat chocolate, until an elderly man with badgerish hair and a yellowing moustache came through a door. He smiled at me in a grandfatherly sort of way.

'I'm afraid the clinic is finished today but if you'd like to make an appointment . . .'

'Oh, no . . .' I began to explain.

'This is Hetta,' Cele said, still occupied with the patient. 'She's with me. Dr Jacobs, Mr Ryan needs a new prescription for his wife. She's still in a lot of pain.'

While Dr Jacobs was attending to Mrs Ryan's pain another man, clearly also a doctor, came into the waiting room. A younger sandy-haired man with the kind of blond eyelashes that make you think of pigs.

'You must be Cecilia's cousin.'

Mr Ryan's worries having been temporarily allayed, Cele introduced me. 'Hetta, this is my other boss, Dr McCowan. This is my cousin Hetta.'

'Your cousin's a godsend, Hetta,' the younger doctor said. He smiled at her and his eyes crinkled in the way they do when a smile is real so that my prejudices about his lashes fell away.

Later I remembered this but what at the time seemed the most memorable part of my stay in London was that Bell bought me my first decent bra.

'What do you fancy doing, dear?' she asked me the following morning.

I was expecting to amuse myself and said so.

'No, let's go shopping,' Bell said. 'We'll go to Harvey Nicks.'

So that's where we went, where, thanks to Graham, my aunt now possessed an account card, and she bought me a new bra. The bra I chose, from a delectable selection, was primrose yellow with cream lace around the cups into which slices of spongy uplift had been inserted. It was kind of her and I can see now that she felt I was in need of some more feminine influence but naughty Bell must also have taken pleasure in knowing that my mother would not have approved: it was so unlike the white cotton serviceable bras I already owned. I have a memory of matching knickers, also bedizened with lace, but Mum must have thrown them out because I never remember wearing them. The underwear my mother bought for me was strictly M & S.

The bra filled me with such pride that I was reluctant to take it off so I was wearing it when Bell took me to a nearby café, where she bought me a Danish pastry and told me about my uncle. And if the bra is incidental to the story I'm trying to tell, my uncle is not.

No one in the family ever spoke about our father and Bell's brother, the eldest of that generation of Tyes. But thanks to Bell, the yellow bra, the Danish pastry and my dead Uncle Nat have become irrevocably linked in my mind.

I doubt if there was anything about me that caused Bell to open this family safe and say, 'Jack would have been fifty-one today. My God, it's extraordinary to imagine him being over fifty.'

I had my mouth full, which was just as well as I didn't immediately know who she was talking about. No one had ever mentioned that Jack was my uncle's family name. I wouldn't have had a clue how to react anyway.

'We called Nat "Jack",' Bell said, observing my puzzlement, 'because he had a craze for toads.' I didn't understand this either but I wasn't going to interrupt a fascinating confidence to further my knowledge of natural history. 'Do you know how he died?' She looked at me with her slant cat eyes. Bell's eyes are extraordinarily blue, bluer even than Grandpa's: the colour as I imagine it of a lovely alien's eyes.

Still chewing stupidly, I shook my head.

'I could do with a cigarette,' Bell said.

She got up and walked over to a table where a man was smoking. I saw her bend towards him and the man hand her a cigarette and light it for her.

'Sorry, dear,' she said, returning to our table. 'It just got to me suddenly. You know how these things can.'

I nodded my head again, though I didn't know any such thing.

'You don't know how he was killed, do you?' she said. 'No, you wouldn't.' And she laughed a sharp, unhumorous laugh. 'He was climbing King's College Chapel. Silly boy.'

'Will's college?'

'And your grandfather's.'

'I see,' I said, though I didn't. I had always believed that my uncle had died in a mountaineering accident.

'There was a lunatic organisation, club, society, I don't know what you'd call it, that was started in the thirties. They called themselves "The Night Climbers" – ridiculous name – and it involved climbing the highest and most dangerous college buildings at night, barefoot sometimes and without proper safety gear. It was revived again after the war by an undergraduate whose father had been one of the original group and Jack got involved.'

'Why did he?'

My aunt expelled a stream of smoke. 'He was an experienced rock climber. He'd been climbing since he was a kid. But this was different.' Bell flipped her hands apart expressively. They were beautiful hands and she had a way of using them like an Italian. I suppose that was intentional.

'Did he fall?'

'They said he died instantly.'

'Jesus,' I said, feeling that this was a suitably grown-up response.

'Jesus would have come in handy,' Bell said. 'If we could have got him to bring Jack back from the dead your grandfather would probably have turned into Saint Paul and become his most devoted disciple.'

She looked at me again with her slant eyes and if you can locate any precise flicker of time when you can be said to have become adult, for me it was in that moment.

We sat oddly together, my aunt, whom I hardly knew, and I, a girl on the edge of adulthood, in the suddenly cruel-seeming Knightsbridge sun, while well-dressed, well-made-up women with high heels and large cardboard carrier bags with the names of expensive shops on them passed by unperturbed by the recounting of this small domestic tragedy.

Bell cadged another cigarette from our neighbour and drank her coffee and I tried to make sense of what I'd heard. I could feel the unfamiliar sensation of my new bra cutting into the rolls of residual puppy fat round my ribs.

'What did he look like?' I asked my aunt.

'Very like your grandfather at that age. Tall. There are photos. You should ask Granny. They're not on show because Daddy can't bear to see them but she has them stashed away. Ask her. She'll show you, I'm sure. You know you're her pet,' my aunt said.

And then she said a funny thing, which when I considered it later that evening in bed, going over our conversation in my mind, faintly troubled me. 'Not that I mind.'

16

Almost a year after this conversation with my aunt, I was lying on my stomach in the garden, on one of the moth-eaten rugs kept for garden use, writing a letter to Omar. My correspondence with Theo had faded and I was in need of a substitute. Omar and I had discovered at Bell's wedding a mutual love of football and I took a sneaky adolescent pleasure in sharing with my sister's husband an enthusiasm which I knew left her cold.

Mum was erecting the cane wigwam for the runner beans in the corner of the garden where we grew vege-tables, and when Dad shouted for her from the window she didn't at once respond.

I saw Dad come out of the back door and from the way he was walking I could tell something was up. He sticks his head forward in an odd way when he's dis-turbed, like a goose. I could hear my parents' voices across the lawn. They went back into the house so I made my way to the kitchen window and crouched by the parsley. I don't know how they never came to sus-pect that they could be heard from this position.

'It's so near his exams,' our mother was saying.

'I'll try to get hold of his tutor,' Dad said. 'What's his name?'

'Just ask for the Senior Tutor.'

'No, Will told us his name, you must remember.'

So Will was in some kind of trouble again.

My parents had given up trying to keep all their concerns from me, as they rigidly did when Syd and Will were about, so when I went inside it wasn't too hard for me to ask, 'What's up?'

They were standing with their backs to the Rayburn which, summer or winter, was kept on. The Rayburn acted as some sort of material pledge of the family's warmth.

Dad said, 'It's your brother.'

Simultaneously Mum said, 'It's Will.'

'What's he done now?' I asked. I was tired of Will corralling my parents' attention.

'He's been rusticated,' Mum said.

'She means kicked out,' Dad explained, in case I'd not got the point.

'Not for good, we hope,' Mum said. She sounded almost pleading.

'What's he done this time?'

It seemed that Will had been apprehended painting on the wall of the college chapel. And there had been other previous misdemeanours. On one occasion he had apparently vomited into a washbasin (not his own) and left the tap running, causing a flood which damaged the ceiling of the room below.

'It's your bloody father,' Mum said. 'I'm sorry, Bert, but it is. His bloody "intellectual" ideals. I'm sick to death of them, if you want to know.'

When Will was brought home by Dad, who had driven down to Cambridge to collect him, it emerged that Mum's instinct was at least half right. A fervent belief in God's non-existence may be as much an emotional prop as its opposite, if opposites are what they are and not aspects of the same need. And if it is a need it is one that Will and Grandpa seemed to share.

But vandalism was never Grandpa's way, and everyone was puzzled by the childishness of Will's act. He had contrived to spray-paint in scarlet 'Blessed are the atheists' before being caught by the college porters. He told me later that evening, when I tiptoed up to his room to take him the rhubarb crumble he'd refused at supper, that he'd intended to continue with 'for they see Reason'. He was unusually nice to me about the crumble.

The Senior Tutor had divulged that Will had been warned several times about drunken behaviour.

'They obviously like him or they wouldn't have been so lenient up till now. But they couldn't really overlook this,' Dad said, when Will had gone off to his room. Poor Dad, he looked so anxious.

It had been a grim supper. Conversation had been stiltedly polite. There'd been an ostentatious jug of water on the table over dinner, which Will had ignored, and when he left the room Mum said, 'For God's sake, let us have a drink at least, Bert' – which was so unlike her that I began to feel really concerned. Dad fetched a bottle of beer from the pantry and opened it clumsily, bruising his hand, which made him swear and throw the opener on to the floor. I was all of not quite fifteen and mentally dismissed this behaviour as 'babyish'.

Mum said again. 'It's your bloody father. I dare say he'll find all this *droll*.'

She sort of spat out 'droll', which was one of Grandpa's words. I hadn't properly grasped till then how angry she really was with Granny and Grandpa.

'It's that Harvey,' I suggested, because I wanted someone for them to blame other than Grandpa.

I was surprised at their surprise. 'You think it's got something to do with him?' Dad asked.

'He's absolutely dire,' I said. 'You must see that.'

What my parents really 'saw' was somewhat opaque to me because their views were always presented in an indivisible formula: 'We've decided', 'We think', 'We believe'.

'I did wonder,' Mum said, 'whether it was Harvey who pinched your port.'

'Of course it was,' I said. 'You never found it at the hospital, did you, Dad?' It was the first time I recall feeling conscious contempt for my parents' limited understanding. To enlarge their comprehension I explained, 'Harvey's a thug and for some reason Will's in his thrall.'

'Thug' didn't adequately describe Harvey. He was more insidious than that. And I doubt that Will was in anyone's thrall exactly. But my remark served its turn because it gave a new focus to my parents' displeasure.

They began to discuss between themselves what they should do while I, feeling smug at my superior powers of perception, helped myself to more rhubarb crumble.

I was angry that Will yet again had stolen the family limelight. Angry that the family peace was once more being destroyed. I loved Will but I also hated him. Of course this condition is commoner than we are encouraged to believe.

Will expressed no remorse for his actions. When questioned about his motives, he remarked that Shelley had been rusticated for atheism, which was the kind of justification that was bound to make Mum spit tacks. I don't recall at what point he went off to London to stay with Bell. But when I next saw him he'd found work as a barman at the Festival Hall.

Bell had got him the contact, through Robert, or maybe through one of the musical friends she had kept up with from the Royal College. However Will got the position, it was a bad idea. Though it seemed OK at first because it was through this that he started his band.

He had formed an impromptu band during the months in Cornwall which had fallen apart when he left for Cambridge. But now, down in London, he'd found among the South Bank buskers some sympathetic fellow musicians and started a new band, Black Tye Boys. I stayed at Aunt Bell's on my way to St Levan that summer holiday and the first thing I heard when I let myself in was the sound of Will's sax.

I don't honestly remember what he was playing then

but in my mind it is 'One Step Beyond'. All I clearly recall was the experience of hearing the plangent notes sounding in Bell's hallway where I stood listening, as columns of sunlight in which dust motes danced out of time pooled on to the pale gold carpet. And while the music sounded mournful I felt somewhere that Will was happy – freed from the restless spirit that had dogged him and that I didn't understand.

Cele was at work. My aunt was out. A key had been left for me with the caretaker so it was only myself and my brother there in the sunny Kensington flat. Unwilling to disturb him, I crept through the sitting room to Cele's bedroom, where I was to sleep, and sat on the bed and listened while he played on.

He played for some time and when the music stopped, and I could hear water running, I went through to the kitchen and the look on Will's face, as he turned from filling the kettle, caught my heart. I would never have considered myself capable of prompting such a delighted reaction in my brother and in a rush of gratitude I flung myself at his unopened arms.

'What on earth are you doing here?' was his more characteristic response.

'Didn't they say? I'm on my way to Granny's.'

'No one tells me anything,' Will said.

This wasn't true. Bell or Cele would have been sure to tell him I was arriving. What was likely was that, drunk or in a drugged haze, he'd not taken in the information or had forgotten he'd been told. But wanting to recover that spontaneous look of pleasure at my presence I said, 'How awful of them, why ever not?'

And I remember what he said to this. 'As you know, Hetta, I'm generally *persona non grata*.'

I've noticed a strange thing about names. Americans deploy them all the time, even at a first encounter they slip one's name into the most trivial communications: 'Hi, Hetta.' 'How you doing, Hetta?' But the English tend to use names more sparingly. Will rarely addressed anyone by name directly. Hearing him voice my name at that precise moment struck me with an almost physical force, springing a sudden gush of tenderness for my prodigal brother.

'Not with me,' I said, disloyally distancing myself from my cousin and my aunt. I must have very badly wanted his good opinion.

I don't know if it was that afternoon. I think not. I believe it was the following morning, when everyone had gone out and we were alone together again, that I confided to Will what Bell had told me about our uncle. We had been brought up to believe that he had died in a climbing accident but no details had ever been vouchsafed to us. I don't now know if it was that our parents wanted to keep the location secret – though I can think of no reason why they should have done – or if, as is more probable, it was simply that Dad couldn't bring himself to elaborate on the event that had so disrupted his own childhood.

It wouldn't have occurred to me then, but it has since,

that maybe Dad's problems with Will had something to do with a resentment over his lost brother, a resentment that he would almost certainly have been unable to acknowledge and which, maybe, had coloured his perceptions of young men and of which my poor brother had innocently borne the brunt. Whatever our parents' motive, even to me there was something disquieting about discovering that Nat had died not on some snowcapped mountain, as I'd always imagined, but falling backwards on to a Cambridge quadrangle.

'You must have seen the tower every day when you were there,' I suggested, tactlessly in the circumstances, since it was his desecration of the chapel that had led to Will's not being there at Cambridge. 'Is it so high? I don't remember.' I suppose I was trying to curry favour with him by imparting this sensational revision of family history.

'It would be one of the spires he must have been climbing. I'll look when I go back. If I go back.'

'Do you think you mightn't?'

'God knows. I don't.'

'But you want to go back, don't you?'

The expression on my brother's face stays in my mind still and I see it now as unguardedly vulnerable and forlorn. And I hear his voice, which when he wasn't angry was low and unusually melodious, saying, 'Honestly, Het, I don't know that either.'

PART TWO
Betsy

I

It is some time since Hetta first asked me for an account of all that I can tell of the history of our family that led up to Will's accident. I understand her asking. And after Will's fall I did write an account of sorts, for my own understanding. I have believed these reflections were best kept to myself. Yet the other day I thought again of Bede, for whom our mortal life is but a sparrow's flight through a lighted hall.

I am old and soon I must be joining those who have flown before me into the dark. Perhaps I shall fly more freely if I leave behind what I know, or what I think I know and what I thought I knew. Maybe it is time.

Beetle called us before they set out for Addenbrookes that dreadful May morning. I was awake anyway. And I don't believe it is merely with hindsight that I recall my hearing the ringing in the small hours as heralding some doom long awaited, the Angel of Death deciding finally to call. There is a part of me that is always expecting bad news.

Fred was dead in another sense – dead to the world in the arms not of Thanatos but of Morpheus, as he would have put it himself. For years, he'd been on heavy soporifics to help him sleep so he was confused when I forced him awake, and he looked so stricken when I explained the reason that I said little more than that I was off to the hospital. Of course I didn't know then where the fall had occurred.

Because I never cared for my son's given name, I still privately call him by his childhood name, Beetle. He was a timid little scrap and his only known act of sadism was when he chased his sister with a stag beetle, one of the few times I knew her scared. He wanted to keep the beetle as a pet and he cried when I suggested that it was kinder to let it go.

But formally he was 'Bertrand' because when Fred was only a small boy he attended a lecture, 'Why I am not a Christian', given by Bertrand Russell to the South London Branch of the National Secular Society. He was at this unlikely event with our Aunt Charlotte, with whom Fred had been parked while his mother was off on honeymoon with her second husband. Aunt Char was the younger sister of our fathers.

Poor Aunt Char spent most of her adult life in a genteel home for the mildly insane. She was given to sudden passions, and at the time she had fallen for Russell and went wherever she could to hear him speak. According to Fred, Russell's arguments so convinced him of the essential folly of belief in a deity that thereafter he rejected religion in all its forms. I used to joke that Aunt Char's fixation on Russell was a symptom of her deranged mental state but I regret that now because I believe that she was not really mad at all.

'Yield on unessentials,' my father always said, when he was letting my mother have her way, which was why, though it was no secret that I considered Russell an old humbug, I let Fred have his way over our son's name.

By the time Beetle was born Fred and I had few secrets between us, though some secrets are vital in any relationship. I'm not a fan of this modern obsession with 'transparency', one of those window-dressing words that cover a multitude of vagaries and stand for an idea rather than the deed. Ideas can do a lot of harm, if you ask me.

Fred and I shared many things besides Aunt Char. Among the most important was Dowlands, the family house in Northumberland, where our grandparents lived.

The house was built for a Tye ancestor who made money in wool. It was not a spectacularly grand house, quite modest by the standards of the eighteenth-century nouveaux riches, and most of the land that was once attached to it had been sold off by our grandparents' day. But it was an elegant house and commanded an uninterrupted view of the sea and the salt-white beach to which a track ran from the bottom of the field that lay beyond the walled garden. The eider ducks which inhabit the cold Northumbrian waters still bob along the shoreline there. Fred and I had a saying, 'The ducks, aren't they ducks?' Reading this now, the joke seems somewhat lame.

Fred and I spent our holidays at Dowlands. His father was killed when Fred was not quite three months old and he and I were both only children. He didn't get on with his stepfather, or his mother much, and I was packed off up there too to keep him company.

It was company for me besides. My parents loved me, I was never in doubt of that, but they liked their privacy. I never asked why they never had another child because I knew in my bones why. Theirs was a perpetual romance and more children might have threatened its intimacy.

I didn't mind. I was happy to be their sole focus. I loved Dowlands and I loved Fred, who was better than a brother to me.

There's a magic in the air of Northumberland which gets into your blood. Those endless wide skies and the astonishing light which favours the east coast, and the wild sea, forever washing with its pulsing rhythms the wide white sands. They call the sands 'white' but they are only white by comparison with the redder sands of the south or the west. Pale sands, I would call them.

Being left to the care of our grandparents meant, in practice, the care of our fathers' old nanny, Margaret, who had come as a girl of fourteen to look after Charlotte. She never married or had children of her own, and all I can hope is that we and they were enough for her. She would have insisted that we were and there is no question in my mind but that she loved all three of her 'first children' better than their parents did. She was the one who visited Aunt Char in her home and brushed her hair and fixed her up to 'make her pretty'. She had a sepia photo of my aunt, aged three, dressed in one of those meringue-puff frocks and the long, lace-bottomed drawers that children wore then, and while she looks very solemn you could see that she was a comely child. Hetta has a look of her.

One of the virtues of Margaret's care was that it was confined to the domestic so we were left pretty much to our own devices when it came to anything other than what we wore or what we ate or when we were sent to bed. We knew all the local beaches intimately, made friends with the fishermen, went out in their boats to set lobster pots and waded through mud to dig out crabs, and came home to nothing worse than a mild scolding and an order to change our clothes. And when the weather was wet or cold, or anyway too wet and too cold for Margaret's permission for us to be out in it, we read. Children don't read now the way we did, though I'm glad to say most of my family are still readers.

Our grandparents were not readers but the shelves of their library, to which we had free access, were stacked with leather-bound books, collected by some more literate Tye, and classified according to subject. The books were still in fairly good repair, with that peculiar smell of undusted dust which is so potent. There were books on theology (our grandfather came from missionary stock), ethology, geology, psychology and other 'ologies', so our reading was eclectic and by present standards advanced. We read all the classics, which are nowadays thought too difficult for children to grasp, I can never see why. From the age of six Fred attended a prep school (such were the times) where Latin and Greek were taught and he read me bits of Homer, which I loved, and of Virgil, who later became his passion but which I liked less. All those military doings in the *Aeneid* bored me. But it was the *Aeneid* which provided our private code. LR, we used to say – our shorthand for *lacrimae rerum* – when we felt anything was too bad. I know that sounds pretentious but I can't help it. That was how we were. One of the features of love is that it creates a private language.

The family myth was that Fred and I had no other loves before we married. Families cultivate myths – I dare say some academic will claim, if they haven't already, that this is an evolutionary advantage. But there was a kind of truth in this one because for as long as I can remember there was a special tie (a 'Tye', we liked to say) between us. Much the same bond as between Cecilia and Will.

Fred, who softened with age, liked to reminisce about the time we had been swimming near St Aidan's Dunes, where the holy presence of the saint allegedly made the sea safe. There was no one about and we'd grown up seeing each other naked, so I thought nothing of pulling off my wet, and hideous, black woollen costume. God knows why we were sent to swim in wool. Fred looked at me and said, 'You look like a Rhine maiden, Bets.' I remember this because he didn't look at me particularly as a rule, or not so deliberately. In the library there was a book illustrated by Arthur Rackham that told the story of the Ring and I laughed, assuming this was one of his teases because among his many strong views was a fierce dislike of Wagner. He never got over his dislike of Wagner.

I was embarrassed to see his expression change and become suddenly serious. He put out a hand and traced a finger down my nose, as if he were a painter and about to paint my portrait, and then he said, 'Dear freckles' which, given what was on his mind, was a cunning thing to say as I was sensitive about my freckles.

He went on looking at me in that uncomfortably serious way, then he put his arms round my waist and pulled my naked body towards him and kissed me on the lips and I was so stunned I didn't have a clue how to respond. He eased us down on to the sand, still holding me, and tried to make love to me, and I lay there like a lemon, with the waves thrashing in my ears, not knowing what on earth I was supposed to do.

What I chiefly remember is that the experience was rather hard on my back. The most erotic part of it, for me, was afterwards. I had a sandy behind because I hadn't properly dried myself, and Fred, very tenderly, rolled me over on to my stomach and dusted the sand off my bare bottom with the flat of his hand.

Fred used to insist that was the first time we made love. But he got that wrong as he often got such things wrong: we didn't manage it then. We managed things better a little later in the Blue Room where we slept. I don't believe it crossed anyone's mind that we were of an age to sleep apart. I was fifteen years and seven months and he was fourteen months older. He would be in danger of a custodial sentence these days but I don't believe I was any the worse for the experience.

If Fred wasn't born political then he had some gene which was waiting to be activated by the political because by this time he was not only reading avidly about socialism but had decidedly thrown in his lot with it. We grew up in the shadow of the First World War and our generation formed a backlash to that terrible exercise in human folly. Class folly, Fred called it. He was sent away to Stowe, a public school, which his mother in later life blamed for Fred's socialist beliefs. 'That progressive school,' she called it. She wasn't a bad woman, Blanche, and quite a looker in her day according to my father, who knew her when she was a bright young thing and his brother Oswald was courting her.

Oswald, as the elder son, had money from his father, because that was how things were done in their day, and as far as I know he never worked. He trained for the bar but I don't believe he ever took an actual brief. My father was cut from a different cloth. As the younger son with no means, he somehow got himself to medical school at Trinity College, Dublin. I never did ask how he came to go there and by the time I thought to enquire he was dying and there were other more important things to ask. I rather hope he was ducking out of the war but anyway Dublin was where he met my mother so if he hadn't gone there I wouldn't be here. I often think about how tenuous most of existence is.

As a physician, Dad subsequently cared for many who bore the scars of that dreadful war and carried, discreetly, his own inner scars. There had been no need other than the false call of patriotism for Oswald to enlist. Dad kept a letter in his desk from Oswald, his last letter as it turned out, written before the Second Battle of Arras where he died. I have it still and I got it out the other day and reread it. It makes such sad reading.

My uncle describes in this letter how he had to set his platoon to gathering up the dead bodies of their comrades – how they dragged the corpses of men they had been fighting beside into a 'shallow depression in the ground and covered them with thin layers of soil, which was the best we could do for them'. He goes on to describe how the limbs of the dead would often come away as they were being dragged to their last resting place in that depression in the ground.

But the worst part of the letter is this:

'The padre gave us a ripping sermon last Sunday. He finished by saying, "Many of you men here today will not be here next Sunday. But you will have given your lives bravely for your country and you will not be forgotten."'

They were, of course.

It was the loss of his brother, I suspect, that formed my father's unusually tolerant character. Once, when my mother was being catty about Blanche, who gave an impression of blaming Oswald for his own death, I remember Dad saying, 'We have to understand that Blanche's world has been shattered and she hasn't your moral fibre, Maudie.'

I wouldn't say that 'moral fibre' was my mother's strongest suit. But she was certainly much pluckier than Blanche.

Blanche married again, Charlie, a vulgar fortune hunter who had a fake coat of arms engraved on the Tye silver. I lay a good deal of what subsequently happened to Fred on that run of bad luck. Compared to Fred, I was blessed in my parents. For one thing, I was sent to a very different kind of school.

I'm not sure how much I've told you about my mother's family. They were Anglo-Irish, originally from Cork but at some point they moved to Dublin. Ma's parents liked to boast that they could trace their ancestry back to the time of Elizabeth the First but, for all that, by the time she arrived they were poor as church mice. So to cut costs, Ma shared a governess with another Dublin family and Nancy, the child of this other family, became Ma's best friend and much later my godmother. The two girls were greatly attached to their governess, Trudy, who held unconventional views and taught them to plant beans by phases of the moon, to listen to the music of Brahms and Schubert and to read Goethe in German.

Trudy went on to teach at Rudolph Steiner's school in Vienna but she left her mark on Ma. In those days,

Cheltenham Ladies' College was considered an 'advanced' educational establishment for girls of my father's class, so Ma set the cat among the pigeons by insisting that I attend the first Steiner school in London. The Tyes regarded this as the height of irresponsibility, but my mother could charm the moon and stars out of the sky so she got her way with my father. And she liked to stir things up a little with the Tyes. As a result I attended a school where we were hardly scolded and certainly never hit, we learned to spot the constellations, to read the Bible as if it was a collection of marvellous stories, to love poetry and music, to dance and to carve. And to the end of my days I shall see even numbers as green.

Fred had a very different school experience. I suppose if you had to be sent away to boarding school to be whacked on the bottom by older boys and told to 'be a man' if you 'blubbed', then Stowe wasn't such a bad one. Although his first love was classics, Fred acquired his taste in literature from his inspiring teacher Tim White, the eccentric alcoholic and hawk lover, who wrote *The Once and Future King*. And he was taught history by a dashing young Marxist, George Rudé, who became an expert on the French Revolution.

Fred was like Will, or rather Will was like Fred: they were both prone to intellectual crazes. I remember a summer when, thanks to George Rudé, all Fred would talk about was the French Revolution and the Terror and how the means justified the end – do I mean that? Or do I mean the other way round? What I am trying to say is that he insisted the revolutionaries were right to have Louis XVI put to death for the greater good. I had been reading *A Tale of Two Cities* so I was all for the other side. I don't much care for Dickens as a rule but I still like that one.

We had a fierce argument about this as we walked across to Holy Island. There was only a rough and ready causeway then and too bad if you got cut off by the tide.

'They acted as if they were God,' I said, when Fred admiringly quoted Danton, saying, 'Let us be terrible in order to stop the people being so.'

The mention of God always got him going. 'Better them acting God than God acting God.'

'Oh Fred, that's an absurd thing to say. Anyway, I thought you were all for the people. Why should Robespierre and his crew speak for them? I think it's insulting.'

We were terribly earnest. It makes me smile to think of it.

There was a piece of synchronicity, if that is the word I want, to do with another pupil at Stowe, a near-contemporary of Fred's, John Cornford. You maybe won't have heard of him but he was rather famous in our day. He was brilliantly precocious and won a scholarship from Stowe to Trinity, Cambridge aged only sixteen, and he was also a poet and a rip-roaring commie besides, so obviously very glamorous. Thinking about it, poor old Blanche had a point about Stowe being a hotbed of radicalism.

I must watch out for the propensity for the 'olden days' nostalgia that tends to overtake the elderly, but I do wonder if characters like John exist now. He bore that hallmark which endows a child with a charged aura for life – he was adored by his mother. She, Frances Cornford, was a poet too. She wrote 'Oh Fat White Woman Who Nobody Loves' which I used to admire, but having reread it, I think it is really a rather snobbish poem.

When I think of Fred's mother it is amusing to consider how very different she was from my own. Where the most sensational writing Blanche undertook was devising elaborate dinner menus, my mother wrote short stories, smoking and wearing a Chinese dressing gown and red silk slippers. None of her stories were of enduring worth but they were published in the magazines of the time and were not insignificant either. She had a turn for the sepulchral and wrote slightly fey but sometimes chilling stories about spirits and old charms and prophetic dreams.

My mother, like many of her contemporaries, had a crush on Rupert Brooke – from what I've read since, rather a cold-hearted man. He had been an intimate of the Cornfords and a special pet of Frances's. Ma wrote a pretty drippy story about Rupert Brooke's spirit haunting the River Cam. I have the manuscript still and I'm sorry to report that it was written in purple ink. The story attracted the attention of Frances Cornford. She must have admired it as she wrote quite a warm card inviting my mother to visit her in Cambridge, and as I had caught her passion for Rupert Brooke I accompanied her on this visit.

I am not sure why Fred joined us on that trip to Cambridge. Maybe it was a weekend when he had an exeat from Stowe and was coming to stay anyway. He rarely went back to Bakewell where Blanche and Charlie lived. He had heard on the school grapevine that John Cornford had put on an anti-war exhibition with his lover Margot Heinemann (another communist convert) and he carted me off to see it. The shock of seeing men's faces disfigured and blasted by war turned Fred into a pacifist on the spot. I can still picture his cornflower-blue eyes blazing with fury. And his determined 'We must put an end to this obscenity.'

And there was that dead father, pointlessly killed and lying in a grave in France, like Hamlet's ghost haunting him.

But you must understand that the true toll of the First World War was only lately being acknowledged and pacifism was very much in the air. Anyone with an ounce of humanity was horrified by the slaughter of those thousands of young men, so to be passionately anti-war was all the thing. In November, that same year, on Armistice Day, a big anti-war march was staged through Cambridge as a protest against the militarism of the Cenotaph celebrations in London, and Fred bunked off school in order to take part. Afterwards, he came on to London to stay with us and my chief memory is of him talking his head off about the demonstration.

'You should've been there, Bets,' he said, lolling on my bed, his eyes alight with the thrill of it. 'The toffs and hearties pelted us with rotten tomatoes and eggs. Bloody idiots.'

It sounded unpleasant to me. I didn't relish the idea of being pelted with rotten tomatoes and eggs but I can see now that for Fred to be the target of the hatred of his own class was a fillip to the spirit of rebellion against Blanche. 'The old order is changing,' he pronounced loftily, 'and they know their time is over.' It didn't seem to occur to him that he was part of this 'old order'.

I found all this disturbing. I didn't like his new attachment to a collective movement. We had done everything together as a pair I would have believed inseparable and I had that evening the first intimation of being abandoned. Well, you get used to it.

I can see Fred now, in my room in our house in Battersea, talking on and on till the roofs outside grew white in the dawn light, enthusing about the wonders of the world to come, and I did my best to listen, not because I agreed with him but because I wanted to understand. I must have dropped off at some point since I woke to find him sprawled like a great scarecrow beside me and I bundled the blankets round him as if he were my baby. That must have been the winter before the summer of the sand dunes. So I hadn't quite lost him yet.

I stopped writing here to try to find the old hat box where Hetta, bless her, stored all the old pre-war memorabilia when we moved to Ely. It took some time to track down and I finally located it under my bed. When I opened it, I found various left-wing pamphlets, including one with a photo of John Cornford on the cover staring at the camera and smoking. I met him that day we went to see Mrs Cornford. He was handsome and bright as paint and no doubt very noble. But to tell you the truth I didn't like him. I felt he was vain.

There were various other, terribly serious, left-wing articles in the box too, which I read through for the first time. In one John makes this rather typical pronouncement: *The transformation of a worried intellectual into an effective member of a revolutionary party does not take place overnight.* He was all of eighteen when he wrote that. Anyway, he was quite wrong as far as Fred was concerned because it was John's own death, when he went to fight for the Republicans in Spain and was killed the day after his twenty-first birthday, which was the catalyst that propelled Fred into the Communist Party.

I suppose it was inevitable. Along with all the other factors, Fred was inclined to hero worship. And even I, who was never a political animal, cannot honestly say that I disagreed with what Communism stood for. You must remember that Stalin's crimes had yet to be uncovered and the call of equality and compassion for the poor and the dispossessed are powerful intoxicants, especially for the young. But maybe because of my very different parents, or maybe because I was born so, I was always too

sceptical to accept any ideology uncritically or to belong
to any movement.

If you had asked Fred later in life he would have
insisted that we were always close. He would probably
have intimated that he always loved me too, though he
wasn't one for declaring love, not that I minded that. But
his memory, like his politics, could be rose-tinted and
there was a period when we were not close at all.

Magda was Viennese and a student at the LSE which
then as now was a political beehive. When war broke out
and the Houghton Street premises were requisitioned by
the War Ministry, the LSE was moved to Cambridge.
But even before this there was a good deal of exchang-
ing of pollen between like-minded bees at other hives.
Magda was bound to attract Fred's interest. She had
joined the Communist Party as a schoolgirl, just as
Hitler was coming to power, and would have held a
particular fascination for an untried, upper-class, dis-
affected young radical fresh from public school.

She was one of those women who most women but
few men recognize: she had the knack of making men
feel that it was a privilege to know her. Way more sophisticated than any of her British peers, she had sailed close
to danger and received the deference due to that condition.

Of course, from that day in the dunes I had been in
love with Fred. Slyly, and miserably, I observed him
watching the commanding figure of Magda at a meeting
at the LSE he had inveigled me into attending while I

was still at school. His gaze rested that second too long on the ripe-bosomed body and radiant, confident smile. My own wiry frame and sandy hair had long since earned me the nickname Weasel. I knew he meant it fondly.

Fred saw me as an extension of himself – and accordingly less entitled to consideration. Magda was other, and therefore, according to his particular moral reckoning, more deserving of his attention. And she was Jewish and with the increasing dominance of the Nazi party she was vulnerable. I couldn't compete with that. The vulnerable like the dead have cards that the hale and living can never play.

I followed Fred to Cambridge and I went simply because he was there – keeping him doggedly in my sights because of Magda. My father used to say I had a measure of his own mother's flinty determination and it is true that when I set my sights on something I can often achieve it. It was a matter of astonishment to all but Ma when, from my dotty school, I won an Exhibition to read English at Cambridge. Actually, the school wasn't as dotty as all that. They managed not to ruin what I was naturally interested in and that in my view is the most important feature of a good education.

I was not altogether surprised when Fred appeared offhand when I arrived, very nervous, in Cambridge in the October of 1937. He could never successfully hide anything from me – emotionally he resembled a mountain spring, quick-flowing and clear as glass. I called round to see him in his rooms at King's and all he said was, 'Hello there, Weasel. You settling in all right?' Perfectly friendly but hardly a lover's welcome. He offered me a cigarette and then said, 'Sorry to dash but I'm just off to a meeting.' I was hurt but I was too proud to show I cared.

A week or so later he invited me to the cinema to see *The Life of Émile Zola* which he described as an 'important film'. I watched it dutifully and we went for a drink afterwards at the Eagle where he talked very excitedly about Zola, who was his current craze. I had read no Zola so I couldn't contribute much, not that Fred really noticed as when another King's man came into the pub Fred started a quite separate conversation with him about collective farms. He left me to walk back to Newnham alone. Even casual male acquaintances tended to walk us women back to college so it wasn't hard to read the signs. It was as if St Aidan's Dunes were in another country, which I suppose they were.

In the summer term we played quite a bit of tennis together. We'd always made a good mixed-doubles pair but it wasn't hard to guess who it was he was dashing off to London to see after a game, leaving me stranded with Peter Shepherd from Trinity. Peter was a harmless chap and pleasant enough and he had a big serve which meant he was in demand on the tennis courts. But he was so dull that once off the court everyone made excuses to get away from him. That was to be my fate, I told myself: the nice girl who puts up with bores.

So the first two years at Cambridge were a bleakish time for me. But it wasn't all bad. I adopted a cheery all's-right-with-the-world veneer, which goes a long way to making one feel more cheerful, and I stifled my jealousy by starting a literary magazine with Giles Truelove from Selwyn, the college across the way, and Marion Stiles, a fellow Newnham student who became my closest friend.

Giles and Marion and I racketed around together and for all my unhappiness over Fred the three of us had a lot of innocent fun. We published worthy articles in our magazine and some fairly humdrum poetry but there was always the odd jewel, including a poem by John Cornford's lover, Margot Heinemann, on what it meant to live without him. One of the twentieth century's great love poems, 'Heart of the Heartless World', was written for her and they must have been almost John's last recorded words before he was killed. It's an awful thing to say, because she lost him in that poignant war, but I envied Margot that poem.

The hardest part for me in all this was that Fred stopped going to Dowlands. At the end of my first Cambridge term, Ma and Dad and I drove up to Northumberland to spend Christmas there as usual. I jumped out of the car expecting to find Fred reading in the library or by the fire in the drawing room. But only Margaret was there to greet me. She said, 'Oh pet, I am glad to see you and what a shame about Master Fred.' He could never get her to drop the 'Master'.

'Why, what's happened?' My first alarmed thought

was that Fred had been in an accident. But the only accident was to my hopes.

'He's not coming up for Christmas. Mrs Tye is most put out. Says he wrote to say he was off to Vienna.'

Bloody hell, Magda! I thought.

I was right about that. Fred had squired Magda back to Vienna to see her parents and to try to persuade them to leave. He wrote me a postcard, making no mention of Christmas or his absence from Dowlands, but enthusing about the architecture of the city and deploring the political situation. The card is not in the memorabilia box because I tore it into pieces and burned it on the Dowlands drawing-room fire.

I spent a miserable Christmas pretending to be jolly and going for long walks by myself, moping over sights that I had shared all my life with Fred. What Fred had done, I told myself sternly, was utterly worthy, utterly right – and utterly dismaying, my more honest self said.

Only Dad noticed that something was amiss. He cornered me one day when I had come back from a lonely trek to Holy Island. 'All right, old girl? Anything up?'

'It's nothing,' I said. 'Really. I'm just being selfish.'

'We're all selfish,' Dad said. Actually, he was the least selfish person alive. 'It's the people who claim to be selfless you want to watch out for.'

That cheered me up a little. At least I knew that I wasn't selfless.

2

In April 1939, with the political situation in Europe darkening, the government introduced conscription and all men of a certain age who were not students or physically unfit were required to undergo military training. When in September war was declared, any man between eighteen and forty became liable for call-up to full-time military service. Fred had by then taken his degree gaining, to no one's surprise, a starred first, and on the strength of this he had been offered a fellowship at King's. I had hardly seen him that year. He was spending all his time with Magda.

On a couple of occasions I spotted them together, once at a play at the ADC, a production of *Saint Joan*, when luckily I had Marion to skulk behind. Another time I saw them strolling along King's Parade, her hand hooked familiarly under his arm, and I whipped into the market and busied myself buying plums. That summer there was a glut of plums and when Marion came to stay with me over the long vacation we experimented with jam.

It was Marion who told me they had married.

If there are love matches made at first sight there are also friendships. Marion and I disagreed about almost everything: I can't read *Tristram Shandy*, while it remains for her a Desert Island book. I love Trollope and she dismisses him as predictable. She can't bear the taste of vinegar while I'm a glutton for pickles. She was reading Moral Sciences, which was the old-fashioned Cambridge term for philosophy, and she and I and Giles used to debate all kinds of philosophical positions long into the night with plenty of beer to add to the gaiety of nations. I remember us once discussing capital punishment, and my saying that I'd rather be hanged for a crime I hadn't committed than for one I had. Giles said he understood this, but Marion suggested it was 'another case of Betsy's fundamental lunacy'. I loved her and we relished our differences.

Marion and I were planning to share digs in our final year and we came back up to Cambridge towards the end of September to look for somewhere suitable. It was still early days in the war and I'm ashamed to admit this but it seemed almost exciting. We had come to look at a house in Round Church Street, which a research fellow at St John's had taken on a lease and wanted to sublet while he trained with the RAF.

After we had inspected the house, tiny and smelling of damp and, we agreed, just the ticket, we took ourselves off for a drink at our regular, the Eagle. Handing me down a tankard of bitter, Marion slopped it on the table, said, 'Sorry,' and then, as she mopped up the beer with her hanky, a little awkwardly, 'I meant to say, I'm sorry about Fred.'

A lightning insight painfully struck. 'What about Fred?'

Marion, embarrassed, said, 'Him marrying her.'

'Oh, yes,' I said, as if that were old news and not a final blow to my lingering hopes, because even with Marion, over Fred, I needed to keep face. 'No good crying over spilt beer. I thought maybe there was something else.'

If Marion had wind of something else she didn't let on. She was always kind. Fred never saw her worth because she wasn't overtly political. It never occurred to him that kindness is an avowal of kinship and in a discreet way its own form of politics.

Some time towards the end of that October, when all able-bodied men between the ages of twenty and twenty-three were being called up, Fred appeared at the Round Church Street house. I had determined that I would not refer to the marriage until he did but in the event he never mentioned it at all. What he had come to say was that he had decided he had a 'moral duty' to refuse to fight.

'There are no just wars, only hideous ones,' he pronounced solemnly.

You must remember that Stalin and Hitler were still allies. Stalin had decreed that this was an imperialist war and it wasn't uncommon to find even enlisted communists, already in active service, campaigning to stop the war. I supposed this was Fred peddling the Party line.

I was angry about the marriage, angry about his not mentioning it, and I didn't hold with the Party line. 'What about John Cornford? He thought Spain was a just war.'

I never quite worked out how Fred's Communist principles married with his pacifism and perhaps he didn't either, though he did in the end leave the Party. But I remember the deadly serious expression with which he met my protest. It had a disturbing resemblance to the expression I had seen on his face that bright July afternoon amid St Aidan's Dunes when we were still children – a lifetime ago it seemed.

'I have to fight in my own way, Bets,' he said. 'It's not that I'm afraid.'

The note of appeal in his voice touched me. There was an innocence about Fred and as a matter of fact I often found him touching.

'I never thought that,' I said, and then felt annoyed all over again as, not for the first time, I found myself backed into a position of reassuring him.

The 'something else' came out when Blanche wrote to my mother referring to Magda as a 'scheming little Jewess'. Ma kept the news from me. She said she wanted to wait till I'd heard it from Fred himself, which I know was also meant kindly.

A week or so later Fred was back. I could tell that something was up because he was awkward with me.

'It seems I am to be a father,' he said finally, after a long diatribe against the military and capitalism, and produced an appeasing smile.

That really irked me. But I didn't comment, as in the past I might have done, with our old asperity. Instead, I congratulated him, in what I hoped was a magnanimous manner, and privately sent them both to hell.

He looked so sheepish that I almost felt sorry for him. He gave an impression of carelessness but he understood people's feelings better than he let on. But I was too badly knocked to feel very sorry for anyone but myself and went back to our house in Round Church Street and got drunk on some green Chartreuse left in the cupboard by our absent landlord. I was violently sick and had an almighty headache in the morning. I've had an antipathy to anything alcoholic and green ever since.

3

It was typical of Fred that he went to prison quite needlessly. The tribunals which assessed the validity of a CO's case were headed by judges and it was common knowledge that the verdicts were shaped by the judge's prejudices. With his Classics background, Fred could easily have been given a role code-breaking, or been allotted some other acceptable non-combat work. There were plenty of dons at King's who would willingly have lent him their support. Had he been a Quaker or any kind of Christian his stand would have been accepted, however grudgingly. But he ditched any prospect of that by mounting his atheist soapbox and preaching the Communist Party line. Deprived by his conscience of other possibilities for glory, he chose to be a martyr. He was desperate to be sent to prison. I see that now.

I left Fred to stew in his own juice for a month or so while he was serving his sentence in Colchester. My excuse was that I had my finals to sit and he had thrown in his lot with Magda and was no longer my concern. But in truth it was pique that made me neglect him. That and the conviction that he had conspired at his own incarceration. The treatment of COs was not openly brutal as it was in the First World War – but after

Dunkirk, as the Nazi menace pressed closer, the popular mood was not indulgent towards those who put their private morality above the country's safety.

I didn't feel indulgent myself. Fred's blessed principles struck me as naive and childish, especially given that soon he would have a real child to support. I don't suppose that I formulated the thought clearly then but subliminally I had begun to believe that principles are more often than not a cover for something less lofty.

But in the end I weakened and Giles drove me to Colchester to see him. Giles by this time had acquired a decommissioned London taxi cab in which he sped about with a blithe disregard for pedestrians or other vehicles. He habitually drove with one hand on the wheel, gesturing with his cigarette as he cursed motorists and cyclists; yet outside a car he was the mildest of souls. He had wangled some deal over petrol. I never enquired what it was but when I offered to pay for the petrol to Colchester he waved my offer aside and said, 'Least said, soonest mended. I have my resources.'

I found Fred very buoyant. He explained how he was giving classes to the other prisoners and although he had been forbidden by the prison governor to discuss Marx or Marxism he was introducing those who attended his class to Tolstoy, which, he assured me would be almost as effective in expanding their world view. He talked animatedly about Tolstoy's attitude to the peasants and about the judicial system and its anti-working-class bias and only when it was time for me to go asked, uninterestedly, how I had been. I left with the conviction that he had had no real need of my visit and hoping his fellow-prisoners would bear up under his enthusiasm for Tolstoy.

He called at the Round Church Street house on his release from prison and when I enquired, rather grudgingly, how the Tolstoy classes had gone, he replied, 'Swimmingly.' I had noticed that he'd said nothing about Magda or when the baby was due when I had visited him in Colchester and he said nothing that afternoon. But he was on his way to London and I guessed it was Magda he was off to see.

When I walked with him to the bus stop that same evening we ran into Rex Napley, a former student at King's, and his girlfriend, Philippa, a student at Newnham.

Fred was a fast walker and I had learned to keep up with him. As we tried to pass them on a narrow section of Trinity Street, Philippa drew her skirt aside and Rex muttered in a pretend under-his-breath voice, 'Yellow.'

Fred stopped and turned back. 'Repeat that.'

'Yellow conchy.'

Fred would have stayed to argue but I dragged him past. As I did so, Philippa said, 'Makes you ashamed to have been at the same university with them. I know what I would do. Cut their balls off.'

To which Rex's 'witty' response was, 'No need, they haven't got any in the first place'.

My final year at Newnham was overshadowed by the

war, which made any personal aspirations seem paltry. I dealt with my feelings for Fred by studying hard because I wanted to prove myself his equal. 'Pride is not a bad thing,' I see I copied into my diary, 'when it only urges us to hide our own hurts – not to hurt others.' But I played hard too. I enjoyed a rather glorious affair with Jock Turnbull, a clever Geordie reading History at Christ's who had won a place at Cambridge from a school even less Oxbridge-oriented than mine.

At this point, I felt I had to resort to my box of memorabilia to search for a card that I suddenly recalled Jock sending me. There was a devil-may-care mood abroad in those days. Fred took life too seriously to laugh at it but Jock, who didn't suffer from the impediment of coming from a privileged background, had a sense of the absurd and knew the value of laughter. I couldn't find the card at first and became quite frantic riffling through all the other cards and letters but when I finally located it it took me right back.

There was a day we went punting and, taking my hand to help me from the boat on to the bank where we planned to picnic, Jock said casually, 'You know, Betsy Tye, we could do worse than get hitched, you and me, when you're done here.'

The card he sent me before he flew to Belgium was a cartoon of some schoolboys saying, 'Coo! Who wants conkers? We're collecting shrapnel.' It seems rather pathetic now and I don't suppose I found it especially funny even then. But reading again what he wrote on the card made me want to cry. There was another, different, life I might have lived with Jock.

On 15 May 1940, the day of my first finals paper (as I see from my diary), we got the grim news that the Dutch army had capitulated to the Germans. On 3 June (the day after my last exam) we heard that the Germans had bombed Paris. Marion and I sat in the cinema, smoking and watching depressing footage showing lines of refugees trudging the poplar-lined French roads, pushing a pathetic cargo of children and old people in perambulators. The brutal Nazi machine seemed to be sweeping across Europe, effortlessly toppling the allies' cities, and the mood at home was growing starker.

Some weeks after a low-key graduation ceremony – a pretty pointless-seeming affair given all that was happening in the world – I was cleaning the house in preparation for leaving. Marion had gone off to drive ambulances in London and my own plans were still unformed. Our front door had no bell but our landlord, Ralph, had fixed up a steel hammer and sickle to act as a knocker and when I heard this rattle I opened the door, expecting to find just about anyone in the world standing there but Magda.

I had my head turbaned in a hideous old scarf and for half a second I experienced a silly feeling of embarrassment. But there was no need. Magda looked ghastly. Her eyes were shrunken in with tiredness and her scarlet lipstick looked all wrong on her unpowdered face.

'Hello, Betsy.' I loathed Bertha, my given name, but in those days only intimates were permitted to use the familiar one. 'D'you mind if I come in?'

I don't believe I answered but she walked past me into the kitchen as though she owned the place, sank on to one of the only stable chairs, put her hands to her forehead and slowly shook her head. 'Do you have anything to drink?'

'Tea?' I offered, inwardly thinking, *Overdoing the drama, aren't you?*

'Have you got anything stronger?'

I would have offered the green Chartreuse only thanks to her I'd polished it off. 'Ralph has some fairly disgusting-looking stuff squirrelled away.'

I dug out a sticky bottle of something poisonously yellow from the back of the kitchen cupboard and poured it into an eggcup. The washing-up was yet to be tackled and it was the only clean receptacle to hand. Magda swigged it down like medicine and made a face.

'I said it was probably disgusting.' I could see that she was no longer pregnant and decided not to ask about the baby.

'Betsy, I need some help. It's only temporary.'

Some far-off part of me experienced a strange prickle of hope but I spoke cautiously. 'What with?' Though Fred never said so explicitly, I sensed that Magda was given to issuing imperious demands.

'The baby. I need to leave it somewhere. It's only for a while.'

Noting the 'it' I asked, 'Your baby was born, when?'

'Three weeks ago, I think it was. I'm not quite myself.'
It was true, she didn't seem the 'self' I'd been so jealous
of.

I must have said something like, 'But shouldn't she be
with you?' because I know I am right in what she said
then.

'It's a him. I left it with one of the porters at King's.
He's sleeping. He didn't seem to mind.'

'The baby or the porter?'

'The porter. Betsy, you couldn't look after him for a
couple of days?'

'The porter or the baby?'

Again she missed the irony and I wondered how on
earth Fred got along with her and how she coped with
his terrible jokes.

'The baby. Would you? Only I don't know anyone else
to ask. He sleeps all the time and I can leave you his
milk. I promise it won't be for long.'

And the oddest thing is that I didn't ask what it was
she had to do so urgently that it necessitated leaving her
newborn child. I went with her to the King's Porter's
Lodge, like a lamb to the slaughter, although it was Nat
who was the lamb and slaughter was what it turned out
I was saving him from.

Magda came back to see him once before returning to
London on her mysterious mission. She left with me his
birth certificate in lieu of a ration book which she hung
on to for herself. She never confided what it was that

detained her and some stubborn element in me – or maybe a need not to know? – never wanted to enquire.

When I rang the number she had left, which I put off doing as I grew less and less happy at the thought of parting with Nat, the young woman who answered said, 'Oh, but Magdalena has gone away.'

And when I asked, 'Do you have her number?' she said, 'No number, no, but there's an address somewhere in Harrow. Hang on, I'll find it.'

The bomb that fell on Harrow on 22 August 1940 was a promise of what was to come, a grim harbinger of the devastating Blitz that Hitler was about to unleash on London. It was some weeks before the news was official and I realized that Magda was not coming back. But by that time Nat had become mine.

4

All families have secrets. Ours was Nat. Nat was not my child but I brought him up as mine. For a long time no one, not even Nat himself, was aware of this. We didn't consciously keep it from him or the other children. But for years Fred never discussed Magda. And it seemed not my place to tell Nat that he was not my child.

Was that it, really? No. I'm trying to write the truth here and that is only possible if I acknowledge the truths that I've steered away from till now. The truth is I didn't want to tell Nat because I never wanted to own that he wasn't mine.

It was as well Magda had left us Nat's birth certificate. When I protested, at the time, about her leaving no ration book she said, 'His name's Tye and your name's Tye so if anything happens or you need more milk or anything, you can say you're his mother and get a green book for you both'. (Mothers with children under five had green ration books entitling them to extra fruit and milk and eggs.) The birth certificate, registered in Hammersmith, stated that Fred's son, born on 1 July 1940, had been named Nathaniel Wilfred Tye and that his father, Wilfred Acton Lancelot Tye, was a 'University Lecturer'. Magda was described as 'student', though she had finished her degree. Perhaps she was about to begin her worthy-sounding Ph.D. on Marx's Economic and Philosophical manuscripts of 1844, which Fred, with an annoying note of respect, had referred to. I never discovered because other than that one further visit, when she turned up with some nappies and a few pathetic items of infant clothing, I never saw Magda again. But I often thought about her saying I could pretend I was Nat's mother.

In all this time the only word I had had from Fred was one letter, in which he wrote that he'd been detailed into farm labouring work and was headed north where help was required. Since then I'd heard nothing and pretended that I didn't care. But now something more than my own dented pride became paramount.

I presumed Fred must know that Magda had had their baby, though to me he'd written nothing of this, and I wrote first to the only address I had to let him know that Nat was with me. I owed him that. I wrote before I learned of Magda's death but I wrote again, after 22 August, a gentler letter, because I felt there might be no one else to break the news and I wanted him to know that his son at least was safe.

When I located Fred at last, I took Nat to meet him. Those were days when you could hitchhike with impunity and a young woman with a babe in arms, far from being in danger, conjured consideration from drivers. It's a well-worn paradox about war, but still worth pondering: the onslaught of terrible destruction seems to trigger a more generous spirit than peace and prosperity has ever brought.

My letters had gone from pillar to post as Fred had moved from labouring jobs, where the growing Women's Land Army was thought aid enough for the benighted local farmers, to more physically taxing forestry work. I found him billeted with some older men, who had not yet been called up, in a makeshift wooden shack on the edge of Hamsterley forest, near Durham. A very basic existence but Fred never minded discomfort.

We arrived, Nat and I, weary from our journey and in my case nervous of our reception. Fred's first words were, 'Did you know how many different species of fungi there are?' which was an ice-breaker because it was so typical. I can see now that he was embarrassed. He conducted me, Nat in my arms, round the forest, pointing out the various species of fungi he'd been discovering, as if conferring on two visitors a tour of his country estates. But I was relieved to judge him apparently happy. He had lost weight but he looked healthy. I suppose, if I'm honest, I was relieved to see no sign that he was visibly mourning Magda.

It was some while after all this before I felt able to raise the subject of Magda and if he was distressed at all he didn't show it. He claimed that he had married her to give her citizenship. She was not at that time pregnant, or at least not knowingly, and was only concerned that she might be interned as an alien. I doubt if this was the whole truth. I suspect he had edited, as much for himself as for me, the degree of his feelings for her. But it suited me to let his explanation ride.

And it was a heady time, prompting many world-without-end gestures which were always likely to prove unstable in calmer days. Already by the time they had agreed on the perfunctory ceremony at a registry office in Marylebone, it was clear to them both, or so Fred maintained, that they were not twin souls. He wasn't a monster and would have been genuinely very cut up over how Magda had died. But I don't believe in those days he allowed himself to find any loss too painfully personal.

Fred's response to meeting his son was to treat him as if he were the child of a close but absent friend. He conveyed no paternal possessiveness and his first words about Nat were, 'Isn't he rather small?'

'Babies are meant to be small, Fred,' I explained. 'It's how we all start. He will grow, you see.'

He held Nat awkwardly at first and when it was apparent that his nappy was wet hastily handed the kicking bundle back to me. I let him off on the first occasion but when it was time for another change said firmly, 'No, you do it. It's not difficult and you'll have to learn some time.'

And Nat, who was never a placid baby (Magda's assurances that he always slept proved about as reliable as the rest of her maternal contribution), lay on a carpet of leaves and smiled contentedly while his father wiped him clean of shit and anointed the two soft cheeks of his bottom most tenderly with Vaseline. Snapping closed the safety pin on Nat's bulky nappy, Fred turned and beamed and I saw gazing up at me two pairs of corn-flower-blue eyes. Somehow, unless she too had some Northern blood in her, Magda's genes had been super-seded by those of the Anglo-Saxon Tyes.

'How about that for a first shot?' He looked boyishly proud.

'Pretty good,' I said, and felt for the first time that all might be well and that an important step in Nat's life had been safely negotiated.

As we left, I could hear Fred lecturing the other men about the advanced position the USSR took over the division of labour between men and women and what we had to learn from this. Very decently, his colleagues made no comment. I couldn't see their faces but instinct told me that this kind of oration from Fred was not new to them.

5

The winter of 1941 was one of unusual cold and for weeks on end Cambridge lay under a leaden sky. Snow like a cheap Christmas-card illustration decorated the colleges and draped elegant feather boas along the branches of skeleton trees, belying the savage effects on the human population of the steep drop in temperature. Ma, who had accepted Nat as her own as readily as I had, came often to visit, trudging gallantly through the sludgy streets and bundled up in shawls like Mother Courage. Among her other accomplishments was a talent for knitting, a skill which gave her a useful common topic of interest with Grandad Tye, who, less bizarrely in those days, had been taught to knit by his old nanny. Ma knitted Nat jerseys by unravelling her own, so that, well-wadded with layers of brightly coloured wool, he resembled a sturdy Inca baby.

The war had transformed my mother, ever eager to embrace any novelty, into a champion vegetable grower. The herbaceous border in her garden had been dug over to make a vegetable plot and Ma never arrived at Round Church Street without potatoes or swedes or Jerusalem artichokes, carrying them, like Alderman Ptolemy Tortoise coming to dine with Jeremy Fisher, in a string bag.

Marion's room had been taken by a Party comrade, a physics graduate and activist, much revered in the student movement and engaged in hush-hush war work. I didn't revere him, or his beliefs, but I liked him. I liked his bounding, puppyish, energy and he was a natural with Nat.

Various student Party members frequented the house. I used to overhear them outlining their plans for the future, and when the subject was literary I was occasionally pressed to participate. The Russian market for 'decent literature among the proletariat', I was assured, was immense and insatiable. No Russian writer was obliged to turn out 'slush' in order to become a bestseller. Miners and metal workers in the USSR queued eagerly to hear decent poetry. At the time I knew no miners or metal workers but I was far from sure that attending readings of modern poetry would necessarily better their lives. But for all their political ferocity the Comrades were always civil to me so I kept my own counsel and appeared to listen politely.

To be fair to my housemate, he put his money where his mouth was – which is to say he made friends not only with the like-minded but with all sorts, among whom were various market stallholders who slipped him foodstuffs and spices I'd never sampled before, which he wizarded into novel culinary concoctions. Nat and I passed many cheery evenings with him, when he was not off discussing how to raise the consciousness of the masses. He had a fine voice and he taught me mill-workers' songs which I sang to all my children and grandchildren and sing to myself to this day.

For the first couple of years after graduating I got by financially doing a modest bit of teaching for Newnham and some translation work for an academic publisher. The pay was pitiful but the work itself was soothing. There was something remedial about the old and lambent language of *The Vision of Piers Plowman*, in which, while Nat slept, I absorbed myself, ignoring, for a spell, the fact that our modern civilization was nightly being hammered from the skies.

Dad, who was up most nights attending to the Blitz casualties, was able to visit less often than Ma but it was he in the end who persuaded me to leave Cambridge. He turned up one evening with a bottle of black-market Scotch he'd been slipped by the father of a grateful patient, and it was like him to take his time, waiting till the meal was over and my housemate had gone out and then choosing his words carefully.

'You know, old girl, I've always let you have your head. But you'll forgive me if I get something off my chest?'

Dad's advice was worth listening to so I said, 'Go on then, fire away.'

'This bottle we've been enjoying was a gift from the father of a lad who'll be lucky to be upright again. I see too much of that kind of thing to be wildly happy that you are so near London.' I understood his concern. London had become the theatre of a monstrous drama. The carefree evenings of the early months of the new-found dark of the blackout, when an amiable gaiety still flourished amid companionable cigarettes and intimate nudges and lingering conversations, had given way to a vast hush as the city contracted to the arena of ferocious distraction.

'But where else could we go?' I asked.

Dad put down his empty glass. 'Between you and me, it would be a kindness if you'd go up to Bamburgh, if only to keep an eye on your grandparents.'

I had gathered that our grandparents were finding the war difficult. Margaret was becoming more arthritic and all the spryer help had either joined the Women's Land Army or had enlisted and were off fighting the war. But it was the thought of Nat's safety that decided me. Northumberland, with its stretches of sand and the seas with peaceable eiders gently crooning and those wide, windswept skies, seemed to offer the promise of a suddenly available paradise.

So after some deliberation Nat and I said goodbye to the physicist and although he was sorry to see us go I could see that he was pleased that the young woman who shared his bed could now move in. For some weeks I'd been encountering her, wrapped nonchalantly in nothing but a towel while conducting a vigorous political debate with her lover as he took his bath. I was rather in awe of her: she seemed so sure of herself, and of her view of the world and how she was going to change it.

When I think of those years now, as I write this, they come back to me as a hallowed time: my young self lying at night, cocooned in the Blue Room at Dowlands, on the lumpen mattress which I'd lugged on to the floor, with Nat curled beside me, his soft moth breath in my ear.

Perhaps it was this, that then there were only the two of us, Nat and me, and not another living soul to distract from my love for him.

To everyone's surprise, Nat was a hit with Grandad. He pulled at Grandad's gold watch chain, an item commanding the most distant respect when we were children, plucked unrestrainedly at his beard and wildly unkempt eyebrows and, to his own vast delight, took his first independent steps staggering towards Grandad's encouraging outstretched hand.

It was more predictable that Nat would become a fast favourite with Margaret. She made him pastry balls to play with, soldiers out of wooden pegs, and cut up an old sealskin jacket, out of which she skilfully made a toy seal, its eyes made from boot buttons which somehow produced a most eloquent expression on the seal's face. The jacket had belonged to Aunt Char so this was a sign of how far Nat had won Margaret's heart.

Grandmother was another story. Nat, with Fred's colouring, bore no obvious physical resemblance to Magda but that would not have been enough to pacify Grandmother. She was anti-Semitic in the manner that her generation was – not easy for us to understand but as much a feature of the times as church on Sunday and servants and knickers with long elasticated legs against the cold.

The presence in her establishment of a Jewish baby represented for my grandmother the conscientious discharge of duty but when Blanche once visited I was grateful for its flinty terms. Blanche arrived hoping, I could tell, for a scene and when she began to indulge her love for melodrama Grandmother coldly put her in her place.

'I don't regard it as tragic at all,' she pronounced. 'Betsy's looking after the child very adequately. He never knew his mother and there's no reason to suppose he'll miss her now.'

Though it was apparent from her tone that what was intended by this was that the absence of a Jewish mother was very much for the best, I admit that I was relieved by her unusual show of support. But I did wonder how far it would prove correct. It would be odd, I reflected, if Nat didn't at some point yearn for the mother he had never known. But I told myself I was prepared to deal with that in good time.

Blanche left rather huffily, promising to send on a parcel of wool for Margaret to 'knit something for Baby'. I was annoyed by 'Baby' and doubly annoyed because Margaret's arthritic hands were paining her. But I needn't have worried because the parcel never arrived.

My Cambridge fantasy of the Northumbrian seascape was tempered by the reality of war. The east coast was strategically prepared for attack and the long bare beaches of my childhood were fortified by ugly pillboxes and strung with repelling barbed wire. Old cars filled with stones stood in the sands defying German tanks to land. And a causeway of concrete giant's teeth now stretched forbiddingly to Holy Island.

But we learned to negotiate these safeguards. And one day, by St Aidan's Dunes, we met Bev and Eddie.

A stocky little dark-haired boy, much of Nat's age, was hurling stones into the sea and Nat, who wasn't a shy child, joined in. Quite soon they were flinging bladder-wrack at each other, leaving me and the boy's mother relieved of our duty as our children's companions.

She introduced herself with 'I'm Bev. Smoke?' and we sat down together in the dry sand of the dunes.

God, how we used to smoke. I'm amazed we don't all have lung cancer. I still sometimes miss the special companionableness of smoking with a friend.

Bev was what in that part of the world is still called 'bonny' – which is to say she was strong-boned, fair-complexioned and grey-eyed and had the carriage of a queen. I instinctively liked the way she looked but when I got to know her what I liked even more was her indifference to anything political. She was all for fighting the war but that was as far as her politics went. I once said to her, pretending to be shocked, though I wasn't at heart and this was simply a position I considered it necessary to adopt at the time, 'But you must vote, Bev. Women went to prison for our right to vote,' and she said, 'They went to prison for their right, not mine.'

That day when we sat in the sands smoking was the

beginning of an important friendship and also an abiding friendship between our two sons. Quite early on I told Bev about Fred.

'His dad's in the Navy,' she said, nodding at Eddie. 'He's a fisherman, has his own boat, so it was home from home really.'

It would have seemed rude not to counter with where Nat's father was so I said, rather between gritted teeth, 'Nat's dad's a CO.'

'A conchy?'

I nodded, disloyally adding, 'Not that I agree with him.'

'He's entitled to his opinion,' Bev said, which is an attitude a whole lot rarer than it should be.

Bev, it turned out, was a great reader. It wasn't that day but some days later when we met again that I had with me a copy of *Jane Eyre*. I was rereading the Brontës, probably as part of my inner campaign of keeping my end up by defying Fred. He had no time for the Brontës and dismissed them as 'hysterical'.

'I like that book. She's a canny one, that Jane.'

I asked, because I was interested, 'Have you read any of her other novels?' and when she said she hadn't I invited her to Dowlands to look at the library.

She read all of the Brontës after that, though *Jane Eyre* remained her favourite. But she also found books I had never looked at, Maeterlinck's *Life of the Bee*, for example, which she recommended to me and which, when I read it, I could hardly believe I had overlooked. She expressed some serious aversions too. *Tess of the D'Urbervilles* she wouldn't hear a good word about. She worked on a farm herself and was scornful of Hardy's professed agricultural know-how. 'Gloomy old bugger' was her verdict. She was against anything that didn't have a happy ending.

Grandmother Tye took quite a shine to Bev, probably because Bev had a natural respect for the old order. She had strong opinions, but not revolutionary ones, and I can see how Grandmother might find that a relief after Fred. She never said so, but if her heart had been softer his avowal of pacifism might have broken it. She had lost her son, his father, in the last war and although Oswald was never mentioned his photo, a portrait of a flat-faced pallid man with a moustache and a monocle, had pride of place on her dressing table.

And I'm sure it had something to do with Bev that the collection of old ballgowns put away in blue tissue paper was made over to us by Grandmother. As a result of her largesse, Bev and I swanned about in revamped silk chiffon and even some mink trimmings which we sewed on to the collars of our coats, so that we became a local byword for style.

It must have been about a year into our friendship, when we were trying on our latest rehabs before the looking glass in the Blue Room, that Bev said, 'Eddie's dad and me aren't married either, you know.' I can see her now, standing there, looking at herself in the glass and twisting the ring she wore on her wedding finger.

'We didn't get round to it before he went. I dare say we will, though, when Ted gets home.'

She never allowed herself the rider 'if he gets home', because that would have been unlucky. But it must have crossed her mind. The dance that evening was in Bamburgh Village Hall, and Bev spent most of it, in the backless dress we'd cut from one of Grandmother's old silks, in the arms of Joseph Bainbridge, the farmer whose land she helped work, a much older man who was a lieutenant in the Home Guard. When we went to dances, we would habitually leave the boys in the care of either her mother or Margaret but that evening she said, as we were putting on our coats, 'All right if Eddie stays over at yours tonight?'

I don't believe the affair amounted to more than insurance because when her Ted did come home Bev made an excuse to call to return a book and with unusual shyness asked me not to mention Joseph's name. I wouldn't have done anyway. Those were world-without-end times and most women had no certainty that they would ever see their loved ones again.

What else can I tell you? Well, there were the animals. Nat was befriended by Hilda and Hexham, Grandmother's current pair of spaniels. Grandmother made no bones about preferring dogs to children. She tolerated children as necessary to the family's continued line – probably much as she had tolerated the means to bring them into the world – but she remained austerely aloof to their enchantments. And besides the dogs and

Margaret's hens there were always cats at Dowlands. There were the outside cats and the inside cats. The favourite inside cat was a big old bruiser of a tabby called Douglas, and one day Nat and Eddie dressed him up in a doll's lace bonnet and pushed him about in an old dolly's basketwork pram, which must have been Aunt Char's. Douglas lay serenely at ease, like a little old lady out for a drive in her carriage, but the bonnet must have stirred in him some memory as not long after this outing Douglas was found to have produced kittens. Grandmother, who believed that a relaxation of any long-held conviction was as improper as the relaxing of manners or deportment, stuck to her guns, insisting that Douglas had been 'seen to', at which Grandad riskily opined that in that case the five kittens 'must have been one of Cuddy's miracles'.

'Cuddy' is the local name for Saint Cuthbert, whose influence is everywhere in those parts. Fred and I had been brought up by Margaret on the stories of Cuddy's chicks, the eider ducklings, named after the saint who protected the nesting birds on his island hermitage, where he also talked to the kittiwakes and guillemots and rescued the little storm petrels, which are said to walk on water like Saint Peter, for whom they are named. Hetta claims that my interest in Cuthbert was one of my acts of rebellion against Fred. But I like to think I would always have been drawn to a saint who loved birds.

Grandmother had no interest in nature outside her dogs (which I doubt she counted as animals) but

Grandad, in his quiet way, liked birds. In the mornings, he sat in the big front window with his heavy military binoculars watching the bird life. Sometimes I requisitioned his binocs and, while Nat and Eddie cavorted on the dunes collecting fragments of shrapnel, I began to watch the waders which animate those bare beaches: oyster-catchers and turnstones, ringed plovers and sanderlings stalking the margins of the sea in search of sand eels. And my heart would lift with the graceful arctic terns, wheeling like tiny white scimitars across the big skies.

Bev and I were exploring the library one wet afternoon when the boys had disappeared off to play submarines, when I discovered a blue-bound volume by Enid Shackleton, a name that aroused my curiosity as I had a friendly association with the famous explorer. His statue stands in a niche in a wall by Kensington Gardens and I used to converse with it when I was a child. Whether Miss Shackleton was a relative of his the book didn't reveal, but what it did reveal was her interest in Saint Cuthbert.

According to Miss Shackleton – I felt she was a Miss – the saint had walked from Holy Island to a spot not far from Dowlands, where he had built a chapel in which he had sojourned during one of his periods of silent meditation. He was a recluse by nature and, according to Miss Shackleton, at such times he spoke only to the sheep and to the birds.

Enid Shackleton had the Victorian woman's gift for

pen and ink. There were some skilful sketches of various Cuthbert landmarks, the cave where he might have gone to meditate, or, in another version, where his body rested when the brothers took it in their flight from Holy Island to escape the Viking raids. But there was also a neat little sketch of this chapel which stood by a stream.

Bev was on duty with the children, and I was on one of the longer walks that I took when free to do so. I had climbed a steep escarpment, through a field of black-faced sheep, when I came upon a spring and followed it on up to where I hoped the water might be less foul with droppings. It was one of those scorching days in September that can drop out of the gods' laps and I was parched.

Just over the top of the escarpment I came upon the remains of what might have been a shepherds' shelter, until I saw the remnants of what had once housed a bell and recognized a tumbledown version of Miss Shackleton's drawing of Cuthbert's chapel. When I'd slaked my thirst, and taken off my boots and socks and cooled my feet in the stream, I sat with my back against a boulder and watched a flock of goldfinches, scarlet and gold, flit through the dark crimson berries of a nearby hawthorn.

'A charm of goldfinches.'

I spoke the words aloud into the deep quiet. The only other sounds were of the plunging stream and the silly sheep below. A trilling lark began to spin high in the air above me and all around there was nothing but expanses of hill grass, threaded with the heavenly blue of harebells. Quite suddenly I was sure that Cuthbert had been there and had sat as I was sitting and communed with the birds.

I don't know if I prayed. I don't know that then or now I know what praying is – or if anyone does – though I have had need of praying and would like to believe in its power. Let us say that I sent thanks into the air that afternoon. For if it was not Cuthbert it was surely some good spirit watching over us who decreed that Nat and I should move up to Northumberland. Because almost a month after we had left the house in Round Church Street, a German plane, cruising home, idly discharged a spare bomb over Cambridge. My housemate, the physicist, was killed outright. His lover all but died, but was dragged out of the flaming wreckage in time to save her life. Not her legs, though. When I wrote to Ralph, our landlord, to express my sorrow I learned that her legs had been too badly burned to be saved.

The news of the destruction of the Round Church Street house had left me more disturbed than anything I had yet experienced because the danger fell so close. Had Nat and I not got out, it is more than likely that we would have been killed or maimed. I had been tormented too, more than ever, by the conviction that Fred, whom I loved and it seemed couldn't help myself from loving, was wrong. There was evil in the world and an evil that should be, must be, fought. His own son's mother had been destroyed by it. His son might have been destroyed by it. His son, my little Nat, had we lived in Europe could have been put down as vermin. The knowledge of this had weighed on me so crushingly, so bewilderingly and unanswerably, that I had not known what to think or feel.

But that afternoon, by Cuthbert's stream, I recovered a sense that there is also good in the world and that it can survive in unexpected quarters – and might still prevail.

6

One Saturday in April 1945, Nat and I had walked down the track from Dowlands to the sands still strung with wire, and were busy digging out a complex waterway, secure in the knowledge that no Nazi enemy would loom out of the sea, when over the dunes a familiar figure appeared. Nat set off at a lick yelling, 'Daddy, Daddy, come and see my harbour. Are you coming to live with us now?' The question I'd never dared to ask.

Nat and I had visited Fred pretty regularly in his forest sanctuary. I had seen it as my duty to Nat to make sure he saw his father but I had not cared to question what my own position with Fred might be. Nor could I have said what I wanted from him now, even if he were able or willing to give it.

But from the hour of that reappearance Fred seemed to take it for granted that we would start a life together. His first words to me were 'Hello, Weasel pet' and he kissed me, quite casually, as if he'd just nipped out to fetch the papers. It was as if Magda and his marriage to her had never been. I honestly believe he had forgotten – or stowed away in a peculiar mental strongroom – the fact that Nat was not my child.

If I found his apparent expunging of Magda disturbing I didn't dwell on it. I was governed by the passionate conviction that Nat and I belonged together and what mattered more to me than anything was that nothing should part us. Together we had coped through those war years and we hadn't done badly. We had made a life for ourselves, and I might have suggested that we go on as we were, but Fred was Nat's father and from the sight of them together, that day when the firm fact of peace fully reached me, I could not in all conscience have parted them.

And, I had to remind myself, I had no right to do so. I was not Nat's mother. I wasn't even his legal guardian.

All this was so long ago it's hard to be truthful about how I really felt. For a while when Fred came home to Dowlands I was in a kind of dream-like reliving of our childhood before Magda and the war and Fred's precious principles got in the way. We most of us secretly desire, I suspect, to return to the conditions of childhood, where there are plenty of questions about life but not, on the whole, questions about how to live. It's the questions about how to live that are so flummoxing.

Although King's had held over Fred's fellowship, he elected to begin his new life much as he'd led the old one by turning down this opportunity for a comfortable existence.

When I queried this all he said was, 'You can't seriously imagine that I'm about to spend the rest of my days teaching Aristotle to privileged public-school kids when there's real work to be done?'

'I wasn't a public-school kid.'

'Darling Weasel, you're different.'

'OK. Jock wasn't a public-school kid.'

Fred frowned. 'Who's Jock?'

'Someone I knew at Cambridge.'

'Was he in the Party?'

'There were other people worth knowing at Cambridge, Fred.'

Jock died at Arnhem. I took Hetta with me once to find his grave.

I learned that during his time as a forester Fred had become involved with the WEA. The Workers' Education Association ran classes for working people and Fred had volunteered to tutor several of these in Durham. He had returned from this experience alight with a new mission to teach.

He conveyed this to me one night in bed in the Blue Room.

'The WEA is a terrific concept.' He was waving his mug about so violently that cocoa spilled over the sheets.

'Fred, do be careful. It's a hell of a job washing sheets and Margaret's got enough on her plate.'

I might have suggested that Margaret was a worker too, but I didn't bother. He simply looked puzzled at this and announced in what I called his political-rally voice, 'Those of us who have had a privileged education have a duty to pass that on.'

'You know what,' I said, by now sufficiently irked by the reiteration of political piety, 'I'm not sure that being shoved off to a public school to be got out of your mother's hair in order for her to enjoy the blandishments of a parasitic stepfather is such a fucking privilege.'

That did silence him. I rarely swore. I have sometimes wondered if Fred maybe felt this was unseemly in a woman, though he would never say so.

But he had a point. With the fresh winds of democracy blowing and men coming out of the services eager for opportunity in their post-war lives, the spurt of enthusiasm for education was refreshing. Through his Durham connections, Fred learned that the Oxford Delegacy for Extra-Mural Studies had linked up with the Staffordshire WEA and had persuaded Josiah Wedgwood, who was sympathetic to the idea of improving the lot of working people, to lease to them an ugly neo-Georgian mansion, the former home of a local bigwig and now owned by Wedgwood. Fred's wartime activities finally paid off. The Wedgwood Memorial College was set up and Fred, to his delight and my relief, was appointed warden.

The three of us moved there in the autumn of 1946. Barlaston Hall was a large house but our attic flat under the roof was cramped, which suited Fred as any discomfort salved his social conscience. It had been the old servants' quarters, boiling hot in summer and draughty in winter, and, so that people could see for themselves that we were not living the life of Riley, he insisted that we hold any parties in our flat, rather than in the refectory which would have been far more suitable.

Living with any other person takes getting used to and I have sometimes wondered if men and women are really suited to live together. These parties of Fred's entailed a lot of beer and raucous singing late into the night. But I was happy enough because it was the first place I could call my own home. What mattered to me was Nat's wellbeing, and Nat, who was a gregarious child, thrived.

The TUC financed weekend and week-long courses, where potters and miners and steelworkers came to be taught social history, Labour history and international history, which ensured that we had an ever-changing extended family of men and women, released from the daily grind of work or from being Hitler's targets – demob-happy and more than willing to kick or bowl balls with an outgoing youngster. I once found Pat Kendall, a corpulent delegate from the Foundry Workers Union, crouched, visibly sweating, in the fork of the prized tulip tree, with Nat shouting at him directions on how best to negotiate his way down.

'He'll make a grand shop steward,' was Pat's slightly truculent comment when he made it back to the ground.

Fred, who lost no time in recruiting other like-minded comrades and fellow travellers as teachers, was in his element, chewing over dialectical materialism with those who shared this enthusiasm. I was no companion for him in this – in the first place I didn't believe in it and the impersonal frankly makes me tired. But I had my own interests. I enjoyed teaching literature and putting on plays and making sure that the less politically enthused students did not feel too left out. Fred, whose warmth with political colleagues was immense, tended to ignore those who didn't share his views. His own disregard for wealth or worldly status, which however much he had rejected he had patently once enjoyed, provoked envy, something I could never get him to understand. He was too generous and too forbearing in some quarters and in others thoughtless and tactless. I should have seen it coming. I did see it coming, but – my fatal flaw – rather than grasping the nettle I let it float down the stream.

Complaints, from one or two disgruntled souls at first, began to be lodged behind Fred's back. But over time the disaffection must have grown and one day he was summoned to Oxford, where the left-wing political bias of the courses was raised. Fred returned from this encounter with an expression which told me that he was going to set his face against any directive that defaulted from his own. When I questioned him over what the meeting was about all he would say was, 'Oh, you know, the usual bureaucratic rubbish.' He had that strain in him which he shared with Will, a compulsion to go too far.

Fred had been put on notice to temper his educational policy but as he kept the edict from me it came as a shock when we were given our marching orders. For two years Barlaston had been a haven, and a future with no jobs or home to go to, one small child to support and another on the way, was a demoralizing prospect. It provoked one of our first outright rows.

When I asked why he had said nothing of this threat before, Fred's reply was, 'I didn't want to worry you, pet.'

'Fred, that is so abundantly untrue it's insulting. You didn't tell me because you didn't want me trying to persuade you to change your behaviour. And don't call me "pet".'

'Something will turn up, darling Guns. It'll all be Sir Garnet Wolseley, you'll see.'

This invoking of a favourite expression of my own mother's, one that featured an Anglo-Irish establishment general who made his name in the Crimean War, was the last straw.

'Fred, you do know who Sir Garnet Wolseley was?'

He looked pained. 'Of course I do.'

I am not as a rule a sulker. But for the next week I sulked. After days with me packing up our few possessions in what I hoped was a speaking silence Fred asked, 'What's up, Bets?' And it is possible he truly didn't know.

At that particular moment, I had been remembering an evening when Bev and I had gone dancing and I had spent the evening in the arms of her cousin Dick.

'If you want to know, I was thinking that I was happier with Bev.'

I didn't mention Dick and was the more annoyed when Fred's only comeback was, 'I was reading the other day that bisexuality is quite normal.'

With nowhere else to go we fell back on my ever tolerant parents. And for the next few years we lived in the basement of my childhood home in Battersea. Fred, who would never knowingly have touched a hand-out from Dad, had no idea that the rent we paid was greatly reduced. His political persuasions, plus his non-existent war record, meant that few doors were open to him, and even fewer that he would agree to walk through. For three years he took badly paid clerical jobs and, at a very low point, did a heroic stint packing sanitary towels in a factory, which to his credit he addressed with aplomb. He liked working alongside 'the girls', his term for his colleagues, and I expect they in turn liked him because it would be only a very stuck-up woman then who minded being called a 'girl'.

In those days, if you were a graduate you could teach without any further qualification. By this time Beetle had been born and even with the peppercorn rent we were paying we could barely manage financially. So it was as well I found a position teaching English and discovered that teaching suited me. Teachers were highly regarded still and in opening up great works of literature I felt that I was helping to foster an inner world that might serve my pupils well when external life became rough. Smoking was not the evil it is considered today and I refashioned the famous Strand cigarette ad to 'You are never alone with a book', which I had the girls make up into a poster for the school library. Imagine getting away with that today . . .

Gradually our life settled into a kind of normality. Fred was recommended for a job teaching at Birkbeck and, after years of being 'delicate', Grandad Tye died at the grand age of ninety and left us enough money to buy a shabby house in Acton with a big untidy garden.

In the summer of 1951 we moved in. It was an unusually hot summer, I remember. I was pregnant with Bell and my ankles swelled. Nat had just had his eleventh birthday and was about to go on to Acton County (which to Fred's delight had a full-blooded card-carrying communist as its Head).

Eleven is one of those pivotal ages when life changes. Certainly the whole chemistry of our family altered then.

Ma was always at heart a charming child herself and during this period she and Nat had become very thick. I was glad of her help but working full-time, and with Beetle still a toddler and another baby on the way, I failed to notice that her childlike traits were developing along more sinister lines.

She had always had her head in the clouds, occasionally losing keys, glasses, books and purses, but she now began to lose them regularly, and indeed to lose herself more than usual. On a couple of occasions she left the gas on when she wasn't cooking, which was dangerous. But what really alerted me to the early stages of something more worrying was when, bit by bit, she began to lose names.

I remember describing one of Blanche's latest paranoid absurdities – the government, she insisted, was introducing hormones into the drinking water as a form of mass contraception – and Ma frowned ever so slightly and began to say 'Who's . . . ?' and then, hastily, 'Oh, *Blanche.*' Another time she seemed not to be perfectly sure who I meant by Margaret. But it was when she began to haver over my own name that I recognized what was wrong.

Writing this now I've had a painful recollection. A couple of years before Ma's decline, we were discussing an injured racehorse that had had to be shot. She was always one for a flutter and there was a horse called Maudie May that we'd backed to win at Cheltenham. Because that was one of Dad's affectionate pet names for Ma we'd staked a tidy sum on this horse, which romped home famously and we dined out on the winnings – and later on the story.

So we were both sorry to read in the paper that Maudie May had a tendon injury that had led to her being put down.

Ma said, 'I hope you'll put me down if it looks as though I'm no longer up to it, darling.'

'I can't see me taking you out for a torn tendon, Ma,' I said.

'There are equivalent human horrors. I might go silly in my wits. I would hate that, you know.'

She died not knowing who any of us were and Dad, unwilling to go on without her, died soon after. Too late to wish that I had been braver.

While my poor mother faded like a bright summer flower dropping petals, flinty Grandmother Tye lived on, ruling Dowlands in single majesty. Still indomitable, she stuck it out there, in that draughty, impractical house, running her life, and the place, with her iron will and the help of the faithful Margaret.

Bev and Ted had married and now had three more much younger children and we had Beetle and Bell, also much younger than Nat, so when our family visited Dowlands it was natural that he and Eddie should pal up again and share exploits.

My friendship with Bev, though always warm, had attenuated with our marriages. While, when alone, we could still share gleeful reminiscences about our wartime escapades, Fred and Ted, whose wars had followed such opposite lines, were awkward together. Ted, to hide either embarrassment or contempt, or maybe both, addressed Fred with a kind of deference that Fred didn't know how to handle; and Fred couldn't talk easily to anyone who didn't uncritically share the views of the *Manchester Guardian*.

But we all agreed that it was great our two eldest boys had stayed such friends and it became a tradition over the years for the wartime pals to holiday together independently. There was a quasi-socialist organization that sent children off in the holidays to learn to sail or climb, and through this experience Nat and Eddie became keen climbers. As they grew older, the two of them made off abroad on climbing expeditions, while Fred and I went camping with Beetle and Bell.

I have thought about this a good deal since and I detect no hint that Nat ever minded the arrival of Beetle or Bell. He never struck me as a jealous child. On the contrary, he was invariably loving with his young sibs, especially so with Bell, but he was also popular at school and occupied, in a normal schoolboyish way, with his many friends. He appeared to move smoothly up the school, passing his O and A levels with flying colours. I suppose we never expected otherwise. Nor did we think much about it when the school suggested putting him in for Oxbridge. As far as Fred was concerned, since this was the local state 'county' school with no public-school privilege to object to, there was no moral reason to prevent this. The truth is that he would probably have been disappointed had Nat not been considered Oxbridge material.

What was a mild shock was that because his history teacher had some connection with the college Nat elected to apply to Peterhouse, to which the LSE was moved during the war. He couldn't have known the significance of Peterhouse and I was nervous of raising the subject with Fred. 'Mightn't there be some memorial or something to Magda there?' I suggested finally.

I can see now that Fred was embarrassed at my summoning this ghost but his reaction came across as callous. 'Why would there be? She didn't amount to anything.'

'Fred!'

'It's a coincidence. Don't go all spooky on me, Bets.'

But what most strikes me now is Nat's choice to read architecture, which I didn't question at all at the time. He showed an early attachment to cathedrals. Fred, for all his atheism, was tolerant of my own interest, and in the days when we were only the three of us we spent many afternoons examining Romanesque arches, clerestories, flying buttresses and stained glass with a thoroughness that the most pious church attender could hardly better. But while I love to explore cathedrals, it is from the vantage point of the ground. One of the most unnerving experiences of my life was watching *Vertigo*. The mere screen illusion of that hideous perspective provoked in me such a visceral terror that I had to bury my face in Fred's jacket.

But from a young age the sight of a steep drop seemed to release a powerful energy in Nat. I can't remember exactly how old he was when we climbed Salisbury Cathedral's tower. I must have been there with him alone or I would certainly have dispatched Fred, who had no fear of heights, in my place. What I remember is Nat capering around like a little monkey while I stood with my back firmly against a support, feebly trying to catch at his jersey to pull him back. I suppose in a sense I have never stopped trying to pull him back.

8

Nat won his place at Cambridge and we were innocently proud and pleased for him. Eddie, who might as easily have got to Oxbridge, was going off to Newcastle. But they seemed as thick as ever and the climbing expeditions continued. Looking through the box where I have all Nat's cards and letters, I found an envelope still containing the dusty remnants of a furry edelweiss which he must have picked and pressed to send to us. I would have said that there was nothing that I had forgotten about Nat; but I had forgotten the edelweiss.

I see from the postmark that was the summer of 1960, the summer before they climbed in the Dolomites and afterwards went on to Vienna, which Nat wrote to us of with such serious interest that it prompted a conversation with Fred.

I remember I had stayed late at school that day and the letter was waiting for me in the kitchen when I got back. Bell was round at a school friend's house and Beetle was in his room playing music. I knew Fred was preparing a lecture but I gatecrashed his study.

'Nat's in Vienna.' Fred was brave but courage comes in discrete forms and when he looked up his eyes flashed alarm. 'Don't we have a duty to tell him now?'

'I thought you didn't want to.'

'Fred, he's twenty-one next July. Some time he'll want his birth certificate.' It was providential – or so I would have put it then – that so far he had never requested this. I don't remember how we managed his passport. He was still young when we applied for his first one, though that would have been the moment for an honest disclosure. If his birth certificate had been required for this then I suspect it was I, damn fool that I was, who had filled in the forms on his behalf and sent with them any revealing documents.

'If you think we should?' I waited, rather meanly, but I didn't feel like helping him out. 'I suppose we should.'

'It should come from you.' He looked back down at the book he'd been studying, *Aeschylus and Athens*, a Marxist commentary on Ancient Greece, and sensing a potential retreat I said, 'You are his father, after all.'

Was this cowardice? Or revenge? Perhaps a bit of both. I'm not proud of it.

'I suppose we should,' Fred said again.

'No. You should,' I insisted.

'Then you must let me wait for the right time.'

But the 'right time' somehow drifted down the stream. And after that summer Nat began a slow but sustained withdrawal from us and from our family life. He wrote from Austria to say he was going back with Eddie to Seahouses and would write again to let us know his 'movements'. This was the era of letter writing. Long-distance calls were expensive and only the wealthy or the careless spoke much on the phone except on local calls.

I was disappointed. I'd missed Nat, I always missed him, but although I was slightly taken aback by the language, which for him was oddly formal, I thought no more of it than that he wanted to extend his holiday with his best friend.

Nor did I allow myself to sense anything amiss when Nat contrived to collect his things from home on his way back to Cambridge at a time when all of us were out. I should have spotted it – indeed, I must have spotted it and set the information aside – because he would have had to calculate the time quite carefully to be sure of an empty house.

He left a note, brief but not obviously disquieting, and then we heard nothing more.

We had been in the habit of visiting him in Cambridge at least once a term and I waited for the usual letter suggesting possible dates. When none came I wrote him a chatty letter, trying not to put on any pressure but mentioning how Bell and Beetle missed him (which was my cowardly way of conveying that it was actually me who was missing him) and, I hoped casually, enquiring when it might be convenient for us all to come. I remember feeling obscurely bothered that I had had to manufacture the casualness. Nat and I had always communicated easily.

He took time to reply, which was not out of character either but it was out of character that the tone of the letter, when it did come, was guarded. Again, not obvi-ously hostile but signalling a warning: he wrote that he was 'working hard', was 'trying not to have any distrac-tions' and would 'look forward' to seeing us at Christmas.

Fred, whose primary relationship was with the world rather than with any individual, never shared my need to be close to the children. Possibly this is an asset. I don't know that children much welcome their parents' need for them. And in my case I am aware that I was looking for an intimacy that Fred couldn't provide. But I tried not to fuss or harass or probe. Yield on unessentials, I told myself, though my relationship with Nat had always seemed ferociously essential. That boy held my heart in a way that felt molecular. But I gritted my teeth, held my tongue and dug into my work. I had just been taken on in the then unusual role of drama teacher.

That Christmas we went up to Dowlands as usual to be with Grandmother. Nat when he turned up was uncom-municative, though he was unusually generous to his siblings, with a present of an enamelled brooch for Bell and for Beetle, an inspired gift, a rain gauge. I was given Schubert's *Winterreise*. I forget what he gave Fred. What I chiefly remember was Nat's *noli me tangere* distance.

I raised this with Fred in bed in our old room, where the blue paper was now a faded grey.

'D'you remember when you came back from Durham how Nat used to tuck into bed between us?'

We no longer put mattresses on the floor. We slept in the old iron-framed twin beds, parallel, side by side, as we had as children. Fred was reading and only smiled vaguely in reply.

'I wonder when he last did that? You never know, do you, when the last time will be.'

'Last what?' Still engrossed in his book he wasn't paying attention.

'Oh, last of anything you used to enjoy, love. I mean, when was the last time he sat on our laps, for instance, when was the last time I kissed him better, when was the last time . . .' I began to weep and Fred could no longer ignore me.

'What's up?'

'Isn't it obvious? Nat hasn't let us near him all term.'

Fred put down his book, a vast volume about the iniquities of the British Empire, the kind I would never read. 'He's probably in love. Love makes you introverted. You don't want to discuss it with your parents. I didn't.'

Fred would never have discussed anything remotely intimate with Blanche. And even I, close to my parents as I was, had never really chosen to confide on the subject of love. I elected to go along with this and allowed Fred's, on the face of it sensible, explanation to damp down my disquiet.

For of course, intuitively, I connected Nat's sudden distance from us with his visit to Vienna. It was sheer cowardly wishful thinking that gave that insight the lie. I was afraid, afraid of what we hadn't said, of what we hadn't done, afraid of what the revelation about his parentage might mean for me. And with that very fear I ensured the result I feared.

We were both of us, Fred and I, guilty and scared, and because of this we messed up our chance ever to make that explanation, to apologize for what we hadn't said and for what, it transpired, so perturbingly had been revealed to a Nat, who was wholly unprepared for such a revelation. You see, it turned out that we had been in error about Magda's relatives. Not all of them had perished in the camps and by a series of coincidences Nat had found this out.

I was told the story months later by Eddie, whom at the time Nat had sworn to secrecy.

It seems that all those years ago Magda had sent a photo of Nat to a second cousin, who, on the outbreak of war, had been at school in Switzerland and had sensibly stayed put. Eventually she had married a doctor and settled in Lausanne. The photo with an accompanying card, on which Magda had written of her marriage and her new name, had been preserved in a book of photos of the cousin's relatives and Nat's photo, his name and date of birth, were inscribed there too.

This piece of family memorabilia had been loaned to a Viennese woman whose family had also perished in the camps and who was compiling an exhibition of memories of Viennese families lost in the war. The album was part of this display. I don't know if it was permanently open at that particular page, or if that was another turn of fate's cruel screw, but on the day when

Nat visited the exhibition it was his own two-week-old image that he encountered gazing up at him from beneath the protective glass.

It was Eddie, as he told me himself, who pointed it out.

Oh, and I do not, cannot blame Eddie. I can only blame myself. I say to myself, had I never moved up to Dowlands, had I never met Bev and Eddie that day on the beach, had I . . . had I . . . But then Nat and I would have died in that night bombing of Cambridge and none of this would ever have been.

It was months after Nat's funeral that I asked Eddie if I could come and talk to him. I was in desperate need to learn more for I knew in my blood and bones that some dangerous matter to do with his birth had finally reached Nat. I haunted Eddie, poor boy, bombarded him with letters, openly blackmailing him, until, I expect to get rid of me, he finally agreed to let me come. I dare say Bev had a hand in this.

I drove up to Seahouses but when I arrived Bev had tactfully gone out and only Eddie was there to receive me. He made tea and tried to make conversation but I was too desperate to let myself be side-tracked.

'Eddie, what happened when you and Nat were in Vienna? I know something did.'

He sat, the cup of tea in his big hand (I recognized the cup as one that Margaret had given Bev when she was clearing out the china cupboard at Dowlands), while he described how they'd gone, quite by chance, to this exhibition after seeing a poster with a photograph that had caught his eye. He apologized for this, poor boy, as though the whole ghastly mess had something to do with his interest in that photograph.

'We were looking round, and saying how fucking – excuse me – bloody the whole thing was and how hard to believe and so on, and we stopped before this case with loads of photos and cards and that sort of thing and I just looked down at this picture of a baby's face and said, "Look, Jack, that kid's got the same name as you." I thought it was just a coincidence, you see.'

'What did he say?' The pity of it.

'He said, "Ah, get over, man" or something. Under the photo it just said "Baby Nathaniel, aged two weeks." Then he looked some more. There was a card pasted in the book beside the photo, with all his names on it, Nathaniel Wilfred Tye. And his birthday. So it had to be more than a coincidence.'

'God,' I said. 'How could we have let this happen?'

I could tell Eddie wanted to stop because it was only with a supreme effort that I was holding back tears but I made him go on.

'What happened then, Eddie? You must tell me.'

Eddie gave a kind of shudder. It has crossed my mind since that perhaps they loved each other in more than just the way of friendship. We never saw a girlfriend. How extraordinary that I hadn't wondered why.

'We found the name of the woman running the exhibition and tracked her down. Jack had to convince her that he was the kid in the photo but he had his passport and it was all there, name, date, everything. So then, after checking up or whatever, she gave him the name and address of the woman who'd loaned the photo. Jack got in touch with her and he went to see her some time.'

'He told you? What? What did she say, Eddie?'

He half hesitated. I could see how hard this was for him. 'I don't think there was much more she told him than what was written on the card.'

'Oh God,' I said again. 'Poor Nat. How could we?'

'You didn't know,' Eddie said. 'You didn't know.'

9

But I *had* known. Blanche and Grandmother, with their genteel, antiquated anti-Semitism, had been concerned to cover it all up. Grandad, in his dotage, had never really taken it in and Ma was always one for live and let live. But my father, I am sure, believed that we were wrong to keep Nat in the dark. Though he would have been forgiving of my reasons, I was conscious that he disapproved. Dad was a moral touchstone, one I had failed to regard.

I've jumped ahead because all this – all that I learned from Eddie – only came out afterwards.

At Fred's suggestion I was putting on a production of *The Trojan Women*, which is a good choice of play for a girls' school because the principal parts are female. The night that Nat died was the play's first night. The Greek gods were said to laugh at mortal affairs, so they must have been vastly entertained that night, because about the time little Alexandra Pelham, as the young Astyanax, was being dramatically thrown from the battlements of Troy by various of my pupils dressed as Greeks in cardboard greaves, Nat was preparing to scale the north-east pinnacle of King's Chapel.

The son of Rex Napley – the student who had taunted Fred about being a CO – had gone up to Cambridge the year after Nat. Evidently Rex had married the dreadful Philippa and they had produced an equally dreadful child. This ghastly son had revived an old Cambridge tradition of climbing the more perilous Cambridge buildings by night. It was the kind of gung-ho undergraduate cult that Fred and I would have utterly despised when we were students. The Night Climbers of Cambridge, they called themselves. This Napley brat evidently dared Nat to join them. His father had apparently recognized the name Tye and had regaled his son with a tale of Fred's 'cowardice'. Or maybe the son simply took the information that Nat's father was a 'conchy' and ran with it. I don't know for sure.

The loathsome Napley boy wrote us a lickspittle letter after Nat's fatal fall, in which he expressed his 'most sincere regrets'. I didn't believe for one second that he was regretful at all, except out of the desire to save his own skin. We learned more from another student, a frantically distressed young man called Bob Craft, who was too stricken for me to hate him and who had also been involved in the climb. He, poor lad, had reached the roof of the chapel and had witnessed the fall. Nat, already angry with us, must have been goaded into a demonstration of his difference from his father.

His father had chosen to turn his back on the fight against the system whose clear and stated ambition was to rid the face of the earth of Jews – a system which had killed his mother, the mother whom he had, in a sense, only just found. The discovery of this shamefully long-concealed truth must have caused an incomparable inner havoc.

To reach the very top of one of the pinnacles of King's Chapel was the supreme aim of this foolhardy, utterly idiotic gang. Nat should never have been encouraged to attempt the climb with no experience of climbing at night. I know how it would have been. He would have boasted of his experience as a rock climber – he was rightly proud of his skills – but for this kind of climbing venture a knowledge of the location of footholds on the buildings is crucial. Knowledge which Nat had either had no time to or had chosen not to acquire. He made the climb with no head protection and, according to Bob Craft, at the crucial point was unroped. My darling boy, thrown into questioning the basis of his whole life – his history, his very existence – must have been in turmoil, and could hardly have helped losing an inner balance, which must in turn have thrown his usually expert judgement, for it seems that on the very last stage of the climb, over a hundred feet above the ground, he fatally lost his outer balance and grabbed on to a projecting stone that time and the weather had softened, which broke off in his hand.

Those roof climbers had a mantra: 'If you fall you still have three seconds to live.' I have tried to imagine and I have tried not to imagine those three seconds. In neither effort have I been successful.

PART THREE
Bell

I

Hetta dear,

*I don't at all mind putting down all I can remember,
provided that's OK by Mum and Cele. There's quite a lot I
don't know about and some you may well want to edit out. I'm
not fussed for myself but I don't want to give grief or let any
feral cats out of the bag. Anyway, you'll know what to do with
this.*

Love Bell

The word among the family was that I was being unusually decent when I suggested Will come to us when he got kicked out of King's. I wasn't best known for my decency. I was the black sheep, the bad girl, the one without 'principles'. When my mother swore blind she had no time for principles she wasn't being quite honest. What she had no time for was my father's political beliefs but she had principles of her own. Not that I hold that against her.

Mum's trouble was guilt. She felt guilty about our brother Nat, who, as you know, I always called Jack, because she believed that his death was connected to her not telling him who his mother really was. His mother was a girlfriend of Daddy's and she was killed in the war and Mum took Jack in.

In my opinion it was saintly of her. If Jack's mother hadn't dumped him on Mum and swanned off to London – nobody knows why she did but it's my bet she was having an affair, which is usually the reason why people suddenly drop everything – what I'm getting at is that if Jack's mother had stayed put in Cambridge with her baby, where she should have been, she'd be alive today. And if she'd taken him off with her to London, Nat would have died aged seven weeks. Either way Mum was a heroine.

But she doesn't like to think of herself like that.

I was eight when Jack was killed. I remember it as a truly terrible time because it was the first time I ever saw Daddy cry. Daddy never cried. He was always the cheery optimistic one and made us feel everything would always be OK. He had been the sun for me since I could remember, so seeing him cry was shattering.

There was a Ray Charles song in the hit parade at the time, *Hit the Road Jack*. Jack had an old 45 record of this. I don't know what happened to it, but I used to listen at night – on a radio I kept under my pillow that I found in Jack's room – to Radio Luxembourg, hoping to hear the song again and hoping against hope that my big brother *would* come back. I always think of him if I ever hear Ray Charles.

For a long time our father was utterly different after Jack was killed. Daddy blamed himself because some little shit apparently got at Jack by saying that Daddy was a coward because he'd been a conchy in the war – and

Daddy had a theory Jack only made that climb to prove that he wasn't a coward himself, to make himself out as different. Different from Daddy, that is. But I don't buy that.

There are two reasons why I don't: I was only eight but eight-year-olds take in impressions as well as any adult, often better – I know I did – and Jack never struck me as someone who would rise to a taunt. That's not how I remember him. Granted, he might well have been angry that Daddy and Mum had concealed the fact of his birth – that's fair enough, they should have told him. I don't really get why they didn't because I would have thought it was bound to come out some time. What I do remember is an atmosphere one Christmas with Mum fretting that we'd hardly seen him and doing her own discreet version of wringing her hands. But I still don't buy this conchy business being the trigger. If you want my view, they were punishing themselves.

The other reason I don't buy it is what a friend of Jack's told me. But I'll come to that.

I must have decided very young that I was going to be different. You hear people go on about the 'innocence' of children but I would say it all depends. I believe I was born uninnocent, or anyway I lost such innocence as I ever had before I could remember any consciously. I was famous for my tantrums and I remember, quite distinctly, enjoying them hugely and the fuss they provoked. I would lie on the floor and scream and thrash about and it was just great. Quite transporting. Beetle was terrified of my tantrums and I used them to get whatever it was I wanted from him at the time. Poor old Beetle. It's horrible what has happened to him. Worse for Will, though.

I always got on with Will. Robert used to say the celestial cards had got muddled and Beetle and I had been dealt the wrong children: Beetle should have had Cele and I should have had Will. Hetta should have gone to Mum rather than Susan, though I'll get into trouble for saying that. Mum's very careful to be even-handed but she has a special tone she uses for Hetta and she takes Hetta along with her on various slightly mysterious trips. Mum can be secretive. She thinks she's an open book but she's not – not really.

As for Sydella – ridiculous name – I never really got Sydella . . .

But Will. Let me put it like this, if we'd been of an age I might well have gone after him. 'Set my cap at him', as Daddy would say. Dear Daddy. He fancied himself as a man of the people but you can't bleed the blue blood out of your veins. I don't mean he wasn't democratic.

I remember Will coming to Staresnest once, when Robert was staying. Robert had a soft spot for Will and I was up for having anyone to stay who Robert warmed to. We were having one of our rocky patches when his wife was being more demanding than usual. She was never too well and, apart from the obviously annoying fact that she was Robert's wife, I suppose because I've always been strong as an ox I found all this ill-health business simply feeble. Robert was also hugely fond of Cele, by the way. He felt, quite reasonably, that I neglected her and he tried to make up for that. Anyway, there was a to-do when Will was with us, about an otter which the children had rescued from the otter hunt. I have a vague idea that Hetta was with us too but I may have misremembered that. What I do remember is that Will and Cele got into a lather about the creature, which Robert and I could see was done for. They were both mad about animals and Will, who we used to joke had a 'will of steel', insisted that Robert drive them to a vet. Robert was tickled by the 'will of steel' and he cheerfully complied.

The creature had to be put to sleep and the children were desperately upset. Will pinched a diamond brooch of mine to engrave the date of the otter's death on a stone they had made to mark its grave. That was very like them – burying it with all the proper forms, I mean. Anyway, this was a most unusual diamond and emerald Art Nouveau brooch, set in the form of a willow tree, which Robert had given me when we first became lovers and I was extremely fond of. I remember Will, when I objected, yelling at me, 'You're so bloody selfish. You only think about yourself.' He was quite right. I do mostly only think about myself. I remember Robert laughing at what Will had said. Robert knew exactly what I'm like and he didn't mind.

So, given my reputation for selfishness, they will all have been puzzled when I suggested Will come and stay at our flat when he was 'rusticated', as Susan insisted we call it. Ridiculous word.

The brutal truth is I was bored to death with my husband. I had only myself to blame for that. I was bored by him from the start but I'd become afraid of being alone for the rest of my life. I'm not saying Graham is a bad man. He is in fact a fairly decent man and at the time seemed devoted to me, which helped. But it can't be denied that he's frantically dull.

I'd grown tired of my old faithfuls, Kenny and Alastair. As for Robert, the family theory is that Robert would never leave his wife but that wasn't how it was at all. What I've never said is that he did, as it happens, offer to leave her. We'd had one of our rare rows and when we were making up I became maudlin. *Timor mortis conturbat me*, as Mum would say, or, in other words, I had got to a point where I didn't fancy becoming an aging former beauty with no one to soften the edges and I said so. And he said, 'Look, Bella, if you really need me to I'll leave Peggy. I can make over enough funds to keep her comfortable for life and, with your agreement, stay her friend to keep an eye on her.'

For about two days I skipped about like a woolly lambkin on cloud nine supposing I would accept. But the part of me I trust said, Hey, my girl, you know damn well he's going to feel guilty as hell. I couldn't somehow face living with a guilty man. I'd resent it; I know myself. So I took my courage in both hands, or whatever the expression is, and said, 'Sweetheart, that's the nicest suggestion you've ever made and you've been nicer than I deserve but it would cut you up so horribly I think I'd better not let you. For both our sakes.'

And I could tell at once that he was relieved so I was right to turn his offer down. Peggy had never for a second looked at anyone other than Robert. He was loyal to her for this reason alone. I liked him for it, as a matter of fact.

So that was that. But it was the case that I'd begun to lose my nerve. And I confess that Graham's pots of money were a lure. Or the comfort they offered, anyway. I'd managed OK with Robert's help but a life with no more money worries was tempting. The consolations of security, I suppose. And then, Graham's flat was fabulous. He offered to sell it so we could buy somewhere I'd chosen myself but I have no silly proprietorial problems of that sort. It's not the kind of thing to worry me and in fact I couldn't wait to get my hands on his flat, to make it over. I'd always fancied myself as a designer manqué.

And I had a ball. I chucked out all the ugly furniture his ex had cluttered up the place with, had her Regency-style wallpaper stripped off and ditched the hideous curtains to let the light in. That makes me think of a line in a Leonard Cohen song Robert and I liked – *It's through the cracks that the light gets in* – sort of sums things up.

Because it was nice for Cele too to have a decent home. My years of tedious house-mothering were pretty dismal for her and the poky flat we had then was not exactly homely. There was Staresnest, but that had been my bolt-hole and frankly poor Cele had been shuttle-cocked between Daddy and Mum and Dowlands. I knew what they thought of me at Dowlands. And they were right: I'd been a fairly hopeless mother and I was pleased that she could now share some of my fortune. She was an ugly little creature as a child but she's grown to be a beauty. She looks like the photo of her father's sister as a matter of fact.

Should I say something about her father? Perhaps I should.

Igor, oh dear, Igor. Igor was older, foreign, therefore exotic, musically brilliant and rather mysterious. The last two were what most caught my fancy. He was a fantasti-cally fierce teacher, especially with those he rated, and I liked that he was hard on me, partly because Daddy had always let me get away with murder, and the young are perversely drawn to whatever makes for the opposite side of the coin of their upbringing, and partly because I understood that the harshness was a compliment. He was so lofty and seemed so indifferent to everything that I had always been sure of that I had to seduce him. I know how that sounds.

For about two and a half seconds we behaved as if we were madly in love and, whatever else, at least Cele was conceived in passion. I always think that must be a good start for a child.

Though it must be said that the passion fizzled out fairly fast. Igor was bisexual. I knew this, and it was an added spur rather than the reverse, another scalp for me, silly creature, to sport. But he was so narcissistic that he couldn't help being competitive with anyone of either sex who matched him in looks. I imagined he was my conquest and he imagined that I was his. When I told him I was pregnant, about which I was absurdly proud (I had never somehow envisaged myself as able to conceive), he looked so appalled that I actually laughed. People tend not to believe this when I tell them, but it's God's truth that I found it hilarious that he'd never considered that the act of sex might produce a living consequence. Come to think of it, I suppose we were alike in this.

I've no idea if this was guilt or what but about six months later, just before Cele was born, he produced four hundred quid in cash, which amounted to quite a tidy sum in those days. We'd always been hard up in my family, thanks to Daddy's blessed principles, and I'd never handled such a roll of notes before. It was rather sexy, if you want to know. And that's not just the money because although Graham's money was useful it wasn't in the least bit sexy.

Daddy and Mum got into a flap when I had to give up my training but, although they used to carry on about how talented I was, I'm not so sure. I don't know that I would honestly have made it beyond an orchestra, and maybe not such a fantastic one at that. And I was never much cop at playing second fiddle. So perhaps it doesn't matter. I've done all right, in my way. 'Never say "if only"', Mum's father always said. He was remarkably sane, was Gramps. He once whacked my bottom with a rolled-up newspaper when I was acting up. I didn't mind because I knew I deserved it and it made us friends. He used to threaten me with his paper after that, which made me laugh. People make too much fuss about smacking children, if you ask me. I far preferred being whacked to being subjected to those 'look at me' grave talks.

When Cele was born I did write to ask Igor if he thought Cecilia a good name for 'our daughter', as I was careful to remind him. He'd been a pal of Britten's (maybe more than a pal) and Britten wrote the music for 'Anthem to St Cecilia' so I was hopeful that my, as I saw it tactful, hint might produce a further contribution of cash. I wasn't too put out that he never replied but years later, I gathered from Will, Igor sent Cele a Collected Auden with the poem *Anthem for St Cecilia's Day* marked with a picture postcard of Stravinsky. She never mentioned this but why should she? Among the many things I had not given my daughter was a father.

So now, Will. I suppose because I was a black sheep I felt for the boy as he turned into a black lamb. There's honour among thieves and black sheep should flock together. I was probably the first to spot that he was drinking.

It was a Christmas when I was dropping Cele off at Dowlands before driving up to Edinburgh with Alastair. I'm afraid this was one of the many respects in which I was a lousy mother. To show somewhat willing, I'd agreed to stay over for Christmas Eve, which was when they celebrated with their festive meal.

My staying over was my nod to family solidarity. Susan, I should say, never liked me. She's a well-mannered woman so she never gave any obvious outward sign but I'm not without Mum's intuition – negative intuition, Robert used to call it, because it's true that I'm better at picking up negative vibes. One reason Susan didn't like me was that she sensed I hadn't much time for what I believe are called 'family values'. We, that is Beetle and Nat and I, grew up in an ethos of care-unto-others, but to do Daddy and Mum justice it had more zip and pizazz in it. For one thing, Mum (who, as I say, did have some well-concealed principles but never showed them off) was able to laugh at Daddy and challenge him when he became too pious. And, to be fair, Daddy was hardly ever pious – he was really quite mad in an understated sort of way. His aunt went off her head, or so we were told, and in my view Daddy's marbles were not altogether there either. All that CO stuff in the war. Mum insists he never need have gone to prison at all but he wanted to be imprisoned because it would look good on his political CV. Insane but like him and kind of endearing. Beetle and Susan weren't exactly endearing, not in my book anyway, and they certainly weren't the tiniest morsel dotty. Susan once said that our family wasn't 'run on proper lines' and frankly that sums them up.

Syd, who I would have expected to take after them, showed her Tye genes by up and marrying her married

Jordanian and good for her. Hetta retired into her imagination. But poor Will was simply frustrated by the goody-two-shoes atmosphere and acted up. That's my reading of it anyway.

As it happened, on that particular Christmas Day when I spotted the drink thing, Alastair's car chose not to start, so when he rang to give me the bad news that he wouldn't be picking me up I was trapped for a second night at Dowlands.

Beetle and Susan did good works on Christmas Day, which was like them, very commendable but I always thought rough on the kids. Cele and Hetta set out with them when they pushed off – my daughter was the soul of tact and was probably compensating for her rude mother – but Will stayed behind. Not too much fuss was overtly made about this but there was an 'atmosphere'.

I loathe atmospheres. I imagine everyone does but I'm more readily vocal about this than most so I expressed a humorous sympathy once they had all packed themselves off in Beetle's four by four.

I still recall Will's response: 'At least we can have a drink now.'

It was around ten in the morning and while I'm no puritan I'm not given to drinking before lunchtime. However, it isn't my style to comment on other people's foibles so I kept quiet and simply continued to read. I was reading Stevenson because I was off to Scotland. I always liked Stevenson as a child. Daddy and Mum used to take us every Christmas to a performance of *Treasure Island* at the Mermaid Theatre in Puddle Dock with Bernard Miles playing Long John Silver. Silver's one of those 'bad' characters who at the same time are very attractive.

Anyway, by this time in my Stevenson jag I had got to *Catriona*, the part where she and Davey run off to Paris, and was contentedly reading in the big sitting room on their highly uncomfortable chaise longue (uncomfortable because it had been there, magnificently unrestored, probably since Dowlands was completed in 1792). With my peripheral vision I couldn't help noticing that in the space of a couple of hours Will must have gone three or four times to the drinks tray, which was laid out on the old sideboard that had stood there maybe not since 1792 but certainly since our grandparents' day. There's a wobbly little N scratched inside one of the cupboard doors which Jack famously did with the point of a compass when he was five and Great-grandad Tye, instead of tearing a strip off him, apparently roared with laughter.

Beetle and Susan didn't drink that much but to do them justice they weren't stingy either and laid on alcohol for themselves and any guests or visitors for Christmas.

I said nothing, but when they returned I saw Beetle eyeing the whisky decanter, and I could tell he was busily calculating the level which had dramatically dropped. So I volunteered, 'Oh, by the way, I helped myself to a drink or two while you lot were out spreading sweetness and light. I hope you don't mind.'

He might reasonably have minded but had he bothered to think about it at all he would have recognized that this was out of character. I was far too bothered about getting a swollen red nose to drink spirits. But if you have a reputation for impropriety then people will attribute to you almost any social sin, however much it might contradict your observable behaviour.

Not that I minded carrying the can. Water off a duck's back. Will glanced across at me but his face gave nothing away. And I wasn't looking for thanks. Actually, if I wanted anything it was to spare Beetle what I felt would be a needless anxiety.

About that I was wrong, I admit. What I had taken to be merely an act of adolescent rebellion, a protest against the goody-goody 'family values', proved to be something more dangerous.

Unless it was made dangerous by the way they took it. But, to be fair, I don't believe either Beetle or Susan were Lady Marchmains. But what I do wonder now, if this doesn't sound too weirdly far-fetched, is if when Jack fell that ghastly night his spirit somehow shattered into a hundred pieces and, like the sliver of ice in the boy's heart in the fairy tale, some dangerous fragment lodged in Will's being.

2

When Will came to stay at the flat that time I didn't, as family legend has it, find him a job as a barman. Family legend pisses me off, if you want to know. I would never have been so daft. What I actually did was find him a job at the ticket office of the Festival Hall through one of Robert's contacts, but in the very first week Will got the sack. From what Robert picked up, Will was late several mornings and also late back from his lunch breaks and, to cap it all, was surly when reprimanded. So it was understandable they gave him the push. He didn't let on to me but got himself taken on as a barman in one of the Festival Hall bars. And of course that was fatal.

He started to drink really heavily. And I guess, if he hadn't already, he moved on to drugs. They were everywhere then in London, and by the time he'd got his band together he was going to hell in a handcart with a vengeance. In my view, this was more of the revolt, a more determined reaction to the Dowlands 'family values', though by this time something had clearly already gone pretty askew. Daddy was an atheist but he would never in his life have defaced a building, not even a hideous one, and certainly never an ancient chapel like King's. He was too respectful of history for that.

I asked Will to stay with us in London for two reasons: I was sorry for him but also I thought it would please Cele. And, as I say, it had got to a point where the more the merrier, as far as I was concerned, anything to help dilute my time with Graham. But I got that wrong as far as Cele was concerned. She hated the drunkenness, the drugs even more, and it didn't bring them closer. Quite the reverse. The drugs seemed to bring out a violence in Will. There was always an element of that – he had a notoriously inflammable temper but there was a sweetness in him too, a delightful charm, and that seemed to have evaporated, or anyway gone underground.

So the atmosphere between them was none too bright already when one day, out of the blue, the unspeakable Colin reappeared.

I'm not easily fazed but I was completely taken aback when the stranger's voice on the intercom early one evening proved to be his. I'd been expecting a delivery from our dry cleaners, which happened to be called Colin's, so when I buzzed to let him up I thought nothing more than that it was my Max Mara suit being delivered. Although I'd never met him I knew at once who this was when I opened the door.

He wasn't bad-looking. In fact more attractive than I'd been imagining and I admit I was surprised. I hadn't expected Cele to appeal to a man like that. What I mean is, I hadn't expected her to be pursued by such an apparently sexually attractive man, which is not to my credit, I know.

But my God, did I go off him fast. Mr Bloody-Full-of-Himself. It was obvious after three breaths that it had never crossed his mind that he might not be exactly welcome. He actually had the nerve to attempt to seduce me, with a load of crap about how beautiful he'd heard I was but I was even more beautiful than he'd been led to expect, blah, blah. I put a stop to that with my basilisk face, as Robert used to call it.

He was not too obviously disconcerted but I'd conveyed, very firmly, that I expected him to leave and I do believe that he was about to go when Will arrived on the scene. He was either drunk or high, you could see the moment he walked through the door, and I could also tell that, like me, he knew at once who the interloper was.

And the very next thing that happened was that Cele came home.

Will was standing there, stock-still in the middle of my sitting room, just staring at Colin. Then he walked towards him and stared a bit more, very deliberately, slightly narrowing his eyes. As a matter of fact, I had taught all the children that trick long ago. It's a trick I employ alongside my basilisk stare if I want to seriously freeze someone out. Will had mastered this art to perfection. I said that Robert said he should have been my child.

With the double force of our basilisk stares and Will's expertly narrowed eyes you'd have supposed Mr Full-of-Himself would have backed off. But he was just too full of himself. He simply stood there, bold as brass, in the middle of my sitting room on my Persian rug and smiled. A horrid condescending smile.

Then, with deliberate slowness, he extended an open hand and laid it on Cele's cheek. Cele shot him a glance, though I couldn't read her expression, then, eyes down, tried to make for her room. And Colin, stretching out and catching her by the crook of her elbow, said, in a horribly creepy tone of voice, 'Celandine?'

The air became electric. If the awful intimacy of that name shocked me to my core it must have primed Will's already simmering rage.

'Cunt!'

Colin just smiled down at him. He was so much taller than Will that it was impossible for him not to look down.

'You can fuck right off! Fucking cunt!'

And Colin, still with that awful smile, said, 'Ah, the brave, bold cousin William.'

I don't know why I intervened with 'It's Wilfred, actually.' I don't mean I don't know why I intervened.

Colin, whose grip on Cele's elbow had been broken by Will's shoving, now patted him on the shoulder. 'Calm down, laddy.'

I can't honestly swear to exactly what occurred next but it seems Will had a spanner in his pocket – something to do with the equipment for the gig the band were playing that night – and he hit out with it at Colin's face. Then Colin was at my feet screaming blue murder and there was blood all over my Charles Jourdan shoes and over the rug. I bought it at Christie's and it was probably the most expensive thing we had in the flat, but I gave it and the shoes away to a charity shop afterwards.

Cele stood there transfixed and I heard myself saying to Will with surprising authority, 'Go to your room, *now!*'

We rang for an ambulance, which took its time coming, and meantime I wrapped a clean tea towel round Colin's face, avoiding his right eye which was frankly a bloody mess. Colin kept up a low moaning whine throughout which left my withers unwrung. If that sounds spiteful then let it be known that I felt, and feel, spiteful, and cruel, and had then as now no desire to find it in me to sympathize.

If Colin and I meet in hell, where we are both likely to land up, I shall be indifferent to any punishment that may be meted out to me in the unbounded satisfaction that I shall take in witnessing whatever is served on Colin. As Mum said when I put this to her, 'Yes, well, we're told that the Prince of Darkness *is* a gentleman'.

3

When Will was taken to court by the vengeful Colin it was not really so surprising that the person who reacted best to this was Daddy. You might imagine, as the circs were so different – Daddy's sentence being the consequence of a principled pacifism whereas Will's was the outcome of unlawful aggression – that Daddy would've been in the forefront of the band of disapprovers. But what this mess of Will's must have activated in Daddy was his longing for camaraderie. If Daddy was a commie my guess is it was because of a need for comradeship, and Will was already a kind of colleague for him. (It only struck me the other day but if you put together the names they went by they make up the single name they shared.) It was also the case that Daddy's indifference to the personal meant that he cared less than most people about any individual's misdeeds and far more about their ideology. Or his perception of their ideology. In his eyes, Will's attack on Colin was a righteous attack on privilege – male sexual privilege in this case – but any privilege unworked for was to be fought against in Daddy's eyes. Good for him for that.

Beetle and Susan, however, were predictably aghast. All their former anxieties about Will now seemed justified. Any career he hoped to have would, in their view, have gone down the plughole. Daddy's attitude, which apparently contradicted his lifelong pacifism to which we had all been tediously subjected, would have just made their outrage worse, particularly in Susan's case. Hetta has hinted that Susan, quite unfairly, held Daddy's atheism responsible for the vandalism that led to Will getting kicked out of King's.

But the person most deeply affected was obviously my daughter.

The difficulty I have is that I cannot claim that I really know Cele. It's a wise parent that knows her own child and in this respect I am less wise than most, though having said that I would bet I have as good an understanding of Cele as Beetle and Susan have of their children. I'd kept Cele at a distance, palming her off on Daddy and Mum, or Beetle and Susan, so it was only post my marriage to Graham that I had time to observe her.

Poor child. She was obliged to appear as a witness, called by Will's defence counsel, and she loyally plumped up Colin's behaviour that day, suggesting that his physical attempt to detain her was rather more outwardly aggressive than it actually had been. I had no qualms at all about endorsing this and frankly I quite enjoyed being in the witness box. Violence is not only explicit and that 'Celandine' was deliberate provocation (though I know it's not an argument that would wash in a court). So I dressed myself up to the nines and laid it on with a trowel.

Cele refused to dress up at all, though the fact that she looked so excessively drab might of course have helped. What she wouldn't do was claim that Colin had involved her in underage sex, 'a potentially mitigating factor', Will's defence suggested. Presenting Will in the role of one endeavouring to protect his cousin from further depredations might have got him off with no more than a caution and would have finally done for the regrettable Colin (and good riddance, I say). But concerned as she was to help Will in every way, Cele bent the truth no more than by that very slight talking up of Colin's behaviour towards her that day in my flat. Will's defence attempted to milk, by implication, the effect on Cele of her affair with Colin and her desire to end it, and Will's concern for his cousin's safety and peace of mind. And he might have got off altogether except that, under oath and pressed by the prosecution, she admitted in court that the sex with Colin was consensual. In her position I think I would have lied.

Will's defence persuaded him to plead guilty to unintentional GBH and the judge was lenient and on account of Will's previous good character gave him only a suspended sentence. In spite of his scrape at King's, one of the dons there wrote Will a testimonial, saying how bright he was, what a promising student etcetera, which shows you that for all his antisocial behaviour Will was popular there. I was a witness that he had been provoked by Colin and much was made by his counsel of his protective instincts towards his cousin, which was ironical as the episode caused a serious rift between them.

It was a condition of Will's probation that he live under the 'supervision of a responsible adult' who could answer for him and he had touched me by rather hesitantly asking if I would agree to act in that role. I was tickled to be considered a 'responsible' adult but I suppose I had Graham to thank for that. Cele's reaction to the fight – and her refusal to sink Colin outright in court – must to Will have appeared a betrayal. I expect he made himself believe that he was protecting her and that she was ungrateful. Anyway, the upshot was that after a couple of tricky months, with the two of them at daggers drawn, Cele decided to take herself off. I wasn't privy to what exactly led to her move, though I'd overheard them rowing. Will probably thought she'd asked Colin to come, or that they were still sexually involved. Maybe they were. I don't really know.

I ought just to add that, given that Daddy and Mum were first cousins, any long-term alliance between Will and Cele would have provoked serious opposition from Beetle and Susan. And I must admit that even I was a tiny bit concerned. As I jokingly said to Mum once (she wasn't too receptive), there were dotty Great Aunt Char's genes to consider.

All of which is my roundabout way of confessing that I didn't try to argue with Cele over her decision to leave the flat. In fact I thought it might be as well to let whatever there was between them cool down. When Cele left, all she said, to my light enquiry, was that she was going 'to live with a friend'. And because I felt that

I had no right to press her, I never had any idea of who this 'friend' might be.

There was one potentially positive thing about this whole period. Will had the musical gene that comes from Mum's mother's family, and he was a very gifted flautist before he took up the sax. A couple of times, when he was younger, we'd played together on those rare occasions when I was at a family gathering. But the sax was better suited than the flute to his present mood.

Will had lost his bar work over the Colin fracas but his jazz band, Black Tye Boys, he kept going. And one evening – Graham had gone to bed and Will and I were still up – I said, 'Have you considered maybe chucking Cambridge and sticking with the band?'

He laughed and said, quite sweetly, 'Don't let my parents hear you say that. Dad's already got his knickers in a twist that I might not be allowed back to King's.'

Trying to be fair, I said something like, 'He only wants you to have all the opportunities you can.'

And I recall very clearly what Will said to that. 'Dad's scared I'll escape the cage.'

He said it quite affectionately but it brought to my mind how, when he was a boy, I used to call him 'Panther' for the way he would climb trees and drape himself, darkly elegant, along the boughs. You shouldn't shut up a panther in a cage. Will was a free spirit. A troubled one, for sure, but a free spirit nonetheless. And he was dead right about poor old Beetle being scared.

At the time we had this conversation I wasn't sure

that King's was prepared to have Will back, which is partly why I made encouraging noises about the band. And he might even have taken my advice, and made his name as a musician, were it not for Harvey.

Harvey was Will's version of Colin. I don't mean they were lovers, though Harvey might have hoped for that. I don't want to indict Beetle and Susan, who, God knows, have undergone enough, but were I to indict them it would be for Harvey. That puritan mental habitat which Will was raised in deprived him of the speck of moral dirt that confers an immunity on a child. Syd's lack of imagination protected her, and I would say that Hetta's wide reading, or good luck, has done the same. But Will, with his missing skin, was perfect prey for a despoiler.

Into the gap left by Cele, Harvey poured his soothing-seeming slime. That's how I read it. Will needed attention and admiration, and without Cele to provide it Harvey made himself indispensable.

Although I've thought about him often I only met Harvey twice. The first time was on a return from Staresnest, where I'd sloped off for a week's 'solitary', as I called it. It wasn't actually solitary. I'd cheered myself up by starting a not too serious affair with Anthony Li. Anthony was a GP at the practice where Graham was registered. Not my own doctor, Anthony was too professional and too canny for that, and anyway I'd made sure to sign on at a different practice from Graham.

I met him at one of Graham's grisly fund-raising dos – and if you ask me what it was that Graham actually did

I'm afraid I couldn't give you an answer. I was frankly bored to tears and Anthony must have spotted this and came over to talk to me. He made me laugh and saved the evening. He was Anglo-Chinese and very bright, which I found terribly attractive, especially after Graham. I was missing Robert, I guess. And while I was never in love with Anthony, nor he with me, he was a good conversationalist. He was also ten years younger than me, which was a boost. And in that uncomplicated way, which can be restful, we enjoyed each other's company, especially in bed.

But driving home, I was looking forward to a quiet evening with Graham in front of the telly, and was annoyed to find a stranger lolling on my sofa. Will introduced him to me and from the first I could tell that he disliked me.

Not that I gave a hoot about Harvey's dislike. But I noted it and I felt alarm. It wasn't too hard to account for the alarm since Will had one of Graham's massive crystal tumblers in his hand and had plainly been downing the contents. Since the court case, he'd tempered his drinking pretty well and, as far as I could tell, the excessive drug-taking. And while I occasionally caught a whiff of dope from his room I wasn't averse to the odd joint myself and saw no serious harm in it. So I turned a blind eye.

I was trying to turn a blind eye that evening until Will got up to refill his glass and Graham made one of his rare objections. It was his Talisker they were making free with, after all.

Graham said, very mildly, 'Will, old chap, if you drink any more you'll be drunk.'

Will turned and I could tell by his eyes that he was on the edge. What I called his necromancer's eyes. 'I want to get drunk.'

'Actually, Will,' I said, 'you *are* drunk.'

Harvey sniggered.

Will said, in that over-deliberate way which is a sign of drunkenness, 'You are not exactly being polite to my friend, Aunt.' I was always 'Bell' to Will. Never 'Aunt' or 'Aunty'.

Harvey sniggered again. I could put up with a fair bit of aggro from Will but not from a stranger I didn't like the look of.

'I don't know your friend,' I said, coldly, 'but from where I'm sitting the pair of you have had enough. It's Graham's Talisker you're drinking, not supermarket plonk.' Because I'd just come from my escapade with Anthony I was unusually defensive of my husband.

Will, who was barely upright, lurched towards me. I suppose it might have seemed as if he was going to hit me, though I'm perfectly sure that that is not what he planned. Graham, who drove me mad by desperately trying to take care of me, leapt up and began to man-handle Will.

I snapped, 'Leave it, Graham, for Christ's sake' but Will had already wrestled himself out of Graham's grasp.

He threw the tumbler on the carpet, shouted, 'Right,

we're off. See you some time!' and rushed out of the room.

Graham picked up the tumbler and started tutting about the carpet. Harvey just sat there, looking pleased as Punch and I waited a few minutes, then went after Will. He looked pale and angry and was stuffing things into a bag.

'Listen,' I said, 'calm down, for God's sake. Graham was only doing his knight-in-armour thing. It didn't mean anything.'

'He's got no fucking right to touch me.'

'I know, but I'm his wife, it's his flat and, by the way, it is, or was, his whisky. And you can't leave or you'll be breaking probation.'

'So?'

'So that's serious, as you'll remember in the morning, so shut up, sober up and go to sleep.'

I pushed him firmly down on the bed and he had already passed out before I returned to the sitting room, where I was relieved to see that Graham had got rid of the repulsive Harvey. He had touched Graham for cash for a taxi. Graham was always a soft touch and I expect the money went on more drink. Or drugs, more likely.

4

All this happened the winter after Will had been sent down, which was when? 91? 92? You can check. I'll say this: I never saw Will so obviously drunk again. My impression, wise after the event, is that part of him wanted to go to the devil with Harvey and another part wanted to get back with Cele. And maybe everything would have worked itself out in time had it not been for what she did next.

I said I had no idea where she was living. She was a dark horse, my daughter, and I was more in touch with Will's social life than with hers. I assumed her temporary home was with some female friend from school, or someone she'd met since coming to London.

We still met occasionally, though she never came to the flat. If there was a concert I fancied, I would invite her and we would have a polite but not too spontaneous evening with nothing of importance said. But one day she rang and asked if we could meet for dinner.

Aware of my past neglect, I was always a little nervous of Cele and flattered when she took the initiative over our meetings. But I could tell when we met at a restaurant in Primrose Hill that she was nervous herself. She looked older, but older to her advantage. If anything she looked more beautiful, more poised.

We exchanged superficialities, she asked after Graham, I asked after her work and neither of us mentioned Will. And we had ordered before she came to the point, which was completely, but completely, astounding.

This was some time in late March and it was cold still, but she must have been sweating slightly because I remember that she took a white lawn hanky out of her bag and patted her face. I remember it because there was a C embroidered in the corner and I recognized it as being from a boxed set Kenny and I had once bought her in Switzerland. A pretty dull present, quite insulting if you think about it, and in her shoes I'd have chucked it out long since.

Anyway, she looked at me very steadily as if she'd been practising this moment and said, in an ultra-calm voice, 'I wanted to see you because you and Granny should be the first to know that I'm married. I've written to tell Granny. She'll have got the letter today.'

I didn't quite spill wine down my front because I was wearing my cream cashmere and even when shocked I'm careful. But I came damn close to it.

'Christ!' I said. 'Who to?' My immediate horrified thought was, Please, God, not Colin!

'You don't know him. He's the doctor I work for.'

Hetta had described the doctor at whose surgery Cele worked.

'The badgery one?'

This clearly annoyed her. 'I don't know what you mean by that. He's called Alec. He's Scottish.'

I remembered then how Hetta had described the other partner. 'The one with no eyelashes?'

'I don't know what you mean by that either. Alec has all the normal body parts.'

This was such a bizarre thing to say I was silenced.

Cele fiddled with some doughy balls she was plucking from her bread roll. The silence became awkward so I said, 'When was this? When did you two marry?' God knows why I said 'you two'. It isn't my style at all.

She said, very casually, sounding almost bored, 'A couple of weeks ago or something. We went to a registry office. It wasn't fancy.'

'So you're living with him?'

'I've been living with him since . . .' She trailed off and fiddled some more with the bread balls and this was the closest she came to making any reference to Will.

I honoured her reticence until it came to settling the bill, which she refused to allow me to pay, 'No, please let me. I asked you.'

I knew I must be gracious so I said, 'Thank you. But you must tell me what you'd like as a wedding present.'

She smiled a little and began to shake her head, indicating she needed no present, which was one of her ways of punishing me, so I risked, 'Does Will know?' It took some courage to ask.

She hadn't, she said, told Will. She maintained she was waiting to tell me and Mum first but although she didn't voice this my hunch was that she was hoping either I or Mum would convey the news to Will.

When later Mum and I conferred on the phone it was agreed that I would tell Will because, as Mum said, 'It ought to come from someone in person and definitely not in writing.' Mum appeared to have taken the news more calmly than me but I could hear from her voice she was bothered.

I have not been asked to do many hard things in my life so perhaps it doesn't mean all that much that conveying this extraordinary outcome seemed to me impossibly hard. I rang Cele and told her that if she had not already told Will I felt that someone should, which is the nearest I have ever come to a reproach.

'Yes, by all means, you tell him.' She sounded relieved.

Still I procrastinated, not wanting to ruin a good mood in Will and in dread of exacerbating a bad one. And just simply not wanting to have to deliver this bombshell. In the end I managed it one evening after pouring us both a drink, which was cowardly.

'Will, I'm not sure if you know' – I was quite sure he didn't – 'but Cele has got married.'

He didn't rant or rave, as I'd feared he might. He didn't in fact express much emotion at all. He just stared at me, with that unnerving, unblinking stare of his, and after some seconds said, 'Who to?'

'Not to Colin anyway.' I shouldn't have mentioned Colin. 'It's the doctor she works for . . . with.'

'When was this?'

'I'm not entirely sure. I've not met him. She's only recently told me. I . . .'

'OK. I get the message.'

She should have told him. I don't, I couldn't blame her – I've hardly been a model of moral rectitude. But she should have told him, for her own sake as much as for his. Because, after that, it was inevitable that she held herself responsible for all that transpired.

5

Mum rang me shortly after we had the surprise of Cele's marriage to say that her friend Bev's son was coming to London and could we put him up at the flat for a couple of nights. I dimly recalled Eddie from our days at Dowlands. He'd been a pal of Jack's and it goes without saying I was eager to meet him again.

Mum didn't specify why Eddie was coming to London, she has this rather exaggerated thing about not divulging other people's business, but when Eddie rang to thank us, very politely, for our hospitality he explained it was for a job interview. He was a chemical engineer by training, about which I knew nothing at all, but it was an executive position he was in for and he was clearly a high flyer as I recognized the name of the international firm he was hoping to join. Alastair had once had something to do with it.

It was a mild jolt to come face to face with a grey-haired man in late middle age but after only a little while in Eddie's company I recognized the boy I'd seen with Jack. He was tall, over six foot, and his face well preserved and with the pleasant open smile I'd remembered. He smelt nice too. I set a lot of store by how a man smells but I sensed at once that Eddie had no sexual response to me.

It's not that I'm so vain, though the family think I am, that I imagine every man I meet is lusting after me. It's that sex lingers on in us, longer than people think, and there's always a vestige of something, somewhere, in any interaction. I can always tell if there's that glint of 'might have been'. Eddie was gay, I knew it at once. Not a misogynist gay like Harvey, but gay for sure.

He was a bit stiff at first. The evening of his arrival we spent in conventional chit-chat. Graham served some of his fine wine (I encouraged him in his wine obsession because it entailed trips abroad to Wine Society vineyards on which I didn't accompany him) and I managed not to overcook or undercook the steak. It was an OK evening, nothing to write home about. But the following day – Eddie was staying on for a second interview, which he thought a promising sign – was Wednesday, Graham's regular evening to visit his mother, so I was hopeful of a more revealing conversation.

I wanted to hear about Jack.

It helped that for us both he was 'Jack' rather than Nat and my impression was that Eddie shared my relief at Graham's absence. I wined him liberally with more of Graham's claret and he took off his tie, which I teased him over. I liked getting him to smile.

He'd already asked after Mum and Beetle, but it was Mum he was more interested in.

'She was great, like a second mother to me when I was a kid. I remember her and my mum dancing together, and your mum got on our kitchen table once and did a can-can. She was a laugh. My mum missed her when she left. She used to make her laugh like no one else.'

This laughing, dancing person was new to me. Mum was never grim but I'd never had her down as the life and soul. 'Did you know Jack wasn't Mum's son?'

I was afraid that was maybe too quick off the mark because he flushed.

'Not then. I did later.'

'Did your mother tell you?'

'I don't think she knew. I was with him when he found out.'

'That must have been quite something.'

'You could say that.'

I thought maybe I was pressing too hard so I poured him some more wine. I was desperate for him to go on.

We sat there and I said, trying to be a good hostess, 'You don't have to . . .'

And he shook his head and said, 'No, it's that I was remembering. We'd been off climbing, you know we used to climb together? And we'd gone on to Vienna – Jack's idea. There was this exhibition which I wanted to go to – my idea that was. Funny when you think of it that if I hadn't . . . Anyway, there was this photo of Jack as a baby and his name there beside it. It was the name that did it, you see.'

'How extraordinary.'

'It took a while before he got hold of the whole story. You didn't know?'

'I knew that he found out before they'd told him that

Mum wasn't his mother – but not all this. Did it upset him?'

I knew it had. That much I'd been told.

'He was very cut up for a while,' Eddie said. The public school phrase sounded funny coming from him. 'Well, you can guess.'

'What did he say? Can you remember?'

'We talked about it a lot. A real lot. It was a shock, as you'd guess. Not realizing he was Jewish, that was what got to him mostly. That and not knowing about all his family dying. And his mum, you know. Dying like that.'

Quite suddenly I thought, You were in love with Jack.

'You must have missed him.' Maybe this was wrong of me, pushing him back to what must have been upsetting feelings. But I was angry that I'd been left so much in the dark.

'I still miss him. He was like . . .' he hesitated, 'a brother,' he finished, untruthfully.

We sat in silence together. I wanted to probe more but began to feel an inhibition. Graham would be home any minute, full of bonhomie and hail fellow well met, and telling us how his mother's cough was better, or not better, and I couldn't risk him blundering into this delicate web of memories.

So I said something like, 'Well you'll need to have your wits about you tomorrow so I won't keep you up late,' and we said goodnight and Eddie went off to bed in Cele's room.

I said nothing to Graham and lay beside his snoring

body thinking about my family. It's quite hard to take in all that has happened when you're a part of it.

I lay awake till I could see light edging the blinds and the buses had long started up and I had settled on a strategy to ask, when Eddie came that evening to collect his case, if I could visit him some time to hear more about my lost brother. But there was no need as he rang me at lunch time.

'Would it be too much trouble if I stayed another night?'

Of course I was delighted. 'Stay as long as you like, Eddie. I hope it means you've got another interview.'

On the contrary, he said, he had been offered the job and wanted to take us out to dinner as a thank you and to celebrate. And by great good luck Graham asked to be excused. 'If you don't mind taking the old lady out for me, Ed,' he said, in his best avuncular style, 'only I've got a call coming in from Oz. She's quite well-behaved.'

I smiled hypocritically at my husband's tedious panto-mime of male authority, but inwardly I rejoiced.

Keen as I was to learn more about Jack, I knew enough to encourage Eddie to talk about his new job first. It was a big step up, he explained, with a much greater salary and far more scope. By the time we were on to our second course I didn't have to probe: he raised the subject himself.

'I wanted to say, I didn't say, about Jack. He knew right enough why your mother never said anything.'

'Why didn't she?' I was curious to hear what my brother had thought.

'She loved him. He knew that. He always felt well-loved, did Jack. He guessed she didn't want him hankering after his other mother. She'd left him as a babe. Upsetting it would have been for a littl'un, you know, the bomb and all that.'

'Foolish of her, though.'

'I guess we've all been that in our time. My mother always says, "never judge anyone till you've stood in their shoes."'

'That's a kind way of looking at it. I'm not kind, Eddie, I'm afraid.'

'I remember you as a littl'un. Pretty as a picture, you were. Smart as paint too, my mum always said.'

'Thank you.' I was touched. His shyness had dropped away with the success of the interview.

'Your mum had some idea Jack was trying to prove himself, on account of your dad being a conchy. That right?'

'That's the story, yes.'

'That wasn't Jack. He wouldn't give a monkey's what some stuck-up Cambridge prick said.'

'I must say, I never thought so.' I was struck by this eruption of vehemence.

'He was more likely trying to prove something to me.'

'Why to you?'

'Things I said. We had a falling-out. Nothing major. We'd've made up.'

'I'm sure,' I agreed. You were lovers, I thought. That's what it was that I knew I had always known about Jack.

'He was different with me, didn't want to go climbing that summer. I reckon now it was something to do with, you know, finding out about his family and being Jewish and all. But I saw it as him keeping his distance. I was young. I took it personally. You get things skewy when you're young.'

'I can drink to that,' I said.

'Yep,' Eddie said, and stared down at his glass of brandy. We'd ordered brandy. I think we both wanted to prolong our stay at the restaurant.

I couldn't bear for him to stop there so I prompted him, 'So . . . ?'

'So I let off steam, said a few things about Cambridge people being gutless, spineless. I don't know what I called them, but I kind of implied he was too. It was just me getting at him. It wasn't true. I was sick as a pig because I was only at Newcastle, you know?'

'Oh God,' I said. 'I'm so sorry.'

I understood: he had feared that Jack would abandon him.

'You can't take words back from the dead, can you?'

His hand on the table was forcing the palm flat and I laid my own over it. 'You can't know, Eddie. None of us does. You and Mum and Dad and me and Beetle, none of us can know what happened or why.'

'No. I nearly told your mum once, you know, about us falling out. She came to visit to ask me about him after he died, but it felt like I would be making myself out to be the important one, you know, Jack dying because of me, kind of. It didn't seem right.'

You were worried about letting on that Jack was gay, I thought. That's what didn't seem right.

'Maybe the best we can say is that he's out of it,' I said. 'It's us who're the losers. At least he was loved.'

Eddie swirled the brandy round his glass. 'There's some things that never leave you,' he said. 'Isn't that right?'

We were both slightly drunk, though in a perfectly civilized way, when we got back to the flat. Graham had gone to bed but when Eddie and I settled down for 'a nightcap' – I found myself using Graham's awful medicinal term – Will appeared.

He'd been back late the last couple of nights, playing gigs with his band, and had not been around in the mornings to meet Eddie. I introduced them now.

'Eddie, this is Beetle's son, Will. Will, Eddie was Nat's great friend.'

'My mother was great with your nan,' Eddie said. 'During the war.'

Will looked intrigued. 'Would you like a drink?' I asked. I was careful, after the Harvey episode, not to offer him alcohol but not to have done so now would have made it appear that there was some problem and suddenly I very much didn't want to show Will up in front of Eddie.

'I'll have a Coke,' Will said. He settled himself on the sofa opposite Eddie. 'You knew my uncle?'

'We were best mates.'

Eddie's Northumbrian accent, which during the inter-view days had been submerged beneath a patina of southern BBC, had surfaced with the drink. Along with a man's smell I take great note of the timbre of a voice. Eddie's had good resonant tones. Bass baritone.

My guess is that, like me, Will also responded to voice because I observed that Eddie was going over well.

'What was he like, my uncle?'

Eddie smiled. He had a lovely smile. He looked in fact a little like a fit Elvis might have looked had he reached late middle age. A fine bass baritone too, was Elvis.

'He was great, man, you know, just great.'

'When did you meet?'

'As little kids on the beach, down by your nan's nan. Old Mrs Tye's house.'

Will got up and went across to the drinks tray, put down the half-drunk Coke and poured himself an Armagnac.

'Dowlands?'

'That's it. Your nan and my mother got talking there one day while your uncle and me got fighting.'

'Did you fight?' I asked.

'You know, just puppy-dog stuff. We started school together. Your mum used to meet us, give us lunch and so on. Boiled eggs and toast fingers. And apples from the orchard. She was just great to me, your mum.'

'Dowlands is where my parents live now,' Will said. I noticed that he didn't say it was where he lived.

Eddie looked immediately taken. 'Yeah? I moved to Hull. Mum and Dad retired to Harrogate. So we've not been in those parts since . . .'

Will said, 'Were you with my uncle when he was killed?' I could tell he was getting worked up because he was fixing Eddie with that very direct stare of his.

Eddie frowned. 'I wasn't at Cambridge. I was a New-castle boy.'

'Wasn't he killed in a climbing accident?'

'He was climbing one of the spires of a chapel. Mad bugger.'

Hetta has told me since that she had confided to Will what I had told her that day in Knightsbridge when I bought her that yellow bra – a hideous bra but she wanted it so much, poor child. So this was disingenuous of Will, though at the time I was unaware of that.

'What was that about?' Will asked.

I saw Eddie's face and decided it was time to give him a get-out. 'Will, dear,' I said. 'Eddie's tired, he's had a long couple of days. I'm sure if you want to talk to him another time . . .' but Eddie interrupted.

'It's fine. Happy to chew the fat with Jack's nevvy.'

'You call him Jack,' Will said, though he must have known this.

6

It was some weeks before I was allowed to meet my daughter's husband. I was beautifully restrained – didn't press her at all, though it goes without saying I was dying to clap eyes on him. When the invitation finally arrived it was for dinner at their flat, a nice enough flat in Kensal Rise.

My first impression of Alec was negative. Colin was a bastard but you had to hand it to him, he was a good-looking bastard. I saw what Hetta had meant about Alec's eyelashes. That piggy blond.

But he had the voice – and, like a lot of apparently ugly men, once you got to know him the attraction emerged. He went out of his way to be exceptionally courteous to Graham. He was polite to us both but I noticed he was making an extra effort with Graham, from which I concluded that Cele had conveyed to him that I didn't. Fair enough. I didn't make much effort with Graham.

The food was excellent – risotto, a plain fruit fool and decent cheese. Nothing pretentious. Graham commented on it, getting a bit of his own back by comparing the dinner with my own efforts, and, not to be squashed, I remarked that Cele must have learned to cook from her aunt Susan because she would have learned bugger-all from me.

Cele was used to our banter and smiled in Alec's direction, as if to say, I told you how they were, and Alec said, 'I was the cook this evening, so any complaints should go to me', which put both me and Graham in our place.

I was always slightly on edge when out with Graham. The brutal truth is I was ashamed of him, which does me no credit, I know. He was socially banal – not that most people noticed as most people are socially banal themselves, but it got on my nerves. Cele would have sussed my unease and I guessed this was why Alec had been detailed to dish out an extra dollop of hospitality to my husband.

I was naturally mad keen to discover how this romance had arisen and by the time we were on to the fool I risked, 'When did you two decide you wanted to hitch up?' That 'you two' again. I must have been feeling uncomfortable.

Alec said, 'Oh, I fell for her from day one. We had an emergency in the waiting room, a schizophrenic patient who'd missed his injection and was hearing voices and disturbing the other patients, and your daughter, Bell,' – he had a rather nice way of saying 'Bell' – 'dealt with him superbly.'

He smiled fondly at Cele and I liked him still more because I could see pride in that smile.

'What did she do, my clever daughter?' I meant this as a compliment but I have a feeling that Cele heard it as sarcasm.

'She took the voices seriously. Luckily they weren't malign – the Virgin Mary, wasn't it, C?' I liked the sound of that 'C' too.

'It was a little unclear,' my daughter said. 'There were three Marys involved.'

'He thought she was one of them, anyway,' Alec said. 'He took her for the Blessed Virgin, or whichever one it was, and she led him into my room and he was quiet as a lamb while I gave him his dose. She was brilliant. It was love at first sight.'

'He's exaggerating,' Cele said. She spoke, I noticed, with a new calm. 'I'd been there well over two weeks and he hadn't taken a blind bit of notice.'

Graham said on the way home, 'Nice chap. Pity he's not better looking.'

Mum used to say of the Communist Party that the difficulty was that unless you were in charge of dictating the Party line you could never predict when it might have changed so you would find yourself, all of a sudden, on the wrong side of the track. Poor old Graham assumed that because I generally cared about appearances I would find Alec wanting.

'You haven't a clue what makes a man attractive,' I said cruelly. He must have grasped by then that I didn't find him attractive in the little least. 'He's delightful, especially after that viper Colin.'

From what I could observe, Will appeared remarkably restrained during the post-wedding-announcement period. This was the period before he was to return, with the college's permission, to King's and I suppose I believed he was trying to be good, whatever that means.

One event, which had nothing overtly to do with him, struck me at the time. Cele, when she left the flat, had also left most of her bits behind. Shortly after the dinner with Alec she asked if I would please bring her stuff over. She was still steering clear of Will so I understood why she wouldn't want to come herself.

After I had carted various boxes and bags over to Kensal Rise, for which she thanked me rather coolly, she rang me to ask, 'Where's Seal?'

Seal was her childhood toy to which she was hugely attached and even when she was quite old it sat at the end of her bed, more recently on the tallboy which had been at Dowlands in my great-grandparents' time. The tallboy was typical Victorian mahogany, too heavy for my taste, but Cele had wanted it so we had always had it in her room.

My impression, if I had any, would have been that she had taken Seal with her when she moved out, but she contradicted me.

'I left him on the Dowlands tallboy. You must have seen him.'

Not having much, or any, interest in toys, I had to confess I hadn't.

'He must be in the room somewhere. You haven't looked properly.'

It was true I hadn't. But when I turned the room

upside down no Seal materialized. Isabel, our cleaner, said she'd seen it at some point but not, she thought, since Cele left.

I have a bit of a blank about the rest of that time when Will was with us. It passed OK, as far as I could judge, though I didn't see a lot of him. My impression is that he was out most nights playing in his band and for the most part I was probably glad he was out of the way. But for the first time in my life, when he was due to go back to King's I had a maternal reaction.

I felt anxious for him. Anxious about how he'd fit in. He was never shy but he wasn't much of a fitter-in. How terrible that I can't claim ever to have felt that for my daughter.

My way of expressing this novel anxiety was to take Will to buy clothes. Not that he ever cared much about clothes; he was generally pretty scruffy. I took him to a place on the King's Road and bought him some T-shirts and a leather jacket. I've had a thing about leather jackets since I fell as a kid for Jean-Paul Belmondo, so I pressed this one on Will and he seemed quite chuffed with it. It suited him. But he was one of those men who look OK even when scruffy. Daddy was like that. Though I can't see Daddy in a leather jacket.

I offered to drive Will up to Cambridge but that was a step too far. He liked me better when I was distant. He said, 'I'm fine, Bell. I've only got one case and it's quicker by train. But thanks. And thanks for putting up with me.'

And I said something idiotic like 'It's been a pleasure', which he probably thought was just fluff. It wasn't fluff. I missed him. It's an awful thing to admit but I missed him as I had never missed Cele.

7

It was Robert who found the diary. I had to go down to Staresnest before I sold it to clear it out. I was selling it with all the furniture to save the bother of getting rid of the stuff but the personal things had to be cleared.

I couldn't face it on my own and it had suddenly seemed that Robert was the one person I could bear to be with. When I rang him he sounded pleased to hear from me, which was a relief.

He drove us down to Somerset in his comfortable Mercedes. It's quite a way and I just lay back resting my head on the leather seat crying my eyes out. Robert had never seen me cry but he knew better than to comment and only patted my hand from time to time. I'd forgotten how he used to pat my hand.

There was a platform performance of *Die Valküre* on the radio. It's my favourite Wagner anyway but the whole Siegmund–Sieglinde drama seemed uncannily apt.

Robert had bought flat-packed boxes and the morning after we got there he put them together and taped them up while I made coffee, very strong. I can't stand weak coffee. And yes, we slept together, made love, had sex, fucked, call it what you will. If I'd not consciously decided to leave Graham, then that night with Robert put the lid on Graham, if that's the expression I want. Never mind.

There was not so much to pack up, when it came down to it. All the kitchen paraphernalia we put into the charity-shop boxes, the same with the clothes. If I wanted to keep anything it was mainly books that had come from Great-Grandad Tye's library and other odd-ments from Dowlands, some old-fashioned dip pens, a heavy crystal inkstand with a silver lid and a blotter, the kind shaped like a child's boat that you rock over the ink to dry it – quite useless these days. And I also wanted the bound volumes of *Punch* and *The Strand*, in which some of Granny Maud's stories had been published.

To the best of my recollection, I'd never read any of Granny Maud's stories and was unable to keep myself from starting on one there and then. Displacement activity, Robert called it.

I suppose I'd expected her stories to be melodramatic affairs, which is why I'd never bothered reading one, but this, called 'The Green Fairy', wasn't half bad. It was about an absinthe drinker who, in a state of alcoholic befuddlement, follows the spirit, who has promised him a 'rest from all earthly troubles', across the Liffey, taking with him his only daughter, whom he loves to distrac-tion, and both the man and his daughter drown.

As I say, it was Robert who found my own daughter's real-life drama.

We'd been sorting books into the 'Keep' or 'Charity' boxes for what felt like hours and I was beginning to flag. Robert casually opened a large tome, with a title something to do with Shipping Forecasts, which I'd put to be chucked out. Inside, the pages had been cut away and a notebook was lodged there. One of those utilitarian notebooks, with a dark blue hard cover. I was on my knees on the floor packing up the 'Keep' books when Robert handed it to me.

From the first sight of the handwriting, before I'd read a word of the content, I could see that the notebook was Cele's. Robert, who would normally have been protective of Cele's privacy, didn't demur when I began to read it. He knew how desperate I was to find any clue that might help. He simply said, 'I'll make some more coffee, shall I?' and a little later, without my asking, he made up the fire. It was a late October afternoon and Staresnest was always inclined to be cold.

Hetta has some of the other diaries and I know from these and her conversations with Cele that she has teased out many of the other events which make up this sorry tale. But it was left to me to discover this account of the last few meetings between my daughter and her Will before the accident that wrecked their lives.

Just before the Easter of 94, about a year after her marriage it would have been, Cele rang and asked me if she could stay at Staresnest. She had, she said, a few days' holiday owing and fancied some 'quiet time' in the country and there was some writing she wanted to do.

Of course I agreed. I was always since my marriage glad to be of help to her and I liked the sound of the writing. I felt guilty that she'd got no decent qualifications and responsible for her keeping her light under a bushel, or whatever the saying is.

She must have brought this notebook with her then and hidden it in the Shipping Forecast on some other occasion.

April 6th 1994

Will rang me at the surgery saying he needed to see me urgently. I've not seen him since A and I married and have dreaded this. But he sounded sober so I agreed. I knew I had to see him sometime. We met in the National Gallery because I couldn't think of anywhere else suitably anonymous. I suggested we meet in the shop but he said 'I hate those shops full of mugs with sunflowers on, as if Van Gogh didn't have enough to bear without being traduced by marketing morons. Meet me by the Rembrandts'.

He was there when I arrived looking at The Woman Taken in Adultery *which was obviously intentional. I'd hung about outside on the steps in order to be on time. I'd guessed he'd be early.*

The moment I saw him I knew it was a mistake to come. He had the old khaki bag we always called 'Jeremy Fisher's' over his shoulder. His shoulder blades looked like wings cropped to the bone.

I would have turned round and hoped to vanish back into the crowd but he felt my stare and turned instead and then how could I go?

I could see him trying not to frighten me off, because he gave a nervous half-grin. There was something so pitiful about that grin.

He was always thin. But he looked ill. He walked over and put a hand so gently under the crook of my arm and said, 'Let's get out of here, shall we, my love?' and I went with him. I couldn't have done otherwise.

We walked out into air so bright that St Martin-in-the-Fields was adazzle in its whiteness. We walked, I haven't a clue where, and he held my arm tight close to his ribs and I found myself remembering how Eve was taken from a rib of Adam's. My hip bone kept banging against his as we walked. His trainers were incredibly dirty, with holes in them.

I'd forgotten how exhausting desire is. In the end I begged to sit down and we landed up in a fuggy little café somewhere off High Holborn, with orange tea and some lardy cake, which I chose as we loved it as children.

The cake stuck to the roof of my mouth – he didn't touch his. He leant down to his Jeremy Fisher bag and said, 'Here, I've brought him back to you' and he gave me Seal.

I said, stupidly, 'I don't blame you.' I meant for taking Seal, though he hadn't taken him, as he told me later, and he said, 'I don't blame you either. I was mad, quite mad and you were scared, I know, but "Celandine", it was hearing that name he called you. I couldn't stand it.'

Oh God, these seeming betrayals.

I said, 'It was an accident. Colin asked me about my family and I told him about Granny because she'd visited me at St N's and he asked what she was like and all I could think to say was how she'd taught me the names of wild flowers, I didn't say she'd taught us, I didn't mention you. Colin said, "Tell me then, tell me about flowers." The celandines were newly out and I told him their name and he said, "How interesting, I've always thought they were buttercups." You know how people do? And then he said, "Celandine, it's like your name. In future I shall call you Celandine." I was appalled if you want to know. But if I'd told him not to he would have asked me why.'

And Will said, 'The man is diabolical in his cunning but I don't believe he's a telepath. He must have read it in a letter I wrote you.'

I'd never even thought of that. All that time I'd been imagining it was a horrible coincidence but of course I had often carried W's letters around in my bag. It never entered my head that C might pry.

I began to cry then, because in my stupidity and blindness I'd caused so much harm and W said, 'Don't cry, my love, or do if you need to' and I wept and wept all over the lardy cake and W pressed his finger into the crumbs and licked it and said, 'It tastes of the salt of your tears.'

I have wasted our lives.

April 9th 1994

I'm writing this in my lunch break and I'm keeping the book locked in the filing cabinet in the file of a patient called Tomlins who, from his records, hasn't been to the surgery for years. I didn't tell A I'd seen W. He knows too much about him. I told him I'd gone to the dentist with toothache, which was as well as my face must have looked swollen when I got home. It was late so I said the tooth had involved root-canal work and I'd have to go back in a couple of days, which is today.

I've asked W to keep Seal. He explained about Eddie taking

him. I'd almost forgotten that Seal had belonged to Nat. But I can't bring Seal back to A's now or he'll ask where I found him. I still think of the flat as A's even though he's put it in our joint names.

I'm meeting W this afternoon with the dentist as alibi. He's rung twice at work but I've asked him please not to except for emergencies.

April 10th 1994

I plucked up my courage and rang Bell and asked if I could borrow Staresnest. I knew she wouldn't ask questions but I felt I had to give an excuse so I told her I wanted to go there to do some writing. She perked up at that. She thinks I'm a failure because I'm only a receptionist. I told A the same. He trusts me unreservedly and I didn't even feel bad about deceiving him. I have some holiday owing and I said I wanted to take it before the summer.

W and I have agreed to meet tomorrow at Paddington at 9 a.m. for the 9.30 train.

When I reached this point in the diary I said to Robert, 'I don't think I can do any more at the moment. I need strong drink, would you mind?'

And dear Robert simply said, 'Wine strong or spirit strong?' and I said, 'Spirit please and lashings of it' and he poured me out about a treble Scotch.

We sat by the fire which he'd got blazing and he said not a word until I did. But he put on some Handel. 'Saul'.

'I never loved like this,' I said. I meant like Cele, not like Saul. 'Not even you.'

Dear Robert. He laughed and said, 'You loved me quite enough for me.'

I still loved him, by the way, but I didn't say so.

Robert cooked an omelette and made a salad, he's a good cook, and we drank some of his wine, which wasn't at all grand for which I was grateful. I have no palate and I never really appreciated Graham's wine. Then he ran me a bath and knew to leave me to soak on my own, which is the thing that I really miss about Robert, I mean the knowing not the being left alone, and after that I went to bed in the huge king-size bed he bought for us long ago, and I lay there, wiped out, utterly exhausted.

That night we didn't make love. But we lay there and talked and talked, or I did, and that was some relief, because we'd never talked in that kind of way before, not just about Will and Cele, but about the whole shebang: Daddy's affair, Jack, Susan losing Will's twin, Great Uncle Oswald's pegging out in France, the Spanish Civil War, the whole damn circus.

At some point I said, 'She refers to me always as Bell or B. Never Mum,' to which Robert said nothing. It may have been after this that I told him I was going to leave Graham. He said nothing to that either.

8

Around 2 a.m. I woke and got up and made myself a large hot toddy with more of Robert's Old Grouse and sat by the fire which was still ember-warm enough to flare up when I chucked on more logs. I was wide awake and I wanted to read more of Cele's diary.

There were some pages torn out and the next entry read:

April 23rd 1994, Shakespeare's birthday

Will went back to Cambridge tonight. I went with him to King's Cross to see him off. It was the last train and so empty we wondered if it was really going to leave after all and then the engine started up suddenly and I had to jump out of the carriage. It felt dreadful seeing the train move out of the station, tearing us apart.

It was too late to go back to A's – and I'd said I mightn't be back till the morning. I've checked into a hotel. It's lonely but I'd rather be lonely here than lonely with A.

What to do?

A sounded anxious when I rang to say I was ill and wanted to stay on longer at Staresnest. But I don't think he suspected anything. I'm sure he was simply concerned about my cough. He would have driven down to collect me if I hadn't stopped him. It hardly seems fair that it's he who's helped me become so much stronger.

I've promised W to tell him, tell A that I made a mistake, that we should never have married.

These days with W – walking to Cow Castle and finding the otter's grave in the garden, not at all where we'd remembered it (unless B moved it?) with the inscription still visible that we scratched on with B's brooch – Otter R. I. P.– all those years ago. They were happy times.

We pledged murder against the hunt that did for our otter then – W cut his wrist with his penknife and made me and Hetta swear on his blood — we laughed about this when we found the gravestone at last but we agreed we would swear so still today – but I am thinking now that the worst murders are against ourselves. We murder our better spirits because we're afraid of what they summon us to do. Or not to do.

I remember a strange thing that Florence, the girl I pretended to meet in Penzance that time I was meeting Colin, once said to me. She said, of Will, whom I'd mentioned to her afterwards, 'But you've known him for ever, haven't you?' as if knowing someone for ever disqualifies them from being important. I have known him for ever and that is why he is important.

I fled to A for safety because I was afraid – but there is no safety to be found outside the kingdom of the heart. Shakespeare knew that. How clever of him to die on the date they say he was born.

At this point I had to stop reading and go into the kitchen.

Cele was right. I did move that otter's tombstone. I moved it because it was in the way when Gareth, the man who saw to the garden, mowed the lawn. I don't know why that so preyed on my conscience. If, as she wrote, she had murdered her better spirit it was because I failed her. It was a cruel awakening, not to my selfishness, I was already alive to that, but to the scope of its reach. No doubt there is some appropriate Biblical saying to do with sowing and reaping. That night, reading what my only child had written in her anguish, I reaped a bitter harvest.

I went to get a pair of Robert's woollen socks from his boots which he'd left by the back door, because my feet had grown icy, before resuming reading.

April 26th 1994

W rang and asked if I'd told A yet. A was in the office writing repeat prescriptions so I had to pretend it was the dentist's receptionist calling with an appointment. 'Thank you,' I said, 'I can't make that date. Have you anything after 6 p.m.?' At 6 p.m. A is deep in surgery.

W rang at 6.10. He remained calm when I said, 'I've not had a moment to yet.'

I didn't tell W this but A's father is unwell. His father brought them up as his mother had MS so it's a bad time. The longer I'm away from W the less brave I feel.

April 30th 1994

I went to Cam to see W this weekend. A has gone up to Glasgow to see his father so I didn't have to make an excuse.

W has a room in college (with the suspended sentence he can't live out) so we had to squash into his narrow bed. Rather different from the huge bed at Staresnest. He asked if I'd made love with A and I lied. I've had to – A wanted to the moment I came back from Exmoor and I could only use the excuse of the cough for so long to hold him off.

Granny says that ordinary notions of truth are overrated and it's the truth in your heart that counts. The truth in my heart is that I make love with A out of politeness, at best out of kindness. I never 'made love' with C.

I would never have asked if W had been with anyone else but he volunteered that there were a couple of girls when he was angry with me. I was angry about that. But perhaps it's as well we have been with other people. We know now what we want – who we want, I should say.

The weekend was very intense. We talked about what we would do when he has taken his degree. He isn't drinking and I didn't either. Neither of us was hungry. He said, 'You are so thin, my love, I can almost see through you,' and I said, 'You can talk, you are like the skeleton of a leaf, I could blow you away.' He sometimes seems so frail, my W.

On a stall in the market we found an old signet ring engraved with the letters CW which he bought for me.

I've asked W to please keep my ring safe until I can wear it.

May 2nd 1994

A rang to say his father is dying. He is going to take some leave and the practice will get in a locum. I feel awful that the news was a relief to me.

I can't get cover while A is off but W is coming to London. He has exams but he says he'll revise here.

May 6th 1994

W was to stay for three nights but after the first night I was nervous. We aren't close to our neighbours but I was in a state in case we bumped into any of them. In the end we went off to a cheap hotel, cheap because W has no money and I couldn't use my credit card because A and I share the account and we have a joint bank account too so I could only afford to draw out a certain amount of £s. But that was hopeless too as I was in a state about A ringing and finding me out. And I felt bad about his father. W became fractious because he guessed the reasons for my fret. The hotel was grisly, carpets with swirly patterns and an avocado bath. We've agreed that in future we must only meet in Cam. Or Staresnest.

May 10th 1994

A's father died yesterday. The funeral is on Friday and I am travelling up to Scotland tonight after work. LR.

My limbs were stiff and the fire had burnt low. I got up, feeling old and creaky, and went into the kitchen and looked out.

The river which runs through Staresnest's garden was in full spate and a wind had got up and an upstart syca-more, which I had always meant to have felled, was releasing a hostile-sounding patter of winged seeds on to the kitchen roof. It made me think of Mum, who wages war on sycamore seedlings. A dense cloud of birds, probably fieldfares, was passing across a pewter sky. And again I thought of Mum, trying to interest us in birds. 'What's the point of knowing their names?' I used to ask her, winding her up. But things stick, even when you don't intend them to. And watching the cloud of birds thin and dissolve against the whitening sky all at once I felt incredibly happy to be able to name them.

What I had read humbled me. It spoke of passions beyond my experience, of a tragedy borne that I could never have undergone. I could guess at what the ripped-out pages had described. Those few days of splendour in the grass that my daughter and my nephew had been granted before the life they had built against the life they had been born into collapsed upon them. So far as I know, they never did have a chance to be here together again.

There was more dismal reading in the blue notebook. I have read it since but see no need to disclose more here. What has been recorded already tells enough of the story.

It was not that Cele lost faith. She would, I am sure – though how do I have the nerve to feel sure about one so unlike myself? – have left Alec in the end. Certainly from her account she was planning to do so. Only 'all in good time', as Mum used to say when we were kids and drive me mad in saying it. Because in this respect my nephew was like me: 'good time' was not good enough for him. I'm no psychologist, but my guess is that Will's nerves were too frayed to manage the waiting. "'Everything comes to him who waits,'" as Daddy sagely used to say 'is a maxim of dubious prescience,' which is probably why he was always such a one for revolution.

9

But all of that, of course, the sale of Staresnest and the discovery of her diaries, came later, much later.

I had hoped to see more of Eddie after his stay with us but, apart from one rather strained dinner, he seemed to dissolve back into the mists of the past. I was inclined to blame Graham. I was inclined to blame Graham for most things. But one day Eddie rang me and suggested lunch.

I met him at a restaurant near his work in Millbank and I could tell from the first sighting of him across the room that the new job had made a mark. He was thinner and looked more prosperous and for a fleet second I found myself regretting that he was gay and simultaneously recalled something that Robert once said, which was 'The reason people are atheists is that they dread the idea that there is a being somewhere that can truly read their minds.'

We took some time over the menu. Eddie ordered sparkling water and I noted that the food he chose was that of a currently fashionable diet and hoped that the reason for this was a new partner and not just new London ways. Over the cured fish he asked after Graham, and then after Cele. I explained about her marriage and although I had never mentioned Cele in connection with

Will he said, as though he knew of it, 'I've seen a bit of your nephew.'

'Will?'

'He's stayed over a few times when he's been down in London.' I had noticed that since Will's return to Cambridge he had not visited us and once again was inclined to blame Graham. 'He wanted to hear more about his uncle.'

'I can understand that.' I did understand – I had felt the same.

'Thing is, his friend . . .'

For a moment I thought he must mean Cele. 'Friend?'

'Harvey, isn't it?'

'Oh God, him.'

The waiter arrived and offered bread, which we both refused.

'Thing is,' Eddie resumed, 'Will brought him one time and he stayed over too. I didn't take to him, to be honest.'

Mum says that when anyone says 'to be honest' you can assume they are lying but in this case she might have been wrong.

'He's a creep,' I said.

'Maybe worse.'

'Why do you say that, Eddie?' He looked awkwardly at his plate while the penny dropped for me. 'Did he . . . ?'

'He's not my type but he tried it on.'

'Eddie, would you mind if I had a glass of wine after all?'

'No, I'll join you.'

He ordered a bottle and as we drank it he told me about Harvey.

'Will had a gig with his band,' Eddie explained.

'How was he – is he?'

'Seemed fine to me.'

'Was he drinking?'

'Not with me. He had a Diet Coke.'

'That's good.'

'It was more this other guy, Harvey.'

Harvey had appeared one evening at Eddie's and, Eddie said, he had the impression that Will was not over-pleased to see him. He expressed some surprise at Harvey's being in London at all but he had obviously given him Eddie's address. Harvey had stayed the night on Eddie's sofa and the next day the two of them had gone off together, apparently back to Cambridge. But Harvey had reappeared at Eddie's flat a few days later, to ask if Eddie had perhaps found his allegedly lost watch.

'It was a pick-up line,' Eddie said, 'or I was supposed to read it that way. But I wasn't interested.'

'So . . . ?'

'So he kind of hung around and I gave him coffee – I don't drink these days, well . . .' We both looked at the half-empty bottle.

'Once in a while won't hurt,' I suggested.

'Sure. Anyway, he wanted to hear about Jack.'

'Why?'

'He's got a thing for Will.'

'But Will isn't gay.' Eddie flushed and I felt I'd been too blunt. 'I mean, I know we all are somewhere but . . .'

'It's OK. It's this. He, Harvey I mean, had worked out about me and Jack, you know.'

I nodded vigorously.

'He's – what can I say – he's . . .'

'A creep?' I suggested again.

'Worse,' he said again.

'How worse?'

You can see why Will was fascinated by Jack's fall. And the fact that it had been kept so secret. In the absence of any other willing ear, he must have confided in Harvey. And for what it's worth I recognized Harvey. I have never knowingly corrupted anyone but I know that I am capable of it and I recognized him as a corrupter – a corrupter of innocence. If he couldn't have Will physically, he wanted him emotionally.

'See, I had this book,' Eddie said. '*The Night Climbers of Cambridge*. It was written by one of the blokes who started the whole business in the thirties. I found it in a second-hand bookshop, in Oxford funnily enough. I wanted to see what climb it was that Jack was trying for and I wanted to work out where he'd gone wrong. I had it in my flat. It was their kind of peak climb, the spires of King's Chapel.'

'I'd love to see it too,' I said. 'If you'd lend it to me.'

'I can't,' Eddie said. 'Harvey took it. I know it was him because . . .'

'Because Will wouldn't?'

'That's right. But I know for sure because I didn't show it to Will. I mentioned it. But then I was worried because he was kind of obsessed and I thought maybe I shouldn't. It was after Harvey was at the flat on his own that it disappeared.'

'What did he want it for?'

'Dunno,' Eddie said. 'But it was the book he was interested in, not me. I mean it was Will he was wanting it for. I was worried for Will. You know he's kind of . . .'

'On the edge?'

'I like him. I like him a lot. But he's . . .'

'Fragile?' I suggested.

'Suggestible,' Eddie said.

'I wouldn't call Will that.'

'OK. Susceptible then.'

Eddie was right. Will was susceptible. There's a family myth that Will was like Daddy, but Daddy was never susceptible, or not in that way.

All this, the conversation with Eddie over lunch, took place before the Easter when Cele and Will found each other again. Harvey must have ferreted out that reunion. I would know this about him anyway because that's the sort of thing I know. But I also have a kind of proof that he wanted to hurt Cele, because I saw him.

I'd seen very little of my daughter since her sudden marriage but there was the occasional concert I could tempt her to. The Nash Ensemble was playing Haydn and Bartok at the Wigmore Hall and Cele had a preference for chamber music, so I used this as an excuse to ring her.

She accepted in her customary cool manner but when I saw her she was different. I doubt that I consciously registered this at the time but I can see it now. The prophet hindsight, as Robert says. It was the one and only time that, on looking back, I could see her father in her: she was rude about him when they met but when I knew him Igor possessed a kind of intensely alluring fire.

We ate in the café below the hall and I can't recall what we spoke of. Trivia, I imagine. She never discussed anything serious with me. On the way into the concert hall, I turned aside to go to the loo and left Cele buying a programme. And when I emerged I saw Harvey.

He was watching her back as she was searching her purse for change. Except that he wasn't watching her back in the sense of guarding it. It looked more as if he was calculating where to stick a knife in. I was caught for a moment wondering whether to tackle him head-on and decided in the end that he was best ignored. And maybe he saw me, as when I looked again he had sloped off. But it gave me the creeps, I can tell you.

And I know, with every fibre of my being, that it was Harvey who persuaded Will up on to that chapel roof that awful night. Harvey was into drugs all right and it may have been those that did for Will. But it wasn't just the chemical drugs that got to him. It would have been a kind of thrill, his way of coping with the hole left after the thrill of recovering Cele, a thrill based on our family tragedy. Harvey was in love with Will, or obsessed anyway. I don't say that Harvey physically pushed Will off the roof (though he had it in him to do so). It was more that he wanted to murder the prospect of Will's happiness with anyone but himself. Very few, very, *very* few people grasp the dangers inherent in being so attractive.

But in this regard I must also hold my child to blame, though I cannot in the end blame her. Knowing Will as she did, she should never have left him waiting, with a space in which the spores of doubt could mushroom and multiply. She ought to have foreseen how the return to King's would tax Will's resources, that there was always Harvey lurking in the background, ready to unsteady any new and unwelcome resolve that excluded him.

And at heart, Will was so unsure of his own worth. It's easy to forget how world-without-end, as Mum would say, everything seems when you are young and unsure of your worth.

10

For months Will lay unconscious, fitted out with terrible tubes inserted into every part of his body – his bladder, his bowel, his stomach, his throat – more dead than alive. I am squeamish and a coward. The sight of Will's body so transformed frankly did for me. After one visit I couldn't bear to see it, not that he could care. But I have never doubted that my daughter is made of better stuff than I am – and it is a matter that gives me pride. She gave up her job at the practice and, to be near Will, more or less moved in with Daddy and Mum in the house in Ely they had moved to from St Levan. I don't know what she said to Alec about this. He would have wanted to help her and maybe his acceptance of her absence was his way of lending his support.

The principal damage had not been to Will's spine, as we first thought, but, far more serious, to his brain. Harvey, needless to say, denied all responsibility for the LSD and alcohol in Will's system but two other students who were also on the roof that night were questioned and reported that Will had suddenly climbed on to the parapet, raised a hand to the moon and declaimed, 'To the spirit of my uncle'. Then, according to one, he swayed and then seemed to topple forward, but the other said it looked to him as if Will were trying to fly. Whether it was the impact of the fall or the drugs themselves remains unclear, but one or other, the medics concluded, had precipitated a massive stroke.

During all that time Will lay in a coma and my daughter sat there, day in, day out, playing on a portable CD player music of all kinds, jazz, blues, pop, country and western, classical. Most regularly, she played stuff he'd performed with the Black Tye Boys or flute music she had heard him play in the past. And she read to him, poetry, bits of the Bible, Homer, fairy stories. Mum says she and Cele pondered endlessly the kind of language, the words and images and rhythms that might reach a shut-down brain.

My guess is that the medical experts had more or less given up and were about to consign Will to a mental rubbish dump when, one afternoon, in December, six months after the fall, she was reading aloud *The Song of Hiawatha*. Mum's idea. Cele was apparently intoning

> *Of all beasts he learned the language,*
> *Learned their names and all their secrets,*
> *How the beavers built their lodges,*
> *Where the squirrels hid their acorns,*
> *How the reindeer ran so swiftly,*
> *Why the rabbit was so timid,*
> *Talked with them whene'er he met them . . .*

when she looked over to Will, as she always did, to include him in whatever she was reading, and saw the faintest flicker around his eyes. Imagine after all those months, seeing those eyelids fluttering like a butterfly emerging from a chrysalis.

I can only guess at what she might have said to him. He couldn't speak but she knew, she said, she just *knew*, that somewhere he was conscious. She would know, of course.

There were still few cases recognized then, let alone studied, of Locked-in Syndrome and if more is understood today then my belief is it is in part thanks to Cele. Because she never gave up hope of reaching Will and she had an instinctive sense of what was needed to bring his drowned mind back up to a point of conscious connection.

She took from their former life his famous 'will of steel' and made it her own. She pressed the loyal Alec into service to find names of all the research and international specialists, oversaw Will's physiotherapy and sat in with the speech therapist, hoping to learn from her how to help Will recover some speech. She pursued all prospects of technological help, enquiring, charming, badgering if need be, insisting and pleading with whoever necessary when it seemed to her that not enough was being done. In short, I observed my meek, diffident daughter become a force to be reckoned with, a campaigner, a veritable ambassador for Will's life.

And gradually, gradually, over many months, thanks to Cele's sustained involvement, Will regained a slight degree of control over his ruined body. In time, they were able to remove the catheter from his bladder and, while the technology was nowhere near as sophisticated as it is today, there came a point when he was able to be moved into an electric wheelchair which, painfully, painfully, by blinking he learned to control.

Because, with Cele's help, Will had slowly learned to communicate by winking.

There was a chart consisting of the commonest letters used at the beginning of words and another of the commonest letters used in the English language. With someone pointing out the letters, through one blink for 'No' and two for 'Yes', Will was able to spell out first words and then sentences. Those close to him learned to foresee what he wanted to say. Cele was naturally the quickest of us; Mum was pretty far ahead too. But Daddy also proved to have a surprisingly easy ability to communicate with Will.

I shall always be thankful that before Daddy died he and Will were able to converse because Daddy would have been one of the few people Will would really have wanted to see. Daddy was so preoccupied with the ethereal that, once he was over the shock of it, he barely took in that Will was mute and paralysed and would have overlooked all this, quite genuinely and not as a matter of tact. Daddy would have just gone on reading the *Georgics* aloud to Will and discussing various points that he felt might also interest him. I hope they did interest him, though I rather fear that Will had matters closer to home on his mind. Dear Daddy. He was always rather an innocent.

Towards the end of that first year, it was proposed that Will could, with the right help, move from the rehab centre and there arose the question of where he should live.

Susan and Beetle, understandably, wanted him at Dowlands but Dowlands was too far from medical aid. Daddy and Mum's Ely house was far too small, even if they could have physically coped, and while Cele would have wanted Will with her, Alec's presence would have made that impossible.

Don't ask me why Cele stayed with Alec. If she didn't leave him it may have been because she was too much in need of support after Will's fall. Or maybe, and who can blame her, she simply didn't have the strength to go through any further emotional turmoil. I didn't of course know then, nor did anyone except Will, that she had been planning to leave her husband.

But it was for Cele's sake that I offered help this time. It seemed to me to make sense. We were in London, I had spoken to Anthony, who was a crack GP and would see to it that the best medical help was on hand for Will, the flat was huge, the lift was convenient, the hall was wide and there were enough spare rooms. It was obvious Will was going to need (awful term) a carer.

To my surprise, Susan and Beetle sounded quite grateful. And Cele seemed not to baulk at the suggestion. As for Mum, for once she was actually pleased with me. She rang when she heard of my offer and I shan't forget her words.

'That is better than generous, Bell, darling, it's gracious. Thank you. And thank Graham from us both, please.'

She knew that I knew how little she cared for Graham.

But let me say, and all credit to him, that Graham was very decent about my proposal. I made the offer without consulting him but I suppose I was banking on his agreeing, as he agreed with practically everything I ever suggested. If I'd announced I was contemplating acquiring a baby elephant he would probably have gone along with it. What I didn't know then was that all the time, under cover of visiting his mother, Graham had been conducting a squalid affair of his own with his PA, Zara, a dyed blonde with a preference for Lycra. (I say 'squalid' but that is me being spiteful. I'd had my fling with Anthony and I'd always held poor old Graham in disdain.) What was truly decent, though, was that he allowed me to make over his study to accommodate the help Will would need. My excuse was that Graham hardly ever used his study, having an office on tap, complete with Zara in her Lycra. But still it was a sacrifice, one he needn't have made. It meant that we still had Cele's old room on hand – and I wanted that for Cele.

If Graham's mother was a cover for Graham, I became a cover for my daughter. Ignorant still, at that time, of the chapter and verse of her passion, I recognized her need to be with Will. It wasn't hard to see the reasons. I noticed that Alec had become only an occasional visitor at the flat but he would not have been surprised at her insistence on being near her cousin. She had never concealed how close they had been. And if Alec didn't hold with her guilt, he understood it, or thought he did. My God, did he go through it, that man. I hope he's over it now.

During most of the year after Will left the rehab centre, Cele stayed at our flat and while she was there she and Will communed. I learned to 'talk' to him a little myself but all the blinking tired him, and, let's face it, he would hardly want to spend time chatting to me, so I never attempted a very long conversation. But I can say this, he said enough for me to confirm that whatever that crack on the head had done there was nothing wrong with his ability to think. To the end, Will absolutely and utterly knew his own mind.

Since I am in the best position to give an account of Noreen then I suppose I had better do it, though it makes me want to vomit. Poisonous bitch.

'Beware, beware of those who care,' as some wise person said. Not that I'm suggesting there is anything wrong with caring. But as Granny Maud used to say, 'Fine words butter no parsnips,' and she might have added, 'Caring should be felt and not heard.'

There exist marvellous carers, selfless, dedicated, modest souls. We had two admirable people with us before Noreen: Amir, a slender, softly spoken rather beautiful Iranian, who looked after Will with the greatest tact, and Dana, an iron-grey-haired middle-aged woman from Romania, very upright, who contrived to weave a certain dignity around those she looked after.

But Noreen 'cared' with a vengeance. From the word go I disliked her. That it was mutual, I didn't give a rap. What mattered was how she took against Cele.

She resented Cele's being attuned to Will's needs, her ability to judge them more accurately than she, 'the professional', ever could have done (she was always on about being 'professional', was Noreen). She would have sussed the nature of Cele's feelings for Will because she made it her business to fall in love with Will herself – and love sensitizes the antennae. If 'love' is what you'd call it. Please understand that I'm using the word loosely.

There were procedures required for Will's comfort and hygiene which naturally he wouldn't want Cele, or anyone close to him, to perform. Noreen took an ill-disguised pleasure in these and in then discussing various intimate matters arising – blockages in his bowel and I don't know what – in front of Cele. Always with that despicable furrowed brow of concern that made me want to slap her.

I don't know how far Noreen is responsible for what transpired. I do know that, though there were other, more serious, reasons, it was partly the irritant of her presence that led to Cele's decision to take Will off up to Northumberland to see them all at Dowlands. Hetta, who was there, will know more about this. I can only speak about their return from Dowlands, because that same evening Cele said to me, 'Will would like us to get rid of Noreen but he thinks it best for you to tell her, if you don't mind.'

That was fine by me. I didn't mince my words and there was a lot of predictable protest and tears bravely held back, and when that performance cut no ice with me, which it wouldn't, there was legal talk. I confirmed that we would pay the wretched woman in lieu of notice but, just to be provoking I suppose, she became hell-bent on working out her notice.

To avoid trouble, it was agreed that Noreen should

stay on for a further week. She spent the time having a good nose around and lifted quite a few items in the process. Some silver napkin rings of Graham's, a pretty cream jug which had been Grandmother Tye's and the odd bit of not terribly important jewellery all disappeared along with Noreen. Cele kept her underwear, nightwear and so on in the tallboy in her room and more weirdly, though I suppose a psychoanalyst wouldn't be too surprised, Noreen also pinched some of Cele's tights.

We were frankly so glad to see the back of her that we didn't bother reporting the thefts. I doubt we'd have involved the police anyway. What I did do, which was a mistake, was inform the agency through which we'd found her, which obviously added fuel to her resentment.

With Noreen's departure, Anthony found for us, through the medical grapevine, Rose, a bouncy Cork girl with a boyfriend in tow, a breath of fresh air after the clammy Noreen and not over-exercised about her duties. So it was not surprising that Cele was around more than usual to lend a hand.

Then, one evening in late September, Cele told me that Mum proposed coming to London for a new production of *Othello* and wondered if I might like to join them. Graham was going to be off on a 'business trip', presumably one of his Zara jaunts, and Cele suggested that Mum might stay for a night or so in her room, that she herself would happily sleep in the study, near Will, which would leave Rose free to go with her boyfriend on the city break to Barcelona that she'd been after.

Rose's boyfriend had booked them on an early plane so she had to stay the night at his place in order to be sure to be off at dawn. Which meant that in the end Cele didn't come to the theatre after all and Mum and I went together, which was nice for me. Since Daddy died, I'd not seen much of Mum. To tell you the truth, I never did see much of her. I see her more now.

From what I remember, the guy playing Iago was OK but Othello was a bit unconvincing. There's something too cringe-making about a white actor blacked up which gets in the way. Mum and I discussed the play afterwards and I remember her saying that Desdemona's only failing was that she didn't see her husband clearly enough and that, had she done so, a good deal of grief would have been spared. 'Real love is also clear-sighted,' Mum said. Not that I disagree but it's a very her-ish thing to say.

When we got back to the flat, Cele was still up and we all had quite a bit to drink, so my recollections of that night are vague. What I do remember is going in to say goodnight to Will and Mum coming into the room after me, and saying, 'I'll sit with you a bit, if that's all right, Will, darling.' A while later, coming out of my room to get some water, I heard her say, 'Goodnight, Will, God bless, my darling. Sleep well.'

I wouldn't have expected to hear him reply.

PART FOUR
Hetta

I

When Granny rang to say that Grandpa was to be buried in Bamburgh churchyard I was so taken aback I couldn't help asking, 'But would he have wanted that?'

I had left Ely only the week before. Since Will's fall, home was not a happy place. Dad had retreated into a twilight depression of limited engagement, with us anyway, though he seemed to function as well as he ever did at the hospital. Mum had become more than ever inclined to dictate the terms of my existence, which grated on my eighteen-year-old self. Will's ability to command our parents' attention seemed more powerful than ever and it angered me that his accident was now serving to restrict my liberty even further. When Mum deduced, from the fact that my red heels were missing from my room, that I had taken them hoping I might bump into Rick Stannock – a boy she considered 'wild' – and interrogated me, we had a blazing row and I rang Granny.

'Not so much a "neighbourhood of voluntary spies" as a household, Granny.' It was the Easter before my A levels. One of my set texts was *Emma* and this was the kind of shorthand Granny would understand. But it was also me getting one over on my mother. As far as I knew, Mum had never read any Jane Austen.

'It's understandable, darling. You must . . .'

'Yeah, yeah, I know. Will's accident, etcetera. But checking up on my shoes, for God's sake.'

'Parents do check up, darling. It's part of their job.'

'You didn't!' There was a pause where I thought the line had gone dead. Our line was dodgy. 'Granny?'

'Yes?'

'May I come and stay?'

'Of course, darling. You know you are welcome to come any time. But make sure it's OK with your mother first.'

My excuse to Mum was that Granny was a help with my English revision. She had been a teacher and we had always talked books together, and while Mum mutely resented this she was also ambitious for me and must have recognized that Granny's love of literature had fostered my own. But in the event I was very glad I went for another reason. Four days after I left Ely Grandpa died in his chair in the sitting room, where he had been reading his beloved Virgil.

About ten days before he died, Granny and I were in their kitchen. Grandpa had gone to bed and it was a time when we tended to chat, over tea for her and cocoa for me, at the red Formica table which they had had for as long as I could remember. In fact when I reflect on my childhood that red table, with a scorch mark where one of us had once carelessly put down a roasting tin, is a visual refrain. The mugs we were drinking from also went way back. Grandpa had a weakness for the kind that are adorned with pithy-sounding quotes, which as children we were always pleased to find as he was tricky to give to and we could mostly rely on examples of these to make acceptable presents. The mug I was drinking from had a quote from Margaret Thatcher, 'The problem with socialism is that you run out of other people's money', and a picture of her handbag. I don't know who gave him this particular mug, or what it was doing in his anti-establishment kitchen cache, but perhaps he found the sheer crassness of this Thatcherism amusing. Grandpa had a bizarre sense of humour.

Granny's mug had a quotation from Oscar Wilde which made more sense to me. 'Man is made for something better than disturbing dirt.'

The mug was on the table and I turned it towards me to read the words again.

'It's from *The Soul of Man Under Socialism*.'

She'd told me this before but I didn't let on. Although her memory was not as acute as Grandpa's, on the whole it didn't slip much.

'Why soul?' I asked. I had arrived at the stage when you are most curious and enquiring about the metaphysical.

'Have you read *De Profundis*?'

I hadn't then, though I have made sure to since.

'He wrote it in prison,' Granny said. 'That stupid pointless case. It drives me wild thinking about it.'

'What's it about, the book?' I knew about the case. I think Granny nursed the notion that had she been around to advise him Wilde would never have got himself into that particular mess.

'People imagine because his wit was so sharp that he wasn't a deep thinker, which is a very English kind of prejudice, Hetta. But he thought deeply about many things, especially in prison. Especially about soul.'

'But do you think we have one?' I asked. Talking about 'soul' in Grandpa's vicinity felt like a kind of sacrilege.

'It depends on what you mean by "soul",' Granny said. And we left it there.

But the following evening over the red Formica table, she said, 'I was looking at this again last night after our conversation.' She produced a battered *De Profundis* from a pile by the lamp. There was always a pile of books on their kitchen table. '"To deny one's own experiences is to put a lie into the lips of one's own life. It is no less than a denial of the soul." I can't help thinking, Hetta, Fred was so pleased and proud when Will was offered the place at King's. And yet all of that represented an elitism he has set his face against his whole life.'

I didn't really understand then what she was getting at. 'Grandpa meant it for the best.'

'Oh, certainly. Fred always does mean things for the best. But it's as if his way of not denying his own experience is to expose others to it. I must have been mad not to have stopped him from encouraging Will to go to King's.'

I didn't like this. 'Granny, Mum and Dad were beside

themselves over Will. You and Grandpa were only trying to help.'

'Yes, well, as you know, "The way to hell is paved with good intentions".' She had got up to fetch the old round cream-and-green tin, the kind that nowadays fetches pounds in fancy junk shops. 'Digestive?' Granny looked young for her seventy-six years but as she offered me the tin her face appeared suddenly aged.

'Are these still Grandpa's favourites?'

'He claims to prefer custard creams but I draw the line at those.'

'Does he still say, "I've lived by the sword and I'll die by the sword"?'

'He would if I bothered him about his diet. But he's not diabetic and with all his other complaints why deny him a few indulgences? Anyway, as you know, Fred's always been his own master.'

It was true. Grandpa never swerved from what he regarded as right – whether for himself or for the world. And although Granny complained about this, and it had often made her life more trying than it need have been, she also loved him for it. Or maybe I mean she loved him in spite of it. It's difficult to say because I suspect those two states often merge over time.

I was aware, anyway, how hard Grandpa's death would hit her. They'd been together, as she always said, 'through thick and thin' almost from the very day she was born. So I felt badly over my tactless outburst on the phone over where Grandpa should be buried because after all it was up to her.

But she took my objection phlegmatically. 'He won't know and besides I like to think of him looking at the sea.' This is quite typical of Granny: having it both ways.

It's a fine old church, Bamburgh, and even an atheist body might welcome its austere hospitality; but it was the graveyard she had in mind. If you stand by the west end of the church and look out, as I did that clear April day when we buried Grandpa, there is an uninterrupted view of the distant horizon, that strange liminal point which our eyes create and has no tangible existence, where the sea meets the sky. And you can hear the call of birds etching the bass line of the sea's thrash and rumble, and breathe in the freshness of the salt-seaweedy air.

I had been making to move off with the others to allow Granny a moment of quiet alone but she gestured me back. 'Listen.'

Far out, over a sea chopped by wind, a bird was keening. 'What is it?'

'Curlew, I think. Wait.'

The forlorn-sounding cry was repeated. Much later that night in bed I remembered her telling me as a child, 'It's us, Hetta, who hear the sounds as sad. To a curlew it's simply curlew.'

We stood side by side at the grave, listening to the unlamenting curlew as the wind from the sea blew into our faces.

2

It is some time before you can erect a stone on a newly dug grave for you must wait until the earth settles. Granny had decided that, when she had chosen a suitable local rock, LR would be engraved there. It was Will's idea. But that was before Will himself died.

I had followed Granny's advice and ignored Cambridge in my university applications. I would have been very happy to get into York or Bristol so I was over the moon to be offered a place, conditional on my A levels, at Oxford, where I had supposed I had badly messed up my interview. I had blushed and sweated, muddled up two Edith Wharton novels, trying to show off my range of reading, misquoted Keats and then revealed that I'd never read *Tom Jones* but only seen the film. And while the man interviewing me at Wadham had laughed very nicely at that and said, 'I wish everyone were as candid,' I was sure I had blown it. He was called Dr Bennet and I discovered much later that it was he who had insisted I be offered a place. I owe him a lot because Wadham was where I found Theo again, or rather where he found me when he came to Oxford to do his Masters in music.

The news that I had the grades I needed had only just reached me when Cele brought Will up for a visit to

Dowlands and seeing him prompted the awful feeling that I have mentioned before, that I've had more than my fair share of our family's luck.

When she last stayed with us in Paris I summoned up the courage to say something of this to Cele.

'I often think that if you'd not had the affair with Colin I would never have met Theo. It seems . . .'

But she stopped me. I should have known better than to mention Colin.

'Hetta, things happen and then because of that other things happen and so on and so on and that isn't just "the way of life", as people say. It is what life *is*.'

My cousin is less obviously beautiful these days. She's older and thinner – too thin Theo says – and her expression if not sad is reserved, sealed off. But she still has a luminous quality about her and her eyes will always be that bewitching green.

She knew what I had been going to say – 'It seems unfair' – because it feels to me as if Theo and I have been happy at her expense. Her expense and Will's.

They stayed during this visit in Old Moanie's old room. Cele slept there too in case Will needed help in the night. I was too young not to be afraid of what Will must be feeling at needing her to assist him in such intimate ways and it made me shy with him at what turned out to be our last meeting, which I regret bitterly now. So if I am trying here to set down as much as I can of the complex set of events that we were all involved in, it is in part my attempt at reparation, my effort to make up for what I never said to my brother then, though I am aware that this is quite pointless since he's not around to know of it and his life anyway cannot now be repaired.

All memory is partial, or just plain wrong – I take that as a given – and there is much of this period of my life of which I've only the haziest recollection and many events that I do not recall at all. If I remember the time of the cousins' last holiday through a miasma of awkwardness and self-reproach, what I do recall, most vividly, is my last holiday at St Levan.

It was the holiday when I'd just discovered the Romantic poets and I was inwardly preoccupied with saving Coleridge from his drug addiction, a preoccupation which, rather obviously, was connected to my errant brother, though I would have indignantly denied this at the time. My fondness for Coleridge has lasted – so there must have been something more substantial than family psychology, though family psychology can and does lead us to more objective affections. But I can see now that the psychology fits. So perhaps it is to Will that I owe my abiding love of Coleridge, as well as to Granny, who on that same holiday gamely read aloud with me the whole of *The Ancient Mariner*.

There was a melancholy feel about that visit, partly because it was goodbye to a place where I had been happy. Being with Granny and Grandpa was a rest from some of the tensions of home, which at the time I felt in my pores but did not fully understand. But the sense of sadness was also because it was the first time I took in the fact that Grandpa's health was failing. He'd been, as he liked to say, fit as a flea all his life, and for all of my life too, which counted more in my reckoning, and I was taken aback by his frailty and visible decline.

There was no corresponding failure of his mind. He was more than ever engrossed in his Virgil translation and read me out long passages, which I hope I gave an impression of enjoying and for which I'm grateful now. But his arthritis was affecting his ability to write – Dad once tried to interest him in a computer and he reacted with, 'I may claim to have some small grasp of Lucretius but in a million years I shall never grasp modern technology' – and the episodes of atrial fibrillation had, Granny confided, increased.

My first real apprehension of the indignity of mortality was when I observed Granny undertaking any physically taxing task behind Grandpa's back. I was at the stage of relishing my youthful strength and was only too pleased to be allowed to help, and they had plenty to pack up. Grandpa was never one for possessions; 'Possessions,' he used to say, 'possess the possessor,' but Granny had her fair share of the barnacles that cling to us from our past.

We sent Grandpa to his study, to be out of our hair, while I heaved boxes of books, which they stubbornly refused to cull, took down ragged curtains and tried to help Granny decide what ought to be jettisoned – difficult, as she was brought up in an era when waste was considered a crime worse than theft and she insisted that the most decrepit and beaten-up articles be preserved. Her 'holey relics', Grandpa called them.

The most arduous task was dealing with the mounds of dusty papers, which had been left untouched for years. The amount of paper we must have burned – at least four bonfires, late at night to avoid annoying the neighbours, with me toasting, on a pea stick, the aged marshmallows I'd found hoarded in the larder from God knew how many Christmases past. Not even the pea sticks were to be sacrificed for the move.

I wish now I had bothered to take time to sort through those papers which may have held secrets sadly long gone up in smoke. But we did at least sort all Granny's notebooks, her more personal letters and her diaries into chronological order and stored them in the old boxes she had retained from her mother's time and in the ship's captain's portable desk, which she says is one day to be mine. The accounts you have read couldn't have been written without them.

At the back of a high cupboard, jammed with junk – an old ballet tutu of Bell's that was shedding sequins, a set of wooden ninepin soldiers with two soldiers missing, a single croquet mallet, six ancient tennis racquets, two bicycle bells, assorted boots, the leather mud-caked and cracking, and, most unfathomably, since we could think of no one who could have had a use for it, a child's crutch – I discovered, while balancing precariously on the top of some dangerously wobbly steps, a black tin box which revealed rather more valuable salvage. Among this was the scarab ring which I have on my desk because it's too fragile to wear. It belonged to Granny's god-mother, Nancy, who left her Staresnest, and she gave it to me as a thank you, 'You should have this, Hetta, as Beetle's child.' I'd not known till then how Dad came to be called Beetle.

Also in the box was a silver watch and chain that had belonged to Granny's father, which she asked me to take to London for Will, and with it, for Cele, a gold locket of Great-Granny Maud's, which opened to reveal a four-leafed shamrock, along with a scrap of paper on which was written in faded brown ink *M & G, Mourne, 1918.*

I arrived bearing these historic gifts at Bell's flat to the immediate aftermath of Will's attack on Colin. The row had left Bell uncharacteristically nervy. She was smoking, though she had, on my last visit, informed me that she was giving it up because of her fear of wrinkles, and almost her first words to me were, 'Hetta, darling, can you help me with this lot?'

And there and then, between us we lugged the rug he had bled all over all the way down Kensington High Street to the Oxfam shop.

When we got back from offloading the contaminated items Bell said, 'I need a drink, would you like one, dear?' She would have been well aware that I was permitted only a token glass of wine at Christmas.

The return home was a return to the ignominy of being a schoolgirl. My parents must have been trying to protect me from any further family tempests, because I was mostly shielded from news of the charges being brought against Will. What they didn't know was that Bell had described Will's assault on Colin, accompanied by dramatic gestures where our cargo permitted, while we were lugging the bloodied rug down the high street. It wouldn't have occurred to her to censor anything out of regard for my age.

Nor would it have occurred to her that I was ignorant of the details of Cele's affair with Colin, which she also described as we walked back along the high street. She was furious with Colin, and, which I didn't quite appreciate at the time, furious with herself for exposing Cele to him.

I had been fobbed off with some watered-down version of events by my mother. Scampering after my aunt, I heard with fascination that my cousin had been expelled for a dangerous sexual liaison. If this was disturbing it was also exciting. More so than the news that Will had been in a fight. He'd been getting into fights all his life and the fact that this had caused bloodshed was nothing new to me – I'd witnessed bloodied noses and bruises countless times. But knowing what I did about his relationship with Cele I did wonder what was going to become of them.

3

The first clear memory I have of anything to do with Cele's marriage was over the Christmas that followed it.

Will had resumed his degree that October. He was in his second year when he was sent down and part of the punishment was that he had to go back and retake the year. Harvey, having completed his final year, 'should by rights have buzzed off', as Bell remarked, and while nothing overt was said you could tell that my parents were not best pleased when Will appeared that Christmas accompanied by his old friend.

If Harvey was there it was maybe because his was a familiar figure in a probably humiliating return to Cambridge for Will. And no doubt part of Harvey's pull, as Theo says, was his apprehension of the side of Will drawn to risk and danger. Harvey used this. Got off on it probably.

And he got off, too, on his ability to hit just the wrong note, to unsettle people. It was during the Christmas Eve dinner that he threw into the general festive chatter a spanner he must have been saving for this purpose. 'And how is Mrs McCowan the doctor's wife faring?'

There was something shocking about hearing Cele's married name, especially from Harvey. Everyone instinctively averted their gaze from Will. Dad, being Dad, ignored what had been said but betrayed his discomfort by scraping back his chair on the unforgiving flags to get up and open a window. Mum, who was always better at confrontation, waved the carving knife and said briskly, 'She's very well from what we hear. More goose, Harvey?'

Granny always says that no one is ever really 'the one' and that this is youth's delusion. A 'pop song fantasy' she calls it. But I would like to believe that I am the one for Theo, as he is for me. And that the same was true of Cele and Will. But I believe that it is also the case that Cele loved Alec, if in a different register.

Alec promised security. Not the security of money and creature comforts, of the kind that had tempted Bell, but steadfastness and quite possibly admiration. Cele had never been made fully alive to her own loveliness, another consequence of being the child of a beauty. Alec was enchanted by her. I doubt if Will had ever thought of paying her a compliment or took much conscious notice of her beauty.

And you have to remember that Cele was Bell's child. She had never had a home to call her own and was living with Alec already, and this may have seemed to settle something for her, after a life that had been one of unsettlement. It looked like a finality, and finalities, good or bad, offer a promise of calm.

Theo, who has the French enthusiasm for philosophy, once tried to explain to me the concept of moral luck.

'It goes like this, Hetta,' – when Theo explains anything he conveys the ideas with a pencil, which he waves about like his conductor's baton – 'you see, it was morally OK for Gauguin to leave his wife and children and go off to Tahiti because out of that came great art.'

'I don't personally regard Gauguin's art as all that great.' This was early in our renewed relationship and I was still, rather pathetically, trying to keep my cultural end up.

'OK, Picasso then. Picasso was a shit but . . .'

'I don't like him much, either,' I said. 'I prefer Matisse.'

He put the pencil down, looking hurt. 'Now you are being deliberately dense, Henrietta.'

I was. And although I grew out of trying to best Theo because I felt inferior, it is still not an idea that persuades me. But if the idea is worth anything then you would have to agree that Cele suffered from moral ill luck.

It was a conversation about this with Theo that led to my trying to set all this down. As the grandson of Granny's great friend Marion, he already knew some of the score.

'From what my grand-maman says, there's an interesting history there, your family. Your grand-papa, for instance. His political views are worth recording. He went to jail, no?'

Too late to ask Grandpa now what he had felt was worth losing his liberty for. 'I wish I'd asked him more about all that.'

'But there is your grand-maman. She will talk to you.

It seems to me worth doing if only for yourself, Hetta. All that stuff swept under the carpet.'

'I'm not sure that I can ask Cele.'

'You can ask. She can only refuse.'

But when, very apprehensive, I broached the prospect, Cele said in her cool voice, 'Do what you like, Hetta. You know I trust you.'

The next time I saw her she handed me some letters and notebooks. 'You might as well have these. I was going to burn them.' And when I began to speak, 'No, please, do what you like with them. I never want to see them again.'

I left the letters and notebooks unread in my desk drawer for some time. I was a minor sufferer in my family's collective injury and I felt reluctant to pick at any scab. But one day, when Theo had gone down to Avignon to organize a concert, I turned on the radio and heard someone playing the sax so eloquently that my eyes filled with tears. It brought Will to mind, that day I saw him in Bell's flat, when he was still his old self and had a chance to find another kind of life – to get away.

I made myself a large cafetière of coffee and sat down on the old green leather sofa, where I had once sat as a shy schoolchild, and began to read my cousin's notebooks. Sad, sad reading. And if I ever divulge the content to a wider audience it can only be when – but I don't know when. When no one can be hurt any further by them, I suppose.

Her letters to Will are naked in their pleas for his

understanding. Equally painful are his replies. Most poignant is his awful stab at being Humphrey Bogart.

Reading Will's "'I'm no good at being noble, but it doesn't take much to see that the problems of three little people don't amount to a hill of beans in this crazy world'" made me weep all over again because we don't live in films with bittersweet endings, however much it might flatter our picture of ourselves to quote from them. Will was right, he wasn't any good at being noble.

At some point, I remember, Cele said to me, 'The worst thing, you know, Hetta, is that Alec would have let me go, ever so nobly. He was like that.' And when I mentioned this to Theo he said, 'That was her trying to be noble by not wanting to seem to abandon Alec. Don't ever try to be noble with me, will you, Hetta?'

As I sat on the Bazinets' sofa, attempting to take all this in, what seemed to me most touching was the revelation of how hard my brother tried. He tried to hang on, he tried not to complain, he tried, and this for me was the strongest proof of his love, to put himself in her shoes but with such a strained jocularity that it made me flinch when I read it. He did his best, or tried to, and as Granny always said to us about exams, 'You can only do your best, or try to.' But on another occasion, when Grandpa was digging in his heels about something, she said to me, 'Never try to push anyone beyond their limits, Hetta.'

We don't know our own limits so how can we judge the limits of others? And what it is easy to forget is that they were so young. Too young to bear all those horribly complicated family strains. I guess Will's resolve snapped. Or maybe all my speculations have nothing to do with it at all. Maybe, in the way that people often stuff themselves with cream cake and chocolate before embarking on a diet, Will was treating himself to a last hedonistic binge before his new life with Cele began. I don't like to suppose that was the case, but then I am a romantic.

4

On the night of the total lunar eclipse in September 1996 I had gone with friends down to the beach by St Aidan's Dunes, where we made an illicit fire and drank cheap wine and smoked and danced and mucked about in the sea. A couple of the boys got thrown in and more than one couple went off into the dunes. I gather the idea was to have sex in tandem with the rare celestial conjunction.

I had no such ambition. School was over for good at last and I was looking forward to a year out, away from the over-scrutinizing regard of my mother and my father's lowering moods.

I was tired of home, tired of school, tired of my friends, tired even of Northumberland. The shadow of the earth, so precisely crossing the pale luminous disc that was weirdly recast upon the glinting surface of the sea, seemed to herald some portentous new chapter in my own history.

I had started to write poetry again. So I ignored the amorous invitation of Rick Stannock, for whom only a few months earlier I would have walked barefoot to Berwick, electing instead to go home to try to convey in words the elusive magic of what I had seen. I reread my efforts recently. I would never have made a poet.

But either the effect of the moon or the prospect of my coming liberation left me wakeful that night and it seemed as if I had barely slept when brilliant sunlight roused me the following morning.

I've always been an early riser, even with little sleep I have never been able to stay in bed. So I biked into Bamburgh to get the papers.

I was reading a review in the *Guardian* when the phone rang. And this time I had no precognition.

Dad answered in the hall and perhaps because by now I was out of the habit of monitoring my parents, I caught nothing sinister in his voice.

He must have gone upstairs to Mum, who was still in bed. I finished reading the paper and was halfway up to the Blue Room but hearing a sudden awful wail turned into their bedroom.

My mother was sitting up in bed holding her face in her hands.

'Mum?'

'Oh, Hetta . . .'

'What? What, Mum?'

'Oh, Hetta. Will is dead.'

I don't remember what I said. I think I simply went over to the bed and we held each other. Dad too, the three of us clutched in a huddle.

It was Granny who had rung. Will, she said, had been found that morning in his chair. They were waiting for Dr Li, the GP friend of Bell's who had always seen to Will. They thought, Granny said, that perhaps Will had choked.

Will had recovered some of his ability to swallow but it was precarious. I had watched him choking when he and Cele had stayed with us when she brought him up for that visit to Dowlands, and it had scared me.

We left immediately for London. Graham was away. As we now know, he was off with his PA, which, given all that happened next, was maybe just as well. Dr Li, who had been to examine Will, had left by the time we arrived.

My brother was still in his chair, very pale, but his face which had been freakishly twisted when I had seen him last looked at peace to my apprehensive gaze and, while I am aware that that is a corny phrase, I cannot find one more apt. I was a bit in fear of touching a dead body but I managed to stroke his face and kiss the top of his head and then I laid my cheek on his hair – his hair was dark and curly, as Bell used to say like a black lamb's. It smelled of the old Will, I remember that. He hadn't smelled good when I had seen him last.

I left Mum and Dad alone with him in his room and went to look for Cele. She had met us wordlessly on our arrival but had disappeared off with Granny and only Bell was about.

It's Theo's view that our family has been hard on Bell. She wasn't much use when it came to her daughter but she was very generous to Will. It must have been dreadful for her, his dying there. Mum in particular, as I came to see, resented it and still punishes her.

Bell was generous to me too. And this is an odd thing to say, because by all normal standards she was selfish.

But it was a selfishness which, while it put her own comfort first, didn't make the mistake of imagining that the
rest of the world would.

She greeted me that day with a characteristic 'Hetta,
dear, this must be utterly, utterly bloody for you. I'm so
sorry.' She was smoking and she hadn't bothered to put
on mascara. I'd never actually seen Bell without mascara
before and I thought, in that absurd way you do when
there are matters too huge to take in, that she needn't
really have bothered with make-up because her cat's eyes
looked as lovely, maybe more lovely, unadorned.

I sat down beside her while she sat and smoked. At
one point she said, 'I'm sorry, dear, would you like one?'
meaning a cigarette, and I said, 'I don't smoke,' although
I did. We all did. I suppose she knew that.

After a bit someone rang the doorbell and three men
arrived and Will was taken away. It turned out they were
undertakers, funeral directors as I believe they are called,
and perhaps that is not such a stupid name since death,
unquestionably, as I observed that day, is a drama. It's
not for nothing they call it 'the theatre of war'.

We all sat about not knowing what to say. Cele looked
dreadful, deathly pale, and I saw she was shaking. Granny
had an arm round her and at some point took her off
again to lie down. Dad, who had spent some time with
Will's body, announced that we three would need to find
a hotel.

'You must let me pay,' Bell said, and when Dad began
to demur, 'Beetle, do let me, please.'

He must have accepted because we spent the night in a fantastically grand hotel overlooking Kensington Gardens, with vast vistas of carpet and dangling chandeliers. Only much, much later did I realize that it was the very same hotel where Bell had held her wedding reception. The rooms had that viciously efficient air conditioning which bites the skin and froze me to the bone, and not knowing how to turn it off, and feeling the need for comfort, late that night I knocked on my parents' door. Mum was still up. She held me to her and her nightie was wet with tears.

The next morning Dad had a call. Will's death had been reported as being from 'unexplained causes' which meant that his body had been sent for examination by a pathologist. And from that point everything became terrifying.

I don't know exactly when the police became involved. I know that Dad and Mum were invited to go to the Kensington police station and that I went with them and sat in a grubby little waiting area which smelled of disinfectant, while they spoke to officers I never saw. They were incarcerated there for some time and when they reappeared I felt more frightened than I ever remember feeling in my life. Which was hardly surprising as what they had been told was that the police were treating Will's death as suspicious.

The pathologist thought he detected evidence of asphyxiation and the contents of Will's stomach had been sent away for analysis. Because there were no interlopers, no sign of forced entrance to the flat that night, because Rose, the carer, was away on her city break and Graham was in Brussels, my cousin, my aunt and my grandmother had overnight become suspects in a murder inquiry.

Shortly before seven that morning, police officers had arrived at Bell's to question Bell, Granny and Cele, who had all been in the flat when Will died. It is not merely in TV dramas that the police work on intuition. I suppose it was inevitable that from the first the greatest suspicion fell on Cele.

There were two investigating officers, a male Detective Inspector and a woman Detective Constable, who questioned her. They bent over backwards to be civil and the questions, to begin with, were straightforward.

'When did you last see your cousin alive, Mrs McCowan?'

'Before I went to bed.'

'And that was . . .?'

'Around 11.30. I can't be quite sure of the exact time.'

'Can you tell us how he was?'

'As he always was.'

'Can you be a little more precise?'

'He seemed OK. I said good night. And I gave him a kiss.'

'Were you in the habit of kissing your cousin?'

'Yes.'

'Where were you sleeping?'

'Next door in Rose's room, the carer. Will's carer.'

'Rose was away?'

'Yes.'

'How did that happen?'

'She was owed time off. She wanted a break with her boyfriend.'

'And who was it who arranged this, Mrs McCowan?'

'Will suggested it. As Granny was coming to stay it meant we had a spare room for her if Rose took her break then.'

'Your grandmother came to stay. Why? Any special reason?'

'She wanted to see a production of *Othello*.'

'Was this her idea or yours?'

'Hers. We go to the theatre together quite often.'

'And you went with her to see *Othello*?'

'No. Rose was supposed to be with Will that evening but she spent the night at her boyfriend's because their plane was very early so I stayed behind.'

'But hadn't you asked your grandmother especially to go to the theatre?'

'No. She invited me.'

'But you had to let her down?'

'She had my mother to go with. She understood that someone had to stay with Will.'

'And were you the obvious choice?'

'Well, Granny had come to London specially to see the play.'

'And your mother? She didn't offer to stay so you could be with your grandmother?'

'Granny wanted to see her too. She *is* her daughter.'

'So it would be more natural for you to be the one to stay behind with your cousin?'

And so it went on. Question after question, always leading to 'Did you in any way assist your cousin to die?'

They had already asked in several different ways if Will had expressed a wish to die.

'His life must have been very reduced by his accident. Cruelly reduced. Did he discuss ending it with you?'

'Sometimes.'

'And you maybe thought that it would be a kindness to help him.'

'I did want to. But Will didn't want that.'

'He didn't want your help or he didn't want to die?'

'He didn't want my help.'

'How did you communicate with your cousin, Mrs McCowan?'

'As I said. He blinked the letters out.'

'That can't have been easy. Plenty of occasion to misread him, I'd have thought.'

'No. I didn't misread him.'

'Not ever? You must have been unusually close.'

'We were close, yes. And I didn't misread him.'

'Can you tell us what he said to you then about dying?'

'He said "I do not want you suffering for me." He said it more than once.'

'He blinked this?'

'Yes.'

'So you would have been willing to help him to die if he had given permission?'

The young DC looked across the table at Cele with comprehending eyes. 'It must have been awful for you. Seeing Will like that.'

'Yes.'

'You knew each other as children?'

'Yes.'

'You must have done a lot of things together. Played together?'

'Yes.'

'I was like that with my cousin Geoff. We got up to all sorts.'

'Yes?'

'We still do muck about. I would miss all that if anything happened to Geoff.'

'I did,' Cele said.

'You missed doing things with Will?'

'Yes.'

'But you never thought to maybe help him? I don't know what I mightn't do for Geoff.'

'Will made it clear that he didn't want anything to happen to me.'

'But he asked you to help him to die?'

'He said that he didn't want me to be involved.'

'So who do you think might have been involved, Mrs McCowan?'

'I don't know.'

'Oh, come on, Mrs McCowan.' This was the DI now. 'There were only you, your mother and your grandmother at the flat. Your cousin is dead and not from natural causes. If it wasn't you yourself, you must have an idea who he would have asked for help.'

All this time, ignorant of what exactly was happening, Mum and Dad were becoming frantically anxious. They must have had more than an inkling of what had occurred. They too were questioned about Will's state of mind when they saw him last, whether he had discussed with them ending his life, his mood, his recent history. Most difficult, I imagine, were the questions about how Will came to be living there, away from Dowlands. It had seemed better for Will to live with Bell for all kinds of practical reasons but my parents will forever believe that, had they not agreed to this, Will might be alive today.

The person I feel for most in this whole tragedy is my mother. When you fall in love, one of the most rewarding aspects is the chance, with a sympathetic other, to analyse your family, that spider's web of which we are all a part and in which we are also trapped and from which we struggle to escape. And, with luck, in time and with help, we may come somewhat to understand.

Theo detects some aspect of affection lacking in my mother. 'Not,' as he said, 'that she is a cold-hearted woman, Hetta, but she has – how would I say? – a guard around her heart.' He went on to say, 'I wonder if your mother perhaps shut down a little when Will's twin died? It would be normal.'

Since Theo's parents retired and settled permanently

in the south, we have rented their Paris flat and this conversation took place when we first moved in and were
painting the bedroom green. (I had always pined for a
leaf-green bedroom but after less than a year decided
this was a mistake and Theo, with only raised eyebrows
and an annoying smile, helped me repaint it white.)

I remarked that I had sometimes wondered if Mum
really preferred girls.

'Or is more comfortable with them?' he suggested.
'But she is right, girls are greatly to be preferred. You
have some paint in your hair, come here.'

Lifting himself from my body he said, 'The dead
might be absent but they don't disappoint your ideas for
them.'

I liked it that Theo never really stopped pondering
things but I also liked to pretend to be annoyed. 'Théodore Bazinet, have you been thinking that up while
making love to me?'

'Hetta, a musician has to be able to do more than one
thing at a time.'

I would never want to hurt my mother by seeming to
impute blame for what must have been an instinctive
retreat, like a hurt animal retiring to the back of its cave.
But it may be, as Theo suggests, that after the death of his
twin she was never quite able to meet Will – for I cannot
say I felt any deficit for myself – with enough of that love,
or maybe I mean enough expression of that love, which
for good or ill shapes us for the rest of our lives. Maybe
some small part of Will was always in want of her.

Certainly, he had a more than usual need to be best. It was why he got into fights about his size, why he fought those he saw as oppressors. And it was the basis of his love for Cele that for her he had always seemed – until Colin – to come first.

Theo, when he speaks of music, speaks often of silence. He is in love, he says, with gaps, with the speaking spaces in a musical score. It's a subject where our interests meet because I am fascinated by the gaps made by people and by the gaps in people, and how those gaps get filled, sometimes to our detriment, sometimes to the detriment of others, for maybe I had been granted more of my mother's love because of the loss of that other sister.

So much of this story has to do with gaps. I hope I see them better now.

5

Granny and Bell were subjected to the same line of police questioning as Cele. When had they last seen Will? How did he seem? Had he mentioned taking his life? Did they or anyone they knew assist his death?

Both answered in much the same way. They had seen Will before they retired to bed, he had seemed much as he always did and, yes, he had mentioned a wish to die to each of them on other occasions but neither recalled him saying anything like that on that particular night. Neither of them had any idea how his death had come about.

Bell, from being initially indignant, took being interrogated in her stride. I wouldn't be surprised to learn that she enjoyed it – though perhaps here I am being unfair because I do know that from this moment she became truly concerned about Cele. And Granny, well, Granny will tell her own story. But at the end of the questioning that long afternoon it was Granny who determined on two courses of action. One was to ring the old firm of family solicitors, who, as she liked to say, had been around so long that God had probably instructed them over the conveyancing of paradise; the other was to take Cele off to a hotel.

Bell went back to the flat alone, which was brave of her. 'The poor child cannot stay another night there,' it seems Granny said. It was accepted by everyone that it was Cele who would take Will's death most hard.

The old family solicitor must have busied himself because the next day he rang to say that he was sending a partner in the firm round in case the police wanted to continue their questions.

Anu Singh, a Sikh with a greying beard and a neat black turban, which, Granny said, inspired confidence, called at the hotel while Cele was still up in their room resting. 'She's had a dreadful night, poor child,' Granny said when she went down to have coffee with him. 'I'm not sure she would be very coherent. They were very close.'

Anu Singh was sympathetic. 'I have heard something of this terrible business. Can you enlighten me a little further, Mrs Tye?'

'I wish I could. My grandson has been incapacitated since a bad fall. We found him dead on Saturday morning. We assumed he had choked. He had Locked-in Syndrome, you know.'

Anu Singh's amber eyes conveyed distress. 'How very sad. An awful business. And problems swallowing, yes?'

'Yes. My daughter called the GP who looked after Will. We assumed that he'd choked. But it seems there is a question over how he died.'

'These pathologists overreact to any faint suggestion that all is not quite normal at a post mortem. But is there anything I should know, Mrs Tye? Any matter, or detail relating to your grandson's death that you might need to tell me before we, so to speak, embark?'

'Not that I can think of. And it's Betsy, please.'

'I am sorry, Betsy, to intrude on your family's grief but you understand I have to ask these questions.'

He promised to return the following day and was present when the police arrived at the hotel and asked if Granny and Cele would be kind enough to come to the police station to answer some further questions.

'A moment,' Anu Singh said, 'while I have a word.'

He came back from a conversation with the two officers looking worried. The analysis of the stomach contents had not yet come back but Bell, he was told, was also being questioned again and her flat was now sealed and being searched.

'They appear to be moving to a position of treating Will's death as suspicious, which I devoutly hope is not the case. Cecilia, forgive me but I need to be very clear. You are sure that you know nothing about how your cousin came to die?'

'No.'

'Nothing?'

'No. I mean, yes, nothing.'

Anu Singh accompanied them to the station where the questioning became more penetrating. Granny, I can imagine, handled the interrogations with seeming composure but Cele found it hard to answer without collapsing into tears.

'Mrs McCowan, we believe barbiturates may have been found in your cousin's stomach. Can you tell us how they might have got there?'

'No.'

'As the wife of a GP, it must have been fairly easy for you to obtain a script from your husband, fill it out, put a squiggle for his name. You must have had many occasions to sign for him.'

'No.'

'You see, Celia . . .'

'Cecilia.'

'I do apologize. Do you mind if I call you Cecilia?'

'No.'

'I was saying, we understand. You were helping your cousin. You were helping Will.'

'I wasn't. He didn't want my help.'

'Let us put it this way, Mrs McCowan, the courts take a dim view of a not-guilty plea when there is compelling evidence of guilt. You tell us what happened and we'll do our best for you. We understand it was a mercy killing. We do understand that you were doing your best for your cousin. We do understand.'

Terrible to be so terribly understood. They were kind, she told me. Very kind. And with Will gone she was more than ever in need of kindness.

'I would like to propose,' Anu Singh said at some point, 'that my client be given a break.'

When he was alone again with Cele he said, 'I am going to suggest to them that you write a full statement.

They have no concrete evidence for anything and you don't look well. I shall request no further questioning pending your written statement. Your grandmother and your aunt too should do this.'

Granny and Cele spent the following day at the dismal hotel, trying to compose statements. I have read these but I am not going to record them here because before long they became irrelevant.

Piecing everything together, I would guess that the pathologist had smelled a rat pretty soon. The analysis of the stomach contents revealed undigested fragments of tablets which led him to suspect, before the results proved it, that Will had ingested some sort of drug. This, plus signs of asphyxiation, were not enough to charge Cele, since in theory any one of the three women could have been responsible. And for this reason not one of them could have been charged were it not for the testimony of Noreen.

Rose was questioned but her stay in Barcelona was a definitive alibi as far as the circumstances of the death went. She was able to shed no more light on things than anyone else had. Noreen was another matter.

Tracked down easily via the agency from which she was hired, and only too eager to help the police, Noreen described how she had seen a bottle of pills, 'Soneryl' she thought it said on the label, in Mrs McCowan's drawer where she kept her underwear. She, Noreen, had been looking in the drawer for a camisole of her own that had gone missing. Not that she was trying to pry. Little pink pills and she did wonder what they were doing there as there was a gentleman's name on the label. Not McCowan, no, another name, but she couldn't remember what it was.

Will was always such a pleasure to look after. Not at all down in the dumps. Quite cheerful, in fact, he seemed when she was with him. But Mrs McCowan was always so keen to look after him herself, which she, Noreen, always thought funny. She did wonder what her husband Dr McCowan made of it all.

When murder is suspected the process is swift and serious. Swifter and more serious than the average person, fed on TV drama, might suppose. On the Thursday after Will's death, the police arrived at the hotel and cautioned Cele, who was taken to the police station where she was formally charged with murder. She was photographed, her fingerprints were taken as well as swabs for her DNA.

She did not, as seemed for a while likely, have to spend the night in a police cell. Thanks to a legal bigwig friend of Granny's, another firm of solicitors, more on the ball, was instructed and they argued successfully for Cele's release from custody overnight, since, rather clearly, she was not a danger to society but far more probably a danger to herself.

Cele was permitted on recognizance to sleep another night at the hotel with Granny. God knows what they talked about. The following day she was rearrested and taken back to Kensington Police Station and from there she was taken to the magistrates' court, where she was formally committed for trial at the Central Criminal Court. I can only guess at how profoundly terrifying all this must have seemed.

6

Granny's friend, Giles Truelove, had put her on to a firm of solicitors specializing in criminal defence and it was Giles Truelove, who was apparently once a barrister himself, who recommended a senior QC called Cuthbert Baines. Granny, once she heard the name, insisted that he was the right man to defend Cele. I don't know whether it was he or the new solicitor who thought they should hear more about Will and Cele's last holiday together. I had already written a statement but I was invited to go to speak to Cele's brief in his room at the Inner Temple.

I had not, after all, gone away. All the plans I had made that night of the lunar eclipse had to be set aside while my family dealt with this new disaster. But I had got myself a job selling programmes at the National Theatre and found a friendly floor to sleep on while I looked for a flat share. I felt for my parents but I couldn't stay a day longer at Dowlands. To be brutal, I felt that that might finish me off too.

I was anxious going to see Cuthbert Baines, unsure what he would want from me. And I was unsure, in my own mind, what to think about Will's death. I couldn't for the life of me imagine killing anyone and found it hard to believe that my gentle cousin Cele could kill. But I had talked, painfully, to Will and I had felt his misery and despair. And I knew that she would have felt it tenfold.

Cuthbert Baines looked to me quite elderly, though he can have been only in his sixties, tall and spare, with jutting eyebrows over little grey eyes. He had hair coming out of his ears, which I found embarrassing because I felt he was aware of my trying not to look at it. When he spoke, which he did slowly and precisely, he had a trick of rubbing his right thumb into the palm of his left hand. The hands, with rather yellowish uncut nails, were long and bony like the rest of him.

'Good afternoon, Miss Tye,' Cuthbert Baines said. 'Would you care for some tea?' The little grey eyes searched mine coldly as if he were suspending judgement on me pending my answer.

I didn't in the least want tea. I didn't want anything as a matter of fact, other than to get away as fast as I feasibly could. But I accepted the tea because I felt that maybe I should; or that maybe I would not be considered trustworthy if I rejected it.

Cele's solicitor smiled at me with a red lipsticky smile in a way that was probably meant to be reassuring. I was not reassured. I was frankly so nervous that I slopped the tea a young man had brought in for me into the saucer and then on to my skirt and over the rug. It was a rug not unlike the one I had helped Bell to lug to the Oxfam shop – composed of very faded muted colours which made me aware that it was probably antique and grand.

Cuthbert Baines flicked an imperious hand at the rug. 'Don't worry about that, tea is good for carpets.' He passed me a box of tissues to mop my skirt. There was a tin on his desk, with a picture of a pair of kittens playing with a ball of wool, and I remember thinking that it was not the kind of tin I would expect a big-shot lawyer to have. It turned out to have digestive biscuits in it and he offered me one, and that was more reassuring because it brought Grandpa to mind.

'I have a grumbling ulcer which I have to keep quiet by feeding it biscuits,' Cuthbert Baines explained and afforded me a chilly smile.

Cele's solicitor was engaged in reading something in a fat ring binder balanced on her knee.

'Thank you for coming here, Henrietta. We've read your statement but we were wondering if you could give us some insight into how your cousin was when she brought your brother up to see you at Dowlands, it is, isn't it?'

'A little holiday,' Cele had said to Mum on the phone. 'Will wants to come up to Dowlands to see you all.'

My memory of it now is sketchy, but Cele wrote about it in her diary. Their last time away together, it must have been.

Jesse Arnedale had taken over *Kittiwake*, his dad's boat, and he offered to ship the cousins over to Holy Island and Farne. I could have gone too but Will's features were all screwed up and he was so crooked-looking that I felt squeamish in his company. Cele never revealed this at the time but it was as well I didn't go along with them as when Jesse saw Will in his chair he said, 'Hey, grand to see you, man' but he apparently had tears in his eyes. Will was always the leader, the guy Jesse followed. Awful, it must have been for him, seeing those tears.

Jesse took them out to the islands, where they saw Cele's friends the seals and puffins and other seabirds.

And quite suddenly, sitting uncomfortably in Cuthbert Baines's rooms, I remembered Cele saying excitedly over supper in our kitchen that they'd seen a fulmar.

'Did you know,' she said, 'that fulmars have a clever system for processing salt from the seawater they drink which they eject through their nasal cavities? Jesse explained it. All these years coming here and I didn't know that.'

She had seemed very bright that evening.

'How was your cousin when they were staying with you?' Cuthbert Baines asked me that afternoon. 'What sort of mood was she in then, can you remember?'

'I think she seemed happy,' I said.

'Was that unusual?'

I tried to consider this. 'Well, she was, we all were, worried about Will mostly.'

'In what way "worried"?'

'I don't know, just worried. He was so different. I mean he'd been very active and he was, well . . .'

'Very maimed?'

'Yes.'

'I'm sorry if this is upsetting, Henrietta,' the solicitor said. She didn't look too upset herself.

'What would be helpful, Henrietta,' Cuthbert Baines went on, in his grave, clear voice, 'is if you could give us some further idea of how your cousin behaved on that visit. She helped your brother considerably, I gather.'

'Yes, a lot.'

'What did that involve? Could you say?'

'With his toilet, his bladder and, you know, things like that.'

'I see. Difficult tasks to undertake, in other words.'

'Yes.'

'And how would you say she was, your cousin, about performing these very delicate tasks?'

'She was great. I never felt, I mean, she never made . . . she never made a fuss about them. She just did them.'

'So she took very good personal care of your brother. Your mother or father didn't help, then?'

This was trickier because I wasn't really sure why it was always Cele who did the things that needed doing for Will.

'I don't seem to think they did those things for Will. But that wouldn't have been because they didn't want to, Mum and Dad. I expect he wanted Cele to see to him.'

I had loathed the thought of it. I don't like to remember this but, truthfully, I think I had wanted them both to go.

'So Will relied on Cecilia, trusted her, in other words?'

'Oh yes. He trusted her more than anyone.'

'Thank you, Henrietta. That is most helpful. One last question. Did your cousin ever make any suggestion that she might be contemplating helping your brother to die?'

'I don't think so.'

'You don't *think* so. Can you say if she ever did?'

'No.'

'She never suggested to you that it might be a help to Will if she assisted him to die?'

'No.'

'Not ever?'

'No.'

'And did he ever make such a suggestion to you?'

'I wasn't that good at talking to him. I mean it took a lot of time, you know, he had to blink everything and it took getting used to. I didn't talk to him much at all.'

'I understand. So he never made such a request to you for help in dying?'

'No.'

'And he never suggested that he might have asked for Cecilia's help?'

'No. No, he didn't.'

'And would you say you were close, you and Cecilia, exchanged confidences, that sort of thing?'

I considered this. Were we?

'Yes, I think so. Not as close as she was to Will.'

'But you would say you were, if not as close as she and Will were, anyway fairly close?'

'Yes.'

'She talked to you about things? Included you in her plans?'

'She was always very kind to me.'

'So you would say Cecilia is a kind person?'

And that I was very sure of. 'Oh yes, immensely kind.'

As I made my way out of Cuthbert Baines' outer office I could hear her solicitor's voice, which was shrill and carried: 'Don't think we can use her, can we? Too unsure of her ground.'

And then I heard Cuthbert Baines say, 'She might go down well with a jury. Clean-faced young woman, seems honest, sounds authentic. Let's withhold judgement, shall we, pro tem?'

PART FIVE

Betsy

I

I have told only part of the story, my story, my part in the story of our family, but only a part of my part. The essence of what you have read already I wrote in Ely, in those dark days after Will's accident when his life hung in the balance and we were unsure if he would live or die. While Fred buried his feelings by working away at his translation and Cecilia worked away at Will's recovery, I found that I too needed an occupation, a means to stay my mind. But there is more to be told . . .

About that mark on Cain. I have been thinking that if there was a mark it was not so much that he killed his brother as that he survived him. Survivors' guilt I believe they call it. I think a good deal about survival now.

The day after Will's accident I went to sit in the cathedral. From the time of our move to Ely I had often retired to its ancient calm and never went without lighting a candle for Nat. That afternoon I lit one for his nephew too and stood and watched the pair of fragile flames burn side by side in the dim quiet before sitting down on one of the pews to – what? To consider what had happened and how it had happened. To try to comprehend.

After Nat was killed, for years it was as if I had been

in a bad accident and to the other children I must have seemed – no, have been – a broken creature. In their different ways they both suffered. I knew it then but I see it more clearly now.

How Bell came about I'll never know, unless she was a changeling. She drove me round the bend because while she was as bright as a button she was also as lazy as all-get-out. I once chided her for not getting on with her exam revision and she shrugged her pretty shoulders, opened the window and threw all her books and notes out into the front garden. I recovered some of them lodged in the thorns of my 'Madame Alfred Carrière' rose. She passed all her O levels fine nonetheless.

Even as a small girl Bell had men eating out of her hand. She had a way of moving her body which was always provocative. It wasn't pert or overtly sexy and I don't believe she was putting it on. I saw a version of this in my mother. Nothing is odder to me than how a movement or gesture will recur in a new generation when it cannot have been learned. But Ma was a fluffy kitten to Bell's tigress.

I was always trying to discover where my daughter's beauty came from as no living relative, handsome enough as some of us were, possessed such features. Dad used to say Bell was a throwback to my mother's Anglo-Irish genes and it was true that she did have a look of Maud Gonne. It must have been this which so often brought to my mind those lines in *Prayer for My Daughter*:

> *May she be granted beauty and yet not*
> *Beauty to make a stranger's eye distraught,*
> *. . . for such,*
> *Being made beautiful overmuch,*
> *Consider beauty a sufficient end . . .*

But Yeats survived his passion for Maud Gonne. It was she, whose beauty had driven him wild, who in the end was the loser.

If there is blame to be levelled over the history of my daughter, and thus my daughter's daughter, then, sitting in the quiet cathedral, I had to acknowledge that it lay with me. For one consequence of the loss of Nat was that I never really challenged Bell. For all my outward scolding, her tantrums cheered me, caused me a secret amusement. I suppose I was impressed that she had the nerve not to yield.

There is some perverse element in human nature which seems to manifest in a peculiar lack of sympathy for those who reflect our own weak traits. Poor Beetle never won from me such admiration. Yet in many ways we were alike. Like me, he was terrified of heights. He was in terror of many things, poor Beetle. Where Nat went off to nursery with barely a backward glance, Beetle clung to my skirt and it was weeks before I felt able to leave him on his own. He was scared of thunder too, whereas Nat was never bothered and Bell could go wild in storms. I can see her, running naked on to the lawn in the midst of a spectacular summer storm, shrieking with Bacchic excitement.

Once at a birthday party Beetle threw back his head to laugh and cracked it on an iron radiator so hard that blood flowed. It was Bell's fourth birthday, so he would have been seven. The little girls squealed in horror but dear Beetle when he saw how the blood was upsetting them just laughed the more.

As I sat in the unjudging quiet of Ely Cathedral thinking about my children, the old reels flickered across the screen of memory: Nat dancing on the top of Salisbury's tower, showing me a grass snake he'd found coiled in a mound of grass clippings, refusing to shout with the other children, that 'Yes,' he believed in fairies, when Ma took him to *Peter Pan*; Bell stamping on her birthday cake because I'd forgotten pink icing, winning the talent contest at the Daily Worker fête, dressing up as the Queen in Ma's satin petticoat – and little Beetle, laughing as blood dripped down his neck on to his clean shirt.

If Beetle survived Nat's loss, I reflected that May afternoon, he did so partly by marrying Susan.

Susan was unexcitable, loyal, capable and her only mild eccentricity, if that is what you'd call it, was her obsession with her sheep. Fred used to call her Bo Peep, which he took for granted she found amusing. I could tell that she found it irritating and I tried to explain this to Fred. But he was never able to see that what was unimportant to him might matter quite a bit to others unlike him.

In truth, Susan found us both irritating, though she

hid it fairly well. But I was aware of it and I was alive to her reasons. I should explain how they came to have Dowlands.

I had always reckoned Grandmother Tye as indelibly steeped in the ethos of male primogeniture. It would never have crossed Fred's mind to speculate on wills or calculate a likely inheritance. But if I ever considered the future I would have bet Ma's brown diamond ring on Grandmother leaving her estate to a male heir.

She died with characteristic aplomb, at close on a hundred and three, all but eighty years after she and Grandad Tye – she in old lace, he in full fig – had married in Bamburgh Church. Her last will was brief. She left Margaret a life tenancy in the house and the dogs to care for. I suspect it was thanks to the dogs that Margaret had the tenancy – Grandmother would never have had her dogs lose their home. But I was wrong about her principles, for ultimately Dowlands was left to me. I suppose she trusted me not to give it away.

After her death, it emerged that over the years, with Grandad having passed on much of the family money to Oswald and their capital draining away, they had taken out loans from the bank, which by now held a substantial charge on the house. The place required attentive upkeep. By the time Margaret died, it was run-down and badly in need of repair. Any sale value was unlikely to be very high.

Sydella had not long arrived and Beetle was training as an anaesthetist in a hospital up in Manchester. One day he rang to say he was in London and could he call round. I remember it made me apprehensive: there had never been any question of the children *asking* if they could call round.

When he turned up he was visibly nervous and suggested we have a drink, which put me in mind of Magda when she came to ask me to take care of Nat. I try to follow my father's rule, which was 'to hold off till sundown', but I had a drink too because I caught his nerves.

He sat there smoking until I couldn't stand the uncertainty and said, 'Well go on then. Spit it out.' As I believe I've said, I was always slightly preparing for bad news.

'It's about Dowlands. Susan and I would very much like to buy it, if you'll let us.'

And I was so relieved that I said, 'Is that all? There's no question of your buying it. Of course you must have it.'

I was touched that the old house mattered to Beetle. But there was this too. I felt I owed him some kind of recompense. I never regretted it till lately, when I began to wonder if maybe some unquiet spirit of Nat's haunted Dowlands.

In those first years after they moved up to Northumberland, we saw precious little of Beetle and Susan, which meant I saw next to nothing of Sydella, which I regret as I never got to know her as I did the other grandchildren. Susan was wary of me. She was always outwardly welcoming and her words were on the face of it warm but you could read 'Keep off' as clearly as if she'd daubed it in paint on Dowlands' big oak front door.

It was partly because of me giving them Dowlands.

Dowlands was where Nat and I had spent those enchanted early years and the very fabric of the walls was imbued with that first love. It seemed fitting that I should pass on what I could of it now to his brother. But for Susan the gift made for difficulties. She had her reasons for resenting me. She didn't hold with the way we had brought up our children. Her own family were in no position to offer financial provision and she was having no truck with any hint of a Lady Bountiful to whom she might be expected to be beholden. I like to believe that I had no such expectation. Nor do I think she would ever have voiced such thoughts. But thought, especially unconscious thought, is real and I felt it.

It must have been doubly hard for Susan that the twin who bore her mother's name was the twin she lost and that the baby named after Fred survived. The idea of naming the babies after their grandparents was hers; it was a dear thought, one that Fred and I appreciated, to give one of the twins his name. Though it's a name that seems not to stick; neither Fred nor Will ever owned to Wilfred.

Because Susan was exhausted by a protracted birth, and then holed by the grief of her lost baby daughter and by Will's ceaseless crying, at Beetle's request I went up to Northumberland that freezing December of 1971 to help out. I was very grateful to be asked. Grateful that they allowed me to be of use. To be allowed to be of use is a privilege that you only truly grasp when you become a grandparent.

For three of the nights I was there I took baby Will in with me so that Beetle and Susan could get some badly needed rest. Once little Will had worn himself out with crying he slept beside me in the bed in the Blue Room, as his uncle had done over thirty years before.

People may get used to terrible things but I don't believe they get over them. They may go on, but that is because they have to, which is not at all the same. I believe that because of that first loss there was some small aspect of life for Will that was never quite right for him. Like his father, but when no more than a scrap, he bore on his tiny downy shoulders the burden of being a survivor. His relentless frantic wail was like no other that I at least have ever heard. It was strangely unchildlike, more penetrating than a baby's usual cries, so that his crying seemed to touch some nervous system, deeper almost than the heart.

'He is lamenting his lost twin, poor little lamb,' I said to myself. I couldn't say this to his parents.

2

To my mind that was what Cecilia was for Will: his lost twin. I do wonder if this love affair they seemed to have had would really have lasted. Who can say? Perhaps it would have done. Perhaps my tendency to anti-romanticism is some defence against the romantic chances that I myself have spurned. But what I do believe – and have no doubt about – is that they were kindred spirits and yes, if you like, twin souls.

They stayed with us many times as children, so I had leisure to observe them, and they had the kind of intuitive sense of the other that you most commonly find in twins.

Those were halcyon years for me and Fred. Fate which had pitched so many horrors at us seemed content to let us graze for the time in pleasanter pastures. We never forgot Nat. But things you have to bear – because what else is there to be done? – will, in time, become perforce bearable. Fred, once he had settled in at St Levan, was happy with his books and his reading and his translation. I was grateful for this as it absorbed his considerable energy. And I, always more lackadaisical and untroubled by idleness, was content with reading and walking by the sea and gardening – and my grandchildren.

Before he left for the RAF, I went with Jock Turnbull to the Fitzwilliam. In one of the galleries there was a Renaissance painting of a Madonna, don't ask me by whom because I forget. What I do recall is making a callow comment about her expression. I'm sorry to say that I insisted she looked constipated because, while I was never a card-carrying atheist like Fred, in those days to be even faintly religious was to be considered reactionary. It's not so different now, I suppose.

Jock, who came from a mining family, and was therefore free of left-wing pretentions, was hampered by no such prejudice. He said, and I never forgot this because it was a kind way of taking me down a peg, 'I reckon she's contemplating all those years ahead of never being able to put things right for her kid.'

I might have told him, had he lived, that grandchildren make up for a good deal because they are a second chance.

This must be why there is so often such a special bond between grandchild and grandparent. And I have come to see that the better you treat someone, the more you love them – which is why you must never let someone treat you badly, for the worse they do to you, the more they will hate you. I had failed Nat, and my other children were the sufferers and for that reason, I knew, I had loved them less well. Fred, I should say, would have dismissed this suggestion as rubbish.

But it meant that free of the anxious tentacles of parenthood I was able to watch with enjoyment as Will and

Cecilia, and later Hetta, grew. And I'll say this, in spite of all that had happened with Nat we never coddled our other children or our grandchildren. When they stayed with us in Cornwall we let them go off bathing and climbing the cliffs and exploring because it seemed to us that common sense is best cultivated by being let loose to navigate the world, not by being sheltered from it.

For years, I put the pair of them to sleep together in the four-poster that was Ma's and too fragile for Fred's big frame (the only time we slept in it one side gave way so suddenly that I ended up on the floor). I would often steal in when the two children were sound asleep beneath the old silk canopy, simply to enjoy the vision of them entwined together or with their limbs flung about in that childish unconscious carelessness. Few sights are as sheerly heart-melting as a sleeping child.

Will and Cecilia more or less learned to read together on the tattered copies of Beatrix Potter that I had first read to their parents. I can't say that this is what gave them their love of animals – I suspect all children love animals until they are taught not to. But the very anthropomorphizing, so witheringly despised by Fred, who had no time for Beatrix Potter ('bourgeois'), gave them that sense of animals being their equals and worthy of respect. Certainly this point of view came naturally to them.

One of the things I love most about children is the way they mind. It is what I loved in Fred, that he minded. 'Never mind,' I often say to myself, but children ought to mind. It creates the oxygen in which their souls can breathe. But even by the standards of children, Will's minding was exceptional. He regularly got into trouble for fights and because he was small he had a compulsion to take on bigger boys. He got into a barney once while staying with us with a local lad who was maltreating a donkey. I never discovered how this unfortunate animal had landed up in this bully's care. But when, to prove his point, Will took me to the bit of scrub where the donkey was tethered, I could see that the poor beast had abscesses. Will, aged ten, sought out the donkey's owner, who was an overweight bulky boy of fourteen, verbally attacked him and, when that produced jeers, physically assaulted him. According to Cecilia, the lout rushed off wailing to his mother. The mother came round to complain but Fred, who had a down on her because she'd got up a petition against some council houses that were being mooted in the village, packed her off with a flea in her ear and a threat to report them to the RSPCA. Fred was always Will's ally.

Although he tended to tangle with older boys, Will was remarkably tender to younger children. I've often thought that small children are like canaries down a mine – they only sing when the air is wholesome. If I was sometimes worried by Will's easily aroused aggression, I was reassured by the gathering of the local little ones who appeared like magic when he was down with us. As Fred said, he was a pied piper born.

That got him into trouble too. Little Tim Trannack,

with his nose running and his bruised knees, whenever Will was staying would arrive first thing at our door to ask if he could come out and play. Although Will could be impatient he was always patient with Timmy, who was a backward little boy with a speech difficulty so it was often tricky to make out what he was saying. Will, however, seemed to follow Timmy's odd locutions with no trouble. He let Timmy tag along with him and Cecilia when they were messing about near home. But he knew better than to let him accompany them on longer expeditions.

Timmy once followed the cousins surreptitiously on to a bus which was going up the coast and then missed the stop where they were getting off. Instead of waiting for the next stop he jumped off the bus after them, and was badly knocked on the head and shoulders where he fell on the kerb. He was hurried off to A and E and Will was desperately upset and blamed himself for Timmy's fall, though he hadn't encouraged him, quite the reverse. He seemed to me always to retreat too readily into some inner place of hurt.

And it was the case that when Will was hurt, and he was easily hurt, he could lay waste all around him. I never knew the cousins quarrel when they were small but as Will grew older not even Cecilia was safe and she was the one most vulnerable to his attacks. Will was always Cecilia's sun. She took her centre of gravity from him.

It's hard to pinpoint exactly when things began to go wrong but if I had to choose a defining moment, when the unravelling of Will began, it would be with Cecilia being sent away to school. I should have tried to dissuade Bell. I knew it was a bad idea. Bad for Cecilia, bad for Bell, bad for all of them. And it led to that monster seducing Cecilia. She must have been so lonely away from them all at Dowlands, poor lamb.

I tried to speak to Fred of this once and all he would say was 'But you were under age, weren't you, when I had my way with you in the sand dunes?'

I could have said, 'It wasn't in the dunes.' I could have said, 'That was quite different because sixty years on we are still together.' I could have said, 'Times were different then and you, after all, for all your faults are not a thorough shit.' But what would have been the use? He wouldn't have understood and anyway I was too annoyed.

3

When Fred died, Cecilia came to see me in Ely. Hetta had been staying with us and had left only days before and I was missing her, as I always missed the grandchildren when they went. But I was missing everyone more sorely than usual, for obvious reasons.

I had left Fred's copy of the *Georgics* on the little table by the chair where he was reading it and Cecilia picked up the book with its scuffed red jacket. 'Do you remember how he used to get us to help with his *Aeneid*?'

'How could I forget. Was it an awful burden?'

She laughed and that was good to hear because she didn't laugh much. 'I wasn't much help but Will was, wasn't he?'

'Oh, Fred loved that Will shared his love of Virgil. But I was saying to Hetta, I feel if it weren't for that Will would never have gone to King's and . . .'

'Granny, please don't.'

'I'm sorry. One should never say "if only" . . .'

'We loved being with Grandpa. Especially Will. I don't mean . . .'

'It's OK, pet. I know Fred was special for him.'

'He still says "LR", like you and Grandpa. It's probably his only joke now.'

She looked so wistful that I said, 'It's not one that many people would get these days.'

'He said to say "LR" to you about Grandpa.'

There was something too painful in this so as she began to flick through the book I didn't say, as I might have done, 'Please don't lose his place.' I had wanted to leave the book marked at the point Fred had reached. It was somewhere in the section on bees, I know, because before I left the room to make tea, I mentioned to Fred how all those years ago Bev had got me to read Maeterlinck. Funny how I suddenly recalled that. He must have died while I was warming the pot because the tea still wasn't made when I put my head back round the door to ask if he wanted a biscuit and saw that he had gone.

It was the last thing I ever said to him and maybe it was not such a bad image to go out on, a bee.

I was rewarded for holding my tongue about the book because, with it open in her hands like a prayer book, my granddaughter said, 'Granny, Will wants to die.'

I had gathered as much. More than once he had painfully blinked out to me 'I do not want to go on like this.' And what could I answer that would not sound to Will like sentimental tripe? 'You must live in hope'? 'Things will get better'? 'The Lord will provide'?

'Yes?' I said.

'Granny.'

'Yes, darling.'

I can see her white face still, with the luminous skin and the Russian bones and those eloquent green eyes.

'He wishes he had never regained consciousness.'

'I see.'

'And I helped him back.'

'My understanding is that you helped him communicate. He was conscious anyway, wasn't he?'

'I don't know. I may have made him come back.'

I doubted that. I still believe there are limits to human powers. But I listened. I have learned to listen, or maybe to listen better. I listened not simply to her words but to the reverberations behind them, the tone. You can hear the truth of a person's words in the tone.

Pretty much from the time Will learned how to communicate after his accident, he had, as far as he was physically able, been badgering Cecilia, entreating her to help him end his life. Everything that had mattered to him had been taken from him, he insisted. He couldn't walk, or climb, or run, talk normally, argue, eat, he couldn't hold her in his arms, never mind make love. Even with her, he lamented, he could barely hold a proper conversation.

'I haven't tried to dissuade him. It would have only increased his anguish for me to seem not to know how he feels. I can't, I can't tell him it will all be all right because it won't be, will it, Granny?'

'Probably not.' Not enough for Will, anyway.

'He wanted me to tell you and I wasn't sure that was right.'

'But it seems so now?'

'It did just then. I don't know why.'

I felt I knew why. It had something to do with Fred

dying. And while I didn't think this then, maybe some part of her saw that his dying had left me more free. 'Darling, I am so, so sorry.'

'I'm sorry too,' she said. 'I'm sorry if this is upsetting for you.'

'I'm upset for Will. And for you.'

'Don't be upset for me.'

'I worry, darling. I worry that . . .'

'Don't,' she said. 'Don't say it, Granny.'

She has changed, I thought. My sweet timid girl has changed. I realized then how the things that open out in us as we go on through life become the very things that prevent us from ever going back.

'It's all right, lamb. I understand.'

I did understand. I understood why Will wanted to go and why she wanted to help him. She would always want to help him and somewhere, for her, he would always come first. What I was less sure of is what I wanted to do about this and before I could consider anything so serious I felt I must bury Fred.

I gave Fred a prayer-book service because – well, basically, because I wanted to. And as Fred himself would have been the first to say, he wasn't there so he wasn't likely to mind.

We sang Bunyan's 'To be a Pilgrim', because Fred had always excepted Bunyan from his atheist's Index and Fred, in his way, had been a pilgrim of sorts. I wanted Bell to play the fiddle but she said she was too out of practice, though my private thought was that she feared she would be too overcome. But it was at her suggestion that we gave Fred 'Joe Hill' as a final rousing send-off. The vicar, a portly young chap with a belly that suggested he would do well to watch his own heart, was quite witty about this and observed, '"I never died, said he" is, after all, a well-regarded religious position, so I think we can approve it for Wilfred.' I had to explain that Fred was never 'Wilfred.'

Cecilia came, bringing a message from Will. She didn't stay for the wake that Beetle and Susan had organized at Dowlands. Hetta was there of course. And Sydella sent beautiful flowers, white lilac, which, sweetly, she had remembered that I love. Eddie had driven Bell up from London the afternoon before in a very smart car, which I was glad of, as I felt Bell might need someone to talk to – she was always closer to Fred than to me – and Bev and Ted came from Harrogate, where they'd retired. And I was touched by other locals who had known us coming to condole, including a nephew of the farmer with whom Bev had her wartime fling. The nephew strongly resembled his uncle, who was a big rugged man, and I caught Bev giving him an old-fashioned look. She caught me catching this and winked.

When I got her to myself I told her about my mentioning Maeterlinck to Fred moments before he died. She laughed and said, 'I can't say I remember reading it myself,' but she seemed pleased. I get the feeling she doesn't read so much now.

Susan had laid on a fine old spread. The dead, notoriously, are good being gone so maybe she was assuaging her guilt with sliced ham and home-made pickle and beetroot (which reminded me of the ghastly paying guest they used to have there, God knows why). Beetle provided beer, and two cases of very superior wine arrived from Graham with a thoughtful note, which was especially generous as he must have been aware that Fred, in his high-minded way, had vaguely despised him.

I was glad to be among my family and friends but after a bit I wanted to be alone. So I took myself off, not too much the worse for wear, to the modest hotel I'd booked myself into because while I'd sometimes visited Dowlands on my own, especially latterly, I frankly couldn't stand the thought of sleeping there that night without Fred. And it's an odd thing but that night my sleep was strangely sound.

The next morning I woke early and drove to the foot of the hill where long ago, as a young woman, I had found Cuthbert's chapel. There had been rain in the night and the sky was washed white and blue and the wet hill grass was gleaming silver. It was a tough walk up the escarpment through the black-faced sheep. I am fit for my age but the years take their toll. When, panting but triumphant, the bottoms of the legs of my trousers drenched from the wet grass, I made it up there, I sat on my jacket on the boulder by the hawthorn, where I had sat long ago, and pondered in my heart many things.

4

I sometimes teased Fred that he might have made a splendid general because when he set his mind to it he had a capacity both to anticipate and to plan. What in his make-up appeared vague, and many mistook for benign, could switch to a decisive ruthlessness when he chose. Will had the same decisiveness. From the moment I agreed to help he meticulously organized the campaign for his own death.

It was Will's idea that I should be there at the flat when Cecilia fed him the drugs and this was the really clever part of his plan. He dismissed the idea of involving Bell, unsure whether she could withstand the questions that might follow. But he had concluded that if everyone present pleaded ignorance – Bell because she genuinely would be ignorant and Cecilia and I because he had demanded that we did so – then there would be a serious evidential problem with any inquiry.

Before I agreed to help I had gone to see Will, ostensibly to give him an account, as I explained to Bell, of the funeral.

'Grandpa's fine,' I told him. 'He's looking out to sea.'

Will blinked back, 'Good.'

I said, 'I got your message. I'm going to have LR, just the letters, on his stone.'

'Good,' again.

'And Cecilia has spoken to me. Are you sure, darling, that this is what you want?'

'Sure.'

'You truly want to go?'

'Truly.'

I had sat and pondered what Cecilia had told me for longer than I could reckon but it was not until the moment my grandson blinked out those letters that I felt sure the decision I had come to was the right one.

'If this is what you truly want, then I will help.'

'Thanks.'

'OK,' I said. 'Tell me what you would like me to do.'

According to Hetta's Theo, Will's last instruction is a version of the prisoner's dilemma, a proposition from Game Theory, which he has since tried to explain. If I have it correctly, two suspects of a crime who are interrogated separately will be best served if each unswervingly sticks to an agreed account of their innocence. Only if one cracks and accuses the other is that other compromised, in which case the outcome for the compromised prisoner is likely to be a worse punishment than a confession would have drawn.

What Will said, once more painfully blinking it out – he confined himself to the shortest possible words – was this.

'I do not want C 2 suffer for helping me to an end I wish for.'

'I understand.'

'I hav made C promis 2 deny it. If C denies it and u are also here and u deny it 2 I do not think police wil hav a case.'

'Go on.'

'If C denies she has done this wil u deny that u no wot she has done? I can not let her do it if u will not agree.'

'I have one question, darling. What about your parents?'

'Must never tell them.'

'I shan't. But your father is my son and they will mind terribly.'

'I can not liv for wot they mind.'

The best laid plans . . . Even the most talented generals may find that their theoretical stratagems are bested by the accidents of reality, and I doubt that Will ever considered what sticking to the story he had devised might be like for us. We loved him. And he loved us. But I cannot pretend he thought much about the comfort of those he loved.

Police officers are skilled questioners. They employ a variety of techniques, designed to break resistance down. Marion's husband, who, before he fled to England, was involved with the French Resistance, once described to me what it was like to be questioned by the Gestapo. He said it was the sympathetic Nazi who nearly did for him. Not that the police were anything like Nazis, you understand. I was an old woman and they treated me with the greatest courtesy. But for all that, I was invited, quite subtly, to betray my granddaughter. It was as if, they implied, I would be doing her a good turn by relieving her of the guilt that she must be feeling. I played the poor old widow woman card for all it was worth because, as Hetta said afterwards, I was after all an old widow woman, and sometimes the truth is our best disguise. But it was an ordeal.

Five days we spent sticking to our story, and five nights Cecilia and I spent in that unlovely hotel to which we'd retreated because, apart from my thinking it would be too much for her to be where Will died, it meant we could speak freely. Bell, of course, was in the dark. I've often wondered what she has made of it all since.

As I lay in bed with my arms round my granddaughter, I found myself in conversation with Fred.

It was as well that he was out of it. With age he had become uncharacteristically anxious and Will's death and all that followed, all that I could see was going to follow, would have set him worrying. But it was not the physically eroded man I conversed with that night but the old antinomian warrior, the Fred I had so often chided for acting out of his blessed conscience and defying the prevailing rules. In my mind, there is no doubt that the spirit lives on, if only in the hearts and minds of those left behind, the survivors, and I have an idea that a person's spirit might be heard more truly once the flesh is left behind.

'Tell me what I should do, Fred. Advise me.'

Over the nights we spent at that hotel, Cecilia had unburdened herself of the details of the whole miserable business. She had obtained the barbiturates from a prescription made out for a man who had subsequently moved away, which had never been collected and which, over a year back, while still working at the surgery she had taken, under Will's instruction, to be dispensed at a pharmacy outside London, pretending that it was on this patient's behalf. That was about the time that Will had begun to implore her more pressingly for her help. The evening he died, after I had kissed him goodbye and left them together in his room, acting under his instructions she had ground the pills down and mixed them with water and a little wine. But his ability to swallow had never fully recovered and in the stress of the moment he had had trouble swallowing the lethal concoction down.

Will had anticipated that this might be the case and had decreed that if there was a problem with his swallowing, when he had ingested enough of the drug to knock him out, as he put it, she should smother him with a plastic bag. He did not, he declared, want his plan to go off 'at half-cock'.

When I think of Will now, it is often of him saying 'at half-cock' in his fierce voice, though of course he never spoke these words aloud.

By this time, Cecilia had disposed of the tell-tale pill

bottle, though not before the snooping Noreen had clocked it, as we were to learn. And the plastic bag was then still to be recovered by the police from the rubbish bin, where she had put it after having rinsed it out and filled it with used tea leaves. Too late to suggest that she would have done better to burn it. If only I had not gone as I was bidden to my bedroom and been there to advise.

I had been told the bare bones of their plan in advance, but hearing from her of the lonely decision to use the bag, her last farewells to an unconscious Will, and then having to peel the evidence off his dead face and wash the bag out, was so appalling that I asked why in heaven's name she hadn't called on me for help.

'We thought the less you knew the better if you were questioned. Ignorance is bliss.'

'Hardly bliss, darling, in this case.'

'I wanted to do it alone, Granny. Really. It was right.'

Which only went to convince me more than ever that Will was right to insist that Cecilia make him that promise never to admit to what she had done.

As my granddaughter sobbed weakly in my arms, the faint intimations of what must be done began to form in my mind. I had at that time not bargained for Noreen; none of us had. But my bones told me the police strongly suspected who had helped Will to die, who in fact had killed him – because she had done more than assist or abet his death, she had bravely snuffed the life out of him. Carrying out the deed, God knows, should be punishment enough.

She fell asleep at long last and I lay hearing her occasional fretful murmurs against the insistent background whine from which London is never free. I called up the many long years with Fred, wishing again – I had wished this so often latterly – that I had been kinder to him. Not that I was ever unkind exactly. But there was some small element of understanding that I was aware I had denied him.

And I considered again those years with my little Nat and how the long shadow of his death had fallen on my poor Will and my poor Cecilia. And all the while the ancient well-worn words ran through my head, *the sins of the fathers* ... Those biblical authors, when they weren't fanatical zealots, or list-makers and lawgivers, were shrewd psychologists.

When I went up to Northumberland to bury Fred, the night before the funeral Nat's friend Eddie called at the hotel where he had discovered from Bell that I was staying. He and Bell clearly hit it off.

He had come, he said, to 'pay his respects' and I laughed at that and said, 'Oh Eddie, pet, don't be so formal,' because, after all, when he was a littlie I had often wiped his nose and his bottom clean. Not that I mentioned this. It strikes me that it is one of those matters which must inhibit men, when they have to deal later in life with the women who have tended to them: the fact that they were once seen by them in a state so nakedly vulnerable.

I made tea from the hotel kettle and offered Eddie a

ginger nut, unable to prevent the thought that Fred would have enjoyed these – and he relaxed somewhat and we chatted awhile about his life in London.

I'd gleaned from Bev's regular Christmas cards that he'd done well and I was always pleased at this news. Bell had mentioned to me that he'd spoken about Nat when he stayed with her for his interview for his London job and I had hoped from her words that Eddie might perhaps renew his acquaintance with us. I had not been surprised that we'd heard nothing – it would have been hard for him and maybe he feared too hard for us to want to rehearse old miseries. But he must have decided a moment had come to speak. Death does that. It opens sealed doors.

'Your Bell was saying you maybe had an idea that Jack's making that daft climb had something to do with, you know, his other mum and all that.'

'I've always felt so.'

'Or something to do with his dad, you know, being a CO.'

'That too. There was this vile other student who we think taunted Nat . . .'

He interrupted me. 'I don't think it was that either. I think more likely he was proving something to me.'

'It's nice of you to say so, Eddie.'

He frowned and said, 'I'm not. Being nice, I mean. I should have said before. But, I don't know . . .'

'It was a difficult time for us all,' I said.

'But you came to see me up in Seahouses and I didn't

say. You ought to know that he did think of you as his mum. He knew his . . . his other mum had left him, left him with you to look after him. Really, he wasn't angry with you for long. It wasn't that.'

I noted how he had avoided saying 'his real mum' or 'his natural mum'. He was always a sensitive boy, Eddie.

'Thank you, Eddie. That really is kind.'

'No, it's true. I mean it. He loved you. And his dad. He was proud of his dad. Really proud. I mean it,' he said again. 'I mean, yes, it was a shock discovering, you know, he was Jewish. But he did understand, I mean about your husband. He didn't, oh, I don't know. He didn't blame him. I'd have known.'

We sat quietly together for a spell. I could hear the sheep mindlessly bleating in the fields outside. Maybe this is why children unable to sleep used to be urged to count them. There is something settling to the nerves about the sheer woolliness of sheep.

Then Eddie said, 'There were these stones we found together, me and Jack, on the beach down here. I found this one in that toy seal he had. The one, you know, your granddaughter found at Dowlings, sorry, I mean Dowlands. Jack used to post things we found as kids inside it.'

He produced something from his pocket. 'They call them friendship stones. We had one each. I thought you might like this one.'

I took from his hand a small dark grey stone, with a hole worn through by the long action of the sea.

'This was Nat's?'

'Yes.'

'And it was in that seal, the one Cecilia had, that Margaret made?'

'We, me and Nat, used to post bits and pieces inside it. I saw it at Bell's when I stayed and I took it. I shouldn't have done. I'm sorry. I didn't realize, you know, that it was still wanted but I wanted to see what was maybe inside. I gave the seal back, but I kept the stone because, well . . . Anyway, I reckon Jack'd want you to have it now.'

'Thank you,' I said again. 'Thank you, Eddie. I shall treasure it.'

We sat some more in silence and when he got up I thought it was to leave and moved towards the door. But instead he walked over to the window and looked out.

'There's something else.'

'Of course. Please, whatever you like.'

Dusk was falling and as he turned I could see behind his head the tea-rose flush of the sky above the hill outside. His face was in shadow so I couldn't see his expression.

'It's about your grandson.'

'Will?'

'You know that book? About the climbers?'

His face was obscured still but I heard the anxiety in his voice.

'I'm sorry, Eddie, I don't know. What book?'

'*The Night Climbers of Cambridge*. You know that Jack . . .'

'The book Will had in his room?' Hetta had shown it to me. She'd collected it when we cleared Will's bits and bobs from King's.

'It gave the moves of the climb Jack was making, you know, up King's. I bought it because I wanted to see where he went wrong. D'you see?'

'I think I do.'

'See, I had this obsession that it wouldn't have happened – I mean I could've helped Jack if I'd been there.'

'Oh Eddie.'

'But, you see, that book, I think Will got hold of that book through me. His friend gave it to him.'

'What friend, Eddie?'

'He's called Harvey. He's not a friend. He's a bad'un.'

I had heard of this Harvey from Hetta and hadn't cared for the sound of him.

'Will was fascinated by Jack. He used to come to see me to ask me about him. There are pictures, photos in the book. I think having that book's what took him up there, Will, that night. To see it, you see? Where Jack died.'

'Eddie, come here.'

I held him and he wept, and I wept, because we none of us knew what had really happened, to Nat, to Will, to ourselves. We don't know. We think we know, but we don't.

I had Nat's stone with me as we buried Fred. And it was in the pocket of my trousers while the police questioned me. From time to time I fingered it and its smooth resilience helped to hold me fast – stonily fast – to my appointed task. Which was to refute, stoutly and categorically, any suggestion that I knew how Will had died, or that I had reason to believe that my granddaughter had had any part in his death.

The little grey relic was by the bed that last night, the night before they arrested Cecilia, and once I was sure she was asleep I gently detached my arm from around her shoulders, picked up Nat's stone and walked over to the window.

When I moved aside the heavy curtain, which stank of a foul room spray, I could see low bars of light already impressed across the bleak London sky. I observed them without pleasure. Light can look very minatory.

I was visited by a profound sense of shame. All these years a silent tribunal in my heart had judged Fred, had held him to blame for what had happened. And he may have been quite blameless after all. Nat may have died through no more than youthful folly and recklessness. It was possible it was the discovery of our deception that had unbalanced him. But it was possible too that Eddie's guess was right and that the fatal climb was a piece of daring, a rash bit of showing off to his oldest pal. I would never know. How far more likely it was that my own derelictions towards my other children had led to the catastrophe of Will. I had never outwardly abandoned them but they had felt my absence; both in their differing ways had been misshapen by it. And, in turn, those absences had defined the lives of their children, the cousins who had loved each other.

Even in that love they were unlucky as a result of my own luck – for I knew now that I had been lucky in my marriage to Fred. Had we not been cousins, Cecilia and Will might well have had the courage to embrace their own love. Or Cecilia might have done.

Because as I stood that morning by the window, watching the bars of light bleed into a tangerine-and-shocking-pink-skeined sky, it belatedly came to me that it was she of course who, of the two of them, must have been the one who held back. Will, like his grandfather before him, would have entertained no such conventional qualms. It must have contributed to her odd flight to Alec, that and her part in Will's attack on Colin, which had plainly scared her. These were the silent burdens she had been bearing since Will's fall. It was why she felt she must at any cost help him.

Like everything else in London, dawn comes on at a pace. Traffic was already groaning in the streets below and I could hear along the corridor the faint bustle and chatter of hotel staff. Someone in the next room had ordered breakfast. I thought to follow their example and had bathed and dressed and put down the phone, having ordered coffee for two in our room, when it rang loudly, making me start, and I was told that there were two police officers in the lobby and that they were waiting, when she was ready, for Mrs McCowan.

5

On that terrible day in September, when the police came and took away my darling granddaughter, I saw to the practical things. I set great store by attention to the practical because, if nothing else, it composes the mind. And my mind was dearly in need of composure. I rang Giles, and Giles agreed that the old family firm, stalwart as they had been, was not best equipped to help us through this calamity. On Giles's recommendation, Bolton's, a firm famed for criminal defence, was accordingly instructed. That done, and with no other distracting duties, I had my thoughts to attend to, to untangle and recast.

Cecilia had confided that she and Will had found each other again in the National Gallery. It was a long time since I had been there myself and with no other guide to follow than my own inclinations I took a bus to Trafalgar Square.

I have a fondness for Nelson on his column and for the general ambience of that island, with its lions and fountains, amid the London traffic, and on another day, in a different mood, I might have lingered there. But it was dead cold, the sky was that bitter white that offers no solace, so I hurried across the square, with no more than a nod to the lions, into the sanctuary of the gallery's warmth.

I drifted through the long rooms, marking anew the magnificent wealth of the offerings and reassured, as if by meeting sympathetic friends, to encounter old favourites: the Wilton Diptych with its heavenly blue angels, Tobias with Raphael and his scrappy little dog, the imposing Man with the Blue Sleeve who in any fight one would want on one's side.

I had come not to look but to reflect, and reflection is immeasurably improved by the right surroundings, but nonetheless passing through a room of van Dycks I stopped before a painting I had not noticed before.

A wide canvas, with a blue bird-crossed sky at its centre, above a lake running to a gushing waterfall, artfully framed by feathery green-brown trees. Clustered upon the hills beyond and nestling by the waterside were all the animals of the ark, except it was not the ark and the human figure, placed slightly off-centre to draw the eye, was assuredly not Noah.

A young man in a rich red robe is seated easily on the ground, his feet casually bare, as if he might have come from paddling in the nearby water where ducks are splashing. By his side, in a companionable sort of way, sits a pelican and by the pelican recline two lions. The young man is playing a stringed instrument.

I inspected the label. *Orpheus* by Roelandt Savery, a Flemish artist I had never heard of.

There are comfortably padded benches for the

bottoms of weary visitors in the rooms of the National Gallery, and I plumped down on one and considered the painting.

It was not too far a stretch into my memory to recover Orpheus. Orpheus and his lyre (for which Savery appeared to have substituted a viol) whose playing was so hauntingly beautiful that it calmed the breasts of wild animals. Orpheus, who lost his dead love for eternity by faltering, faltering and looking back. I do not believe in mystic signs or emblems but I do believe that in certain circumstances we are given a sight of what it is that is needed.

Error is all in the not done, all in the diffidence that falters . . .

6

The solicitor from Bolton's who had replaced the courteous Anu was cut from very different cloth. Sharply dressed, well made-up, the steely-looking Shama Bhatti arrived at the police station perched on very high heels. It was a situation that required steel. She argued, after Cecilia was formally charged, that her 'client' was both harmless to the public and a serious suicide risk and, on the grounds that she would be with me, her most respectable grandmother, Cecilia was released back into my care.

I was thankful my granddaughter had been spared a night in a police cell for, looking at her wan face and bruised eyes, I was not at all sure she would be able to hold out for long.

And the thing was, Cecilia would willingly have gone to prison. She longed to confess, to get the whole terrible business off her chest and out of the way. The idea of prison, she kept repeating, seemed welcoming – to be put away, out of it all, to be left alone. But she had given that solemn promise to Will. She had not faltered. She had done as her beloved cousin asked.

We spent one further fraught long night in that hotel before she was due to appear at the magistrates' court.

The child's body in bed that night was so cold. I never knew another living human being so cold. But the court appearance was thankfully brief. As we had been warned, the case was referred to the Old Bailey and we were advised it would take months to be heard there. Shama was again splendidly persuasive. Cecilia was deemed sufficiently safe to the community and unsafe to herself not to be remanded in custody. Recognizance was granted, and with the court's agreement Cecilia came to Ely with me. As she said, she never wanted to go near Bell's flat again as long as she lived.

I will say this for Bell: she did finally do what was needed for her daughter. I imagine she could have had the funds for Cecilia's defence from Graham but instead she decided to sell Staresnest.

'You don't mind, do you, Mum?' she asked.

I'd almost forgotten Staresnest had ever been mine. 'Of course not, darling. It's very good of you.'

'No, Mum. It isn't good of me.' She was aghast at what might happen to her daughter but I think too she was somewhat admiring of her.

While Bell, with Robert, who I was glad to see had reappeared, was off seeing to the sale, Cecilia and I spent some days together in Ely alone. Alec drove from London once to see her. I don't know what was said, and I didn't ask, but they went for a long walk together and when he left to return to London he shook hands with me very formally and thanked me for looking after her. I never saw Alec again after that day. He was a kind man and loyal and I feel sure he would have stayed to be with Cecilia had she wanted that.

Cecilia and I spoke very little of what she had done for Will, as if by keeping it to ourselves, between ourselves, we were keeping the knowledge from a more dangerous audience. She looked ill and I was constantly aware of what an enormous task Will had laid on her.

One morning, over the Formica table, she said, 'The solicitor has asked me to write a statement for Mr Baines. I don't know what to say.'

I had not at this point communicated personally with Cuthbert Baines, who came highly recommended by Giles, but I too had been asked for a statement.

'Say just as I shall – that you were asleep. That you saw and heard nothing. I shall back you up.'

'It's harder than I expected.'

'I know, lamb. But hang on.'

Although Giles and I had not kept up after our Cambridge days I had occasionally read in the *Guardian* about his civil rights cases and had had oddments of news from Marion. It was Marion who gave me his details and, knowing in advance of Will's plan, I had made sure to get in touch myself.

It was partly to ask him about Cuthbert Baines that I decided to invite Giles to dinner. I would have gone to London to see him – as a matter of fact I would have gone to the moon to see him – but he claimed to have business in Cambridge anyway, so in the end we met at a pub in Grantchester.

When he walked in I recognized him at once. To my eye, he had hardly changed.

He must have recognized me too because he hailed me with, 'Did we come here as students? I don't recollect.'

'I don't remember ever coming to Grantchester as a student. I came as a schoolgirl. Did I ever tell you? I came out here with my mother to meet Frances Cornford.'

'If you did I've forgotten. Don't you find that one of the joys of age is that you can be fascinated all over again by ancient news?'

And I had forgotten how much I had enjoyed conversations with Giles. 'It's good to see you, Giles.'

'It's good to see you too, Betsy, though I'm sorry it has to be in such beastly circumstances. So tell me,' he said, after we'd ordered bangers and mash with wine for him but only water for me because I was driving, 'how are things? Is old Cuthbert doing his stuff?'

'I've not met him. He wants me to write a statement.'

'Oh, you'll meet him. He's a canny old bird and he likes to get a feel for his witnesses. If you were there, in media res, he'll be sure to want to hear your angle. Is she sticking with the not guilty plea?'

I shrugged, hoping to steer him away from this. 'What else can she do?'

'I suppose that rather depends.'

Giles always did lack Marion's tact but he had enough not to spell this implication out.

'She can't plead guilty, Giles, for something she didn't do.'

'I seem to recall a passionate conversation – what, sixty-odd years ago? – when someone suggested she would be prepared to do just that.'

'How funny you remembering that. But you haven't quite got it right. What I said was that if I had to be hanged I'd rather be hanged for a crime I hadn't committed.'

'And Marion said you were off your rocker. Have you seen her lately? She's gone blonde.'

'You always said that Marion's hair was her crowning glory.'

'Did I say that? I seem to recollect it was you I was smitten by.'

'Flatterer!' He wasn't at all. But it was not unpleasant to hear this.

'But to be serious, what your granddaughter should take on board, I mean Cuthbert'll see to this but so that you know, is that a plea of not guilty goes down badly with a jury – and with the judge – if there's any solid proof to the contrary. I just make the point.'

'The police don't have much.'

'They must have enough to satisfy the CPS that the charge would run.'

'The only thing that points solely to Cecilia is the word of a snooping carer who claims she saw some pills in her drawer. Bell says she was a thief anyway.'

'Cuthbert will make mincemeat of her testimony if that's true.'

'Apparently she correctly identified the kind of pills they were.'

'He could swallow then?'

'It looks as if there was a plastic bag.'

Giles pulled a face. 'So is the charge murder?'

'I'm afraid so.'

'That's not so good. There's a statutory term for murder. See what Cuthbert says but I would advise a guilty plea. It's a mercy killing and the judge can amend the sentence.'

'But she's not guilty.'

'So these pills were innocent?'

Which is when my half-formed plan crystallized.

'Might I have some of your wine after all please, Giles?' While Giles was gesturing at the waitress to bring another wine glass I rapidly composed my story. My memory is not what it was but luckily my wits are still fairly sharp. 'As a matter of fact, I think they may have been my pills. Or Fred's rather.'

Giles, who was pouring the wine, looked at me over his glasses. 'What were Fred's drugs doing there?'

'He was on barbiturates for years. They dished them out like sweeties then, and he got, what d'you call it?'

'Addicted?'

'Acclimatized was the word I was searching for. The GP never suggested his not taking them.'

'Probably he assumed Fred was on the way out anyway so it didn't matter.'

I was actually amused by this but it allowed me to assume an air of being slightly affronted.

'Fred can't have been addicted. For the last months, he had stopped taking his sleeping pills, partly thanks to Will. When Will and Cecilia were younger Fred got them on to his *Aeneid* translation.'

'I'd forgotten he was a classicist.'

'He always taught a Latin class while he was running the Birkbeck programme, to keep his hand in, he used to say. But he really went back to it when he retired. He never said so, but I think it was his way of detaching himself from a political system that had let him down.'

I'd not really analysed this before, but talking to Giles I became aware that I had felt embarrassment for Fred at the collapse of Communism and all it had seemed to offer.

Giles waved his wine glass in the air. 'Here's to Fred. I wish I had such energy. I doubt I could read the *Aeneid* these days, let alone translate it.'

'Oh, Fred's intellectual energy never flagged.'

'And did he finish his translation? I'd like to see it.'

'He did. And, being Fred, he was already preparing to start on the *Georgics*. He said the pills were making his mind woolly. But I went on collecting his prescription, just in case.'

'Yah. But the police will ask what they were doing in Cecilia's drawer.'

'I used to take one from time to time, after Fred died

when I had trouble sleeping. I must have left them at Bell's when I stayed there the time before last. They always insisted on putting me in Cecilia's room.'

And the great virtue of this was that by and large it was true. There were a few of his pills left over when Fred died. Who was to say how many? Despite what I had suggested to Giles, the truth was that Fred had relied on the drugs to the day he died and his mind remained as sharp as a pin. But the police could hardly interrogate my dead husband to disprove my story.

I crossed my fingers mentally that my last but one visit to Bell's had overlapped with the poisonous Noreen's term. I was almost sure it had because I had in that split second consulted Cuthbert. Not Cuthbert Baines, whom I had yet to meet, but the other Cuthbert. My friend the saint.

'But why,' asked Giles, looking at me more pointedly, 'haven't you divulged all this before? I mean it's neither here nor there to me but the police will want to know.'

'I'm pushing eighty,' I said smoothly. 'I simply forgot I'd left the pills there. Just as you forgot that I'd visited Frances Cornford, Giles.'

As we parted Giles said, 'Look after yourself, Betsy. And do send me Fred's *Aeneid*, if you trust me with it.'

I didn't go straight to Cuthbert Bainbridge's. I needed to gather my wits and prepare my ground. Once Bell was back from arranging the sale of Staresnest, I left her to look after Cecilia and drove up to Northumberland. I wanted to see Beetle, and Dowlands, again.

It was not an easy visit. Beetle and Susan were in mourning, and not only for the son they had lost. Cecilia had been like a daughter, especially to Susan.

'We should never, *never* have allowed him to live with Bell.' Grief had heightened her anger.

'You did it for his comfort,' I attempted.

'And that Cecilia could have done this to Will. She was like . . . oh!'

She wept and it was awful seeing her so distressed.

'Susan, love, come here.'

I was glad to see Beetle embracing her.

'But she was,' Susan said. 'She was like his sister.'

'But she didn't do it,' I insisted. 'She has sworn not. And did you ever, all the time you've known her, know that girl to lie?'

'Anyone might lie if they are in line to go to prison for murder,' was Beetle's rejoinder. 'And if she didn't do it then who did? You? Bell? The cleaner? And the police wouldn't have charged her unless they were fairly sure. They don't. They can't. They have to have good evidence.'

I have always been of Forster's party when he said that if he had to choose between betraying his country and betraying his friend, he hoped he would have the courage to betray his country. But I had to choose between betraying my son and betraying my grandson, and that is an even harder choice. If there is a Saint Peter at heaven's gate (if there were a heaven and I were to get there, which is doubtful) the most dire sin I would have to own up to is not that I lied before the law of the land but that I lied to my own son.

Before I left Northumberland I went again to Cuthbert's chapel. And this is the moment to correct a misapprehension which has lingered in our family too long. More than a misapprehension, an injustice. It concerns Aunt Char.

When I decided to write what I knew about the terrible events that overtook our family, I had to have recourse to my ship's captain's desk, where with Hetta's help I had stashed away any important family papers. While I was looking through my own letters and notebooks, I happened on a bundle tied in old tape, which had been among the items from Grandmother's desk when we cleared Dowlands. I had put this with other papers to see to later. It was typical that I had never done so. The bundle was not, as I supposed, a collection of old legal documents but carbon copies of letters from Grandmother Tye, addressed to the authorities at the home where she put away poor Char.

The 'insanity' for which Char was put away was apparently based on her repeated report that she heard the voices of saints. In particular, this correspondence relates, it seems that Charlotte claimed a friendship with Saint Cuthbert.

I read with distress the stern ink phrases written in my grandmother's firm hand.

'Charlotte claims again that the Sainted Cuthbert was with her. She claims he visits her regularly in her room.

She appears to "take his counsel" and has several times refused to do our bidding on the grounds that "Cuthbert advises me not to."'

'Charlotte was reasonably docile on her visit to us but then started up at luncheon exclaiming loudly, "He is there outside. I must go to him."

'Both Hubert and I feel that it is best that she not return here to Dowlands again, which appears only to make her excited. We should like you, with Dr Mallory's approval, to increase the dosage of her sedative.'

Oh, Aunt Char. All those years cruelly shut away because you spoke with Cuthbert who became my own friend and adviser.

'It's like this, Cuthbert,' I said, the last time I sat on the boulder by his chapel, having said a last goodbye to Dowlands. Cuthbert doesn't muck about and over years of acquaintance you get to drop a measure of formality, even with a saint. 'My dear granddaughter gave a solemn promise to my equally dear grandson that she would never admit to what she had done, done for him, at his request. But, you see, I made no such promise. My friend Giles says if she is convicted it will be for murder, not simply aiding and abetting a suicide but murder, because my grandson was helpless and could not raise a finger to take his own life. Murder, Giles tells me, carries a mandatory sentence. Who knows who might be sitting on the jury, over-convinced of their right to evaluate the sanctity of life and keen to have a chance to occupy the moral high ground, or ready to be persuaded by some specious legal argument.

'So what should I do?' I asked. 'You know something about the sanctity of life but is there not a sanctity of death? There are occasions where there is such a thing as a good death, wouldn't you say?'

I don't want you to suppose that I saw Cuthbert. He didn't appear to me, with his tonsure and his sandals and long monkish robes. Nothing so crude. I like to hope that perhaps he did appear in seeming person of some sort to my Aunt Charlotte, for no other man visited her bedchamber. But to me he simply spoke in my mind, in a roughish low voice with a Northumbrian accent. Always cordial. The kind of voice that the sheep would be sure to be calmed by.

That was the last time Cuthbert spoke to me, though I hope he might visit me again before I go. But thanks to him, when on my return from Northumberland I went to the Inner Temple, to the rooms of that other Cuthbert, I was well prepared.

I had ostensibly come to give a verbal statement of what I knew of the night of Will's death, and of Cecilia. Her solicitor, perched on even higher heels, was there to greet me. She escorted me to Cuthbert Baines's room, where he offered me coffee.

'Thank you for coming here. I find a conversation often helps. As someone present at the scene, we are particularly interested in your account of events, Mrs Tye.'

I drank the too weak coffee, waiting for him to finish. You would think that a man like Cuthbert Baines might rise to better coffee.

'Yes,' I agreed. 'I was present.' He was about to speak but I held up my hand to forestall him. 'I was more than present. I've come to explain.' I had Nat's stone in my pocket, the pocket of my good jacket which Bell made me buy for Fred's funeral. I had felt that for my confession I had better present a respectable figure. 'I killed Will,' I said. 'I killed my grandson.'

I've always rather regretted that Bell didn't have these lines to deliver. She would have appreciated the reaction.

'I am so sorry not to have come forward sooner but you see I never for a moment supposed anyone would – could – imagine that Cecilia could do such a thing. It's out of the question. Completely out of character, poor child.'

I said that day at the chapel was the last time Cuthbert spoke to me but it was not the last time I felt his presence. I felt him by me then, and much later in court. Stalwart at my left shoulder.

'So,' I continued, as neither of them spoke and I was keen to move matters along, 'I would be grateful if you would inform whoever you need to inform so that my granddaughter can be released as soon as possible from this charge. It's really quite shocking,' I said, warming to my part, 'that that girl, who loved her cousin more than anyone in the world, should have had to go through all this and be treated as a criminal. Shocking, really,' I added again, for good measure.

Cecilia's solicitor sat there still speechless. But Cuthbert Baines, who had no doubt coped with odder reversals, recovered his sang-froid. 'It would be helpful if I could impart some details to the police when we inform them of your, er, admission. The barbiturates for example . . . ?'

'They were mine, or I should say my late husband's. He took himself off them before he died – he was about to begin a new translation of Virgil, you know, and it mattered to him to have his mind clear – and consequently I had a supply. I left them at my daughter's. I'm afraid I cannot account for what they were doing in my granddaughter's drawer but I customarily used her room when I stayed there. They can ask my husband's GP. He will confirm the regular prescription.'

'I see. And you . . .'

'I pulverized them and fed them to him in a drink, with wine.'

'And the plastic bag?'

'Will begged me to make sure. He was unwilling that the affair should go off "at half-cock".'

The adrenaline of acting a part must have caught hold of me, as I felt a sort of frisson as I spoke Will's unuttered words. And I also felt the atmosphere shift and change as if they had hit some impalpable target.

'I was unsure whether he had imbibed enough of the drugs so when he seemed to be asleep I did as he asked. It wasn't easy.'

The odd thing was that by this time I had begun to

believe I had actually been the one who had accomplished Will's death. My eyes were welling and I was shaking. But you see, there was a way in which I believed that I had.

'Well, in that case,' said Cuthbert Baines, massaging his palm with his big thumb, 'perhaps, Miss Bhatti, you had better inform the investigating officer.'

Miss Bhatti had still said nothing but I saw her take out a bejewelled phone from a glistening patent leather handbag as Cuthbert Baines showed me to his waiting room, where, rather endearingly, he ordered me a second cup of his very bad coffee.

I had prepared the ground for my confession. Before I left for London I collared Bell and asked her to pass on a letter to Cecilia but not to do so until the following day. She raised her eyebrows but she asked me no questions. She was good like that. Then I wrote to Marion. She was aware of the situation and had rung several times to see how we were.

My dear M,

Cecilia may get in touch with you. If she does, please will you describe the argument we had all those years ago in Cambridge about capital punishment. If you don't recall this, or what I said then, you should ask Giles. He remembers.

I may not see you for a while but do write when you feel like it.

Much love,

B

The letter to Cecilia took more considered thought.

My dearest Cecilia,

I need you to do something hard. But really it will not be too hard as it is for Will that I am asking. You did an extremely brave thing and you made him a promise and I think it important that you keep that promise, both for him and for yourself. But I made no such promise. So I am going to ask you to allow me to confess to helping him to his death without attempting to refute this because I am quite sure that this is the best thing to do. And that Will would agree with my decision.

I am an old woman. If I plead guilty the sentence will be very much lighter than any sentence likely to be laid on you, especially with a not guilty plea. For you there is a dilemma: you must either plead not guilty and risk a longer sentence in prison, or break your promise to Will.

Admission of guilt is taken into account at sentencing and there will be no potentially sanctimonious jury to punish me if, as I plan to do, I plead guilty.

And, and it is important that you understand this, it will help me to set some things a bit right. Or a bit righter, at least. You must take my word, and I have never lied to you, that it will be a comfort for me to do this and not a sacrifice. If you are in any doubt, please ring Marion and ask her about the argument we had years ago over capital punishment. I have not changed my mind since. And, my darling, you see it will also put me on a par with Grandpa. He would be immensely chuffed, as he would say, at the thought of my joining him in his career as a gaolbird.

By the time you read this it will be too late to stop me. I will have made the confession and if you then try to put the record straight it will put us both at risk and ruin everything Will worked for.

I have it on the highest authority that all shall be well. So be of good courage, darling. You did as your Will asked and he would be proud of you and that is enough. I am proud of you and Grandpa would be too.

All love,

Granny

7

The police questioned me again of course. They were rather bemused, I could see, and for a time they were hesitant about accepting my story. I imagine that they wondered if perhaps I was dementing. But I stuck to my guns. From Cele's account I had the scene pat and, although I had my heart in my mouth, so anxious was I to be believed, it wasn't too hard to carry this off because, you see, I was innocent. It was a corollary of that position I took with Marion all those years ago.

I had hoped that Cuthbert Baines might defend me. But when I called him at his chambers he explained that, 'Regretfully, Mrs Tye, that would amount to a conflict of interests. But I should have been honoured to act for you.'

I had half a mind to tell him why I had so warmed to him but instead merely mentioned that I had a special fondness for his name.

His tone audibly brightened. 'Ah yes, I owe my forename to my mother whose family hailed from your neck of the woods.'

He wished me luck in his grave courteous voice and later gave Anu Singh – to whom as my solicitor I had reverted, for I felt that I was not in need of the might of

Boltons – the name of a young QC who had only lately taken silk and who Cuthbert Baines described as 'very effective in defending Human Rights cases'.

Hetta found him cold but there are times when coldness is appealing.

As you know, I was tried and sentenced. But it was only me, the prosecuting counsel and my defence counsel that day at the Old Bailey. My young QC was alight with a mission to place my actions in the most humanitarian light and by the time he had finished delivering his plea on my behalf I felt myself quite a moral heroine. It was all very bizarre.

There is, as Giles warned me, a statutory term for murder. But thanks to my age, the fact that I pleaded guilty and the circumstances of Will's health, the judge, a sympathetic-seeming soul, recommended the sentence be commuted to eighteen months. In the event, I was out of prison after nine.

And after the first month in Holloway, an experience I cannot recommend, it really wasn't so bad doing time. I was moved to a pretty decent open prison in Kent and I acquired a certain cachet among the other inmates, who were impressed by this elderly murderer. The Governor, a fair-minded woman, placed me in the library where I catalogued the books. I did a bit of teaching there too, helping some of the older recidivists to learn to read. I often thought affectionately of Fred and his blessed Tolstoy classes.

And I read too, of course. Prison is not a bad place in

which to read. It was there that I reread Bede and I sometimes used to laugh to myself at the idea of what Fred would have thought of my diet of prison reading. I think it is safe to assume that he would not have approved.

I no longer see Beetle or Susan, or Dowlands. They refuse to have anything to do with me but for that I do not blame them. It was a price I was aware I might have to pay. And I feel no need to visit the two graves looking out to sea where Fred and Will lie side by side. I like to think of them there but it is enough that I see them in my mind's eye.

Cecilia goes there often. She is working now on Holy Island, on a dig that is hoping to uncover the remains of the original eighth-century monastery where Cuthbert once presided.

It was last autumn, after Cecilia had been to plant on the graves some bulbs that I had sent her for the purpose – snowdrops and daffodils, the kind called Lenten Lily that you see growing wild in those parts in carpets of pale gold – that she came to visit me in Ely.

Cecilia has referred only once to my decision to take the punishment for her. I had written to her before my trial, reaffirming that she was not to see this as some act of heroism on my part but a way of attempting to settle certain difficult matters for myself. *So I hope you will try to understand,* I believe I wrote. *It would be a shame and spoil everything if you allow it to be an occasion for any more guilt.*

When I emerged through the prison door, not too

much the worse for wear and grateful for my liberty, she was there waiting for me with flowers, freesias, whose scent she knows I love.

'This is hardly a thank you, Granny, but . . .'

'My darling,' I said, 'you have had your own sentence to bear, a far harder one than mine.'

From that day we have never spoken of this; nor do we ever speak of what really took place the night that Will died. It is our way of honouring Will and our pledge to him. But we speak around it and it was inevitable that both Will and Fred were in our minds as she described planting the bulbs.

She gave me a progress report on the dig over coffee at the red Formica table – she has completed her archaeology training and is now in charge of overseeing the volunteers whose efforts make that dig possible.

'We live in sorry times when the government no longer cares enough about the past to provide the funds to uncover it. I'm glad that Fred isn't here to be disillusioned,' I said, offering her a digestive biscuit.

She took one, which pleased me as to my mind she is far too thin. 'But would he be, Granny? It seemed to me that the important thing about Grandpa was that he was always optimistic.'

She was right. Fred never did give up hope. He was bigger than me in that.

It was then that she confided something strange, so strange that I do not wish to enquire too closely into the reasons for it but I think it right to set it down. She told me that the night after she put Will out of his misery the compulsion to count that had ruled so much of her life ceased altogether. For all those years, from the very moment she awoke, she had been daily tormented by the voice of a relentless demon in her head threatening her world and all she loved if she did not submit herself to its demand. Will's death must have called time on the demon, for from the moment she snuffed out the life of her beloved cousin it vanished altogether and so far she has never again suffered from those symptoms that had so plagued and harried her.

Next time, I must remember to ask her to plant some rosemary on the graves.

Acknowledgements

In a book of this nature there will be many sources and resources which I have either knowingly plundered or unconsciously imbibed. Those who know me will recognize certain details that are taken from my own parents' histories and their time as members of the British Communist Party, when they formed many friendships which survived their disenchantment with communism. All my 'godparents' remained lifelong Party members and while I have never shared their political allegiances I remain persuaded of the virtue of an outlook that pursues equality of all kinds for all sorts. Their several loving influences have enriched my life in important and lasting ways.

I am extremely grateful to Lord Blair, former Commissioner of the Metropolitan Police, who advised me at length on police procedure and was kind enough to read the relevant sections of the book, and also to Edmund Newell who made the introduction. I am grateful, too, to Lord Hoffmann for putting me in touch with Patrick O'Connor, QC, who answered my many questions about legal matters, specifically about criminal law on 'assisted suicide'; in 1996 this was governed by the Suicide Act of 1961, which made it a criminal offence to aid, abet, counsel or procure the suicide of another or an attempt by another to commit suicide.

His Honour Judge Owen Davies, QC, confirmed that the events described in the book would lead to a charge of murder but reassured me that a High Court judge would be in a position to recommend in passing sentence that, in certain circumstances, such as a mercy killing, the statutory term for murder be significantly reduced. And my thanks to Professor Ray Tallis, patron of Dignity in Dying, for our valuable conversation about Locked-in Syndrome. Where these subjects appear in the book any errors will be mine.

My publisher, Venetia Butterfield, who has been a staunch champion of this book, and my agent, Jonny Geller, stood by me through some difficult patches during the writing. I know how lucky I am to have a support that many writers today sadly lack. And Petrie Harbouri has been the best and most punctilious of copy editors, saving me from many lapses and solecisms and generously offering advice of the most tactful kind.